# The Unknown Puppeteer

By

# Deborah DR Kralich

# The Unknown Puppeteer
## A Lieutenant Sinclair Plate in Sand Waves Mystery
### Copyright 2016
### By
# Deborah DR Kralich

Published by Ruskras Corner
The United States of America

The Unknown Puppeteer - A Lieutenant Plate in Sand Waves Mystery
ISBN 9781942542100
TX0008426861
Fourth in a sequence of stand alone mysteries
All cover designs, artwork and photography by Deborah DR Kralich, copyright 2016

# The Unknown Puppeteer

# Cast of Characters

**Joanna Scarpartti-** A temperamental Italian princess, her Egyptian fiancé would like to cut her movie career short by less than pleasant means. Her flight to safety in America puts people in grave danger. Her position tempts criminals to action.

**Stark Wynter-** A famous producer-director, he is determined to transform Sand Waves into the new Hollywood. Yet he does not believe murder is good publicity.

**Castroe Zopev-** A serial killer on trial, it does not look like he has much of a future. But is he on trial for the wrong murder? What will happen if he is set free?

**Sally Monroe-** A nondescript housewife, mother of a toddler, labeled the first victim of a serial killer, her murder 11 years ago changed more lives than anyone realized at the time. More than one person believes it could have been prevented.

**Buddy-** Sally's twin, listed as MIA Vietnam. Did he disappear in the jungle or is he keeping his survival a secret to avenge her murder? Is he in disguise or in the open?

**Ted Monroe-** Sally's husband, he disappeared after her death, along with their child. Has he resurfaced to seek revenge for his wife? Will he be revealed as an impostor?

**Chief Robert Brecken-** Police chief in Sand Waves, his men look up to him but is he truly worthy of their devotion? How much does politics influence his judgment?

**Daphne Martin-** As a single career woman she has up to now managed to completely control her life. On the eve of her wedding she is no longer sure she knows what's best or what to do next when a killer stalks the wedding party.

**Lt. Plate-** Security for a princess, a royal Japanese VIP, a producer staging a Hollywood wedding, and the trial of a serial killer all have to take a backseat to unimaginable tragedy within the police department, which proves no one is safe.

**Officer Skaar-** By default he finds himself once again behind the gates of Sand Waves, looking after the rich, famous, and infamous as only he can.

**Officer Willhouse-** Trying his best to serve and protect in such a way that makes up for a lack of diligence in his past career, he may be too trusting of those around him.

**Officer Jordan-** Not the best liked cop in Sand Waves, he is forced to take his job more seriously when a serial killer comes to town and romance must be sidelined.

**Officer Fondrem-** Truly ahead of the times, this police officer made a courageous stand in an era where deviating from the norm usually brought censure or dismissal.

**Darica Daniels-** Her news career thrives on tragedy. An unforeseeable murder gives her an opportunity to move up in her profession. A mysterious man derails her gain.

**Eduardo Pauliza-** In the past he failed to protect his wife from an attacker. He is determined that won't ever happen again. His diligence creates a theatre of murder.

**Sarah Pauliza-** Assaulted almost 14 years ago, she would like to put it behind her. Vengeance that went wrong and fear of the future still can be traced to her pain.

**Sheik Abdul Mahlah-** Humiliated by Western romance, he turns to his own. A voice across the ocean demands that he seek retribution that backfires into murder.

**Mr. Shiameto-** This mysterious man speaks English well. Why be accompanied by a translator who seems to have no usefulness? His secret talent holds the future.

**Elizabeth Lopez-** A translator at home in Sand Waves, she's surprised to find she still has to relocate to do a job & more than language is needed to cope with death.

**James Juan-Paublo II-** A college student & poster child for poor judgment, he's sure his charms will entice a princess. He sees his motives for attacking her as pure.

**Kareem Makikz-** His future is dependent on a strange Middle East prince. If his plan to embarrass the royal's enemies fail, he will need to find another place to live.

**Fabrizio-** His love for a princess puts him in grave danger. He is not above trying to capitalize on her predicament but when it comes time he steps up to defend her life.

**Mr. Ito-** Skilled translator, he eyes a colleague, sees trouble but does not dare speak up when his boss is tripped up by a beautiful insurance agent and her reporter sister.

**Emilio Cardioxa-** Grieving husband of a murder victim, he finds comfort sailing on his yacht where he can plot revenge in many different ways. Does he cruise alone?

**Yolanda Cardioxa-** It is her death that holds the key to bringing a serial killer to justice. Nobody can bring her back but it can be hoped that she did not die in vain.

**Klaus Lewegz III-** His sailboat was a happy home for him & his wife until a serial killer boarded and destroyed his love for the sea. Now he prowls the land for justice.

**Donna Lewegz-** Her death yields no progress in stopping a killer from killing again. Her husband's determination for justice borders dangerously on a thirst for revenge.

**Kate Traval-** An interior decorator, she has become a bright light in the life of a lonely police officer. He has reservations about making their relationship permanent since they have both been burned before but she is sure she can reshape his world.

**Elisabeth Morgan-** A consultant, she use puppets in her workshop for counselors and educators. Her devotion to the technical detail of her craft leads her to become valuable witness to murder but an unexpected risky attraction changes her life.

**Drake Plate-** A retired Texas peace officer, he is certain of his own detective skills, certain of his son's proficiency, but wants to keep him from making a grave mistake.

**Vivian Plate-** Practical and down to earth, she is hoping for the best for her son and his fiancée but worries they are rushing headlong into disaster with their eyes shut.

**Debralyn Martin-** The failed marriage of one daughter makes her reluctant to give her blessings to the upcoming nuptials of another despite night and day differences.

**Frank Martin-** A traditional father, he is at a loss as to how to proceed in the 1980s. He is overprotective of his single daughter when it is his divorced daughter in need.

# For so many of these characters after love comes murder...

# Prologue 1972

"Ever feel like you have no control over your life?"

Sally Monroe dangled her toddler on her knees as she watched her brother pick at his uniform in the hallway mirror.

"No," replied the soldier. He finished flecking pet hair off his pants and turned his attention to his shirt. "You might have an easier time with the housework, and keeping your clothes clean, if you kept the dog outside."

"I wasn't talking about housework. I was talking about life itself. I mean, here we are, just a few years out of high school. Remember all our big plans? And here I am with a baby and bills, Ted unemployed, and you on your way back to the war. Both of us in circumstances over which we have no control."

Sally took a moment to shoo the dog out the back door. She did not want her brother to have to worry about anything right now, even pet hair on his uniform.

"It isn't like you to be philosophical, Sally," said her brother, upon her return. "And it isn't forever. The kid will grow up. Ted'll get a job or, more likely, get drafted. The war will end. I'll come back. Not necessarily in that order."

"Doesn't seem like this war will ever end," said the young mother.

"It will. Peace talks in Paris are on again. And I'm going back. I'll lick 'em single handedly."

Sally laughed wearily. "Idiot."

Both siblings lit cigarettes. The baby fussed.

His uncle picked up a toy meant to be used by adults to

distract infants. It was a hand puppet in the form of a kitten.

He tossed it to his sister. She put it on her hand and interacted with the baby.

"You are happy with Ted? Right? He takes care of you?"

"Oh, yes. The one light in it all. I have him to protect me. There's nothing that makes you feel more protected than being married to a cop turned lawyer. Even if he is between jobs."

"Lawyers can always find jobs. Just because it didn't work out at the last place means nothing. What did happen anyway? When was he let go?"

"It's been three months. Officially, he never was employed because they let him go in their trial probation window. He signed off that he was never there so they would not give him a bad reference. He had choices on graduation and he just chose the wrong firm. They were edgy and his personality didn't fit in. When one of their older clients took a dislike to him, they blamed him and fired him. He took it okay, at first. Now it's different. He's getting worried. If he lists them as a reference, he has to explain. If he doesn't, he has to explain not working for such a long time after passing the bar. Our savings are almost gone."

"Look. He can always go back to the force. They're desperate for police these days, with all of us drafted right out of high school and the hatred society has for the police. All forces are short. If I weren't in the army, that's what I would be doing myself. They are even hiring women now. Did you know that Volding Brook, just a couple miles over, has a female cop now?"

"He doesn't want to go back to police work. He's a lawyer now. It was a lot of long hard work and I supported him quitting the force 18 months ago so he could focus full time on getting his law degree finished. We both got fed up with the abuse our society heaps on the police these days. Many are targeted just because they're in uniform."

"Soldiers don't fare any better."

"But you've got more protection."

"I fail to see how."

The soldier surveyed his mirrored image once more. This time he was satisfied. He put on his beret. He was leaving for deployment soon and he had a drive to get to base.

"Oh, Buddy!" Sally put the child down, tossed the puppet aside, and rushed to her brother. "Don't get killed in Vietnam!"

She embraced him and started to cry.

"I won't, silly," he said, gently pushing her away, wiping pet hair that had transferred from her clothes. "You haven't called me Buddy for years." He tickled her chin.

"I could call you by your real first name," she threatened.

"No! Anything but that!" He feigned mock horror.

"Don't push me away, then." She grabbed him and hugged him again.

"You know, I tell the other men I have a twin and they automatically assume it's a man and usually identical. One of these days, I'm going to adopt a pseudonym and pretend to be my own twin. Some men are named Sally, you know."

She laughed. "That's hysterical."

"None of them would believe my twin is as lovely as you. Now, don't cry. I can take care of myself," he said. "And I've got to go."

"It's not fair you have to go and not me. Just because you had to be a boy." She faked a pout. "I so wanted a twin sister, not a twin brother!"

He laughed this time.

"I'd much rather go and see you stay here and raise that child and more to come," he said. "You know I'm not the marrying kind. After Mom and Dad pass on, and I know they are not well, you and your family will be all I ever have."

"I don't believe that!"

"It's true. I've already decided. No brides for me."

"Wouldn't surprise me if you came home with a Vietnamese girl in tow."

A dark look came over the soldier's face for a moment.

"Just kidding! Come on. Don't be mad. Buddy!"

8

The looked passed and the soldier smiled again at his old nickname.

"I'm single for the duration, kid," he said. "Already set in stone. A confirmed bachelor-soldier for life. I'll never marry or leave the army."

"A long life, and career," his sister pleaded. "Stay safe over there."

"I will return, in the famous words of MacArthur. Keep the home fires burning," he said. And his salute to her was only halfway lighthearted.

He knew living as a housewife with a small child and an unemployed husband was almost as stressful as what he faced.

At least he could fight back.

All she could do was wait for better times.

And he was doing what he wanted to do. He was not so sure about her.

He reached in his pocket and pulled out a $20.00 bill.

"Go to the movies tonight. Find a babysitter. Have some fun."

"Oh, no, I couldn't!" She made no attempt to reject the money.

"Yes, you can! Go see *The Godfather.* It's good. It's bound to be playing around here somewhere."

"I heard it's so violent."

"Nah. Just like the old 1930s movies on late night TV. Just in color. It's good. Go see it. The real violence is where I'm going."

Sally kissed him goodbye, still clutching the money in her hand.

As her brother drove off, Sally Monroe walked outside and watched as long as she could see his car go down the end of her street before having to turn off to the main thoroughfare. It was a bright sunny day and she was able to see the street clearly.

"Your husband off to war, ma'am? A fine looking soldier."

The voice came from nowhere as Sally walked back towards her front door. Her modest tract home was baby-proofed but she did not like to leave the child alone very long. She did not have time to talk to a neighbor.

"Yes," she said. "But that's my brother. My husband is not in the service, not yet. Mr.-"

"Zopev," said the man. And he hit the nearest tree with his knuckles. "Knock on wood. On a college deferment?"

"No, he's a lawyer," said Sally with pride, not mentioning Ted's employment problem.

"A lawyer? That's impressive. With a baby and all, maybe he can get out of it if he tries."

"My baby's inside-" Sally began, as she tried to place the man. Zopev. The name was not familiar. Did he live on her side of the street? A couple doors down? Or was he part of the new family that just moved across the street?

"I'd love to chat but I really can't."

"I'm expecting a draft notice any day, myself," said the man. "Just divorced. So that bumps me up on the list. I don't have a degree or kids, so..."

He spread out his hands and sighed deeply.

Sally looked around to see if anyone else was outside. More and more homes in her neighborhood were vacant during the day as more and more women went to work to earn a second paycheck, needed in the appalling economy of 1972.

The worst downturn the US economy had suffered since the Great Depression of the 1930s, with massive unemployment and, differing from four decades ago, vicious inflation instead of deflation.

Prices doubled and tripled at whim and only the fortunate few had secure jobs.

Sally bit her lip anxiously.

No one was visible.

She felt uneasy.

The man stepped between her and her front door.

"Could I come in for a cup of coffee? We just moved up here from Wilding Falls in East Texas. My - uh- girlfriend's at work and we don't have a thing in the house."

*Living together,* thought Sally, distracted by the man's gossip about his own personal life. Her other concerns faded as she contemplated the arrangement. Her eyebrows rose unconsciously.

"Just economics until our divorces are done and we can get legal," said the man, seeing her expression and reading her mind.

"Oh, of course." Sally felt guilty for judging him. Everyone had to do what they had to do in these hard times. "Come on in. Welcome to the Panhandle."

After all, it was 1972 and times had changed.

He stepped back to allow her to precede him into the house. She had only a moment's cognition after he shut the door and before his hands closed around her throat.

A brief recollection that the new family that had moved in was from Mexico and awareness that this man was blonde...

As he forced the life out of her, she had a moment of spiritual union with her unknowing toddler and then she was gone.

# April 1983

Chapter 1

Fitted with her wedding gown for the last time, the bride-to-be stood before a wall of mirrors framed in tall white columns.

Beside one column stood her father, happy and smiling.

Ready to pay for the dress.

Before the other stood her intended husband, dark and handsome, bearded, with deep brown eyes of approval, surveying her image.

Ready to take possession.

The attendant brought the veil.

The princess was never sure later at exactly which second she decided to run. It might have been the moment the attendant mischievously arranged the satin panels on either side of the lace veil in such a way as to resemble a niqab, covering the lower portion of her lovely face.

On the other hand, it might have been the moment she caught the eyes of her turbaned fiancé and saw a rare smile and triumph in his eyes.

In the end, the trigger for her subsequent actions was irrelevant.

Somewhere within her emotions, she uncovered the stark fact that throughout her whirlwind romance with Sheik Abdul Mahlah, she had been looking for disapproval all along.

Someone to stop her.

However, her father enthusiastically endorsed his daughter's romance with an Arab oil prince who was immensely rich.

Her mother petitioned the Catholic Church for dispensation so their planned secular ceremony would be approved.

And the Church said okay.

Her publicity agent put out stories of how her upcoming marriage would affect her rising career as a star of Italian movies and television if her husband forced her to abandon her craft as most expected.

It was a drama. Fans ate it up.

Felicitations poured in.

Advice abounded. Advice about the dress. The cuisine. The venue.

No one saw beyond the potential glamour and entertainment of the union.

Her former boyfriend, a good Italian Catholic journalist, who should have fought to the blood death in defense of her hand, instead extended his to the oil prince in congratulations and hinted around for a position in the Arab sheik's TV production company in Egypt.

Finally, at the last bridal fitting, the realization, forming for weeks, crystallized.

There was no one left to object except herself and God.

After the dress fitting ended and the men left, she phoned her personal maid with instructions on where to send clothes and personal effects via international transit.

She promised to mail the maid a good reference upon their receipt.

She had her passport in her purse.

Then, gown and veil left behind, she diverted her chauffeur from the bridal salon exit to the Rome airport and a plane to America.

With a simple stop at that new modern convenience, the ATM machine, simultaneously money was flying through the airways to an American bank as her plane winged its way across the ocean.

Just prior to boarding, a call to a Hollywood producer had paved the way for a royal landing.

Italian actress Joanna Scarpartti, descendant of Sicilian royalty, was traveling to the new Hollywood- Sand Waves, Texas. She would make her American debut in the first movie produced in the new studio that was being built to compete with, if not displace, the old-line establishment in California.

The studio owner and movie producer, Stark Wynter, had placed a standing offer at her feet months ago and he was delighted to get her message of acceptance, unexpected though it may be.

He would take care of all arrangements. She only had to arrive safely in Texas.

The movie studio was practically on an island, adjacent to one of the most exclusive gated communities in the world, itself tucked inside a moat-like border of solid middle and upper class Americans.

Texas would become the princess' new domain, with Sand Waves her personal castle.

Safety was purported to be superbly enhanced there for celebrities in the aftermath of a recent political assassination. Whereas in Italy assassinations were a part of the normal crime activities, generally met with a bored reaction from police, never provoking any positive change.

This small command design colony was now practically a fortress, so she was told by Stark Wynter.

Joanna was sure that enclave of the old west, home of knight-like rangers, site of the famed Alamo victory, and promoted as uniquely different from the rest of America, was the perfect place to shield her from the parental threats of her father and potential violent tendencies of her betrothed.

She knew Texas was warm and dry like Sicily.

She had seen many movies where the Texas Rangers had ridden into sweltering sunsets in the hot dusty desert.

They protected all persons in their realm regardless of their nationality or origins, anticipating the needs of all good people instinctively.

She was not naive enough to expect protection from the Texas Rangers military force itself. But she was sure Sand Waves had the best police force in Texas.

She envisioned a squadron of 75 to 100 men patrolling the colony, probably on horseback.

Carrying large rifles.

Wearing big white cowboy hats.

Competing to serve her needs.

The princess was sure she could make her every security desire known.

Even though she could not speak a word of English.

Chapter 2

The woman drove slowly into the motel parking lot.
It was 2:10 AM. He was late.
It was raining.
Warm April Texas Gulf Coast rain.
But rain.
Texas weather was stereotyped by Hollywood as being hot and dry. This part of the Gulf Coast was hot. That was true. Dry was an adjective that could sometimes be used to describe it in July and August, maybe June and September, sometimes other parts of the year. Occasionally there were droughts.
Usually it was humid and prone to substantial downpours of rain, afternoon thunderstorms, occasional tornadoes, and rare but certain hurricanes.
Today there was only rain.
The waiting woman felt extremely frustrated. This relationship, so full of potential when it began, but stalled for so long, was on the verge of fulfilling its initial promise.
The trial was almost over. The verdict would soon be in.
The rest of their lives would begin.
Her pulse quickened. The car was lumbering into the parking lot. Yes. It was him.
He already had the room key.
"Darling!" He kissed her fervently. "I have missed you, too."
She did not mind the cheap Houston motels. She never had. The way he made love was worth it! Such passion! Such vitality! Like a man possessed.
They entered the small, already smoky cubicle and began undressing.
"Do you know how much I love you?"
"Yes," he said arrogantly, pushing her down on the bed.
She murmured automatically. "I love you so much. You are the best damn liar."
"Now, we are both free. It was hard to get away without

anyone noticing. But I did. Soon, I will not have to sneak around."

"Yes, I know." The woman smiled broadly but a faint annoyance touched her brow. "There should not be any reason why our relationship cannot be public now."

He bent over her, grasping her shoulders.

"If I only thought I was the only one."

"You are! There is no one but you! No one can compare to you. Why do you think I waited so long? Do you think I would do for anyone else what I have done for you?"

He laughed and relaxed. "No, I guess not."

"I know not!"

"Sometimes, I feel that when we are married, your career will come first."

"Now be fair." The woman lit a cigarette. "Would not your career come before me? Is not that why we are still hiding."

"My career is different from yours," he insisted. "A man with my job needs a full-time wife."

"I do not see where your work is more important than mine."

"I've a lot more responsibility than you. A lot more worries."

She sighed with exasperation. "Oh, let us not argue."

He brightened at those words. "Let us not. Let us not waste our time. I know the trial is almost over. I have no doubts about the result. It will still take some time for all the details to be ironed out in the end."

"How long before all the final papers are done and we do not have to keep our love a secret anymore?"

"The court procedures are not the problem at the moment."

There was one worrisome development. He decided not to burden her with it. He did not want to dampen the mood.

She regarded her lover with trepidation. "I do not see that we were really arguing. We were just discussing the merits of a justifiable solution to an almost impossible situation."

"We have to discuss two different things at the same time? In English?"

"We can be intelligent enough to do that. In English. The

present question is- why should I go on meeting you at motels? Keeping you a secret? It is nerve-racking, not to mention inconvenient." She caressed his chest.

"Temptress," he said.

"If I were a temptress," she said. "Then surely you are the most powerful tempter."

"I work with ruthless people. I have to maintain their respect. I have to maintain control. I need to be above suspicion. You have these one-on-one situations. You only have to keep a few people content."

"My new job starts soon. I may only be dealing with a few people but I am going to be extremely busy for the next week. That is why I wanted so much to see you."

"Oh, I thought you were not going to take on another job until everything was finalized."

"You just indicated that could take weeks if something goes wrong. I have to eat."

"Nothing will go wrong." He spoke with uncertainty.

"And my career brings in good money. I do not see why I should quit after we marry."

"We don't need money. We just need patience."

"And that is your response to which situation? The present? The quandary that is keeping us from making our relationship public? Or the future? The question- what am I going to do about my career after we're married?- is just as pertinent. We should resolve it now."

"Damn your career. It's not all that high class you know."

"I suppose you think yours is? Others with your experience do better. With more prestige to go with it and less danger."

Angry now, he pushed her away from him. "I will have more prestige soon. More acclaim than you ever imagined anyone having. You just wait and see."

"You are a fool," she said. "Your talents are just being used."

"A fool?"

"A fool."

"Damn you, you little wench." He grabbed her by the shoulders and shook her.

She winced, but emotionally she was untouched. "Do not act like a child."

He let go of her. "It is time to go."

"I am not ready to go yet."

"Then I will leave you here alone."

"Do not go away angry."

"I am not angry. It is all going to work out."

"It is just that this has been going on between us for too long. You think I am not really in your class. But it is you. You who are not really worthy of me."

"Ha, you, little lady, are not in my league. You may have the first name of an English queen but your real last name is as Mexican as my alias."

"I guess when we are married, you think I am going to move in with you. That is what you think. You are going to be moving in with me."

"I have got the better place. Why do you think that I would take a step down? My boat is superior to your house."

"All right! You think you can get away with saying that?"

She started attacking him with a pillow. And in the ensuing pillow fight and its resulting consequences, they forgot their present and future problems while the physical consumed all their intense attention.

They concentrated on what had to be done next.

"Let us just forget both our careers," he laughed. "Now with this new movie studio coming to Sand Waves, we will just become stars."

"I am going to get to be an extra in the big scene."

"I think everyone in Sand Waves is going to be an extra at that event. I am going to be there."

"Yes, but I will be able to get a prime seat that will guarantee my getting in the movie. You will probably wind up on the cutting room floor."

They stared each other down until he grabbed his pillow and they went at it again.

Chapter 3

"Everything is all arranged for the wedding. All you two have to do is show up and follow directions. Well, you, as the bride, will have to be fitted for your costume the Monday before the event."

"That would be this Monday?" Daphne asked incredulously.

"Yes. The costumes are all done. We just have to fit you and make sure no alterations are needed. If they are, we will get them done the next day."

"So my wedding dress is already chosen?"

"The movie is set in the 1940s," explained Stark Wynter, "so you will be dressed as a postwar bride. With a severe long sleeved high neck dress, draping skirt, and no lace, all satin bodice with a scalloped moiré taffeta overlay. I had it especially designed by the finest costumer in Hollywood at a cost of over $5000. It is stunning."

Wynter paused.

"And you will just wear a tuxedo."

The famed movie actor from Hollywood's golden-silver age, now still famous as a producer-director in the 1980s, was treating Lieutenant Plate and his fiancée, Daphne Martin, to an early breakfast at the most popular Sand Waves eatery, the Toy Museum Restaurant. Most popular because it was virtually the only gourmet restaurant that had secured a coveted permit to operate in the command design colony.

Sand Waves was north of Galveston, south of Houston, and contained about 25,000 people. In the different sections referred to as colonies, homes were separated by size and price. Never in Sand Waves would a lower price house be built next to a quarter million dollar property. That sacrilege frequently happened in the highly populated city to the north, Houston.

"After all, you are just the groom," Stark Wynter was saying to Plate. "No one will be looking at you."

Plate brushed the water beads off his police uniform shirt. April showers were almost a certainty in this Gulf Coast climate and downpours had been relentless lately. An intermittent day of sunshine every so often gave the water a chance to run off and held back the threat of a flood like the one the previous November.

He and Daphne had met during that weather event although their romantic relationship had not gone into full swing until after the first of the year. Engaged less than six weeks, they were being offered a chance for a dream wedding, all expenses paid.

They had not set a wedding date. Nor had they completely informed their families. Only their parents knew of the seriousness of their relationship. They had asked their parents not to talk about it with their siblings yet. They were taking time to enjoy each other and get to know one another better. They were discussing the possibility of a fall wedding date.

This event would only be a week away.

And it looked like it would be a rainy day wedding. The forecast showed no letup in sight.

A relatively dry preceding winter also meant the ground was not saturated to the point of flood risk. When the warm winter sun of Texas had plenty of successive days to shine, the ground dried out despite cold temperatures.

The flood in November had been deadly for Sand Waves. Now in the early spring of 1983, rains had come back but in a more benign way. At least for the time being. The worst effect so far had been over-watered lawns. Many very foggy mornings with low visibility contributed to a rise in fender benders.

Daphne had come to breakfast with an umbrella but Plate did not even have his jacket, as, after an early spring cold snap, the temperature was warming up enough to threaten extreme humidity on the horizon.

"A theme of the movie will be the hot Texas weather with the deserts of East Texas as the background," said Stark Wynter.

"Is this going to be a fantasy?" Plate asked.

"Certainly not! We're aiming for realism here. There will be, of course, a stunt marksman for the shooting scene in period dress," Stark said. "He will be costumed just like any other extra for when the shooting starts, in case we decide we want a glimpse of him on camera. Right now in the script the killer is anonymous. But I think I might reveal his identity in the end. Have to decide who and soon. I have hired a pro extra who is a real marksman, served in Vietnam, to fire shots at the bride. Of course, they'll just be blanks but this guy's got all the good movements. He will be isolated on one wall on a short platform balcony designed just for him to take his shots. Like most of my Hollywood-based personnel, he's going to be flying in for just overnight. I'm trying to find him a room."

"I'm not really sure this is the way I want to get married," Daphne said.

"I don't know why the designers of this place did not allow at least one small hotel inside the boundary," said Stark Wynter.

"I always had in mind a church wedding," Daphne said.

"It would be so much more convenient if there was just one small hotel. I could rent the whole thing. I cannot even find apartments to rent," Stark said.

The only apartment complex was a very small set of units hidden in the back of the colony. There was a long list for the next available unit.

"Powers-That-Be believe this discourages riffraff," Plate commented.

"I do have an idea of what type of dress I want and I'm not sure it's the 1940s style," Daphne said.

"You just have to make a slight alteration to your appearance. A dark wig. Elicia is not a blonde. There will be two identical dresses, one with the blood on it and one you can wear for your ceremony. The princess will be wearing the blood stained dress," Stark said.

"Wait a minute," said Daphne.

'It will start like this, you will make your entrance and we will film it, then you can go on with your real wedding. After the ceremony, we announce to the congregation that we will be filming a short sequence for the movie, give simple directions as to how we want them to react, and ask them to join in the fun. We should get it all in one take," Stark said.

"Taking *Murder as the Organist Plays* and setting it in the

1940s is one thing. But I don't recall any shots being fired at the bride," Daphne said.

"Huh?"

"I've read the book and I don't think it was that way," Daphne said.

"Oh, the book. All we wanted from the book was the scene with the bride with blood on her dress. As I said, it is being updated to be set in the 1940s and rewritten for modern audiences," Stark said.

"I don't see how this book could possibly be rewritten for modern audiences," Daphne said.

"The princess is making her American movie debut as a bride in this movie. Problem is, she doesn't speak a word of English so we had to cut her character a little short. In this version the bride, Elicia, gets killed on the way down the staircase," Stark said.

"Does the princess know this?" Daphne asked.

"What do you mean?" Stark asked.

"In the book she's a main character throughout the story," Daphne said.

"My great-grandfather told my father the writer of the book was more interested in her," Plate commented.

"I know," Stark said. "We don't really care what the book was about. But it's just wonderful that your great-grandfather was a primary character. This is the perfect angle to launch the film. We shoot the wedding sequence at the real wedding of the descendant of a real character in the movie. That will be great for publicity. We've got to do something to counter all this sci-fi stuff. And this is going to be the pivotal scene. The rest of the movie is mostly made."

"What do you mean? I thought the Italian princess hadn't even come to America yet," Daphne said.

"Her arrival was a secret. I just got her to the compound with a hired companion. Before that, we didn't know who would be the bride. So we shot all the action around her," Stark said.

"Officer Skaar is there, providing security until I can take over," Plate explained to Daphne. "The rest of us are involved one way or another in the Zopev trial. Willhouse was the arresting officer.

In addition, Jordan was called as a witness because he was up for the next call and he had to go explain why he let Willhouse take the call instead. The chief and I had to testify as to departmental procedures. These lawyers try to make something out of every little thing. Jordan has a bad ankle that was bothering him that day. One of the defense lawyers wanted to make a federal case out of that."

"What action?" Daphne asked Stark Wynter.

She ignored Plate's comment, already knowing all about the well-publicized trial.

She was sick and tired of hearing about it.

A fan of mysteries, both in books and movies, she detested plots focusing on serial killers. They tended to be too graphic. The ones where she knew who the serial killer was from the beginning were boring because she knew who the serial killer was from the beginning.

She found the ones where the serial killer turned out to be the least likely person who could ever be suspected to be a serial killer too far-fetched.

Daphne thought sure she would know exactly what a serial killer would be like if she ever met one.

There was no way she could know people for years and years and it turned out they had been secretly murdering people here and there, everywhere, since adolescence.

"We considered a plot with a serial killer. But there's too much of that these days. We decided to go for something more direct and simple," said Stark Wynter.

"I thought the book had pretty good plot with a good twist at the end," Daphne said.

"Movie audiences don't want to sit through a long engrossing show just to wait for a quick twist at the end. That would force them to think and they don't want to do that. They just want to feel."

"Can't they do both?" Plate asked.

"Plus, you have to allow for the effect commercials have on mood when it goes to television. Some suspense is okay but we need action, action, action," Stark said.

"So what is going to happen in the movie?" Daphne asked.

"After the bride is killed at the wedding, the preacher grabs the sister and tears her clothes off of her. He has been lusting after her for years and the sight of blood on the bride's dress provokes him into sexual action," Stark said.

"What?"

"One thing leads to another and in all the chaos they become handcuffed together- never quite worked out that detail yet- but anyway, they're handcuffed together. They spend the rest of the movie roaming through the desert, with her naked," Stark said.

"That sounds terrible!" Daphne exclaimed.

"Big market for that type of stuff," Stark said. "We are taking the movies in a direction those sci-fi adventures cannot follow."

"Why not?" Plate asked.

"I'm working with a hot new star from Europe to get him to play the preacher, rather than do one of those sci-fi movies. They are just a fad."

"Why would they stay out in the woods handcuffed together? Why not just come in?" Daphne asked.

"Okay, this is the brilliant part," Stark said. "This is a spur of the impulse thing for him, see? What happens is- he doesn't dare go back. Remember, this is the 1940s. He'll be disgraced and lose his collar. Unlike today. Nobody would pay any attention. Once she is stripped naked, it's revealed Coria has a bodily defect, one breast being significantly larger than the other. She doesn't want to be found without clothes because this defect causes her deep psychological anguish and she shall become suicidal if the world finds out."

"Won't the fans of the book be upset about all of this? Have you read this book at all?" Daphne asked.

"No, I never read books. It cost me a fortune to acquire the rights to this one. It took private detectives weeks to track down the actual rights owners. They were descendants of the writer. Happy to get money. They didn't care what I did with it. As for fans of the book, well, readers ought not to expect movies to follow books. That's old hat."

The server brought their lunch and they ate quickly, each trying to envision exactly how the wedding within a movie would work out.

"I have to have a decision by tomorrow morning," Stark Wynter warned.

Plate caught Daphne's eye.

She frowned.

"I will let you know by then," Plate said.

Stark Wynter went to pay the bill.

"Peter, we need to talk about this," said Daphne urgently. She took Plate's arm and pulled him up from his chair.

"It'll be okay," he said, seeing that the look on her face was giving way to panic. He finished his Coke quickly and followed her through the restaurant towards the exit. They waved farewell to Wynter, still in the middle of settling the bill.

"This is going to ruin our wedding!" Daphne protested, as they climbed into Plate's car.

"Calm down. Look at what we're getting out of it. An all-expense paid gala wedding. You're getting an incredibly beautiful expensive dress. All for free. All it is going to take is about 30 minutes to an hour for them to shoot. This means they shoot, then they leave, then we get on with our wedding. It'll be worth it."

"I don't like it. I won't have any control. There's only a week to prepare!"

"That's the beauty of this. We don't really have to prepare. Other than the fittings, all we do is show up on Friday. No stress. No preparations. Everything done for us. And first class all the way."

"I always wanted to have a church wedding. A big church wedding with hundreds of people."

"So it won't be in the church. He is going to use a real minister. I have already given him the names of those we know. We will have hundreds of people there. The entire community is being invited to show up as extras. Everybody in Sand Waves will be there. Look, and for our private guests they're giving us a $25,000 reception. All they want is to shoot a few scenes before, during our ceremony and at the very end. You're going to stand at the top of the stairs in the bloodstained dress-"

"No, not me. The actress," Daphne corrected Plate. The image his erroneous words invoked caused her to shudder.

"Right. That's what I meant. The part that is our wedding will be a normal wedding. Just filmed on Hollywood quality film. They'll just be taking excerpts as they need it for various backup and flashback scenes, not showing our faces," Plate said.

"I'm going to have to wear a dark wig. And you're not going to be able to wear your uniform!" Daphne complained.

"I can put on a uniform and you can take off the wig at the reception. We get to invite anybody, have everything we want at the reception."

"I think we're rushing into this."

"Look, I had not told you this yet. And I will try to get out of it. But for the next month I'm probably going to have to spend most of my time worrying about this Italian princess-actress and her safety in Sand Waves. Why not go ahead and get a great wedding out of it?"

"I think you're just doing this because Chief Brecken wants you to do it. I wouldn't be surprised if that was his idea. He's put out cause he can't send you out on undercover romances anymore and this is his revenge on me."

"A $25,000 wedding reception any way we want. All expenses paid formal wedding. No hassle. Nothing to do but be there. We just have to wear the right costumes and have some extra bridesmaids and groomsmen. Think of the money we're saving."

"My parents would've paid for my wedding," Daphne said.

But she knew it would have been a strain to pay for the elaborate extravaganza she wanted.

And her father would have been ashamed to let her pay for it herself.

"Even if your parents wanted to pay for the wedding, turning this down would be terribly unfair to them." Plate was using his most persuasive charm. "We are so shorthanded. I don't know when the chief is ever going to hire anyone to replace the two men that left. We might not have a chance to do a real wedding until after the first of the year. Think how much money I'm going to be paying on the apartment rent. When we could go ahead and be married and I could let that apartment go. Is it because you're worried about the extras that are going to be the bridesmaids?"

"No."

Daphne hesitated.

The idea of Hollywood providing extras as bridesmaids would have been objectionable to most young brides. But Daphne had no doubt she would not be overshadowed by any actress Hollywood could produce. Especially in the 1980s.

She would have had a harder time competing in the pre-1970s era when actors and actresses still had to look good.

She was not troubled that they would all be towering over her in height. That, she felt, was an advantage. A set of tall bridesmaids would show off a petite bride like herself.

Seeing hesitation in her objections, Plate tried again. He was driving her home so he could get back to work.

"Wynter has promised us that we can ask our own family and friends to be groomsmen and bridesmaids. They'll be fitted in the same costumes as the extras in the wedding party and might even get in the movie. I've already lined up Skaar, Jordan, and Willhouse. I'm going to ask my brother as soon as you give the okay. They're going to get free tuxedos, which they're going to get to keep. And they'll get to be first, the extras will follow. You can do the same thing with whoever is going to be your bridesmaids."

Daphne bit her lip. Outside of her sister, Darica, she had no one to ask to be bridesmaids. It was hard for her to admit. Even to herself.

She had cultivated few close friends in high school and college. They had drifted away, most marrying young and slowly dropping her as she became a mature single career woman.

None of them bought any insurance from her.

She shared a close relationship with many of her clients. There were some she was even going to invite to the wedding. But there were few single women near her age and it would have been a bit too much of a push at the social barrier to ask an insurance client to be in the wedding party.

Asking a person to be in the wedding party indicated a degree of intimacy that Daphne just did not have with any other woman her age, client or not, married or single.

"I guess it will be all right," she said reluctantly. "Do you think Mrs. Skaar and Mrs. Willhouse would like to stand with their husbands?"

"I'm sure they would be delighted. That's very thoughtful of you." Plate was touched.

"I'll try to get a hold of Darica and see if she can be my maid of honor."

His numeric pager went off just as he pulled into her driveway.

"Fine, I will finalize the details with Stark this week."

He went inside her home to answer his page.

Using her new antique French style phone in her home office, he called his answering service and received his message without replying as Daphne watched.

The look on his face told her he would not be staying.

He hung up the phone and stepped briskly to her front door.

"I have to get to Houston. The Castroe Zopev murder trial is over at last. There's been a verdict."

Chapter 4

The case had been prepared with care. Vietnam Veteran, Castroe Zopev, manager of a distributing-servicing company for typewriters and copy machines located in a small set of offices in a strip center in Houston, was also a serial killer.

Or so law enforcement authorities had said since the mid-1970s. Police from all over Texas had tracked his movements for years without success. Several victims had been traced to him but with no real evidence.

Finally, at least ten years into his horrific pastime, he had been caught. His arrest came inside the gates of Sand Waves, where he had recently moved.

He was charged with the murder of a neighbor's wife, Yolanda Cardioxa, and this time the husband, Emilio Cardioxa, had seen him on the premises.

The manner of death was nearly identical to all those Zopev was suspected of perpetrating.

Several sets of parents who had lost daughters along with several widowers from throughout the country had come to Texas to attend the final session of the trial and see the verdict handed down.

Emilio Cardioxa's testimony was expected to nail Zopev at last.

Everyone involved congratulated themselves. They had removed a dangerous manic from the streets of America for the rest of his life.

They knew it.

Lieutenant Plate knew it also.

Yet he worried.

Authorities knew the identity of the killer, had a list of supposed victims, but did not understand just how he selected his victims or his ulterior motives for killing in the first place.

Nevertheless, those elements were not necessary for the killer to be apprehended and brought to trial.

Full credit for capturing and bringing this monster to a court of justice quietly went to Officer Timothy Willhouse, who had quickly responded to the husband's call and identification of his neighbor, arresting Zopev peacefully at his home.

And it was on Officer Timothy Willhouse that the burden fell hardest when Zopev was acquitted after a short trial.

"Not guilty," said the jury.

Castroe Zopev walked free.

Blood pressures soared inside and outside as area humidity spiked. The temperature broke 85 degrees at the same time the early morning verdict came down.

Acquitted on the evidence of one witness who provided Zopev with an alibi, Zopev did not seem celebratory. He looked anxious as he was congratulated by his few supporters.

A policeman watched him closely as he ducked out of the courtroom in the rain into the waiting car of his lawyer. Shortly after, that same policeman joined at least one other vehicle in shadowing the freed defendant.

The haziness produced by the raindrops bouncing off hot asphalt in the humid weather made it easier to follow undetected.

"We knew Eduardo Pauliza was going to alibi Zopev but we didn't think the jury would believe him," said Plate to Daphne.

They were relaxing at her house enjoying freshly delivered pizza for lunch.

The TV on mute.

The rain coming down.

They were safe and dry in her den.

The unexpected twist of a not guilty verdict made the trial become interesting to Daphne.

"It was thought the victim's husband's testimony would trump Pauliza. But the jury bought the Zopev's defense attorney's idea that Cardioxa saw somebody that he later identified as Zopev to get a conviction. Ordinarily a defense attorney would attempt to suppress suspicions about a client, but this one cleverly turned the tables. He made our valid beliefs that Zopev has killed before appear to be persecution of an innocent man and was able to impeach the testimony of Cardioxa. He pointed out all of the relatives of the victims in the courtroom and said they had been brought there as a staged show and to get them off the backs of police. Especially to neutralize Klaus Lewegz."

"So he said it was a conspiracy to get Cardioxa to identify Zopev?" Daphne asked.

"Yes. He cleverly argued that Cardioxa saw someone. And later that his identification was manipulated. Pauliza, on the other hand, was a disinterested party with no reason to lie," said Plate.

"Then why did everyone think Cardioxa would be believed over Pauliza?"

"Pauliza is a resident of Sand Waves' lowest price colony. He's Hispanic. He's a blue-collar worker. He moves furniture for a living. Hard work. Does not participate in society much."

"Probably too tired after he gets off. You're a snob, Peter. Isn't Cardioxa Hispanic, too?"

"I wasn't giving you my opinion. That is what was thought. And I don't think Emilio Cardioxa is Hispanic. I don't know what he is. He does have a very slight accent that I haven't been able to place. His wife was though."

"So you are sure Zopev is a killer?"

"His first victim, we think, was a young mother, housewife, wife of a former policeman in 1972. Her name was Sally Monroe. Then there are several others over the years. But with little in common and not enough evidence in any of them."

"How many are you, that is YOU, actually sure Zopev did?"

"I did look over all the files. I would say four. IF you count the one he was just acquitted for."

"Really? You are telling me you are not sure about that one? You're not sure he killed Yolanda Cardioxa?"

"I've been troubled by the fact that no one has tied the victims together with a common ground."

"No other police wives?"

"No. All except Yolanda were housewives."

"What did she do?" Daphne asked.

"Oh, nothing. She was an heiress from Mexico," Plate replied.

"So she had no career?"

"That's accurate," said Plate.

"Then she was a housewife, too," Daphne concluded.

"I've never really thought about it that way. I would just call her a socialite, not a housewife. After all, she did not keep house."

"Being a housewife does not imply that you keep house."

"I thought it did. I thought that was what it meant- a woman whose primary function in life is to keep the house. I thought that is where the word came from, you know like the wife of the house, married to the house…What? Why are you looking at me like that?"

"I'm contemplating exactly how I will strangle you."

"What did I say?"

"I keep my own house. Does that make me a housewife?"

"No, but you have a career. And you're not married yet."

"You just defined a housewife as a woman who keeps the house."

"A married woman who keeps the house. With no career."

"So what does that make me?"

"I'm confused."

"Housewife is just a word to describe a woman who is married and has no career. It has nothing to do with a house. She might not even live in a house. She might live- live on a boat. It has to do with being dependent on your husband's income."

"Yolanda Cardioxa was not dependent on her husband's income. And they did have a boat."

"Plate, you are making me very angry."

"How? What am I saying?"

Anger popped inside her eyes. "Ooooh. Plate- I-"

" 'Peter', remember," he interrupted in self-defense. "We are in love. You call me Peter now."

She folded her arms and glared. She had forgotten for a moment. It scared her a little.

"I think we had better skip this discussion," he said cautiously.

"Yes, I'll file it away for after we are married."

Plate felt a sudden wave of panic as he envisioned a large file cabinet containing every dispute they ever had taking up a preponderance of space in their living room.

"Let's get back to murder and deception. Serial killers. Less stressful topics," he suggested hopefully.

"Yes, I agree." She took a deep breath. "I was thinking about the two other victims of Zopev you are sure of. Tell me more about them."

"One was married to a lawyer. Jan Smith," he said, with gratitude in his voice. Daphne's eyes were becoming normal again. "Same as the one here. The other was married to a children's advocate. Her name was Donna Lewegz. Remove the Sand Waves lawyer, and no connection there either. Three different occupations, police, lawyer, advocate."

"Advocate sounds like a lawyer."

"But it's not. It's more like a social worker."

"Maybe Zopev didn't know that. This was some time ago right? He was younger."

"1979. Not that long. But still. It's a thought. But still doesn't explain the policeman."

"All connected to the law, somehow?"

"That's a stretch."

"And the others that you are uncertain about?"

"All housewives, uh, homemakers, with husbands in various other professions. Nothing in any way connected to a legal job. I think really they have just been included because of the time period and locations. My analysis, strictly unofficial- it was Willhouse's case- is that we could be certain Zopev killed the first mother of the toddler- Sally Monroe, the cop's wife in 1972, also the advocate's wife in 1979, Donna Lewegz, wife of Klaus, and the first lawyer's wife in 1980, Jan Smith."

"So you think Cardioxa killed his wife?" Daphne asked.

"I have no thoughts on that case. I had no involvement with it. I just don't see the connections between the victims."

"So most of those people in the courtroom really probably were not family members of this guy's victims? They were brought in to watch some strange guy get convicted that probably had nothing to do with the crimes against their loved ones?" Daphne asked.

"That's what the lawyer argued and that's what I think also. Except of course, the family members of Zopev's true victims."

"Their families were there?" Daphne asked.

"Sally Monroe has no traceable family," said Plate. "Her parents are dead, died just months after she did. Those inexplicable deaths of broken hearts apparently. She had a brother who was reported lost in Vietnam. Donna Lewegz's parents were there along with her husband, Klaus. He still lives on the boat where she was killed. It's docked somewhere in Galveston. Jan Smith came from a missionary family. They're all in Asia right now. Her widower has remarried and moved on. He did not want to be a part of this. I don't remember his name. Or nobody ever said. Yolanda Cardioxa's family sent English speaking representatives. Who knows what they will report back to her family in Mexico?"

"Say, you did say Sally Monroe's husband was a former cop?"

"He was unemployed at the time, according to the records."

"An unemployed cop in the 1970s?"

"Maybe a bad cop. Or personality problems? I don't know. Lots of reasons. He could have just been between departments. Wanting a change or something."

Something suddenly dawned on Daphne. "So what happened to her husband and child?"

"We don't know."

"Don't know?"

"As I said, we have not been able to trace him. We know the Smith husband went off and started a new life. We assume Sally Monroe's husband did also. But we don't know."

"I'd look into it."

"I don't have time."

"Why not?"

"Our wedding. Computer conversion at the office. This actress

35

who just arrived, having jilted her Arab fiancé who might want to kill her. Plus, we have just learned we have a Japanese VIP arriving soon, who is some relative of Hirohito."

"That sounds like it could be code for agent. One you don't know what he's doing here, exactly when he's coming or even his real name. You know, that sort thing."

"Nonsense," said Plate.

"Well, I can look into the medical insurance aspect," said Daphne.

"You know, if we got a modem for your computer, you would not have to use your general manager's computer to access the insurance data bank."

"A what?"

"A modem. That would allow it to connect with other computers via the phone lines."

"Look, right now my computer is working just fine. I am not tampering with anything. It's a wonder in planning the wedding. I have a file for the guest list, their addresses-"

"You won't need all that. We're letting Stark Wynter take over."

"I don't see it that way. I intend to keep up my files. Something could go wrong. And no tampering with my computer. No modem or whatever. I got that computer put together and it works. Remember, I had to assemble this computer myself and keep it on the fireplace hearth for a long time until I got my office remodeled and turned my closet into a little computer cubbyhole."

"You could connect to other computers. Don't you want to be able to access other people's information?"

"From my house? That's doesn't even sound legal."

"Your company computers do it."

"That's different. Insurance companies do all kinds of things that aren't- I mean that are legal only to them. I think. Anyway, I cannot get in trouble if I have the client's permission and the few times I don't- well- there's not a way to trace what I do."

"I'm not sure about that."

"At least if I do something with the company computer, it's defensible in that I am just trying to get better odds on making a sale. Anybody would understand that. It's a perfectly innocent motivation. But if I start accessing information about total strangers from home-"

"You may be right."

"I know I am. You do not want your future wife to get arrested. It would not look good."

"Okay, let's drop it for now. I don't have time to get information about real criminal cases much less investigate laws concerning computer espionage. In fact, I have to go. I forget. Do you get the morning or evening newspaper?"

"Morning."

Plate sighed. "I need to pick up an afternoon edition. They're supposed to be putting out a special on the trial verdict."

"Oh. When they put out a special, my carrier usually delivers one to me. He knows that's one of the things that gets him good tips at Christmas. So check my porch on the way out. Take it if you need it."

"It would save me a stop on the way back to work."

Daphne's newspaper carrier had come through. The special edition of the *Houston Chronicle* was at the edge of the little square cement platform in front of Daphne's front door, which she referred to as a porch.

The enclave did have a cover, so Plate was able to look at the newspaper for a moment before going on out into the rain.

He scowled as he quickly scanned the new lead story, then rolled up the paper and dashed out through the raindrops, sprinting around Daphne's right angled sidewalk to her driveway where his patrol car was parked.

Despite his efforts, water splashed on the newspaper causing the headline containing the word 'shocking' to blur and disintegrate when he tried to brush the moisture off.

Chapter 5

The antique shop customer could not resist the old newspaper from 1972. It was the year his life changed and somehow as the time had passed, he found himself collecting mementos with that date on it.

He smiled when he saw the article predicting the day people would receive their newspapers electronically.

Through some sort of pneumatic tube installed in exterior walls of houses, the feature writer speculated.

In addition, the article predicted someday there would be computers in the home.

The latter prediction was beginning to come true.

The man became sad, reflecting on all the many changes in the past decade never dreamed of, never experienced, by those who had passed on.

He looked over the display in case he had missed anything.

In the old Galveston shop, this display of hundreds of papers lined a magazine rack. The expensive ones- announcing the death of Elvis, the Vietnam peace treaty, détente with the Russians, and so forth- were most prominent on the top row. But he could often prowl through the lower tiers and find something from his favorite year.

The display was only one variety of hundreds in the shop, which occupied an old warehouse that had once been used for production during World War II.

Every possible collectible and antique imaginable was represented in the store.

This customer never went beyond the small front corner that held the newspapers. Adjacent was a display of dolls, all kinds, from Madame Alexanders to Barbies.

He would window shop the doll display for amusement but he never bought anything there. It was just near the newspapers.

He wondered how the dealer acquired the old papers. They were from all over the country. And every so often true antique newsprint would appear. Something from the Civil War, priced high. Or World War I and World War II, the latter selling for higher prices than the former for some strange reason.

But he was only interested in 1972.

Today he was in luck.

He shivered a little as he paid for the paper even though the weather was very warm. His luck was running so well that he was beginning to get a little superstitious about everything he needed, wanted, and thought of, just somehow falling into place.

The verdict was the one element in his plan he could not be sure he could control.

It had been perfect. And now there had been another development that had landed valuable information into his lap.

Almost as if God had seen his plans and decided to make them complete.

Except he had stopped believing in God long ago. So he just took it as really good luck.

Or bad luck, depending on whose point of view.

He was unconcerned either way.

Passing the doll display on his way out, he stopped for a short moment to peruse a new type of figure that he had not seen there before. Prominently displayed on the center shelf inside a small stage was a collection of antique puppets. They were miniatures on strings and they had to flop in lopsided positions, as they had no master to guide them from above.

The newspaper collector could not help but compare them to the people he dealt with every day.

And it briefly came to his mind what an expert it would take to make these puppets interact in such a way to accomplish a certain goal.

Just as skillful as he needed to be to get his mission accomplished.

*I am the director of this project. I pull the strings.*

He felt rather silly.

And it was a total impulse.

He purchased one of the puppets.

Clutching it, he smiled as he prepared to exit into the rain.

Upon stepping out of the store, he also purchased a newspaper on the street. A special edition had been rushed out.

The press has been prepared. The verdict in the Zopev murder trial was on the front page.

*They must've had two mock-ups already prepared. One for a guilty verdict. One for a not guilty verdict.*

He laughed as that train of thought continued. *Wonder if anyone had cleaned up in the newspaper office pool by betting against the odds?*

He wrapped the 1972 paper carefully in the plastic courteously provided by the vendor. The small puppet doll was slipped inside of the newspaper, it strings casually wrapped around its body.

He stuffed the current copy of the *Galveston Daily News* in his raincoat pocket and hunched his shoulders.

The weather was warm but the rain felt a little cold.

A few moments later, he picked up a phone receiver. He was in an obscure corner of Galveston where he had found a working pay phone on a long sidewalk on a barren street holding only warehouses with workers who cared not what went on anywhere else in the world.

It was one of the few rare phones left that had a complete enclosure, like the ones where Superman changed clothes in the old black and white movies and TV shows. Most 1980s phones now sat on hanging on a half shelf with only a seashell like canopy protecting them from the elements, and not giving much protection from the rain for the customer.

He went out of his way to access this old fashioned structure whenever he wanted to make a completely private call and take as much time as he wanted.

He knew, despite crime movie plots, that any call could be traced to any number, domestic or long distance.

Keeping a phone call short to prevent its tracing was a myth.

Anonymity, seclusion, and a rarely used isolated forgotten pay phone was the best protection.

He also took precautions against being easily recognized. An old fashioned hat, dark glasses and usually, if the weather justified it, a coat of some kind.

And the weather certainly did justify a raincoat today.

"Operator," he said upon getting a connection. "I want to put in a person-to-person call to Egypt."

It was hot and stuffy in the booth.

He carefully placed the older paper on the little shelf underneath the pay phone but carelessly stretched out the current newspaper and propped it against the glass partition so that he could read it with ease while he waited for the operator to put the connection through.

Outrage from families of supposed Zopev victims blasted from the front page.

Houston- A verdict of not guilty was reached in the murder trial of Castroe Zopev, openly suspected in the serial killing of several women. Zopev was vehemently condemned by numerous relatives of women allegedly his victims over the past 11 years. Prosecutors thought they had him for the murder of Yolanda Cardioxa, wife of Sand Waves resident, Emilio Cardioxa. But an alibi provided by a local furniture mover, Mr. Eduardo Pauliza, proved the undoing of the prosecution's case. Pauliza testified that on the evening of the murder, Zopev was there at all times Pauliza and another moving company employee moved office furniture at a complex rented by the accused. Pauliza's account was discounted by the prosecution because the associate allegedly working with him that night vanished before he could be questioned. Zopev's defense maintained the associate was most likely in the country illegally and fled to Mexico in fear of exposure as an illegal immigrant if he testified. The prosecution maintains no such associate existed. Supporting the prosecution was the deceased victim's husband's testimony of having glimpsed Zopev fleeing the scene on the same night the victim was killed. The jury obviously believed the defense. The accused seemed dazed after the verdict and left the courthouse without issuing a statement. Also Emilio Cardioxa was visibly stunned after the verdict. A spokesman for victim's families, husband of victim Donna Lewegz, E. Klaus Lewegz III, a children's advocate, blames police for careless procedures and the district attorney's office for past lack of thorough investigation and follow-through on tips from the- *continued on page 19*

"Your party, sir." The operator's sharp Texas twang came through the phone, interrupting his reading. "Please deposit $5.00 in coins."

He poked quarters into the slot methodically until he heard the connections click loudly. Getting through to his ultimate target was easier than he thought it would be.

A person-to-person call from America still had mystique.

"This is Abdul Mahlah. You say you have a message from Joanna Scarpartti? Who are you? I do not recognize the name the operator gave me." His smooth English, with only a faint accent, nevertheless could never be mistaken as native to Texas.

The American caller had made an effort over the years to make his voice as accent free as possible. He had been successful. Few people could have placed his home state by listening to his voice.

"I'm giving you an opportunity to get at Princess Joanna."

"Get at her?"

"Get her back. Kill her. Whatever you want to do. I know where she is and how to get to her."

"Preposterous. I know where she is. The whole world knows where she is."

"There's a flaw in her security. If you are willing to send someone after her at a specific time, I can guarantee he will get in."

42

The caller spoke with some speed as he only had a limited quantity of quarters and the expense of the call caused the operator to sound a warning in his ear more frequently than he had anticipated.

"I'm no longer interested in this princess. I have decided to marry a woman of my own faith and country."

"I'm one of your faith and I am outraged by the insult she has perpetrated on all of us. You may not want her anymore but if you don't exact revenge, we will all lose face in the sight of the whole world. You're going to let her make millions of dollars in America using her insult of you, our country, and our religion as her base for her fame and success. If you do not take some kind of revenge, the revenge will be taken on you."

"Preposterous! How dare you threaten me! Do you know who I am? Obviously you know I have a reach to America. I'll find out who you are and kill you."

"Then I will be a martyr to my cause. More will rise up behind me to demand satisfaction. Will you take action or not?"

The prince paused for a moment.

His first initial reaction, after he got over the wounded male sexual aspect of Joanna's rejection of him, had been commonsense thoughts that it would have never have worked out anyway.

In addition, he was probably well rid of her without having to pay a lot of money to accomplish the same end after a few short years of marriage.

His childhood sweetheart had been waiting patiently for years. Princess Joanna had faded from his mind faster than he thought possible.

However, he had been the object of some vicious ridicule from some of his friends. Not a particularly religious man, he had failed to consider how his embarrassment might reflect on some sects, and how some of the more devout might view it.

Maybe a small token of revenge was called for, after all.

"Please deposit-"

The caller did not bother to listen any further but rapidly exhausted his supply of quarters into the slot as quickly as he could.

The voice of the oil prince came back after another noisy click.

"How much do you want for your information?"

"I'm not asking for any money. This is a matter of integrity. I just want a guarantee that revenge will be exacted by your operative at the place and time I name."

The lack of a payoff demand flustered the prince. Maybe this was a religious fanatic. If so, he could be dangerous.

"If you are so devoted to this idea, why don't you just do it yourself?" the prince asked. He mentally ran down the list of people in the United States who he might be able to call on for a small favor.

"I cannot do it without considerable risk and exposure. I wait my turn for a much more important operation. Then I might be bound to reveal under torture your complicity."

"That won't do." The prince knew where Joanna was hiding behind the gated section of Sand Waves. The son of an old friend was nearby as well. An old friend whose family owed him a few favors. Not to mention, trying to live the Sand Waves lifestyle, the friend's son, a college student at a nearby institution, would probably welcome a little extra cash.

However, the prince was not sure how law-abiding this contact might be.

"Give me your information and I will get back to you to see if it can be arranged."

"Surely you don't think I'm that stupid, Your Royal Highness." The last three words were heavy with sarcasm.

The caller had paid scant little attention to news reports about the Iran hostage crisis four years ago but it had saturated the newspapers. He had just scanned a story about it in one of the older papers for sale at the antique shop.

Now he echoed some of the rhetoric of the hostage takers to the Arab oil prince.

The jilted lover's attitude changed at once and his voice began to shake a little.

"I have to at least know when. If there's a specific time

44

element that the security is going to be lax, I might not be able to get somebody at that point in time," said the Egyptian.

"Only at a specific time or your operatives will be caught."

The caller from America relayed the exact time the princess would be vulnerable.

"Give me 24 hours at least. To make arrangements."

"I'll call you back this time tomorrow."

The caller hung up. He had no doubt the prince would be able to arrange something. And he laughed a little at the vulnerability of the Egyptian to the old ideas that he had borrowed from movie plots of the 1930s combined with a few memories he had of recent troubles in the Middle East that had made the news.

Now convinced the caller was of the same ethnicity and religion, of which he was actually neither, the millionaire would not dare back out.

The phone made a sound.

Metal striking metal.

Two quarters fell back down in the change slot.

The caller hesitated. He hated to call the person he had designated in his mind as the lowlife.

He did not have a choice.

One more quarter went into the phone. This would be a collect call so the coin would be returned upon contact when the recipient accepted the call. Which he did.

"What the hell happened?" demanded the designated lowlife. "We were so sure. How could they get the wrong verdict?"

"I don't know. We have to talk."

"You are damned right we have to talk. That sonofabitch walked free. What are you going to do?"

"Before I can do anything, I'm going to need a little money."

"Money! Hell, I cannot afford this call!"

"Calm down. Not money from you. I know you must be broke. I have a plan to make a score due to this Italian princess, here to do that movie in Sand Waves."

"The actress?" The lowlife sounded surprised.

"Yes. It's a con. I already have it going. I'll get enough money out of it to take care of everything once and for all. I need just a little information and cooperation."

"What can I tell you? What can I do? Now my girlfriend knows nothing about you or how this all came down."

"I know but she can help without knowing what's going on."

The lowlife took a deep breath. He was beginning to catch on to what his compatriot was saying.

"We had planned to announce our engagement. This verdict may cause her to reconsider."

The caller took a deep breath. He could not image why any decent woman would consider marrying the lowlife.

"Do I need remind you of the consequences of not doing what I say?" asked the caller.

"Okay, what do you need to know?"

"I don't want this call to go on too long. If they ever check your phone records- "

"Okay, let us meet. Can I call you back at this number?"

"Yes, if need be. Come on down to Galveston. You know where. Wait for me if I am not there yet."

The phone booth occupant hung up and retrieved his quarter.

It would be a while before the lowlife would get to their destination, while it was close by to him.

He needed to wait just a little longer for the sociopath to call. He knew the sociopath would ring on time for his instructions. As soon as that aggravation was done, the inhabitant of the phone booth knew where he would go next.

A small antique projector located nearby showed a short documentary film every 15 minutes about the Great Storm that had destroyed Galveston in 1900.

He had seen it several times but it always fascinated him.

Almost forgotten by history, the storm has killed an estimated 12,000 people and destroyed most of the city in the worst natural disaster ever to strike the United States. It happened in the era that coincided with the infancy of motion picture technology and someone had gone to the island and filmed the destruction.

In 1900 the movie camera was so new that the cameraman was able to fool authorities that he was a surveyor with the government and his strange apparatus was newfangled surveying equipment.

Twentieth Century carnage from the world wars and modern photography had combined to make his work obsolete. There was much more death and destruction filmed in better quality, and with sound, to supply those entertained by true-life disasters.

When Hollywood mushroomed two decades later, the story of Galveston's Great Storm did not make the big screen.

But someone had salvaged the footage and made it into a documentary that could be seen for a couple of dollars in a small dark storefront museum. Enough tourists pursuing the fun-in-the-sun experience overflowed into the city to make the museum survive.

On rainy days, there would sometimes be several curious who paid the small admission price.

Seeing the old film would kill just about the right amount of time. The museum attendant knew him by sight.

That would give him a hint of an alibi if it was ever needed. He had carefully noted that the attendant did not keep track of how many patrons attended which showing each day.

There were a small handful of people who came and watched the film frequently. Like he did whenever he was in Galveston.

He could always insist he was at an earlier or later showing on this particular day if need be. It would be his memory versus the attendant's. If she disputed him.

As he waited for the phone to ring, he mentally reviewed his plan. He would give precise instructions to the sociopath. Like the lowlife, the sociopath was clever, but unlike the lowlife, the sociopath was sick, needing less intricate manipulation. The conversation would be brief. Then he could look forward to the rest of the evening at the museum.

He looked at his watch. Not much longer. He pulled out the newspaper and began rereading the Zopev murder trial story.

Chapter 6

Plate picked up a late supper to go from the Toy Museum Restaurant. He returned to the police station with it, finding Chief Brecken still alone.

The rain had previously let up a little.

It was getting much heavier again.

"The question is, Plate," said the chief. "Are we going to give Pauliza some kind of protection?"

The two men were now conferring in the reception area. The wide shallow room had a small unused desk on one side, reserved more than ten years ago for a never hired receptionist. Two picture windows faced the street. Parallel to the entry door, an interior door in the middle back wall opened to a hallway with offices on either side.

Plate and Brecken were anxiously watching the picture windows. They were vulnerable to shattering in wind driven rains.

Like the torrent now pounding against the panes.

"Have there been threats against him?" Plate asked.

"Nothing officially reported. The verdict is only a few hours old."

"I think it's much more likely that something's going to happen to Zopev. We only have so many resources. We're short on men. We would have to call in the county personnel and we would have to pay them."

"True. The budget is tight for the year and, despite Stark Wynter picking up most of the cost for this princess, we're going to be responsible for the Japanese VIP. Nobody is going to help pick up the tab for that," said the chief.

"I think I know a way I can get Wynter to help out there."

"How?" Brecken asked.

"He has got the princess on the third floor. He is using the second floor for housing the equipment he needs to make this movie since the soundstage is not finished yet. The first floors have been turned into the movie set. He is staying in one of the four cottages on the grounds. The other he's reserved for us."

48

"For you," said the chief.

"Whoever. Anyway, that leaves two vacant cottages."

"Surely he has them reserved for his stars coming in from Hollywood," Brecken said.

"Probably. But they haven't arrived yet. The only star he's got on hand is the princess. The actress playing the sister, the actor playing the groom, and the actor playing the organist have already done a great deal of their work back in Hollywood. They may not even have to come to Sand Waves at all. Wynter is using stand-ins for them as of this point in time."

"By all means, ask him if he'll let us put the Japanese visitor in one of those cottages. We wouldn't have to go to the county for extra men. It would save a bundle."

"I have a little leverage with him since Daphne and I are doing this wedding within the movie for him. I think I can get that little perk added to our compensation," Plate said.

"Wonderful." said the chief.

"And as far as Pauliza is concerned, the final decision is up to you, of course. But I'm not inclined offer him any extra protection other than that given to any law-abiding citizen in Sand Waves. I'd be more inclined put him under surveillance. In a way, that would be a different means to the same end."

"There is no justification for doing that. All the man did was testify in the trial. We've no evidence, despite looking until our eyes popped out, that his testimony was bought, corrupted, or false in any way."

"It's completely unverified and totally contradictory to what Emilio Cardioxa testified."

"Everybody knows that. And keep in mind, it is only our point of view that the jury members were totally out of their minds by believing Pauliza over Emilio Cardioxa," said the chief.

"One of them had to be lying."

"Or one of them was mistaken. I think pretty much it's being summed up in the papers that the jury believed Cardioxa was mistaken. He had just found his wife dead. There had been a little smattering of publicity about Zopev living in the area. Emilio Cardioxa put two and two together and made five. He probably did see the killer. But you know how unreliable emotional eyewitness testimony is."

"Are you telling me that you believe Pauliza?" Plate asked.

"I'm just trying to look at it from the objective point of view. The official point of view. Pauliza was hired by Zopev to work at night, so that the business was not interrupted during daytime hours. Pauliza swore Zopev was there, letting him and his employee in, supervising the move which took place at the exact time Yolanda Cardioxa was killed and Emilio Cardioxa thought he was seeing Zopev in his back yard."

Plate was contemplative for a moment.

"I still think it odd that Zopev picked the night that Yolanda Cardioxa was murdered to suddenly decide he needed his furniture moved from one office to another."

"Coincidences happen in life. If Zopev was innocent of this murder, how could he possibly have known it was going to take place?" Brecken asked speculatively.

"He lives alone. Most any other night he would've had no alibi. He happens to hire nighttime movers that specific night?"

"Pauliza has the only such business near the colony. So his rates are lower here."

"I would bet you that Willhouse did not consider looking into why Zopev wanted his furniture moved in the first place."

"I could well understand lax attention to that detail. Have you ever considered that the man just wanted to redecorate his office? It does happen."

Plate recalled Daphne's redecoration of her office that resulted in it going from looking rather junky to having a classic Victorian motif. Not only had the effort gotten her computer off her fireplace hearth, but also she had a wall safe installed behind a new oil painting Plate had given her.

She was waiting on a Pulaski desk that Plate owned to complete the look. They had competed to purchase it earlier in the year and he had beat her to it.

He smiled as he envisioned the desk in her office. The room was visible from her den. She kept it neat and orderly at all times, actually having a work desk inside the wide and shallow closet. She could leave that messy and just close the closet door.

It was a very deceptive room.

The Pulaski would complete it.

"We're missing something. How thorough was Zopev's office searched? Maybe something was hidden there. Something which escaped us," said Plate.

"Zopev's offices were completely searched," Brecken said.

"Under Tim's supervision."

"Are you saying Willhouse missed something?"

Plate did not reply. The chief was subtly reminding him that Yolanda Cardioxa's murder was not his case.

Plate knew if he continued to pursue the conversation, the subtlety would be dropped.

The phone rang and the chief went into his office to answer it. A moment later he came back out.

"That was a complaint."

"From?"

"Mr. Edward Klaus Lewegz III."

"Is Edward his first name? Did we know that?"

"Goes by Klaus. We did know it," said the chief. "Lives in Galveston, drives to Houston every day for work. Spends half his life on the freeways, a quarter at work, the rest seeking justice for his wife."

Plate recalled the anguish on the sandy haired man's face when Zopev walked free.

"What is his criticism of us? We got the guy. We're not the jury."

"He wants to file a formal complaint against Timothy for mishandling the arrest."

"It won't get anywhere."

"No, not unless you keep on about how he might've missed

something in the investigation."

"I won't say another word."

"Good. Now let's go over the plan for you moving into the compound and taking care of the Italian princess. I know Skaar is a good man. But he's the youngest, least experienced of us. Her father's important enough in Sicily that if something happens to her we're liable to have an international incident with the Italians. Actually got an inquiry from the State Department. So I intend to reply that I've got my best man on the job and everything is going to be okay as long as she is in Sand Waves," Brecken said firmly.

Edward Klaus Lewegz III had been busy on the phone in the immediate hours following the acquittal. In addition to his complaints to the authorities, he was calling all the family members of the possible victims of Zopev that he could find.

A significant number of them, having already grieved for their lost relatives several times, rebuffed his approaches.

They wanted to bury their dead and get on with their lives.

Lewegz already had three people lined up to meet with in coming days in hopes that they could come up with a plan to expose sloppy law enforcement tactics and other inefficiencies of government officials that had failed to take the Zopev off the streets and put him in prison or the death chamber where he belonged.

Klaus Lewegz did not mind the rejection of most of the people he had contacted. He understood. If he had been blessed with children, he would have probably felt the same way. But he was alone in the world and as far as he could see, there was another husband of a victim also alone in the world that had no reason to reject his plan.

And on top of that, Emilio Cardioxa was a lawyer. He could be an immense help in the pursuit of the course of justice for his dead wife, Klaus's dead wife, and the other women.

The death of his wife of 15 years had devastated the social worker. Born wealthy, he had forsaken an easy life in his family's business for a stressful job advocating for children in need. He and his wife had transferred their love of children into care for the disadvantaged when they found she was infertile.

They often brought his small clients out to their boat for a fun-filled sail, giving the wards of the state a relaxing experience on the water.

A fresh break from their anxiety-filled lives.

Now Donna was gone and it was Klaus who lived the anxiety-filled life.

The boat, also his only home, had remained in port since Donna's death. But while having abandoned active sailing, Lewegz had not forsaken his professional calling.

He had added a second passion, justice for his wife.

Therefore, Klaus Lewegz was extremely agitated when Emilio Cardioxa rejected his idea of getting together with other victims' family members to plot strategy.

After a term of blinding anger, Klaus Lewegz's emotions settled down when he considered the possibility that it was just too soon after the trial for Emilio Cardioxa to do much of anything.

He resolved to contact the lawyer again after his first meeting with the other family members, enlisting them to help convince Emilio to join with them in taking some kind of action.

He planned to pursue new avenues with the press. He had contacted a woman reporter and had a historical angle he wanted to pursue from a feminist point of view.

It was just another ploy but who knew what it might yield?

Something had to be done before another woman died at the hands of this vicious killer, vindicated over and over again by legal technicalities and liars like Pauliza, who gave him alibis.

Eduardo Pauliza.

Lewegz wrote that name beside the list of the family members who had consented to engage with him in the cause.

There was strength in numbers.

There was strength in a common cause.

Maybe this group could do something about Pauliza as well.

Somebody had to have paid him to give Zopev that alibi. Klaus Lewegz was a reasonable man. He was sure that the authorities had investigated thoroughly enough that a payoff by Zopev was no longer a viable theory.

But that did not mean that somebody else did not compensate the furniture mover to testify as he did. It was just a question of figuring out the guilty party. And how it was done.

Klaus Lewegz had known where Zopev had stored his automobile in the unlikely event of an acquittal. Getting that information had cost Lewegz quite a bit of money and now that the unlikely acquittal had come, he took a perverse pleasure that the expense had not been wasted.

Like collecting on costly catastrophic insurance he had hoped he would never need.

Lewegz exhausted his list of numbers of other family victims.

He hung up his car phone.

He picked up his binoculars and trained them on the Zopev's vehicle.

There was no way the killer could retrieve the car and exit without being seen from the parking space occupied by Klaus Lewegz.

Lewegz had a clear view of the defense lawyer's car when it pulled up and let Zopev out.

The murderer had a small suitcase with him.

He made a phone call from the pay phone before getting in his car.

Lewegz got excited.

He started his engine in anticipation. Maybe something was going to happen today.

Maybe time in jail awaiting trial had more than exhausted the serial killer. Maybe it had whetted his appetite for another victim.

Klaus Lewegz patted the camera and the gun resting on the passenger seat. At least he would know where the freed serial killer was going to be staying.

If he watched closely enough he could prevent him from striking again.

Klaus revved his engine a little. He was ready.

Chapter 7

Zopev drove over the only bridge that connected Galveston Island to the mainland with much trepidation. He was not worried about the high span of the bridge or the wolfpack of rapidly moving cars switching dangerously from lane to lane to get around larger trucks or slow moving station wagons like his.

He was a good defensive driver.

He literally feared being murdered upon arrival.

He had been less worried before the acquittal. In fact, he had not expected the acquittal. He knew his alibi was solid and would hold up on appeal.

He had expected to be convicted by an irrationally emotionally charged jury. He then expected to enjoy the free police protection provided by the entity charged with both incarcerating and protecting him until some time had passed.

After the publicity had died down, and his conviction was reversed when a total, thorough investigation could find no fault with Pauliza's testimony, Zopev planned to slink away to some other area where he had less fame.

The acquittal meant he walked out of the courtroom completely vulnerable. The paperwork bought him some time as it was afternoon before he was released. His court appointed lawyer had helped him elude the press, dropped him off at the parking lot where his car was stored, and wished him well.

The lawyer had handed him a phone number from an anonymous caller, who had said Zopev would recognize the number as being from someone who wanted to help.

Otherwise, he was on his own.

Before retrieving his car, Zopev risked being exposed at the outdoor pay phone.

He did not want to wait to make the call. He did not want to make it from a hotel room or any other place it could be traced.

The car lot had no tall rectangular phone booth with a bifold door ensuring privacy, if not total safety.

That structure had recently been demolished and the pay phone hung on the side of the attendant's hut to make room for another valuable parking space.

He picked up the receiver to make the call, desperately hoping the phone actually worked.

The attendant eyed him with peripheral vision, then turned his back.

Zopev deposited his quarter and dialed the number. Relief flooded him when the connection clicked and he recognized the voice of the person answering.

"I know you are in trouble. I can put you in a safe place," assured the person on the other end of the line. "Just follow my instructions."

Still, Zopev was nervous. The assistance came from a most unexpected source. Granted, this person had helped him before, out of some extreme sense of Christian conscience, he guessed.

But he strongly felt the disgust of this person towards him.

Only preventing a perversion of justice could have been the motivation.

But now an offer of more help? Maybe a continuation of Christian charity meant that he should be kept alive. However, his benefactor did not seem the type to be that devout.

Nevertheless, Zopev felt he had no choice. Everyone else was treating him as if he had leprosy. And he feared the wrath of Klaus Lewegz. He had no money to hire security.

He was scared. He got in his car, still wary of being followed, and headed to Galveston.

Once on the island city, he picked out a random motel, located on the beachfront, down a little from the seawall, to spend Friday night. He cautiously parked in a paid lot a few blocks away so if his car was spotted in the middle of the night, nobody would know exactly where he was.

As soon as it turned dark, he walked to the marina. It was a fairly long walk but he felt sure his car was being watched.

He rather enjoyed the walk. He had a good umbrella.

And it was not cold. Just wet.

The water lapped gently at the boats in the harbor. Most boats were fishing boats or speedboats. Sailboats were in the minority but still the most picturesque, even though most were made of fiberglass and had lost the classic teakwood décor that had been the source of so much of their charm and mystique.

A few antique sailboats and a few extremely expensive new vessels retained the teakwood exterior. They stood out like genuine topaz among plastic pearls floating on the blue water.

The marina was well lit.

Even in the dark and the rain, the boats lined up in their slips, a wooden dock on one side with an extended pier, and endless water on the other, combined to make an artistic impression.

This idyllic postcard setting struck Zopev in sharp contrast to the gray prison cell and the brown prison courtyard where he had occupied space awaiting his trial.

*I could live on one of these boats,* he thought. *If I knew how to sail them, I could sail away out on the ocean where there was no temptation.*

He was contemplating how such an existence would be possible as he walked down the uneven ramp towards the boat he was looking for, per instructions from his unlikely benefactor.

He stopped before a nondescript sailboat, blue and white fiberglass like hundreds of others in Galveston and the surrounding Gulf Coast area. It had the correct name. But no one was in sight.

There was a note, sealed in plastic and taped to the railing on the deck.

He carefully stepped aboard, his inexperience causing the boat rock a little bit.

The note was for him.

"Working tonight. Be there tomorrow. Hatch is unlocked. Pull the cover straight up and climb down. Provisions down below. I will be on board shortly and we will wait for our chance to slip out to the Gulf."

*Of course, the safest place for me! Out on the water!*

Zopev felt a rush of gratitude towards his benefactor.

*Must be religious fanaticism,* he thought. *Nothing else could explain this amount of generosity.*

He debated going back to his car and getting his suitcases. He had left his vehicle in the small parking lot that bordered the marina.

Lewegz was out there waiting for him somewhere.

He was sure he had shaken off the car that had been following him from Houston.

However, there was always the risk that his shadow would guess where he was going.

This boat was close to the bay.

The walk back would take nearly ten minutes.

Even if anyone following him found his car in the parking lot, it would be a long time before they could ever figure out which boat he was on.

By that time, they could be out to sea.

He was almost sure he had lost Lewegz. Almost.

He decided to get his belongings later. He followed the instructions on the note.

Entering the tiny cabin, he was dismayed at how little space there was to move around. The entry led to a small eating area with a fold-down table and cooking provisions on the side of one wall. The other opened into the small head. Seating for the table obviously doubled as an extra bed and there appeared to be a closed off bedroom in the bow section.

It had a short vinyl coated door with a metal handle.

He turned the handle and poked his head inside the small triangular room, seeing the narrow beds lining either sides of the wall and touching each other as they came to a point.

He was wondering just how uncomfortable they were when darkness fell all around him just as he felt the sharp pain at the back of his head.

Chapter 8

None of the stiff chairs at the police station were comfortable. Tolerable, perhaps. They were designed to keep the occupant alert.

That design was failing as darkness descended.

Despite the lateness of the hour, Brecken and Plate could not close the station and go home.

Both men were exhausted but an unexpected dilemma was keeping them on the job, slumping in their rigid chairs.

Even when their small force was at full capacity, they did not aim for 24-hour coverage. The county took care of hours they were not able to cover and, after 1 AM, private guards patrolled the gates that led to the highest priced section of Sand Waves until near dawn.

Any emergency call made to the police department's number was automatically rerouted to the county when the station was closed. The county personnel were always on duty.

Closed was not exactly a word used. But Brecken rarely worked weekends. Plate tried for Saturday or Sunday off. The 40 hour workweek was a goal, if not a reality, for all personnel.

With only five active men and one tied up at the Wynter estate, there were frequent segments of time when no one was at the station.

If something happened commanding their presence, they were not above being dispatched from home. Brecken, Skaar, and Willhouse rented homes in Sand Waves and were allowed to drive their patrol cars home. Jordan lived beyond the distance limit for that privilege and Plate lived in the Sand Waves Apartment Complex, which prohibited professional vehicles of any type in the parking lot.

The two unmarked cars were kept at the station and used as needed. Jordan had one of them now.

"Jordan was instructed to follow Zopev," Brecken told Plate upon calling him back in. "Both to keep track of him and make sure nobody kills him. And he hasn't reported in."

*So much for it being Friday. No time to spend the evening with Daphne tonight. I'll be here all night the way this is going. At least we got breakfast and lunch together*, Plate thought.

Plate was back at the police station conferring with Brecken and Skaar as to what to do about Jordan.

They did not want to call in other law enforcement agencies prematurely. But time was passing. The weekend, with only skeletal agency support staffs usually available, loomed.

Just as they were about to give up and contact the county, the missing patrolman limped inside the police station.

Jordan claimed a weak ankle from an old injury that he milked for sympathy whenever anything went wrong.

"Why the hell didn't you call?" Brecken snapped.

"Sorry, Chief. Fouled up and I was trying to fix it before I had to tell you."

"You lost him!" Brecken exclaimed, angry now.

"It was as simple as that. I lost him in traffic. Galveston traffic, no less. I do have some interesting things to report, though."

"Plate, start alerting other law enforcement agencies as quietly you can. We're walking a tightrope as it is, continuing to keep Zopev under surveillance although he's been acquitted. Jordan, you and me, in my office. Right now!"

"Did catch sight of Lewegz following Zopev. And I saw Emilio Cardioxa lurking as well. Lewegz was on his car phone and Cardioxa was coming out of a pay phone. Not far from each other or where I lost Zopev. Talking to each other, you think?"

"I don't give a damn if you saw President Reagan and Nancy strolling on the seawall. We know where they all are! It was Zopev you were supposed to track!"

Jordan reluctantly entered the chief's office. Brecken followed, slamming the door so hard the building shook.

Plate slipped into his own small office, sat down, put his hands behind his neck, and closed his eyes. Plate had been on the receiving end of the chief's wrath more than once in the past and he did feel for Jordan at this moment, despite the probability that Jordan more than deserved whatever treatment the chief meted out to him.

Plate was not an overly arrogant man. He had enough ego and machismo needed to be a police officer. However, his true skills were in detection and, being human, he could not help but think that this entire situation would have turned out completely different if he had been allowed to take the Castroe Zopev case from the beginning. But the chief had wanted to give Willhouse a chance to prove himself.

Jordan and Willhouse had both been patrolmen for many years and, in Plate's opinion, that was the position they needed to remain in for the rest of their law enforcement careers. Patrolmen were the vital workhorses of the law enforcement community.

Not everyone could be a chief. Or a detective.

*If churches were successful in recruiting all the congregation members into the choir, there would be nobody left in the audience. Without the audience, or in this case the patrolmen, what was the use of having the service?*

This somewhat confused analogy was going through the lieutenant's mind as he began routinely informing all interested law enforcement agencies that Zopev had slipped away. He diplomatically endured their reactions to the news, detaching himself emotionally so that he did not take any of it personally.

Lieutenant Plate liked his job very much.

Pay in the Sand Waves Police Department was not as good as in the big cities. Ordinarily limited to investigating burglaries and other property violations, the Sand Waves Police Department was a department ideally suited for the retiring espionage agent, the idealistic crime fighter with an inheritance in his pocket, the older cop who was burned out on drugs, prostitution, and other common crimes in the big cities, and needed a place to hide until his retirement. Types of crime fighters who could make do with less money.

Sand Waves Powers-That-Be frowned on crime. They could not control the behaviors of criminals with more regulation like they could control the actions of homeowners. This irked them. They simply declared crime nonexistent in Sand Waves.

Lieutenant Sinclair Plate knew different.

Crime was in Sand Waves just like crime in any other human environment. It was simply covered up.

A concentrated campaign to keep all crime quiet was the

continuous work of the local Sand Waves newspaper, the real estate agents, the powerful elite, the advertising department of the newspaper, and as much as he hated to admit it, the police department.

Between the influences of all of those entities, the high rate of property crime in Sand Waves was kept below the radar. There was so much crime in the greater Houston-Galveston area the traditional newspapers and television shows did not have time to fight the red tape needed to get the facts about what went on within Sand Waves.

After all, Sand Waves residents were a very small percentage of the population. They began at upper middle class and went all the way to ultra-rich. But it was the type of ultra-rich that kept a low profile, and the type of upper middle class that had to work to maintain that status. Those in between also had little taste for outside attention. What went on in Sand Waves, good or bad, rarely reached outside the community.

From the beginning, there had been one exception.

That exception was murder.

There was a small exclusive section of the colony that backed up to the bay, a stretch where the undercurrent could be especially vicious. When someone utilized those treacherous waters to commit a capital crime, it made headlines all over the state of Texas.

That was how the supposed second victim of Castroe Zopev met her death. But not from a pier connected to Sand Waves, which only had private docks and one small perimeter of houses in the gated section with water access.

Donna and Klaus Lewegz lived on their yacht docked at a high-end marina in Galveston. Donna Lewegz's body was found in 1979, murdered much in the same way as Sally Monroe. Then in 1980, Jan Smith was killed in her house in a small outlying town west of Houston.

The primary facet of the modus operandi of Zopev was firmly established.

He killed his victims in their own homes. If a body of water was handy, he used it. If not, he just used any means necessary to effect a kill. A blunt instrument could always be found.

His trespasses apparently fell next on a home in Sand Waves. The Cardioxa house. When Yolanda Cardioxa was murdered behind the gates of Sand Waves in March, her husband picked out Zopev in a lineup.

Secondary details were murkier. There was one detail kept back that was consistent with Yolanda's death that matched the other three concretely traced to Zopev. But did not match numerous other cases in which Zopev was a suspect.

There were no signs of sexual assault.

The press and public assumed the two went together so police did not let on that those particular victims were not sexually assaulted in any way.

The lack of such behavior at the death of Yolanda seemed to fit. Privately officials started to consider Zopev a suspect in only the three Texas killings that matched Yolanda's death in details.

Then Pauliza provided an alibi.

Maybe the details matching was truly a coincidence.

And maybe Emilio was truly mistaken. Or lying.

A new detail, seen at the Cardioxa murder site only, was kept private still. There were unidentified footprints indicating a peculiar way the killer had of standing.

If they were the footprints of the killer.

No footprints in the cases of the Monroe, Smith, and Lewegz victims were found.

This isolated evidence had led nowhere and was determined to be of no use in promoting a conviction so it was not mentioned. And footprint evidence would not have carried the day against the Pauliza alibi, anyway. At least this was the summation of Lieutenant Plate, based on what he had quietly studied about the case.

Regardless, he believed Sand Waves, as a community, had changed forever due to this trial. Combined with all that had happened earlier in 1983, the command design colony had gained more notoriety in the past six months than it had seen in its almost 12 year existence. And it could no longer be seen as the safe haven from crime it once claimed to be.

Chapter 9

The Italian princess had counted on Sand Waves to be crime free, but full of adventure. When she had first arrived, going on four days ago, Joanna had been excited.

She had expected a fabulous dressing room on the movie studio lot.

It had taken some time, and spurious translation, to get the princess to understand the movie studio was still under construction and there were no soundstages ready. Therefore, the movie was being shot in several local scenarios, including the residence of the producer, where the princess would be an honored guest.

"Sono Italiano," the princess had said when she finally got through it all. Her limited knowledge of English meant, in her mind, everyone else around her had a limited knowledge of Italian, especially the translator, so she kept her words short and irrelevant.

Just saying she was Italian was one of her favorite replies to any information.

Joanna managed to convey her feelings completely despite the absence of fluency. She was delighted with the security on the third floor of the Wynter estate.

She was instantly enamored of Officer Skaar. He appealed to her preconceived image of a Texas lawman- tall and handsome in the rugged American way with his slightly large nose, big eyes, wide teeth, and closely cropped coarse hair.

In Italy, those attributes could not have possibly been combined in as attractive man as Grant Skaar.

Not impressed by the police under most any circumstances, her companion was less than thrilled.

Stark Wynter had hired Elizabeth Lopez for the time Joanna was in Sand Waves. It was simpler and more convenient to have a translator on hand 24 hours, seven days a week.

The third floor at the mansion had three bedrooms. The princess was assigned a luxurious room formerly occupied by Amelia Mattworks.

Stark Wynter insisted Elizabeth Lopez move into one of the smaller bedrooms on the third floor with the princess.

She was not too pleased with this but the money was really good.

Elizabeth Lopez lived in Sand Waves. She was one of the few single women in the colony to own a home and she was not in one of the lower echelon colonies or behind the gates.

She was in the middle.

Approaching 40, her work was her passion. She had turned her gift for languages into a profitable career that carried her out of the barrios of Houston. Her first inclination was to decline the job of catering to the temperamental princess.

Then Stark Wynter offered her so much money for such an easy job that wasn't going to last very long, she could not refuse.

She had actually met the princess in mid-flight on the runaway bride-to-be's way to the United States. Wynter had arranged for Elizabeth to catch up with the princess on a layover and fly the rest of the way back to Texas with her.

The following day Elizabeth moved to the Wynter compound, occupying the adjacent room.

A room obviously designed for a servant.

The police officer was privileged to stay in a cottage on the grounds. His abode was the size of Elizabeth's house.

Fortunately, it was only going to be for a few days until the wedding scene could be shot.

Elizabeth then knew she would find herself at a crossroads. She would have to decide what to do if Stark Winter asked her to remain on as a translator when the princess left for Hollywood.

She was planning to say no.

However, just in case her other plans did not work out, she took care to get in the good graces of Princess Joanna from the beginning of their relationship.

When Elizabeth was going to do more than one translation for an individual over a period of time, she had learned it was wise to get to know the person so that she could communicate more than just words when it came time to do her job.

Personality, attitude, use of language, comfort zone levels, and intellectual depth were among the traits she liked to have discerned before she had to relate the first conversation.

On the flight from Italy, which she joined midway, she made sure to sit next to Joanna.

They had been seatmates for no more than ten minutes when Elizabeth sized up the lovely Italian girl accurately.

*She is lonely and frightened,* Elizabeth had thought. *Lovesick for somebody but too proud to give in to whatever it is he wants. Intelligent, headstrong, and tenderhearted underneath.*

In addition, after speaking with her for a few more minutes, Elizabeth added one more trait to that mental list.

*Extraordinarily prone to hyperbole.*

By the time the plane had touched down in Texas, Elizabeth had decided that not only did she like Joanna, she admired, and envied a little, the Italian girl's strength of mind.

Particularly where romantic liaisons were concerned.

She did not envy the ease at which the princess adapted to near 24-hour seclusion in a luxurious but small living space.

Elizabeth Lopez still did not like being stuck on the third floor in a virtual fortress, even if her companion was likable and fun. She felt constrained by the intense security. She did not like her movements being tracked. A sense of freedom and independence that she had nourished since girlhood caused her to feel stifled.

And she needed to be able to go outside to smoke.

Smoking had become a discouraged habit in her profession and she had started to hide her addiction.

She immediately started looking for a way to slip in and out of the compound without being noticed.

When she confided her feelings to the Italian princess, Joanna was most sympathetic and agreed to help her bypass security whenever she needed.

Getting around in the house was hard but getting in and out was not.

The house consisted of a T-shaped first floor. The cross of the T was at the back of the house. It was divided into two wings, bracing the middle section of the house, which reached to the front circular drive. The third long section had two floors above it and formed the core of the structure.

For the infamous masquerade party earlier that year, walls had been knocked down to connect the entire downstairs interior of the York mansion.

Barriers that had once made separate rooms now were gone.

Only necessary loadbearing partitions such as where the elevator was located, the bathrooms, the open staircase, and the enclosed stairwell remained intact.

The house had few windows.

A large picture window looked out at the back yard from the kitchen, as did a couple of smaller windows in the den. On the second floor, a few scattered high windows would be impractical for anyone to view the back yard, unless they were quite tall. On the third floor a row of moderately low matching windows were recessed over the extended second and third floor roofs beneath.

The assigned police guard was staying downstairs during the night. While the movie was being staged during the day, he was sleeping in one of the back yard cottages.

Sophisticated monitoring from the cottage ensured no one entered or exited without his knowledge.

When the movie crew arrived and departed for work during the day, those alarms were turned off. Shooting was on a seven day schedule with no weekends off until the final scene was in the can.

An alternative system, allowing anyone with a magnetic card identifying him or her as an employee of Stark Wynter to come and go at will, was switched on each morning.

It functioned as the primary security for the next 16 hours.

Joanna was not issued a badge. Her face was her recognition and all that was needed. Other employees were under instruction to let her piggyback on their entrances and exits.

This meant someone knew every time the actress entered and

left the house.

Elizabeth was to be her companion and remain with her at all times so she was not issued a badge either.

Joanna threw a fit.

Why should the lowliest member of the crew have something she did not?

It was an easy demand to meet. Stark Wynter had an ID made for Joanna, admonishing both Skaar and Elizabeth to make sure she did not use it.

Neither man ever thought about Elizabeth, not Joanna, wanting an escape mechanism.

Joanna had no desire to sneak out into a strange area, where she knew no one and did not speak the language.

She merely gave the pass to Elizabeth. Elizabeth only had to make sure she got out at the same time the movie crew left before Skaar took over security at night.

Therefore, with her entry and exit strategy tested successfully, Elizabeth relaxed and decided to enjoy the short time left on this lucrative job.

She now suspected that Joanna's service as an actress would no longer be needed once the wedding sequence was shot. Stark Wynter did not plan to take Joanna to Hollywood.

Elizabeth figured Joanna did not even contemplate that possibility. The translator was looking forward to the amusement she was going to feel at the reaction of the princess when she found out.

Meanwhile, she started teaching Joanna some important English words.

In addition, she contacted her real estate agent about the sale of her house.

She may not get to go to Hollywood, but she was moving one way or another.

Chapter 10

"Are you moving out of your apartment into her house? Or is she moving in with you?" Chief Brecken asked Plate.

"Now what sense would it make if she left her home and moved in with me?"

"You could rent her house out. Maybe get more for it than the mortgage. After all, you are the man. The house is going to be her separate property unless you take certain steps. Since she bought it before your marriage, whatever equity she has in it will remain her separate property. How are you going to feel, living in her house?"

Plate hesitated. He did not dare tell his boss that Daphne had no mortgage. That the house was, and would always remain, completely hers. Bought and paid for before she ever met him.

He had not spent a lot of time dwelling on that situation.

"Nevertheless, she works from home. My apartment is too small to accommodate that." Plate tried to put end-of-conversation finalization in his tone of voice.

"You realize you've only known this girl for a few months?"

"Almost six."

"Sure you want to rush into this, Plate?"

"How long had you known Mrs. Brecken?"

"That was different. It was love at first sight with us. You just made up your mind you want this girl a few weeks ago. Before that, you wanted Grace York."

"It's much more complicated than that. And, I am sure."

"Yes. Complicated by that other woman you were seeing. Okay, well, don't say I didn't warn you."

"I won't say that. And seeing the other woman was in the line of duty."

"Hmm. Remember, now that the trial is over, you are now on assignment to court and watch this Italian princess."

"I'm about to be married. I cannot openly court women anymore. I don't want to place my wife in a perpetual state of embarrassment or defense of me. I simply cannot take on assignments like this routinely any more. And is this actress suspected of some sort of criminal activity? Why does she need to be watched? I thought she just needed security."

"She does. But she's foreign. Here on an emergency work permit. Too many foreigners in the country. And she was involved with an Arab. Just got over the Iran hostage crisis, you know."

"Stark Wynter already spoke to me. He says the fiancé was Egyptian and there is no real evidence, despite his anger, that the man will do anything to her. Stark said her security needs will be routine."

"I want you on this."

"She's at the York- I mean the Wynter compound. She is on the third floor with her translator. In addition to all the security, the Wynters have added a modern security system since buying the place from Grace York. So why am I needed?"

"I would just like you there on the grounds. You can move back into that cottage where you stayed previously when you were needed there."

"No. I don't want to go. Couldn't you reconsider and let Skaar stay? He is already there. Or send Jordan. Or Willhouse."

"Skaar is married. He needs to go home to his wife. Willhouse just got married. Remember the wedding? It was out of town where his bride lived? You took off."

"That wasn't me. I didn't get to go to that event. I had to work. Jordan was the one who took off to represent the department."

"That's right. I forgot."

"Jordan is still single. Send him."

"Look, Plate, you're moving out of your apartment anyway, aren't you? Why not move a month early and save a month's rent. Then you can marry and move where you like. I'll even pull you off the princess job after your wedding. That is, if you go through with it."

Plate had no answer for that statement.

"The wedding is going to be right there. What more convenient location could you have? You'll walk across the back yard to your wedding ceremony."

Plate had no answer for that logic either.

Brecken was his superior.

"Good. It's settled. Move out to the York- I mean the Wynter compound as soon as possible. Strike up an acquaintance with this princess and see to it she is safe and see to it she is not a danger to us as well," said the chief.

Shortly after, Plate called Daphne. He wanted to firm up her acceptance of the wedding situation.

And ease her into the idea that he was going back to the York compound, now the Wynter compound, to reside once more as he had done earlier in the year to protect an important personage.

She was not pleased.

"At least it solves the problem of Vandal. For a short time at least," said Plate. "I don't think I can keep that cat a secret much longer. Wynter won't object to a cat in the cottage. And when apartment management finds out about him, I'll be evicted anyway."

"I still don't like it," said Daphne.

"Grace York is gone," said Plate. "She's living in River Oaks now and her campaign headquarters is in Houston."

"I meant I don't like it that you changed the cat's name."

"Vandal is a better name for that cat than Midnight. He needed a name that did not constantly remind us of those events. Everything else had changed. Time to move on."

"Forrest Pointpar is there, still next door," said Daphne.

"So?"

"I've heard rumors. That's all."

"Rumors?"

"Forrest and Grace. Probably just vicious gossip."

During a past period of Plate's life, Grace York had been important to him. Daphne still felt some unease about that era.

Seeing this, Plate turned the talk back to their wedding.

"You've got to admit Brecken is right about the convenience. I can get a key to one of the other cottages so that your real bridesmaids can give you a party there. Maybe even stay there. I'm sure some of your college friends will be coming from out of town. That's a lot better than their staying with you. Or your parents. Way out in Katy."

"Um, okay." Daphne bit her lip. "I don't think there's time for all of that. I telephoned Darica and she says she can't get off. Neither can my brother."

*At some point, I've got to tell him I do not have any real bridesmaids. He's seen too many sorority sister movies.*

"My brother said the same thing. We can have small wedding reception later for the family. My parents are out of the state at a school reunion. Neither of my sisters can make it either," said Plate.

"That's going to have to do. My parents had their vacation trip planned and they can't change it. And I don't think we're going to really be able to expect our friends to come with such short notice. So a family and friends reception later in the year?"

"That's right. We'll just get together at somebody's house and have a little punch and cake or something."

"It might be for the best."

"I'm going to give notice that I will be out by May 15th. That will give me a week to move after the ceremony. He might give me back the deposit even though I won't have given 30 days' notice. They have a long waiting list and I know he didn't raise my rent because I am a police officer. So he'll be happy. He won't feel guilty about charging a higher rent to the next tenant."

"Are you going to be able to come over this evening?"

"Probably not. I'm going to be here late tonight and back early in the morning. Listen, he's probably long gone but, just between you and me, we've lost Zopev. He slipped under the radar. I know so far he's only killed married women, but be careful anyway."

"I will keep my doors locked," Daphne promised. "And, although losing my single status may put me on the serial killer's list, I'm looking forward to the day when I have 24-hour personal police protection."

Plate grinned. "I don't think they're going to pay me for staying home 24 hours a day. But at least, after next week, I can change my address on my driver's license from those apartments to your house and I'll be a legal resident of the Maple Leaf Colony."

Chapter 11

In an odd way, losing track of the serial killer created a temporary vacuum of chores for the Sand Waves officers. They could not follow Zopev if they did not know where he was.

Attention could now be focused on a more pleasant event.

Plate and Daphne's upcoming wedding.

The men were able to take time later on Saturday to attend to the not unpleasant chore of being fitted for costumes for the upcoming movie scene. Willhouse, Skaar, and Jordan all proclaimed they were looking forward to serving as Plate's groomsmen.

Plate already had his costume. He had gone for his fitting the day after Stark Wynter and Chief Brecken had first spoken to him about the idea of having his wedding within the movie.

Chief Brecken had decided he could better help out by being one of the many extras that would be seated in the congregation. That would also give Mrs. Brecken a chance to sit with her husband if she wanted to attend. She was undecided, unsure if she could get a satisfactory babysitter lined up in on such short notice.

Even before Daphne and Plate had given Stark the go-ahead, the event had been announced in the papers. Even before he knew the princess was going to play the part of Elicia, plans had been made to shoot the scene as a publicity stunt in Sand Waves, location of the soon to be built studio that was intended to rival Hollywood's best.

Had the real life engaged couple turned him down, Wynter would have simply used a stand-in for the actor signed up to play the groom, as he was unimportant in the plot. A stand-in for the bride became unnecessary as soon as Princess Joanna contacted Stark.

If Daphne and Plate had declined, Wynter would have let the princess play her own character in the dress intended for Daphne. Then Joanna would change into the throw-away dress that would be ruined in the second part of the sequence.

Area residents who wanted to be extras were instructed to mail an envelope with a self-addressed stamped postcard containing a picture, plus their name and address, enclosed. Then, upon receipt of the postcard, obtain 1940s style clothing appropriate for an upscale wedding guest and just show up at the compound at the proper time. The properly marked returned postcard would be their admittance, beyond the gates and into the Wynter compound. Participants would then be selected based on their clothing. And there were a number of Sand Waves VIPs who were invited guests, along with a small selection of guests Daphne and Plate were allowed to invite.

Plate felt a little guilty for hoping that Castroe Zopev was so far away that no new murder would interfere with the wedding scene.

Stark Wynter had even considered how he could possibly benefit from publicity about the Zopev murder trial. Although the trial was held in Houston, the victim had been a Sand Waves resident.

But the famous producer-director could not decide on an appropriate tie-in and abandoned that idea when Joanna fled Italy.

The jilted Arab lover angle was making good copy and generated more interested than serial killers or victims ever would.

Plate hoped Zopev's next victim, which there certainly would be one, was far away from Texas.

Most Texas Police Departments believed Zopev had slipped out of the state and a surreptitious search for him was underway nationwide.

By Sunday morning, it was not long before there were sightings of Zopev all over the country and even internationally.

The other trial participant possibly in danger from public wrath over his testimony, Eduardo Pauliza, had apparently gone back to his normal life as if nothing had happened.

Klaus Lewegz had openly threatened Eduardo Pauliza, according to some newspaper reports. Aware that Zopev had slipped through the unofficial net, Lewegz was busy preparing more complaints against the police and district attorney.

Emilio Cardioxa was in seclusion. He no longer spoke to the press. He now spent most of his time on his yacht in Galveston, which heretofore had only seen occasional frivolous use for pleasure. He was no longer cooperating with police who still considered him a valuable witness despite the acquittal seeming to impeach his testimony. He was refusing to take calls from the district attorney's office, telling them that he had decided to accept the verdict and move on with his life.

Journalists' attempts to track him down only found an empty slip where his boat usually rested. Apparently he was enjoying prolonged therapeutic sailing on the bay, no longer obsessed with the killing or killer.

Eduardo Pauliza apparently was either unaware the alleged killer had gone underground or was unconcerned.

That morning the two police officers supervising the Sand Waves contribution to the investigation rehashed their conversation from the previous day and made a final decision.

Brecken and Plate decided against any contact with the furniture mover for any reason.

Very early Sunday morning the colony's lawyer had informed Brecken that they needed to stay as far away from Pauliza as possible, for he had grounds for a lawsuit if he chose to go in that direction.

"If he asks for police protection, we will have to take it to the Colony Federation Board," the chief told Plate. "Otherwise, it's best if Pauliza does not even see a patrol car cruising down his street, lest he think it's police harassment."

This meant serious business. Rarely did the Colony Federation Board lawyers interfere in the Sand Waves Police Department's business to the point of pulling rank on the chief.

Especially taking time to get the message relayed on a Sunday.

So for the next few days, it appeared only the protection of the princess was going to add to their regular duties.

The cutoff of personal contact from both Zopev and Pauliza created a lighter atmosphere in the departmental offices immediately. In addition, a previously planned sprucing up, including a complete cleaning and touch-up painting, brightened up the place considerably. That had been completed during the night hours of Saturday and Sunday, when the station was empty.

It was shortly after Plate and Brecken concluded their discussion about what to do concerning Pauliza that two of their fellow officers arrived at the same time at the station building.

They were not coming to work but to take care of red tape paperwork. Willhouse had three vacation days he needed to take from the previous year or they were going to expire. The paid days off were hard earned and nobody was going to let that happen.

Willhouse and Jordan were walking across the newly polished hall floor when Jordan slipped.

Jordan uttered a mild profanity.

"Damn this weak ankle!"

He was the younger of the two patrolmen by five years. But at 33, broad and husky, Eddy Jordan looked older than the slender dark-haired man that shared his rank and position in the small department in Sand Waves.

Jordan's mishap was witnessed by their boss, Robert Brecken and their other boss, Brecken's subordinate, Sinclair Plate.

Brecken outranked both patrolmen in both years and title. Plate was a little more than three years younger than Jordan.

Nevertheless, both patrolmen feared the lieutenant's scrutiny more than the chief's monitoring.

Willhouse grabbed Jordan and pulled him up by the latter man's broad shoulders. For a brief moment, they appeared to be dancing clumsily in the hall. Trying to avoid some wet trim on either side of the corridor, painted a few hours ago, made their movements look slapstick.

Willhouse's laughter could be heard all over the building. Also laughing a little, Jordan still had let out a cry of pain in the midst of it all.

By the time Lieutenant Plate got to them, both men seemed to think it was more humorous than painful.

"Just the same, he has to take a couple of days off," said Chief Brecken, who was the authority on such matters. "Disability leave. Monday and Tuesday. I'll get the paperwork started. See a doctor about that ankle."

Those were the current civil service rules, a different rule for every occasion.

Brecken knew them all by heart in the same way Plate knew the criminal code.

Unofficially, the two men in charge had long ago divided their duties towards personnel. It was Plate's responsibility to keep the subordinates coordinated and working hard. It was Brecken's job to keep them content with their work and assure that the department ran smoothly with as few personality problems as possible.

"I'm going to have to do without another man this week?" asked Plate, indicating this was unbearable maltreatment. "I can't be ten places at once. I've got to deal with the Italian princess actress. The Japanese VIP coming in at the airport. When?"

"I'm not sure exactly when," said the chief. "The feds are to let me know."

"And just because we've got these special events going on, doesn't mean all the criminals are going to take a break because they know we don't have time and manpower enough to deal with them."

"I have faith in you," said Chief Brecken. "Lots of faith in you, Plate. You'll manage all your crimes anyway. Take two days, Jordan. If you need them. Plate, you should be happy. This delays your move to the Wynter compound one more day. I am taking Monday off. So you cannot move until Tuesday. You will need to stay at the station and do some patrol."

" 'Manage my crimes'…'two days if you need' ", Plate muttered. "Spending these last few weeks at your desk working with this new computer system has made you forget what it is to be out there in the field. Even if you jump back in the trenches, we're too busy for this."

Hearing all this, Willhouse and Jordan had the distinct look of two little boys let out to play. They were certainly going to ignore Plate's complaints and go with what their chief said.

"Tim, what say we take a day and go sailing?"

"Willhouse has just got married! Surely he plans to spend his vacation with his bride," Plate said.

"I have already been married three weeks. I haven't been fishing in months."

"Don't be a puppet on a string," advised Jordan. "Women will take over and rule if you let them. They are like master puppeteers. The man becomes the puppet on a string. Remember that old song?"

"Jordan, you don't know what you are talking about. I don't recall you ever seeing the same woman more than a month or two. Willhouse, you are not really adjusted to married life yet," said Chief Brecken. "When you've been married for several years, like I have, you'll learn better."

"My vacation starts tomorrow," said Willhouse. "I can swing one day at least. Alice will understand."

"You have not been married long enough to learn," Brecken said, without making eye contact.

"If you can handle the ropes, I can handle the rudder, despite this ankle injury," said Jordan.

"I would think you would need bed rest," said Plate.

"Working out the pain will be good for me."

"Then you should not have to take off," said Plate.

"Suppose my ankle gives out while chasing a suspect?"

"It could give out while tacking and you could capsize. You're not able to sail," Plate said.

Jordan pointed. "Tim here, can handle all the rough stuff. I am definitely able to go fishing on my sailboat, if nothing else."

Jordan kept his boat docked in Galveston and spent as much time on it as he could. He had upgraded from dry docking his craft, to an in-the-water boat slip in the past year.

"That boat will soon be my real home. The apartment I keep as near Sand Waves as I can afford, is just a convenience to avoid traffic jams. Traffic has gotten so bad with all these Northerners moving down here, that it no longer makes enough difference. I'm going to get rid of it and live on the boat. I'll just leave for work at four o'clock in the morning."

"I'd like to have a boat if I could afford one," said Willhouse. "If you can afford it, it doesn't make any sense not to have one. Living this close to the water. A necessity almost. In addition to a house, of course."

"That would cost a fortune. Like having two mortgages. Despite the proximity to the bay, few people in Sand Waves keep private sailboats. If they did, we'd have to have a marine officer," said Brecken.

"Most everybody works in Houston or Galveston. Driving to and from work at least five days a week, they have no time to sail a boat, much less care for one," Plate commented.

"Or they are so rich they just hire yachts or go on cruises when the sea beckons," said Brecken.

"I have found a happy medium. It is possible to maintain a modest sail craft and find time to keep it in shape without it bankrupting you. One trick is to have a boat that uses an outboard instead of an inboard engine. Saves a bundle, and if the engine goes kaput, then it is easy to replace."

"We are all in awe of your sailing acumen," said Plate.

"Since I am the only one making an effort, I do graciously offer a standing invitation to my fellow officers," said Jordan.

"I would come for a sail but I don't think I have ever shared a day off with you," said Plate.

"I can't come without Betty and the kids," Brecken stated.

"I do apologize, Chief. I'm just not equipped for children, not really for women either. That may change in the future. I'd love to see us all go down as a group. We would not be able to go out on the boat at the same time but the others could make a picnic of it while we take turns."

"We are only a seven man force," Brecken reminded him. "And we are down to five due to the two recent resignations."

"It is rare for any two of us to be off at the same time," Jordan admitted.

"It takes a lot of manipulation and compromise for us to get our vacations coordinated in the slower periods of the 12 month calendar timeframe," said Brecken.

"Good friends and we never get same day off even," Willhouse said to Jordan, simplifying the problem.

"But for once we catch a break," Jordan said.

Willhouse grinned at Brecken. "Thanks to the chief."

"Maybe Grant can go with us?" It was a risky joke but Jordan could not resist.

"He is not going to take off!" Plate exclaimed, his temper flaring higher.

Brecken spoke up, deadpan. "He does have a vacation day coming."

"He cannot go off anywhere tomorrow. He cannot leave the princess until I can get over there and take over," Plate insisted testily.

"That's okay," said Jordan thoughtfully. "That works out just fine. We'll include Grant some other time. Tim and I need some best-buddy quality time. I'll see about this ankle tomorrow. I think it's just a mild sprain. But maybe I should have it x-rayed. Assuming that turns out okay, we leave Tuesday, early morning. No ankle problem is going to keep me from the bay."

"Just don't come across any crimes at sea," said Plate, who was in a bad mood by now. "Don't call me no matter what happens anywhere. Call Skaar, who is NOT going with you. He's going to have to pick up routine duties when I get to the compound to hold hands with the princess. I'll be busy with Her Royal Highness."

"Perfect," Willhouse spoke directly to Jordan, ignoring Plate. "Just perfect."

The two patrolmen went away laughing. Plate stared after them thinking Jordan was not limping half enough. But Brecken laughed also. Plate could tell Brecken was enjoying the power to make somebody happy with a popular decision for a change.

Plate scowled at Brecken, wanting him to see that it was not unanimously popular.

However, Plate knew Brecken's leniency would not last. As soon as Willhouse got over his disappointment with the verdict, things would be back to normal.

Plate looked forward to a normal day of routine work and patrol.

Even if it was only going to be one day.

## Chapter 12

"I don't understand why we can't be in our own home yet. Even if we can't just move in together without consequences, we should at least be able to spend time together at your place or mine. I still don't understand why we have to sneak around like this. My divorce is final."

"I just want a little more time put between the divorce and our relationship being known. I'm making progress here socially. And the Powers-That-Be in Sand Waves are sticklers for propriety." Eddy Jordan lit a cigarette. He took a puff and then handed it to the woman who sat in bed with him, Kate Traval.

She held the warm tobacco between her fingers and returned it without it ever touching her lips.

"I think you're being unnecessarily cautious. This is 1983. We are two adults who have committed no crime."

"Just be patient a little longer."

"And your first time off in ages! I have to go to work in the morning but I could've gotten Tuesday off. And you've got to spend Tuesday with Timothy Willhouse?"

"Yes. I've got to. He needs the interaction. I may be back earlier than you would think. We're taking two cars in case he decides to pack it in early. It's just one day. But he's real down over that verdict. A good sail would do wonders for him, is my opinion. I don't think he is sure."

"I am sure I could use a good sail. A day you could spend with me."

She pouted.

"Soon I could be spending every day with you. I promise."

"Ed, I'm serious. It's getting really hard to wait. I can't stand it any longer. I fear that-"

"You fear what?" His voice was suddenly sharp.

"I don't want to make you mad. But I fear our relationship is going to be hurt if this keeps up. I'm tired of these cheap motels. We could at least be on your boat."

"I'm not going to let our relationship suffer over this." Jordan took a deep puff on the cigarette. "I've been racking my brain trying to figure out how we can get our relationship out in the open without any repercussions. And do you realize how small the boat really is? And there is always somebody watching at the marina."

"We haven't done anything wrong. We're not criminals."

He sat up and extinguished his cigarette in the ashtray next to the bed.

He pulled the thick Sunday *Houston Chronicle* out of its plastic wrapper and spread it out on the bed to read.

The acquittal of Castroe Zopev was still on the front page but the article was mainly concerned with background of Yolanda Cardioxa and did not mention the police. At least not before the jump to the inside pages.

"This stint is just a little handholding with him until he gets over the emotional strain."

"I wish that killer had been convicted and sentenced to the death penalty."

Jordan pulled out the financial section and opened it up. An advertisement featuring a drawing of a jagged rock caught his attention.

"That's it!"

"What?"

"How do you feel about taking out some life insurance?" He turned and dropped his feet over the side.

"Life insurance? I have life insurance in my job. As soon as we're married, I'll make you the beneficiary. I already got my ex-husband off the paperwork. Right now there's no named beneficiary, pending our marriage."

"No, I don't care anything about that. You can make the Red Cross beneficiary for all I care. My boss's fiancée is a life insurance agent. If you were to buy a policy from her that would be a great connection. I could introduce you as a friend interested in a policy. She sells you insurance. Then we start publicly dating. It'll almost look like she set us up. A short time from now, nobody will remember who knew who first."

"Well, at first glance, I don't see anything wrong with it."

"It's brilliant, if I say so myself. It just came to me when you said the word crime. You know that old joke that ends with 'and the biggest crime is life insurance'?"

"No. I never heard any such joke." She grabbed him and pulled him back towards her. He wound up in a semi-fetal position with his arm under his head, gazing at her sincerely as she reclined flat on her back, staring up at the ceiling.

"Never mind. You don't have any problems that would keep you from taking out a private policy, do you?"

She turned her head towards him and they were nose to nose on the pillow.

"Problems?"

"Health problems?"

"No, of course not."

"Great. Listen, I'll mention to my boss that I ran into an old friend and we got to talking about all kinds of things and the subject of life insurance came up. I'll tell him you were planning on taking out a policy and I mentioned that his fiancée was an insurance agent. That will get the ball rolling."

"So I have to call this fiancée of your lieutenant and ask her to sell me life insurance?"

"No, don't worry about that. Rest assured. She will call you. Just make sure that she gets through to you."

"She's going to call me?"

"You can count on it. I'll give my lieutenant your number and make sure he gets it to her. Then when she calls you, set up an appointment with her and buy a policy. Don't make me the beneficiary. Don't even mention me unless she mentions me first. Then act like you've just casually run into me and let the conversation take its course. If she doesn't mention it at all, that's okay too."

"All right. If you think this will get us in with your boss and get our relationship out in the open."

"It's the perfect way. I'm surprised I didn't think of it sooner.

Look, remember when I had to go on those engineered dates that were part of a plan to entrap that political assassin?"

"Yes." Kate pushed herself up on her elbows.

"I was set up with the insurance agent then. Her name is Daphne Martin. The lieutenant's been seeing her since last November. She's got him hook, line, and sinker. When I was pretending to be her date, he was sitting there watching every move I made. She reached over and touched me one time and the look on his face scared the crap out of me. So anything you do to help her out will score points with him for me."

"I thought Sinclair Plate was involved with Grace York last year. And then later that journalism person. It was in the news."

"Those were blinds. There might have been something between him and Grace York at some point in time. Then he met this woman during the flood. He was trapped with her in that Christmas store, and I don't care who he was dating, he's been talking about her ever since." Jordan rose up also. He started looking around for his shirt and pants as they were talking.

"It just goes to show you never know about people. Publicly they're doing one thing and privately something else. When I get a job at a private home that's usually what it's all about. Putting up a fake appearance."

"You can say the same thing about both of us."

"That's true. All right, I'll make my debut into your little social world of the police through your lieutenant's fiancée. I hope you're not expecting me to take out a high priced policy."

"No no. Just let her sell you an average policy. Don't do anything to attract attention or make it look like this is contrived. Remember, don't make me the beneficiary."

"I remember. I'll leave everything to my cat. You have to get dressed already?"

"You don't have a cat. I've got to meet Willhouse, remember?"

"I'm going to get a cat. Just for this purpose."

"You've been watching too many cartoon movies," he laughed.

"At least I don't watch that science fiction nonsense like you do."

"It is almost morning. I can catch Plate and give him your number. He's on station and patrol duty today. It will go over better if I do it in person rather than over the phone. He will remember it. You know, I think I really have stumbled upon the answer to all of our problems. Get in tight with Daphne Martin before she becomes Daphne Plate. You'll be her client before any of us get married. And hopefully by then, a good friend. The little scandal about your divorce will be totally and completely irrelevant by the time everybody realizes that you and I are together for real."

"Oh, Ed, I so hope so. I'll instruct my answering service to put any call from Daphne Martin right through. Normally they are instructed to perpetually divert any calls from any sales agents."

Kate got out of bed and started dressing also.

He grabbed her and kissed her. "Good girl."

"I'm sorry my life was such a mess before I met you. My personal life that is. Somehow, my professional life has always just sailed along in smooth waters. Finally, I found you to give me some protection."

"I think I scared that bastard off the last time he beat you."

"You did. That's why he consented to a divorce without much problem."

"It's just that any report of domestic abuse investigated by me, and then I marry the victim- it is going to look bad. Unethical."

"I understand. The preoccupation with ethics this day and age has even permeated the interior decorator business."

"Our regulations and restraints these days are a nightmare. But I won't let that stop me from running him off, if he shows back up."

"I don't think he's going to give us any more trouble. He has left the state and found another woman, from what I've heard."

"Yeah, I been keeping tabs on him. He's shacked up with a woman in Florida. Still, he could be back here in a matter of hours causing trouble if he finds out that you and I are involved, were already involved, when I was threatening his ass with a tail whipping if he didn't stop battering you."

"He actually told me he was grateful to you for talking me into not filing a formal complaint."

Kate and Jordan looked at each other for a moment and then laughed together, a little bitterly.

"He was lucky I did not kill him," said Jordan, caressing her hair.

"Sometimes it's hard for me to realize I'm really free now." She nestled close to him. "I know we don't agree on what to do about my career after our marriage. I know we fight sometimes. But I feel so safe and free with you."

"I know it's been a long hard road for you," he said. "It has for me, too."

"If Daphne Martin is the key to getting us down the end stretch and across the finish line, she's going to be my best friend forever," said Kate, as they prepared to depart. "I'll buy whatever she wants to sell me."

She did not see the grim look on his face or the distant look in his eyes.

"Are you taking this newspaper with you?" Kate pulled out the *Women's Section*. She scanned it with mild curiosity.

The lead feature was a story about an Italian princess arriving in Sand Waves to begin work on a movie.

"Naw, nothing in it."

"I'm going to take this part with me." She picked up the section, folded it, and stuffed it in her satchel-type purse.

"A long hard road," he repeated softly.

And he could not help but contemplate that the end of the journey might not be any more smooth then its beginning.

Chapter 13

Joanna woke up at about 3 AM Tuesday morning.

She woke up angry. The more she thought about the injustice she had suffered, the angrier she got.

She switched on her lamp.

She looked at the previous Sunday's newspaper.

She had expected to be featured in headlines on the front page but instead her picture was below the fold and there was no story. Just a caption.

Her story was buried in the *Women's Section*.

How humiliating! Only women would be reading about her arrival in America.

And it was raining again!

Joanna stayed in bed, but could not get back to sleep. She knew the newspaper was just an excuse for her anxiety.

She was regretting more each day coming to America.

Especially this part of America.

The continuous rain made Joanna terribly homesick. It was more rain than she had ever seen come down so long and so steadily.

Home was sunny and warm Sicily. Here it was warm. However, the Texas sunshine had been seriously overrated. This sunshine could not effectively fight off the constant rain.

She added up the pros and cons of her situation.

She had already decided Sand Waves was the most boring place in the world.

She still liked her translator-companion. But Elizabeth was spending more and more time sneaking out to be with her lover whenever she knew her language skills were not needed.

This left the princess alone too much.

Most of the hours Elizabeth was on scene were taken up with costume fittings, makeup experiments, and press interviews.

Joanna was also feeling the lack of men in her life. Previously she was always surrounded by male siblings, cousins, and her father, plus a plethora of suitors.

Then there was her serious journalist boyfriend.

After him, the oil prince.

She was celebrated in Italy.

Here in Texas, she felt neglected.

Stark Wynter paid her scant attention now that he had her signed and housed on site.

And her nice police bodyguard stayed downstairs all the time and wore a very thick wedding ring.

Broadcast and cable television shows were almost all in English. There was one Spanish cable TV station. Joanna had a hard time understanding the Spanish dialect of most of the shows.

She could read Spanish much better than understand it spoken.

And the station carried almost nothing but love triangle based soap operas.

She liked faster action in her plots.

Wynter had promised her some Italian subtitled movies in the mansion's home theatre, recently installed on the second floor.

He had not delivered on that promise.

The princess had taken to reading books for entertainment. She had found an unauthorized Spanish translation of *Murder as the Organist Plays* on sale at the airport when she arrived.

Since she could read Spanish fairly well, although she could not speak it much, she consulted with Elizabeth whenever she was confused about a word. She finished the book quickly.

She had also brought several Italian murder mysteries with her from Italy. They were her emergency pastimes. Now into her second week in Sand Waves, she was almost halfway through her supply.

Being a fast reader, and fearing she would run out, she had sent Elizabeth in search of Italian or Spanish language literature on one of the translator's clandestine adventures.

The local bookstore had nothing like that in stock.

Elizabeth had told Joanna the store would order some mystery books from Mexico that could get to Sand Waves much faster than anything ordered from Europe.

The order was placed the previous day.

In Italy, Joanna Scarpartti was used to her every desire being granted as soon as possible.

At any time of the day, any day of the week.

So this Tuesday morning, when the knock came at her bedroom door and a male voice called out in Spanish that he had a delivery for her, the princess forgot where she was and opened the door without hesitation or trepidation.

Two dark Latin-looking young men forced their way into her bedroom.

One went immediately for the phone and placed it out of her reach.

The other grabbed her arms, pinned them behind her back with one hand, and put his other across her mouth.

He dragged her to the outside corner of the room.

"Quick! Get the shot! Hurry up!" the man holding Joanna said, low and urgent.

"Just a minute," said the other, and he was fiddling with something in his hands. "Don't let go of her mouth."

Taken off guard, Joanna had offered no resistance until now.

She deftly pulled her right leg forward, her knee up, and then plunged her entire body backwards, aiming her shoe heel at the vulnerable parts of her captor.

She hit the mark.

He yelled, then let go of her.

She fell face forward to the floor but swiftly turned on her back and slipped out of his reach to the opposite corner of the room so fast the second man did not have time to react.

The kicked man rolled forward on the bed, still yelling.

Joanna climbed the furniture nearest the corner window, grabbed a lamp, turned it upside down and started smashing the windowpanes, yelling and screaming in Italian.

The man writhing on the bed looked up at the commotion and started to protest.

"Hey, we just wanted-"

"Let's go!" The first man grabbed his companion and shoved

him towards the windows.

"Don't come near me!" The princess held the lamp over their heads and screamed in Italian.

The phone began to ring loudly.

"Let's go!" repeated the first man. "It's a bust."

"What about the shot!" the other cried. "We didn't get the shot!"

"It's a bust. We've got to get out. Go go go!

Vaguely understanding that she had the better of them somehow, the princess relaxed her guard and lowered the heavy lamp slightly.

Instead of turning to the exit, the first man shoved his partner in the direction of the princess.

"STOP!" she screamed as they came in her direction.

She threw the lamp at the man who had manhandled her.

But he ducked.

The lamp crashed to the ground.

Sparks flew.

The bulb burst.

The first man grabbed the second again and pushed him towards the window the princess had just broken.

She jumped to the other side of the room and they passed her on their way to the jagged glass framed opening.

She was running out into the foyer simultaneously as they were diving out the window and Grant Skaar was bounding up the stairwell.

Chapter 14

Harbor Shadows was a busy residential street running through Maple Leaf Colony. The houses lining it were barely eight years old. Yet it was considered the older section of the neighborhood.

Outer framing styles had changed completely but the structures were similar. The prevailing style was still many large windows covered with miniblinds or semi-sheer drapes. Harbor Shadows was the corner street for Elisabeth Morgan who could see ten Harbor Shadows addresses from her formal dining window.

Elisabeth was a pioneer in the trend of counseling using puppets. Nearing 40 and tired of teaching, Elisabeth was carving out a new career. Rather than work directly with children, she dusted off a minor in acting to combine with her education credentials, and pulled together a presentation on the effectiveness of theatre in therapy.

She used paper dolls and puppets in her presentations, which were in strong demand by school counselors and child psychologists.

The paper dolls were no trouble to maintain and inexpensive to replace. Not so the puppets. Not hand puppets, but marionette jointed dolls activated by strings, they were costly and fragile. But she loved them. They were about the size of Barbie dolls and she had a portable wooden theatre where she brought them to life.

Like most toys, they were always in need of repair and like most dolls, always in need of new clothes.

She spent off days mending them and redressing them, using her dining room table, which stood near a huge picture window looking out on her side street.

This afternoon, spring showers came to Harbor Shadows drive. The rain started with fine light patter but soon became a steady drenching. Elisabeth Morgan decided to open her miniblinds, take a break from the puppets, and watch the rain. Listening to Tchaikovsky on the stereo, she was enjoying the scene.

The huge raindrops sparkled as they struck the steaming pavement. The street was like a river of diamonds flowing through the exquisite little homes.

The largest dominated that part of Harbor Shadows. A masculine house, it had a New England style front. Although a two story, the house was only 1900 square feet, with a square footprint. The kitchen, living area, and attached garage took up the downstairs. The master bedroom upstairs overlooked the front yard, sharing space with two small bedrooms and an open game room at the top of the stairs. A balcony jetted off the master, accessible by French doors.

As Elisabeth Morgan gazed at the rain, thinking how good it was for her lawn and how her water bill might be a little less because of it, a man ran from the street, climbed a tree, and swung open the French doors on the two-story. He entered, then immediately came out. He backed up to the balcony railing and raised his arms almost as a casual gesture of conversation. Another man appearing from inside, facing him, followed him onto the balcony. As he did so, he raised a long black rifle and deliberately shot the first man who crumpled, grabbed the railing in a bear hug and took it with him over the side.

As her eyes followed the man falling to the yard below, Elisabeth Morgan automatically pulled a chair from her dinette table and sat down before the window as though it were a television screen.

She switched off the stereo.

A minute later the man with the rifle came running out the front door. The rain seemed to slow at once. In the urban quiet, now disturbed only by frog chirps praising the rain, she distinctly heard the gunman yell. "Policeman, policeman!"

*All this activity violates Sand Waves deed restrictions*, thought Elisabeth, as she watched with detached curiosity.

Then the homeowner seemed to go crazy on his landscaped Sand Waves front lawn, completely shattering the image of subdivision perfection so treasured by the colony.

Sand Waves was advertised as being unincorporated, free from city taxes, answerable only to county commissioners, who governed with a hands-off policy.

In truth, ruling through rigid deed restrictions, avoiding incorporation and its ensuing rights, powered by implied consent via purchase of property, the iron hand of the colony board had the power to enforce rules at the threat of fines, liens, and in extreme cases, foreclosure. This made living in Sand Waves more restrictive than Houston, Galveston, or any other community nearby.

Deed restrictions strictly governed the outside appearances of homes. Yards had to be green, which caused high water bills in the frequently drought stricken area. Lawns had to be strictly mowed, no stray grass feeders were allowed over the curb.

It was said, only half-jokingly, a regulation was once drawn up prohibiting the generation of exterior garbage. Trash cans visible on garbage day tended to detract from the aesthetic quality of the colony and cause property values to fall. But the proposal was abandoned when it was noted that the only alternative was for the sanitation men to enter houses to retrieve trash. This might cause liability problems. Plus none of the elites wanted to let a garbage man in the house.

Sand Waves residents did justifiably fear unscrupulous people attempting to get into their luxury homes.

A common ruse was a fake package delivery. Sand Waves had one small post office to serve the entire colony. Lines were long and hours were short. It was open from 9 AM to 4:30 PM weekdays and two hours on Saturday morning.

People at work during regular business hours only had a two-hour window each weekend to go to the post office.

So when it seemed a considerate carrier was delivering packages above and beyond the call of duty, either extra early or after hours, most residents were tempted to open their doors.

Fake package delivery was a common trick used by professional thieves to gain entrance and burglarize a residence, or worse. But the unofficial gag order about any lawlessness in Sand Waves prevented this from being common knowledge.

There was a package left at the front door of the Pauliza residence the morning that Elisabeth Morgan witnessed the drama on the Pauliza balcony.

It was a fake, an empty box marked fragile.

The first clue in the mysterious shooting that would rock the colony even more than the death of Yolanda Cardioxa.

# Chapter 15

At the same time Elisabeth Morgan began looking out her window, a black covering blocked the light from a window on the third floor at the Wynter mansion.

Seated on her bed, with rain splattering against the plastic covering causing her to jump periodically, Joanna spoke directly to the translator. Standing beside Elizabeth Lopez, Lieutenant Plate blankly watched Joanna's lips and her hands, so perfectly synced in communication.

The princess said in Italian- "The murdering devils breached this pathetic excuse for security in this hovel. I smashed out the window after they grabbed me from behind, planning to rape me. This pathetic attempt failed due to their lack of manhood- I beat them back with my bare hands- then they attempted to throw me down three stories to the ground and kill me. It was only the quick intervention of this wonderful police officer, Skaar, who saved my life, which kept me from being murdered. I will be his slave forever and the blessing of my ancestors and all the saints in heaven will shower down upon his descendants."

The princess paused to let the translator do her job.

The translator reported to Lieutenant Plate in English- "The princess says that despite the excellent security system in the mansion, two men managed to get to the third floor. Uh, I think she says they accomplished this by breaking the window from the outside. She is not very coherent right now. Anyway, they grabbed her from behind and attempted to rape her. She resisted and they pushed her towards the window. Officer Skaar intervened at that moment. She will always be grateful for his excellent work."

Plate's gaze went from the indignant actress to the slightly agitated translator.

Elizabeth spread out her hands helplessly.

"I understand. Thank the princess on behalf of Officer Skaar," said Lieutenant Plate. "I apologize for not being here yet. I do take her safety with the utmost seriousness. But she could be in no better hands than those of Grant Skaar. Experts are examining the security system now to see what happened and will take whatever appropriate measures are necessary to fix the problem."

The translator nodded and said to the princess in Italian-

"The lieutenant knows the valiant police officer who heroically saved your life will thank you forever for your gratitude and blessings on his progeny. Lieutenant exceedingly regrets that he could not have been the one to have saved you. Experts are examining the security system and whoever was at fault will be struck off the rolls of security personnel forever, prosecuted, and jailed. The problem will be resolved to your satisfaction or the lieutenant will personally resign. Should any harm come to Your Highness, the lieutenant will throw himself out the third floor window in despair."

Slightly mollified, the princess responded in Italian-

"That is hardly an adequate response but I suppose it will have to do. Just be sure and let him know that if any harm comes to me it is his responsibility. My father will come over from Sicily to spill blood. Probably his. Thank you," said the princess.

She rose to show that the interview was concluded, as far she was concerned. She indicated her intention to go to the second floor and watch a movie.

If she could not understand it, would Elizabeth translate the show for her?

Elizabeth nodded. She said to Plate-

"The princess needs to relieve the stress of this ordeal by some private time alone. The princess thanks you for your prompt response. She is grateful you feel strongly about taking responsibility for her safety. And she hopes there won't be any more trouble."

"Grazie," said Lieutenant Plate, addressing Joanna.

There was silence as the officer started towards the door.

"They came to shoot me," the princess yelled in coherent English that surprised both the translator and the policeman.

He stopped with his hand still on the doorknob.

"They yell over and over, 'shot! shot! shot!' " The princess let out a little whimper as she saw the reaction on Plate's face to her words. She only showed her fear for a few seconds before biting her lip and freezing her face into an angry expression again.

"I will do my best to see no harm comes to you," said Plate with some tenderness. He walked away from the door and stood closer to the princess.

Elizabeth translated, then added, "I'm going to go watch a movie with her on the second floor. Wynter has a whole assortment of them down there. I just have to translate the dialogue."

Plate nodded again, his mind on the possibilities of getting any identification from Joanna.

"Could I ask-?"

"NO!" The princess yelled at him in the one word understood in both languages.

"I just-"

"NO! Talk LATER! Movie NOW!"

The princess tossed her head, jumped up, pushed Plate aside, and left the room.

"Unfortunately, this is my fault."

"Don't blame yourself, Miss Lopez."

"Thank you. And I prefer the title Ms.," she said cordially.

"Forgive me, Ms. Lopez," said Lieutenant Plate politely.

"I told her I had ordered some books. Apparently she expected them to be delivered the next day."

Plate and Ms. Lopez shared a good long tension-breaking laugh.

"Unfortunately fake delivery attempts are sometimes more successful than the real ones in this area," Plate said, after he had recovered from laughing.

"I need to talk to Stark Wynter about when that window is going to be fixed," said Elizabeth Lopez, when her mirth had subsided.

"Make sure you don't get it fixed until we get county forensics here to process the scene," Plate directed her.

Chapter 16

Plate and Skaar were still discussing the situation at the mansion when a call came from the chief. Lake Charles authorities had reported that two male suspects had been apprehended across the Louisiana state line.

The assault on Joanna had taken place scarcely two hours previously.

County forensics was still at work on the third floor, where was an extension telephone plus an extra line.

Plate was spoke to the chief and relayed the details to Skaar.

"The two college boys managed to climb to the third floor from the outside. They smashed the window and got in. From the preliminary interview it looks like they are freshmen college fraternity pledges and this was part of their hazing. They had to find a princess and give her a kiss. Unfortunately, publicity concerning this actress's arrival and that she is descended from Sicily's royal family hit at the same time they received their assignment. She presented them a perfect opportunity."

"And where are they now?" Skaar asked.

"Louisiana State Patrol picked them up at the border. They've already indicated they're going to refuse extradition so it's going to take an extra day to get them back here. They are talking off the record only, apparently to the Lake Charles Police Department. Trying to bribe them into letting them go."

"So they are rich kids!" said Skaar. "They probably won't be charged. That's one of the things I hate about this place."

"It may be a blessing in disguise," said Plate. "We've always been so concerned about people getting up to the third floor from the interior of the mansion. I don't suppose it ever occurred to anybody that someone could climb up from the outside."

"I would not have thought it was possible," said Skaar.

"It is, though. If you're young and athletic, stupid, have no fear of heights, and are highly motivated," said Plate.

"I don't think they really intended to harm her," said Skaar.

"They probably wanted publicity," said Plate.

"And how were they going to prove success?" Skaar asked.

"According to Louisiana officers, they had a camera. No weapons. No equipment designed for kidnapping. Not even duct tape. Each planned to photograph the other kissing the princess. Apparently, it did not occur to them that she might resist their charms."

"You think that's what made them turn violent?" Skaar asked.

"You were first on the scene. What was your analysis?"

"To tell you the truth, I didn't see any real evidence of a struggle. Just a broken lamp and the window they broke to get in. If they did manhandle her, I think they just panicked a little, and were probably just trying to get her out of the way to get back to the window once she started screaming."

"That all sounds plausible. It's probably the truth, but let's check it out absolutely thoroughly. And let's get more men over here to patrol the exterior grounds. Call the county and borrow from them."

"And if there's no one available?" Skaar asked.

"Go to the outer-lying counties. Small towns. Anywhere anyone is available. Wynter is paying us enough to offer at least time and a half over what most departments pay."

"I know. Geralyn and I are going to make good use of the extra money next paycheck. Still, I will be glad to turn the princess over to you tomorrow."

Police working security at the mansion were getting a check from Stark Wynter on top of their regular salary.

"Sure you don't want to keep her?" Plate asked hopefully.

"If we had this type of extra work more often, the department would not be down to five people. Higher pay lured away McMillan and Bronxton. Most of the nearby towns are paying more these days."

"Chief Brecken has not had a chance to interview applicants yet," said Plate. "We're all pulling extra duty with very little time off for anyone."

"Except Ed gets disability time for his ankle?" Skaar scoffed.

"And Willhouse has to take his vacation days or lose them. Civil service rules," Plate acknowledged.

"I will be enjoying the money but I am getting very tired of being at work all the time. Tomorrow the princess is yours."

"I'm going to try to get Jordan to take over the princess as soon as he gets back from his disability leave," said Plate.

"Hard work is not his middle name," said Grant.

Such bluntness was unusual for the youngest member of the force.

Plate smiled.

"I think he may have a girl," said Plate.

"You're kidding! Somebody serious?"

"Maybe. He's not been making those 'never me' statements since Tim got married."

Plate reached in his pocket for his notebook, pulled it out and looked at the name and number that Jordan had given him to pass on to Daphne.

It was a Sand Waves phone number and the name was decidedly feminine.

He had known Jordan to date a few women over time but had never known him to be serious about any one of them. He would have said Jordan was confirmed bachelor but discussing life insurance with anyone indicated a slightly deeper degree of intimacy than just mere acquaintances or casual dates, in Plate's opinion.

Jordan had been a little too emphatic about the part where he had just run into his old friend after several years and they had just happened to start talking about life insurance.

*Still all the better if this is somebody Jordan is seriously interested in, that Jordan was willing to recommend Daphne to her,* Plate thought. *Daphne is pretty friendly with a lot of her clients, especially the few young single females. All the better if she and whoever Jordan winds up with become pals.*

"Jordan made a special trip to the station yesterday to have me ask Daphne to call this girl and set up an appointment with her."

"That sounds just like Eddy," said Skaar. "He would want to

make sure the girl had plenty of life insurance before he married her."

Plate laughed. "If Jordan gets married, Chief Brecken will have no single male officers to date suspects."

"Whatever will he do?" Skaar grinned.

"Maybe get some applicants lined up for the vacant positions," said Plate hopefully.

"He can put out an ad, 'Wanted: experienced Texas law officer, must be licensed, dedicated, proficient with firearms, single, and attractive to women. Prefer youthful vigor. Attach list of references from conquered females'."

Plate and Skaar laughed heartily.

By this time, both police officers were on the first floor of the mansion. They were walking towards the door.

Plate was intending to instruct Skaar to go on home and meet with him the next day at the police station when both of their pagers went off simultaneously.

They looked at each other.

Something significant had to have happened. Together, they constituted nearly one third of the Sand Waves Police Department.

Only in case of emergency were two officers summoned at the same time.

"I'll call in," said Skaar.

He walked over to the phone sitting on a marble top table near the front door.

Plate watched with mild concern at first as Skaar spoke.

As he read the changing expression on Skaar's face and saw the color drain from his skin, the concern burst into pure fear.

Chapter 17

There was no choice but to leave Skaar with the princess.

Plate was on the scene within minutes. It was outside the gates, all the way across Sand Waves.

Plate knew the fastest way to weave through the colony and he did not even have to think about directions as he drove.

He saw immediately that Chief Brecken had the crime scene well in hand.

So Lieutenant Plate started his role in the investigation by listening to Elisabeth Morgan's story, while watching the crime scene activity from the same window that she had witnessed the incident.

The sun was shining brightly now and everything was very visible.

She had almost finished her recounting.

Staring at a broken puppet and a stack of paper dolls on her dining room table, Plate was wondering if there were any other witnesses.

"The puppets and paper dolls are tools I use in my educational presentations," explained the consultant. "I was mending this one when it happened."

The van came to take the body.

Plate excused himself brusquely and exited through her front door.

Drawn irresistibly, Plate crossed the street and looked at the dead man again, before they could cover his face. Irrationally he thought there might have been a mistake.

But no. The dead man was Timothy Willhouse.

As the van left the scene, Plate looked down at his hand and realized he was somehow holding Elisabeth Morgan's puppet. He had unconsciously picked it up and carried it off.

He hastened back across the street. She was standing in her yard now. The grass was glistening in the sunshine.

"I am so sorry I took this puppet," he said. "I don't even remember picking it up."

"That's all right, Officer. I knew you would bring it back."

It was only when he handed it back to her that he realized it was dressed in a police officer's uniform.

Eduardo Pauliza was informed of his rights, informed he had killed a policeman, and would say nothing without his lawyer. His wife, Sarah Pauliza, a registered nurse, was near hysterical.

Plate ground his teeth as he began to knock on doors in search of more information. He wanted badly to interrogate Pauliza and find out what possible reason Pauliza could have for killing the officer. That would have to wait until Pauliza's Houston lawyer could get to Sand Waves.

There was no answer at any of the neighboring doors. No one was home yet. An empty box had been left at the Pauliza front door but no nearby houses had any packages, legitimate or fake, at their doorsteps. County officers arrived to help.

Plate decided to ride to the station with Brecken and Pauliza.

The morning rush hour proceeded from Sand Waves in two directions and was just beginning. The tsunami of cars heading towards Houston was significantly worse than the avalanche going to Galveston. It would take the lawyer more than a two hours to travel the short distance from his office at this time of day.

Reluctantly, as if leaving the crime scene and taking Pauliza on to the station somehow finalized the death of the police officer and left his colleagues with the concrete realization that they could do nothing to help him, the officials were completely silent en route.

Eduardo Pauliza kept apologizing, protesting that he never intended to hurt anyone for the duration of the short drive but no one answered him. He was put in one of the department's few cells and left alone.

Plate and Brecken waited in the chief's office for the lawyer to arrive. Plate was very much wishing he could talk to Daphne. He wanted to call her right now and tell her what happened and have her by his side.

But he kept that desire to himself.

While the chief was more than tolerant of the role Daphne had come to play in Plate's life, now was not the time.

The two police officers tried to maintain a crisp professional attitude. Brecken pulled out an official form and started writing a report. Plate opened the file on the Zopev case, planning to read once again the original affidavit Pauliza had given about the activities that gave Zopev an alibi.

However, they were men who had lost their colleague. Despite not knowing exactly what happened, each felt like it could have been either of them.

They abandoned their efforts after a few moments and gazed at each other, then away, lapsing into lethargic silence.

The lawyer arrived and Plate was left alone while Brecken began the interrogation of the suspect.

Plate reached for the phone on the chief's desk and dialed Daphne's number.

She was unavailable.

He pulled out his notebook from his pocket and looked at Elisabeth Morgan's number. Then dialed it.

Plate rarely pressed people over the phone. He much preferred face to face contact.

He was chained to the desk for the moment.

"I don't know that there's much more that I could tell you," said Elisabeth Morgan.

"You said Mr. Pauliza was running from the house in what seemed to be a hysterical manner. Could you describe that in more detail?"

"He ran out his front door, waving his hands and arms wildly. He was jumping up and down in an extremely erratic manner. Almost as if he were dancing."

"Dancing?"

"Yes, you know. Like people jump up and down when they celebrate when they're extremely excited."

"Celebrate?"

"Yes, like somebody who had been the recipient of very good

news and was jumping for joy. You know."

"Jumping for joy?"

"Yes. I had switched off the stereo. That was when I heard the desperation in his voice and he was screaming 'Policeman! Policeman!' Over and over again."

"What was the look on his face?"

"It was hard to see his face, Lieutenant. It was raining. I was looking through a window. A very clear window. I could see his movements well. They were definitely not that of a sane person in my opinion. His arms were jerking up and down. He was jumping haphazardly. Moving about in an erratic fashion is the best way I can describe it. Then right as his wife came out, quite sometime later, I thought. Considering what had just happened. Anyway. When his wife came out, he sort of collapsed like a rag doll. Like one of my puppets after I'm done manipulating them."

"I see. Thank you, Mrs. Morgan. Your description has been helpful."

"Anytime, Lieutenant."

As soon as Plate hung up, the phone started ringing again.

He sat and looked at it for a short time before picking it up again, all the while gazing at the notes he had taken from the phone call with Elisabeth Morgan.

Celebrate

Hysterical

Dancing

Jumping

Erratic

Haphazard

Rag doll

Puppet

Joy

What had Elisabeth Morgan actually seen?

Chapter 18

Plate was at the chief's desk much longer than he thought he would be.

Politicians and public officials clustered at the police department.

Brecken had to handle them all.

They wanted him. He was the chief.

Plate was left to field phone calls coming into the chief's office.

And contemplate a situation he had never experienced before.

The death of a fellow officer.

With open files scattered on his superior's desk and the chief's computer screen on, Plate was beginning to think it was not a waste of time to try to access various computer data banks for general information about everyone remotely involved.

He wished he knew better how to go about that chore.

He was not against the computer age. He was trying hard to learn.

Unfortunately, at this time he had a perpetual distraction.

In addition to personal calls from other department heads across the country, which were brief and dignified, he was also taking incoming calls from the members of the press who were privy to the chief's personal number.

These were the more influential and cooperative members of the fourth estate in and around the Sand Waves area who could normally be trusted to handle sensitive information diplomatically. And who were called on for services from time to time.

In return, they received a higher level of access than the general media.

It was part of Brecken's job to handle these people and Plate rarely dealt with them. He could tell them nothing right now.

The best he could do was stall them with assurances that the chief would get back to them as soon as possible.

They were not happy with that response.

When he answered the calls, a number of these reporters, realizing he was not Brecken, either did not give their names or did not give their correct names.

Plate recognized most of their voices anyway and some of the ones that used pseudonyms caused him a little amusement at some of the satirical handles they created. His amusement would have probably been much greater had it not been for the circumstances.

One female reporter obviously gave a nom de plume that did not amuse him at all.

He was not one hundred percent sure he recognized her voice but he was sure she was not one of the journalists entitled to the chief's special treatment. Somehow, she had gotten the number and was trying to slip into the inner circle.

He was suspicious the moment she started to speak.

When she started dropping lines about the public's right to know and freedom of the press, he was certain she was not one of Brecken's regulars.

They didn't care anything about that.

And when the tension in her voice increased considerably after she heard his voice, he started trying to place her.

He could only come up with one serious possibility- Daphne's sister, Darica Daniels.

She hung up the phone before he could pursue the matter. It rang again immediately.

After one more session with a woman upfront about being from *The Houston Post,* Plate took the phone off the hook.

The sympathy expressions could come later.

Any emergency calls would have to go through county dispatch.

It was several hours later, and several conferences with lawyers and the Powers-That-Be in Sand Waves, when Brecken returned to his office.

Brecken indicated Plate should just remain seated at his desk.

He perched on the side.

"I've been looking at everything I can find. Which is not

much. I talked to the potential witness again," Plate reported to the chief. "At least, she saw something strange. The way she described it to me it was almost as if he were celebrating having killed a policeman. Now, for a conviction, I think we need to find a motive."

"Plate." The chief glanced down at the pencil Plate was twirling. "Officially, we believe Pauliza's story that he shot a home invader coming through his second-story balcony. And all evidence supports him."

"What?"

Chief Brecken stood and went to his office window. "Pauliza says he and his wife were sound asleep. They had just gone to bed a short time before."

"They went to bed at eight o'clock in the morning?"

"They both worked nights. She is an RN on the night shift at Sand Waves Medical Center. He serves the niche market for nighttime movers. The Paulizas sleep days. According to him, he was awakened by the noise. He saw a man coming at him from the balcony. He reaches for his gun. And believing his life and the life of his wife were in danger, he justifiably defended them."

"Chief-"

"Let me finish, Plate. The fact is- Willhouse climbed to that balcony. He was seen."

"That's ridiculous. I'm going to talk to Elisabeth Morgan again. There's got to be some hole in her story."

"That's what we said about Pauliza's alibi for Zopev and look where we ended up. The serial killer back on the streets."

"In both those cases, something is wrong. Somebody has to be lying."

"We know that, Plate. You and I. But only you and I, unofficially. Now- why, we don't know, but evidence is Willhouse climbed up a tree next to the balcony to enter the house."

"That's crazy."

"That is irrefutable. Determined. Fact."

"It doesn't make sense."

"I know."

"An experienced policeman would not climb to a balcony in the rain in the morning and get himself shot without a reason," Plate declared.

"I know. But he did. There is no evidence that Willhouse had any sane logical reason to enter that house. No evidence that he tried to enter it any other way. Back door, front door, downstairs windows, all untouched."

Officer Jordan limped into the chief's office unannounced.

"I just heard. I can't believe it. I want in on this one. I have to be."

"Jordan, weren't you and Willhouse going sailing?" Brecken asked.

"Tim canceled our sail date. He gave no explanation."

"Didn't you think to check on him?" Plate asked.

"I just thought he changed his mind. Are you saying there's the possibility this was some type of weird suicide?" Jordan asked.

"He just called and canceled?" Brecken asked.

"Both of you were here Sunday. He was in a good mood. When he called me and said he didn't want to go sailing, he didn't sound upset or anything. Just didn't want to go."

"We don't know what happened. We are not saying anything definitive about whether or not he was depressed or not, we just don't know," said Brecken.

"I do know Pauliza," Jordan said.

"You know Pauliza? Beyond his role as a witness in the Castroe Zopev case?" Plate asked incredulously. "Why did we not know about that?"

"We did. I did. The defense didn't bring it up for some reason. Neither did the prosecutor," said Brecken.

"And I wasn't told? Why?" Plate asked.

"I was getting to that," said Brecken. "There was no need for you to know about it. We thought it would harm the prosecution."

"May I be told now?"

"Yes, it is just society stuff. Irrelevant, really. Pauliza knows several Houston officers as social acquaintances, you might say, from when he lived there until a short time ago. He is still an active supporter of the Houston Police Association. He contributes to all their causes," said Brecken.

"I can't believe I'm hearing this," said Plate, rising from the chief's desk.

"I can," said Jordan.

"Officer Jordan, just wait, please. Wait please, outside."

"Yes, Chief. My apologies." Jordan left the chief's office and went out into the hall.

"Plate," said the chief, after Jordan left. "I know this is one of our men. I'm just telling you on the surface it appears that a sleeping husband, with his wife asleep beside him, was awakened by a noise and thought it was a prowler. It appears that Pauliza had no way of knowing Willhouse was a police officer."

"He knew who Willhouse was from the Castroe Zopev murder case."

"No, Pauliza was never in the courtroom when Willhouse testified. Willhouse never made the papers. He was just another police officer doing his job. It would make no sense Pauliza would want to kill Willhouse. In fact, the other way around would make more sense. Pauliza mainly knew the officers involved in civics club and the like. You know Willhouse never went out for that. Until he got married, he was somewhat of a loner, save for his friendship with Jordan. And I always had the impression Jordan pushed that a little."

"We can't be sure."

"Yes. But I'm only saying unless we can come up with a good explanation of Willhouse's actions, this whole thing is going to be turned over to the grand jury without charges. A man has a right to protect himself in Texas if he can show good cause that he felt his life was in danger." The chief paused. "So far, Pauliza has a good case."

"Meaning just precisely what from your point of view?"

"Well, I don't believe personally that Willhouse was moonlighting as a daytime cat burglar. But I'm saying the obvious is out. Pauliza did not lure Willhouse onto the balcony and kill him. Willhouse did not go on to that balcony from inside the house. He climbed up a tree to get there. He climbed up there of his own free will. Apparently."

"No," said Plate." I don't believe it."

"Policemen have cracked up before," Brecken said.

"Yes, but there's so many more normal ways to crack up," Plate said. "Don't look at me like that. You know what I mean."

"Willhouse had a bad time once before. That is one reason why the arrest he made in the serial killer case was so important to him."

"What? When? I never knew anything about it."

"That's because you don't have access to everyone's confidential files. And I'm not obliged to tell you everything."

"Please skip the lecture."

"All right. Before Sand Waves was developed, and you and I were hired to build the police force here, Willhouse was with Houston."

"That much I know."

"Well, before he was there, his first job in 1969 after graduating from a private police academy, was with a small police department in East Texas. In 1974, there was an incident. His judgment was questioned."

"He jumped the gun?" Plate asked.

"No, just the opposite. He was accused of moving too slow. And costing another officer's life."

"What were the circumstances?"

"He was reprimanded in a departmental hearing. I read over that report again today. I had seen it when he applied here and felt it was not an impediment. He took the officer's death very hard and was on a long leave after the investigation. A voluntary leave. Then he did the hardest thing. He gathered his courage and moved on to the Houston police. You know there is a huge difference between our mostly white collar crimes and the life of a city officer. And Willhouse was, well, a good old boy. Didn't have any malice in him. No mistrust of his fellow man, you might say. I felt Sand Waves was the place for him."

"So what happened in the small town?" Plate asked.

"The details are sketchy. The only report surviving is that of the hearing. It was a three-man police force. Their chief, now deceased, Willhouse, and another patrolman, now living in Arizona."

"I've been looking through the files and didn't find anything about anything like this."

"That's because I have it locked away." Brecken reached behind file cabinet and pulled out a small wooden box. He fished a key from a drawer in a different file cabinet and opened the box.

The 9-x-12 box was four inches deep. It was full to the brim.

Brecken thumbed through it and pulled out a single sheet of paper from the middle of them all.

"Read this report," he said, handing it to his lieutenant.

Plate took the report and looked at it. It was printed in rather crude English but the events were clear.

*Report concerning the events surrounding the death of Officer K. Fondrem, Neches, Texas. January 1974.*

Previously employed by Volding Brook, a small town in the Texas Panhandle, Officer Fondrem's second law enforcement position was in the town of Neches where the officer had the misfortune to have a wreck with a tanker.

The details of the car wreck were delineated in the report down to the measurements of skid marks left on the highway.

*Officer T. Willhouse, from nearby town of Wilding Falls Police Department dispatched to the scene at 1:10 PM.*

The small departments of tiny East Texas towns, like Sand Waves police, used county dispatchers, not having budgets for 24-hour dispatching services private to their departments.

Modern technology meant this was insignificant in 1983 but in 1973 there still was a delay.

Nevertheless, the report indicated Willhouse had arrived as promptly at the scene as could be expected.

He was the only officer available in the area at the time.

Thereafter, accounts differed.

One witness who stopped to watch at peril of his own life said the officer seemed to hesitate.

*Officer K. Fondrem was clearly trapped in the car, aware of the grave danger, and screaming for help.*

Another witness said Willhouse moved slowly at the scene of the accident.

*Smoke was already coming from the tanker's engine.*

*The smoke suddenly turned black. The curious onlookers and the truck driver ran.*

By this time, a fire department official noted in all capital letters, not to run would have been suicide.

*The only death in the explosion was that of Officer K. Fondrem.*

The report contained a brief paragraph containing the truck driver's statement that the officer had pulled out in front of him and he attempted to swerve but was not able to avoid hitting the patrol car.

There was no one to contradict him and no way to tell from evidence at the scene whether he was telling the truth.

*A tragic accident for which there was no blame assigned. Officer T. Willhouse did receive a reprimand for his slow movement, but no blame was assigned to him for the outcome.*

That was the official conclusion.

The sketchy report did not contain the name of the witnesses. The truck driver was listed by his initials.

Illegible signatures and an official stamp completed the paper.

Plate put the report down on the desk.

"How is this connected to what happened today?"

"Let's say for argument's sake, the second obvious didn't happen."

"What you mean- the second obvious?" Plate asked.

"You say this witness says it seemed like the shooter was celebrating killing a policeman?" Brecken asked.

"She did not say that exactly. But that was the impression she seemed to have."

"That's dangerous talk. It's a double-edged sword that cuts both ways. Killing us just because we wear a uniform, it's probably more common than we care to admit. But it's a tightrope walk when there's no other motive."

"I don't believe he lost his mind," said Plate.

"We cannot get around- there is no proof, no evidence Tim identified himself as a policeman. No sane reason for him to climb onto their balcony and break into their bedroom. More motive for him to have a grudge against Pauliza, than vice versa," said Brecken.

"I still don't believe it. It doesn't add up."

"Between you and me, I don't believe Tim's death was an accident either. I may have to deny I ever said that. Unfortunately, the empty package on the porch does not help us. In fact, if it could be proven Tim left it, it would point to premeditation."

"Premeditation!"

"I don't believe it either. I have to stay with the official findings as of now. But not if you are successful. I expect you to find out what really did happen."

"Yes, Chief. You can count on it."

Chapter 19

"Darica! What are you doing here?" Daphne opened her front door to see her sister with a suitcase in hand.

"I have come for the funeral."

"Did you think you might have given me a call first?"

"I would of thought it would of been expected of me. After all I dated the man."

"You had two prearranged dates, which were part of a setup for an investigation. The two of you didn't even like each other. He married his girlfriend a few weeks later. You are telling me you are here solely to attend the funeral? Not for a story?"

"I promise. I am not writing a newspaper article about the death of Timothy Willhouse. I have taken a leave of absence from the newspaper to reassess my future. When I heard about Willhouse's death, I thought about coming down here to stay with you for a few days and go to the funeral. It's completely a personal private act on my part. I may not of actually had a relationship with the man, but we were acquaintances, and in a way, coworkers during the time we spent together."

Daphne regarded her sister with skepticism.

"Magazine article?"

"Daphne! I've told you before. It's impossible to get published unless you know someone. I can't make enough as a freelancer. I'm currently looking at other options."

"I can-"

"And don't start saying you can get me on with an insurance company," said Darica. "I'm not a salesperson. I'm a writer."

"How long is your leave of absence?"

"A month. Without pay of course."

*Oh, no!* thought Daphne. *Surely, she's not expecting to stay here a month!*

"Don't worry. I'm only going to be visiting you for a few days. I admit I do need to stay with you, if it's okay. A hotel would seriously cut into my savings."

"You've been saving up to take this leave of absence?"

"Actually I was saving up to buy a new car. But I decided this was more important. I'm almost 28 years old, divorced with no children, working in a job with a limited future and endless aspiring journalists coming out of college, fresh faced, willing to work for less money, trying to take my place."

Darica's brief marriage upon graduation from high school was like a fond memory of a dream for Daphne. Memories of the event often sprang up in her mind at random. And when provoked, like now.

*Darica in her long-sleeved white gown with satin cuffs and a V neck, making her look even taller, next to her short twin in green chiffon with a large brim hat. Their mother in a blue satin formal. Scott and their father in tuxedos, along with the new member of the family, the groom with the humorous name- Dan Daniels.*

*Everyone laughing, almost ten years younger than today.*

The marriage had not survived college. Darica had become jaded and slightly embittered as she plunged into the highly competitive journalism profession while living her private life alone.

She worked in the declining print journalism field, not the lucrative television news platform.

"I'm giving up several hundreds of dollars in salary to come to this funeral," said Darica.

Daphne thought of the thousands of dollars she was about to forfeit just by taking a long enough break from insurance sales to marry and have a honeymoon.

The dramatic contrast in their careers was never more apparent. Darica lived from paycheck to paycheck. She rented the cheapest city apartments where a woman dared live alone. She drove a salvaged car. Daphne had a house fully paid for in an exclusive community with a healthy savings account and a nice vehicle. Yet it was Darica who was constantly in danger of losing her job if her bosses found out that she had a twin sister who moved in the higher echelon of society in Sand Waves.

Daphne had clients whose privacy she had to protect to keep their business. Frequently Darica needed to pry into the private lives of that same group of people to create headlines.

So for professional reasons the sisters usually pretended to not know one another. And did not let anybody know that they were sisters.

They had different last names as a result of Darica's failed marriage. They did not look alike. Daphne, standing up at just over 5 feet tall, was a natural wavy blonde. Her sister's 5 feet, 10 inch height contrasted as did her dark straight brown hair.

Seeing Daphne's distress at wedding memories and economic disparity, Darica sniffed in annoyance. She interpreted her sister's forlorn look a different way.

"Don't worry. I kept my apartment. As soon as Officer Willhouse's funeral is over, I will be on my way."

"Then you really are here to get material for a magazine?"

In Daphne's mind that was not an ambition quite as suspicious as a newspaper story aspiration.

Darica did not reply.

"Don't worry. He was not one of my clients. So I don't care. Just, for P-Plate's sake, don't do anything sensational."

"And why should I care what he thinks? Are you still so enamored of him that you now stutter when you speak his name?"

"Darica." Daphne took a deep breath. "Sit down."

"I've been sitting all the way from Dallas." Darica went into Daphne's kitchen and opened the refrigerator.

"Darica, I have something to tell you."

"What?" Darica popped open a Coke and sat at the dinette table, remembering with some consternation that Daphne did not allow any eating or drinking anywhere else in the house. Except for the kitchen and dinette, all the floors were covered with white carpet. Even the bathrooms.

Daphne sat at the table across from her sister. Sitting down did give them a more equalization in height.

Daphne took another deep breath.

"We're going to be married," she said.

"What did you say?" Darica almost spilled the soft drink in her confusion. "Who's going to be married?"

"I am," said Daphne.

"You?"

"Yes."

"To who?"

"To P- Plate."

Darica was speechless.

"And in private, I now call him Peter. But that is strictly in private, you understand. You had better ask him what he wants you to call him."

"You are getting married?"

"Yes."

"To that cop?"

"Yes."

"He asked you to marry him?"

"That's pretty much the way it went. Yes."

"Oh, well. He's not serious. Don't take it seriously. He's just trying to get in bed with you. Oh, no. You haven't? I mean- don't fall for it!"

Daphne buried her head in her hands. She did not know whether to laugh or cry. She looked back up at her sister and took another deep breath.

"He is serious. We are going to be married. Remember, I called and asked if you could get off this coming Friday?"

"Yes, I said no way. Which was the case until Willhouse died."

"You used his death to get bereavement leave?"

"Maybe I exaggerated my relationship with Willhouse. But, hey, we did date."

"Twice."

"That's not much more than you have seen of Lieutenant Plate. Especially when you consider all I am doing is going to the guy's funeral and you are committing for life."

"Are you sure this leave of absence was voluntary? It sounds long for a bereavement leave."

"They have an intern from one of the local colleges in Dallas who is working for them for free as she finishes up her journalism degree. So they can afford to spare me. When is this set for anyway? Did he get you a ring?" Darica asked.

"Not yet," Daphne admitted.

"Oh, well, see, he's just playing with you. Surely, you have not set any date or made any arrangements. Have you?"

"I was going to tell you, in fact, ask you to come be in the wedding party. It is this Friday."

"THIS Friday? Day after tomorrow! Oh, you really wanted me to come all right!"

"It's not that I didn't want you, Darica. It's rather complicated. The wedding is going to be part of a movie. The producer is gifting us the rings. And I- well, I have told Mom and Dad. But they are leaving on their trip tomorrow. And Scott couldn't make it either for some reason he made up. First time I ever asked him to visit my house and he didn't even ask why. So when you immediately said you couldn't come- I know you don't really like Peter. I- I just dropped it."

"You dropped it? Real important to you, is it?"

"Plate, I mean Peter, says we can always have a second reception for family later and there is a lot of money involved."

"Daphne! Are you telling me you are marrying that guy this Friday because somebody is paying you to dress up and act like a bride? Who on earth would do that? I knew you were mercenary, but I would not have thought- " Darica stood up, towering over the shorter woman seated before her. "Daphne! What's happened? Are you on something? Drugs? Or did you have a breakdown and nobody told me? Have you lost your mind over that cop?"

"No, listen-"

"You went to bed with that cop didn't you? Now, he's dumped you for some other of his flings, probably someone he was seeing on the side, like Serena Towers, and you can't take his rejection. You've lost your mind."

"Darica!" Daphne rose from the table also. She still felt helpless, thinking if she got on a chair to be taller, Darica would just climb on another chair and be taller still.

That was the way it went all through their childhood.

"I'm calling Mom and Dad right now. They haven't left yet."

Darica dashed into Daphne's Victorian parlor style home office. She grabbed the French provincial reproduction phone, which had push buttons instead of a rotary dial.

She pounded the buttons, which made loud musical notes.

"Please don't damage my new phone. Or my furniture," Daphne called. "It all cost a lot of money and I would have a hard time replacing any of it."

Daphne waited in the den as her mother reassured her sister that all of what Daphne had claimed was true.

"I don't suppose she's planning to pay the long distance charges," Daphne muttered to herself. Although Daphne and Darica's parents also lived in the greater Houston area, it was long distance to Sand Waves, which kept Daphne from talking as much as she liked to her parents. She could afford it.

But they protested the high rates by refusing to spend any time talking long distance even if they were not paying for it.

"I see... Thanks, Mom... Yes, if she won't listen to you, she sure won't listen to me... Dad thinks what?.. MEN!.. No. I'll call back later." Darica's tone had become much softer and a little defensive as she concluded her conversation with their mother.

Standing in the den with her arms folded, Daphne locked eyes with her sister.

"The next thing you say is 'Daphne! Congratulations! I'm so happy for you!'," Daphne said.

"The next thing I say again is- Daphne, are you out of your mind? You are going to really marry that jerk?"

"Darica, I would appreciate it if you would consider that this is the man I love and he is going become your brother-in-law."

"He's an arrogant jerk!"

"Darica. Did I say anything about Dan Daniels when you married him? Even though I didn't even have a boyfriend, I was not jealous. Even though I barely knew him, did I not congratulate you? Stand beside you as your maid of honor? Welcome him into the family and wish you both the best of happiness in life?"

"Yes." Darica gritted her teeth. "As smart as you are, I would of thought you would of learned something from that."

"You are very fond of pointing out that you are not like me and I'm not like you. You're not being fair. What have you got against Plate?" asked Daphne.

*He's a man,* Darica wanted to reply. But she knew that answer would not fly in this day and age.

It was the 1980s.

"You're my sister. I love you. I don't want to see you hurt. I don't want to see you made a fool of."

"You're my sister, not my mother. Not even my older sister. In fact, I was born first. I'm a big girl. 30 is just around the corner as you just recently pointed out," Daphne said.

"A man as sophisticated as Plate-" Darica stopped, unable to continue verbalization of her thoughts.

"Wouldn't be interested in somebody as socially inexperienced as me? Or sexually inexperienced? Which are you trying to say?"

"I'm sure I don't know anything about your sex life. But I have observed. All you have ever done is go to college and sell insurance. You've never wanted to go to parties. You've never hardly dated anyone. I'm the writer. I should of been the loner. But I was always somewhere out there in the crowd, making connections, while you sat at home. Nothing's changed. You sure you don't want to just marry somebody so that you can have a wedding ceremony?"

"I'm well aware of your opinion of me as a social outcast."

"I didn't say outcast. But it always seemed like you cared for nothing but school and later your career."

"There's more to me than you know, Darica," Daphne said.

Darica started to protest that idea. Then she recalled the events of the past few months and the role Daphne had played in them. For the first time she was unsure of her judgments.

Daphne took advantage of the pause.

"Let's just drop it right now. All the details have not been set because this movie deal situation may be delayed by Officer

Willhouse's murder. As I said, I don't know how that's going to complicate everything. Peter worked directly with him. I don't think they were extra close friends or anything, but it is bound to affect him. He's been so busy the past couple of days he has hardly had time to talk to me," Daphne said.

Darica pondered advancing that last statement as an argument for her previous assertion that the police officer was not serious about the marriage.

Seeing the quiet anger growing in Daphne's eyes, she thought better of it.

"Okay. I agree. We will drop it. Am I welcome here still? Or not?"

"Of course, you're welcome here. You're my twin sister. What a silly question!" Daphne's anger dimmed. "I don't have the guest room ready. I'll need to change the sheets."

"Thanks, don't bother."

"Now, I cannot have you sleeping on musty sheets."

Daphne did not tell Darica that Plate sometimes spent the night in the guest room when he worked very late and very long hours. She could fix him a meal, help him undress and get in bed when he would have been too exhausted to do anything other than collapse on his couch at his apartment, still wearing all of the uncomfortable paraphernalia connected to his uniform.

It was a service she rendered for him gladly, even though he was usually up and gone the next day without a word before she ever left her own bedroom.

While Daphne fixed the guest bed, Darica sat alone in the den and contemplated how much of the truth she had actually told Daphne. She could admit only to herself that she was burned out working as a print journalist. That her hope of getting an exclusive story on the strange death of Officer Willhouse, which would help her break into the higher paying freelance levels, was the true reason she was back in Sand Waves.

While she had previously contemplated that Daphne might be somewhat sympathetic to this goal, and was actually hopeful that

Daphne might help her out, she felt sure that her new potential brother-in-law would bar the way.

She had recognized his voice when he had answered the phone at the police station on Tuesday. He was an obstacle that she had not anticipated. She had been aware that her sister was still seeing him. Despite knowing how Daphne felt about him, she had convinced herself that he was only toying with her twin and the relationship would soon die out.

"I was wrong," she said aloud, just as Daphne was coming back into the room.

"You were wrong? About what?"

"I was thinking, maybe I was wrong in coming."

"No. Don't think that way. We will work it all out. It might be a blessing-" Daphne stopped herself just in time from saying '*in disguise*', which is what she was thinking. She continued, "-a blessing after all. Peter's going to be very busy in the next few weeks and you might be just what I need to help me get through a difficult time. I will get you in the wedding if you will agree."

"As a bridesmaid? I'm not sure- "

"You may need help getting into Willhouse's funeral."

Daphne lowered her head. She was bluffing. She had no idea if she was going to get into the funeral herself.

"Well, okay, I guess so. As you said, you walked the aisle for me."

"Darica, please try to be happy for me. If it's any consolation, I'm sorry it didn't turn out any better for you."

Daphne's feelings for her lost marriage were not a consolation to Darica.

She expected her sister's sympathy.

Felt entitled to it.

For a sharp second, Daphne's words brought back to Darica all of the pain she had first felt when her marriage had failed.

All her aggravation faded into sadness.

Chapter 20

The hard task of informing Alice Willhouse that she had lost her husband of less than a month had fallen on Chief Brecken.

He spent much of Tuesday night with her.

Wednesday morning he returned to the station a depressed man.

"Skaar will have to stay with the princess for the time being. I need you here for the investigation into Willhouse's death," Brecken told Plate.

Brecken had done no more than verbalize a decision Plate had already made.

As second in command, Plate deferred 97 percent of the time to Brecken. But he did have a small degree of autonomy which he exercised frequently.

He had already determined this would be one of those times.

"Any concrete details on the funeral yet?"

"Mrs. Willhouse is in no state to decide. She left the details to me. I have decided it will be a hero police officer's funeral. Regardless of what the official verdict is, we are going to show solidarity in the face of this death. It was the only way we will ever get justice for Tim. Otherwise- otherwise Powers-That-Be will want to sweep it under the rug. I have already phoned chiefs and sheriffs in other agencies. Fellow officers will be coming in from all over the country. Some from quite a distance and on a limited budget."

"I can allow somebody to stay the night at my place. But unless someone wants to be on the floor, I've only got room for one."

*I'll take the couch. I sleep there half the time anyway,* Plate thought.

"About the future Mrs. Plate. Doesn't she have a big empty house?"

Inadvertently, the question caused the floorplan of Daphne's house, so crucial to his last major case, to run through Plate's mind.

Daphne's house was a simple elegant design. The front door opened to a slightly raised foyer, bordered on the right side by a wall that harbored a coat closet. Directly in front was the large den, to the left was a formal dining room with a small formal living room attached. Off the den, also to the left, was the kitchen and dinette area.

There were no walls separating the spaces.

A partition did give a little semblance of a barrier to the kitchen area.

Stepping off the foyer, the dinette adjacent to the den and behind the kitchen was completely open as well. The small room off the front of the den behind the coat closet wall was Daphne's home office.

A hallway hit the den at a right angle and led to three bedrooms in total, with the master bedroom being separated on one side from the den by a huge wall that ran three quarters of the way through the house.

"If you had enough rollaway beds or air mattresses, she could accommodate 15 or 20 overnight guests," Plate thought aloud, then instantly regretted it."

"Then she could take several?" Brecken asked hopefully.

"I cannot commit for her, Chief. How many female officers are coming?"

"I'm not quite sure, but usually they are the hardest to find accommodations for. Most married police officers have a full house, or if they don't have any children, they are still in apartments themselves."

"I'll ask her. I'm sure she will be happy to help."

"There's one other thing about her that worries me."

"Yes?"

"You know you've only known her a very short time. And from what you tell me, she's hardly ever even been stopped for a traffic ticket, much less known any police officers personally. And there's none in her family right?" Brecken asked.

Plate was silent.

Robert Brecken was his commanding officer. His chief.

In the midst of an onerous task.

"All I'm saying is- she can't possibly have any idea what it's like to be a police officer's wife. She needs to get to know some of the other women who are married to cops. I know I said it before but I still think the same thing. You need to consider that you just might be rushing into this."

"Thank you for your advice, Chief."

Brecken sighed. "Anyway, I'm going to see Willhouse's widowed bride again later this afternoon. I need to make final arrangements for synchronizing funeral details with the release of the body. It may be some time. I'm going to ask for plenty of time for the autopsy and forensics to be performed with care. It will be a strain for Mrs. Willhouse to drag it out like that. So I'm going to try to talk to her and in some way console her with the idea the delay will help us find out what really happened. I guess I'm feeling fatherly. Ignore me if I'm getting too personal."

"Yes, Chief."

Outside the chief's office, Brecken and Plate returned to the police department to find Jordan waiting for them in the hall.

Plate and Jordan barely avoided colliding.

"I'm sorry, Lieutenant," said Jordan, steadying himself with a hand on Plate's shoulder. "It's the sprained ankle of mine. I moved too slow."

"Both of us moved too slow," said Plate, irritated.

"Yes, sir. I guess we both did. I'll try to see to it that I am more careful," said Jordan. His tone of voice that indicated he thought Plate was making a big deal out of a little thing.

"And determine it won't happen again," Plate said evenly.

"Yes, sir," said Jordan. A little sarcasm crept into his tone.

"Pardon me, Jordan?" Brecken spoke with agitation.

"Chief, Lieutenant, I really would like to help with Timothy's killing. What is going to happen? Will the grand jury indict? Do we have a case against Pauliza? All the men in all the area departments are talking about this. We'd all like to know what you think."

"Jordan, if I need any help, I'll let you know. You're still off-duty with that ankle."

The phone rang and the chief, expecting more conversation

about Willhouse, suddenly motioned for both men to keep quiet when he heard different news.

"Let county bring them in. Stay with her," he barked into the receiver, then dropped it from his ear.

"What is it?" asked Plate as Brecken hung up the phone.

"That was Skaar. There has been a second attempt on the princess. Kareem escaped custody on his way back here and went right back to the compound try again. Skaar caught him outside the house."

"Always a mistake, to take on a job bodyguarding a celebrity. I know there is a little extra money in it for us but we should have let the county or a private agency handle it. It's been nothing but trouble," said Jordan with some smugness.

"Skaar's waiting for county to arrive to bring him in. He's staying with her," Brecken said, ignoring Jordan.

"We should have let the county deal with the princess from the beginning or told the movie producer to hire private detectives," Jordan continued.

Plate and Brecken glared at Jordan but the higher ranking officers had to silently agree.

They could have avoided all the headaches of dealing with the rich and famous and their needs. It was always a time consuming endeavor.

And now they had more important matters before them, causing the hazing incident and the princess' discomfort to pale in comparison.

"Always a mistake," Jordan repeated.

Despite their short-handedness, Brecken curtly told Jordan to go back home to finish his disability time.

Chapter 21

Reunited classmates, Kareem Makikz and James Juan-Paublo II, sat in the police station in Sand Waves.

They were both extremely ill at ease.

"I had never even been inside a police station before," Juan-Paublo whined.

His partner looked at him with disgust and remained silent.

"You can't keep us here without charging us, I know that much." Juan-Paublo looked around at the bare room. The Sand Waves Police Station was nothing like anything he had ever seen in the movies. It was much too plain and simple.

The Lake Charles Police Department had been worse.

In a different way. Barren and ghostly.

He was a little spooked by Louisiana.

"You will be charged," said Lieutenant Plate. "You will certainly be charged."

"I don't know on what grounds," Juan-Paublo protested. "I didn't do anything."

"You were caught trespassing, if nothing else. Breaking and entering, most likely."

"We were lost! We had no idea we were on private property."

Plate laughed. "After that first fiasco. We can still go back and charge you with felonies- attempted rape, kidnapping."

"I wasn't even there the second time."

"Shut up!" Makikz spoke for the first time.

Plate smiled to himself. It was time to separate them. Juan-Paublo had exposed signs of fear and weakness. Once Makikz could no longer see or hear his partner, he would be easily convinced that Juan-Paublo had told all.

Plate very much wanted to find out what Makikz knew. He doubted that Juan-Paublo would be of much help in finding out what was going on.

Plate figured Juan-Paublo did not know anything.

He was right.

As they were simultaneously interviewed, Makikz by Plate and Juan-Paublo by Brecken, it became obvious that Juan-Paublo actually thought he was participating in a hazing activity for a fraternity. Makikz, he said, had convinced him that in order to get into the elite social society, this was what they needed to do.

"Getting a picture kissing the princess," Juan-Paublo insisted. "That's all it was about."

It took a little longer for Makikz to tell his story.

"My parents are from the Middle East. Our family owed the family of Abdul Mahlah a favor. All I was supposed to do was put a little fear into her. It needed to make the newspapers. It was just for the prince to save face. I wasn't going to hurt her. The first time we got in should have been enough, but there was nothing about it in the newspaper yesterday. So I had to try again."

Expensive lawyers, hired by the well-to-do families of the students, showed up at this time and the interviews had to cease.

Makikz made only one more statement in front of his lawyer imploring Plate to get an article in the newspaper about the attack.

The lawyer promptly grabbed both the young man's arms, pulled him up out of the chair, and yelled at him to shut up.

"Because an arrest is been made, I suspect the newspapers have already picked it up," said Plate to Chief Brecken, after the interviews were concluded. "Otherwise, I'd do my best to see it got kept out of the papers."

"So you think this is pretty much a dead end?"

"I don't see how it could possibly have anything to do with Tim's death."

"Does the princess want to press charges? What about Stark Wynter? It was his house they broke into. You talked to him. What did he say?"

"The princess thinks we should take them out back and shoot them. Stark Wynter would like to hush up the whole thing."

"I thought all publicity was good publicity."

"Stark Wynter's old-school Hollywood. He may like bad publicity but only if he can control it. Frankly, I think he feels that a headline about two junior college students harassing the princess might cause her status to actually drop. He needs elite special forces sent in by either the Italian or some Arab government to abscond with her back to Italy or Arabia. That would be publicity he could sink his teeth into."

"God forbid," said Brecken.

"No indications of anything like that in the works, I hope?"

"As far as I can tell, and this is pretty much confirmed by my sources, all governments in Europe, the Middle East, and North Africa are singularly uninterested in Princess Joanna Scarpartti, except possibly for any taxes they might could collect on any money she might make here in America."

"I see," said the lieutenant.

Plate glanced out into the hall.

Ignoring his superior's order, suspecting it was made out of frustration, Jordan was still limping around restlessly, apparently hoping to get some word about how the interviews with the suspects went.

Brecken invited him in the office.

"I was thinking I might could get some things for Alice before I go on home, if Tim had any personal possessions stored in the lockers," said Jordan.

Thunder sounded outside as the three police officers contemplated the death of their colleague.

"I've got some things to do, Chief," said Plate. "Why don't you go ahead and fill him in on what is going on. Just because he's out on disability doesn't mean he can't contribute verbally to the investigation. He might have some ideas."

"Thank you, Lieutenant. Chief, I apologize if I shot my mouth off earlier about the princess."

Both men ignored Jordan's words but their annoyance at him disappeared.

"Okay. But, Plate, don't you be gone too long," said Brecken.

Chapter 22

The thunder sounded again as Plate left the station. Soon it would rain. Plate always liked dark rainy days.

He started home. But the murder location enticed him.

Plate drove to Harbor Shadows. Now rain streamed down in sheets. The streets of Sand Waves lost much of their suburban charm.

*This was an eerie setting for a murder,* thought Plate as he drove down the street where Timothy Willhouse met his death.

And Plate was sure it was murder.

Small lights glowed from a few of the houses like silhouetted fire. Very few, Plate reflected. It was the age of the working woman. Most of the houses were dark and dreary in the rain, their expensive landscaping cowering before nature's drenching.

Plate stopped before the Pauliza house, envisioning them asleep in their bedroom. He tried to re-create the events that led to Timothy Willhouse's death. While struggling with the complex evidence, including the barbecue pit and the abandoned puppet, he had almost forgotten the scanty evidence of the neighbors. Elisabeth Morgan had seen the shooting.

But there was no real question about the literal shooting.

There were always minor inconsistencies in every situation that were like crumbs that had fallen from a well-set table and usually were swept under the rug.

Sometimes those crumbs were unearthed and made the difference when a case went in a different direction than expected.

More door knocking by county officers at nearby houses after work hours had produced a few such precious crumbs.

A second neighbor had earlier noticed a car parked with a man in it on Harbor Shadows. This was unusual in the middle of a weekday but she paid no attention to it, other than taking note because it was unusual. Later it was gone, she recalled.

A third neighbor saw a man on foot running near the Pauliza home. He saw the same man. Probably. He hailed another man in a car. Maybe the witness saw a package left, not by a postman. Maybe.

Again, occurrences to capture the attention only momentarily. Only because this was Sand Waves, where hardly any pedestrians were ever seen in the daytime on weekdays.

There was no vehicle visible at the Pauliza place. But Plate knew that did not mean they were not home. All types of vehicles, except for family passenger cars and passenger pickup trucks, were prohibited from being visibly parked in driveways or on the street near houses. This meant that any service vehicle had to be kept in a garage hidden from public view.

Real estate agents patrolled seven days a week for violations that might hamper sales. A homeowner might pull his trailer out of his garage to work on it on a Friday in his driveway and find a violation notice in his mailbox Monday, after he had already pulled the trailer back in the garage and gone off to work at his job.

Sarah Pauliza drove an ordinary car but Eduardo drove a small moving van with the company name on it.

Both vehicles could be inside the spacious garage.

Plate circled the block and drove down the street a second time, again scrutinizing the Pauliza house. The whole business was somehow against common sense, against human nature- as if it were contrived, a carefully staged plan.

As if a master manipulator had been pulling the strings that day and Timothy Willhouse had merely been dangling at the end.

Plate stopped the car in front of the Pauliza's house and gazed at the balcony.

What scenario had induced Timothy Willhouse to climb up, kick open the door, and call Pauliza a liar?

Or was that what happened?

What lured him up to that balcony?

Plate sat up a little straighter behind the wheel.

Or was there in the midst of all this an unknown puppeteer, pulling the strings, above it all.

But who, how, and why?

Chapter 23

Plate debated taking the risk. If he antagonized Mrs. Pauliza, he could face an accusation of police harassment in light of the official review of the matter.

He could be fired.

A few moments later, Plate was in the dining room directly under the master bedroom in the Pauliza house.

Sarah Pauliza watching him from the kitchen.

He knew the exact layout of the house before he stepped into it. From the outside, the homes in this colony all had differences. But the interiors were a subset of four different styles. Each style was instantly recognizable as soon as the front door threshold was crossed. It was this way in all the un-gated colonies, except the upper tier where custom homes were allowed.

This was a great advantage to the police. In all but a very few of the neighborhoods, where some older homes had been surrounded by the colony, the police could memorize the various floor plans and know exactly where they were when they entered a home.

Plate was very diligent about such matters. And he insisted the men underneath him do their best to memorize them all.

"Do you really believe my husband murdered your officer in cold blood?" Sarah Pauliza asked softly.

"I believe my officer was lured onto that balcony and murdered."

"By my husband?"

"Yes. Or by you." Plate looked at her evenly. He had no use for formal protocol right now.

Sarah Pauliza sat down at her kitchen bar. She seemed very lost in this puzzle. Finally, she met Plate's gaze and said, "I'm a nurse, Lieutenant. I help people. I could not kill. My husband could not kill. We are just ordinary people."

"Your husband is going to be released. The case will be referred to the grand jury without charges."

"Thank God." Sarah Pauliza went to her dining room window

and pushed back the soft white shears that shielded poorly against the hot Texas sun. "He has checked himself this morning into the hospital for chest pains over all this. That is why he is not here."

"Then I appreciate the fact that it is very considerate of you to let me see you right now," said Plate. "Especially knowing our investigation is still underway."

Sarah Pauliza did not reply.

"Would you do me the courtesy of telling me what happened one more time?"

She turned her head and looked at him through the corner of her eyes.

"You're very attractive, Lieutenant. Very charming. I'm sure you're used to getting exactly what you want. But you won't get what you want from me."

Plate sighed with exasperation.

"Mrs. Pauliza, I do not consider myself handsome. I try hard NOT to be charming. And I hardly ever get anything that I want, I can assure you."

She frowned at him.

"Please, Mrs. Pauliza. Look at it from this point of view. If you and your husband are telling the truth, then don't you want to find out what happened?"

"I told it all the first time."

"Just the basics. Just a skeleton version."

"All right. We were asleep. Just like you are in the middle of the night, I presume. Only we sleep days. A tremendous noise, a banging on the balcony woke us up. Then my husband jumped up. The glass on the French doors broke. The door swung wide. By this time, my husband had his gun. I think I screamed and pulled the covers up to my neck. Then the man, the intruder, he was- was- desperate looking. Maybe surprised also."

"Surprised?"

"Yes. And then he called my husband a liar."

"Called him a liar? Why? Did your husband say something? Or do you think he was referring to his testimony at the trial?"

"I don't know. I didn't know this officer was even involved with the trial. That's why I thought the man was a crazy burglar or seriously disturbed. We had never seen him before in our lives but there he was, calling Ed a liar. And not just like I would say to you- 'you are a liar'. He was screaming it desperately, frantically. 'Liar! Liar!' Then they- he went backwards. My husband ran after him. He had shot him."

Sarah took a deep breath.

There was a long pause.

"Are you sure he said 'liar'?" Plate asked.

"Well, yes. And at first, I thought he was saying 'don't fire'. But I really didn't hear the word 'don't'. I'm sure of that now. And he wouldn't have been telling my husband TO shoot him. Quite frankly, Lieutenant, I don't think he even saw my husband's gun."

"Did he have his own gun drawn? We found his gun beside him. But we are unsure, the way it fell, it could have fallen out of his pocket, or he could have tossed it there. He was not in uniform so we are not exactly sure how he was carrying it."

"I don't know. I did not see."

"Tell me, why did your husband have a loaded gun beside his bed?"

"Because of what happened before- " She stopped suddenly.

"What do you mean? What happened before?"

"Lieutenant, I've talked too long to you. I have to go to work soon. You have got to go now."

"What happened before?" Plate resisted an urge to shake her.

Distressed now, the nurse shook her head. "Go, please go." She sat down at the formal dining table and clasped her hands over her mouth.

Plate started towards the door.

"Lieutenant Plate, I do have one more piece of information for you, for whatever it is worth."

"Yes?" Plate turned around. He was not expecting much help.

"We found later, after it was all over, someone had used our barbecue grill."

"What?"

"Someone had recently used our barbecue grill. You see, we could tell because we had just cleaned it Sunday. After Eduardo was questioned and released Tuesday evening, we didn't go to work because of the shooting. And I thought I would grill some hamburgers on the back patio. It's covered so it didn't matter that it was raining. And that's when I found it had been used. Someone had cooked a meal on it. There was grease. And a little burnt wood."

"In your back yard? Without your knowing about it?"

"Well, you see we have a plank fence, like is required in our subdivision, and behind us is the section running through Sand Waves reserved as natural forest, the green belts, they call it."

Plate shook his head, bewildered. "I don't understand. Can I see this barbecue pit?"

She hesitated.

"That is why we never mentioned it. We were afraid you would not believe us."

"What do you mean?" Plate asked.

"It is gone. It was stolen later than night."

"Mrs. Pauliza-"

"There was one other thing. I'm sure it was just tossed over the fence by some kids. But I found this."

She opened a drawer and pulled out a small marionette puppet.

It was similar to the ones Elisabeth Morgan used.

Except it was older.

It was a soldier.

"May I take this?" Plate asked.

"Yes. Take it. Now you must go. I am going to the hospital to see how my husband is doing. Please get out."

Chapter 24

"Sorry I haven't been able to see you for the past three days. But I did talk to Stark. Everything is set for the wedding Friday morning. Are you mad? Is that why? Why we are meeting here?"

Plate stared at Daphne across a small round table at the Toy Museum Restaurant.

"No, don't be silly. I understand. Calling me and giving me a referral makes up for that." With a poignant pang, Daphne recalled the time when not hearing from him for three days was pure agony.

Not that long ago.

Like childhood, it was now a fond memory. Also like childhood, she was glad those days were over.

"Why- why then the sudden desire for me to take you out to eat? And why can't I pick you up at your house? Scared the neighbors might see me? I crashed there just a few nights ago."

"No, it's not any of that. Darica is here. She's off working but I don't want her showing up unexpectedly when you drop by."

Plate picked up his menu. "Indeed? So she's come for the wedding after all?"

"She's come to go to Officer Willhouse's funeral."

"Indeed!"

"Now don't get mad at me. His death has made national headlines. And I didn't call or anything. She just showed up on my doorstep with a suitcase. She's taken a leave of absence from her job."

"So she's not here to cover Willhouse's funeral as a reporter from a newspaper?"

"No, why do you ask that?"

"She called directly to the station right after his death was announced, using a newspaper's authority, and asked about it."

"She did? She asked for you?"

"No, I answered the phone. I don't think she was sure it was me. Somehow she had the chief's private number."

"Oh. Maybe then, it was just routine."

"Maybe. A lot of reporters called."

"I convinced her to be a bridesmaid. A costume is already ready for her."

"There's Hollywood magic for you."

"I think you should consider she's coming mainly for the funeral. Being in our wedding is a byproduct," said Daphne.

"Mainly for the funeral? How is she going to get in? Entrance to the service is by invitation," Plate said.

"I don't know."

"Maybe she hasn't thought of it. No, that doesn't make any sense. She is a reporter. She would know that such funerals are usually by invitation especially when they're taking place in a small chapel like Willhouse's is. Most of the police coming out of respect aren't even going to expect to get inside. They'll be forming an honor guard along the street."

"I don't know. She said something about because she dated Willhouse a couple of times, she thought it would be expected that she come for his funeral."

"She cannot be that naive."

"She's not. She thinks I'm that naive. She's been asking to use the word processing program on my computer. She was complaining that I did not have a hookup to a phone line. She bought some floppy disks of her own and she's been typing away. I think she's come in hopes of doing a freelance article on the whole situation."

A dark look came over Plate's face.

"I don't see how she could possibly do any kind of article on the situation when we don't really know what situation is."

"What do you mean?" Daphne asked.

Plate relayed his feelings and impression about an unknown puppeteer to Daphne without any hesitation or embarrassment.

She accepted his considerations without any skepticism or criticism.

"A puppeteer?" She reflected. "It sounds like a daydream but your daydreams do have a good record."

"It hasn't come out yet publicly that the police officer killed was the police officer who had handled the Zopev arrest. The press is been preoccupied with a lot of news coming out of Houston. They're just now getting wind that the homeowner that fired the shot was the witness that gave Zopev an alibi," said Plate.

"You know what they're going to say?" Daphne asked.

"I know exactly what some people will say. They will say that Willhouse went to Pauliza's home to confront or even kill him and Pauliza fired in self-defense."

"Is that what Pauliza is saying?"

"No. not even close. Both he and Mrs. Pauliza claim they were sound asleep when Timothy broke into their bedroom through their French doors off the balcony."

"So if he had gone there, even just to talk to them, and the situation had gotten out of hand, why would they come up with that story?" Daphne asked.

"The only thing I can think of is that they somehow lured Tim to the house."

"Why would they do that?"

"That's the problem. To me, that's the only thing that makes sense. But you are right. Why would they do that?

"I can see where people might think that Officer Willhouse might have a motive against the witness, but why would the witness want to harm Officer Willhouse?"

"Regardless of whether or not Pauliza's testimony was true, how could he have any motive to even talk to Willhouse, much less harm him? I can't get past the ridiculousness of the idea that Pauliza initiated the meeting."

"And if Officer Willhouse initiated the incident-" Daphne could not think how to finish that sentence.

"Yes, what was his motive? And what went wrong? We are still faced with the question- why did Willhouse climb that balcony? If we could just explain that."

"I see the dilemma."

The server came over to take their order. As they waited for their meal, a plan came to Daphne's mind. While they were eating, she shared it with Plate.

"I might could help," Daphne concluded.

"I don't think it's much like your computer," said Plate.

"I have some experience on my general manager's setup, remember?"

"That's true. I'd forgotten. Maybe tomorrow. I'll talk to the chief and see what he says. I'm going to have to go. I still got the several things to do tonight before I can call it a day."

"Sorry I cannot ask you over. It's not just Darica." Daphne smiled. "Tonight I have to work late. I have an appointment. I was actually about to run you off because I'm meeting my client here and you might intimidate her."

He reached over and kissed her lightly.

"See you later then. It'll be less hectic when we're married. I promise."

Daphne had her doubts about that. But at least they would be living in the same house.

Plate was not looking forward to the evening before him.

He needed to phone Alice Willhouse. After that painful duty, he planned to drop in on the Italian princess.

Plate was still residing at his apartment. Plans for he and Skaar to switch positions still on hold.

Plate was thinking more and more that he was going insist on leaving the guarding of the princess to Grant Skaar permanently. He wanted to make the death of Timothy Willhouse his top priority.

Despite his grief for his co-worker, a more practical problem presented itself urgently now.

He was losing his apartment on the 15th of May.

He had thought he and Daphne would be married in plenty of time for him to just move into her house.

He was beginning to fear something else would go wrong.

Chapter 25

"I hope you don't mind meeting in a public place," Daphne said to the woman seated opposite her at a different round table in the Toy Museum Restaurant. This table was farther away from the front door, near brighter light, which would make the paperwork easier.

"Not at all."

"It's just that my office in Houston is so far away that I usually meet with my clients who live in Sand Waves, either in their homes or somewhere in the community."

"My place is a mess right now."

That statement was not true.

The small house located in Sand Waves was always in impeccable order.

Its owner was an interior decorator.

Kate Traval had opted for the meeting in the Toy Museum Restaurant rather than her home because she had the house up for sale. She had just managed to erase all evidence of her ex-husband's presence and get it in perfect showable condition. She was hoping for a quick sale so that she and Ed Jordan could purchase a new house when they married.

Ed had specifically asked her not to mention any of this to Daphne.

Kate spent as little time at her house as possible, mainly dropping in only at night to sleep, leaving for her office in downtown Houston as early as possible in the morning. After her abusive marriage, it was still a house of horrors for her. She had already decided if the house did not sell within the next few days, she was going to move out anyway.

"This is a wonderfully pleasant environment. I think you chose one of the most comfortable places in Sand Waves," Kate said to Daphne.

A truthful statement this time.

"So you're interested in an individual life insurance policy?"

"Yes."

"Do you know what type?" Daphne asked.

"No. I don't know anything about insurance."

"Um, hmm. When I called you, you said your occupation was interior decorator."

"Yes. That is correct."

"Are you in business for yourself?"

"No. I work for one of the larger interior designers in the Houston area. I have a base salary plus commissions pay structure."

"More than 50 employees at your company?"

"Oh yes. I think we're about at 75."

"Then you're bound to have life insurance at your company."

"That's true."

"You have any idea how much?" Daphne asked.

"I'm not real sure. But if memory serves me well, it's equal to two year's salary."

"I see. You do know that you probably can take out incremental amounts over and above that for a very low premium."

"No. I've never thought about it. I mean- uh- I wanted an independent policy."

Daphne paused for a moment while a server brought their drinks. As she drank her Coca-Cola, she kept her eyes focused over the rim of her glass on the woman before her.

*She looks healthy. Appears a bit nervous, but doesn't look suicidal,* Daphne analyzed silently.

"And you tell me you are unmarried?"

"Actually, I'm divorced."

"Oh?" Daphne perked up and set her drink down on the table. "You have children?"

"No, no children."

Daphne picked up her Coke again and shifted in her chair.

"Elderly parents that would be left without support if something happened to you?"

"No. My parents are deceased."

"Okay then. I'm happy to write you a policy. Of course. We just have to find the right product for you. There's dozens of different types of life insurance policies. Are you familiar with the concept of whole life versus term insurance?" Daphne asked.

"No."

"Your insurance at your job would be term insurance and that would mean it would have no cash value."

"What does that mean?" Kate asked.

"It means the only way anyone gets any money is if you die. You can't get any type of payout while you're still alive and you can't borrow against it."

"I think someone once told me I could sell it."

"No, there are some exceptions but not normally. Not term insurance. Not unless it's guaranteed renewable with a level death benefit and that makes it almost as expensive as whole life. Unless someone knew you were about to die there would be no reason for them to pay for a policy that might not be renewed before death. Or might be seriously diminished before you die. And if you are about to die, you are not likely to want to sell the policy."

"I see. I'm just thinking of having a policy that belongs specifically to me. One, if I changed jobs, I get to take it with me."

"Your company insurance almost certainly has a provision that allows you to convert it to whole life insurance if you leave the company. No matter what the circumstances of your departure are. The disadvantage would be that the premium would shoot way up for you. And unless you have a new higher paying job lined up, you would suddenly be faced with a large monthly bill that you might not could afford. You might likely drop the option to pick up the death benefit."

"That's exactly why I'm here," said Kate. "Exactly why I want an individual policy. You never know when something might happen. Look at that unfortunate police officer."

"I wish all of my clients were as forward thinking as you," said Daphne.

*I may have lucked out and this might be a legitimate sale*, she thought with a tinge of optimism. *There have to be some single women out there who see the benefit of purchasing life insurance at a young age before they began to have health problems. This woman appears quite educated and sophisticated. I just may have lucked out. If she just doesn't happen to be dying of some cancer or other invisible disease.*

"How much life insurance were you considering purchasing?"

"Oh, just an average policy."

Daphne attempted to control her frustration. "Why don't we consider what you envision the purpose of the policy to be?"

"I don't understand."

"Okay. Think of it this way. In term insurance, the policy only pays off in case of your death. But the premiums are going to be much cheaper. A whole life policy will build up cash value over your lifetime. If you decide to cash it in, you can get that money, after a certain amount of time. You can also access the cash value by borrowing."

"How long would it be before I could access the cash value?"

*Bingo!* Daphne mentally crossed term insurance off her list.

*This woman is more concerned about living than dying.*

That was a relief. It meant she probably did not have a terminal disease.

"It's a trade-off. You take a lower death benefit for the advantage of having cash buildup within the policy. Usually there's a one-year waiting period before you can borrow any cash. And you're usually limited to borrowing either 70 or 80 percent of the full value. I can have a sample printed out showing your cash value under any given type of policy as it accumulates through the years. We can determine just how much you could borrow at any given time. I just have to plug in various variables like your age, face value of the policy and so forth. I can order these from my general manager's office computer and have them for you in a couple of days."

"I'd rather not have to wait that long. I really wanted to get the policy today. Is that possible?" Kate asked.

"Certainly." Daphne paused.

Another red flag.

Rarely did she have so many red and green flags in the same

interview.

Kate looked very calm and businesslike.

Daphne decided to proceed.

"Then, I can just show you examples. The actual figures will differ. But you will get the general idea of how each policy works."

*This woman is intelligent enough that if the figures don't correspond exactly from the sample to her actual policy, she will understand. And not sue me. I hope,* thought Daphne.

"That sounds good. It would be nice to have some extra money accumulating on the side. I make good money at my job but I never seem to be able to save a dime."

"If you're truly interested in savings, we can add an interest-bearing annuity rider to several of our policies that allows you to put in extra money that goes into an annuity, which earns interest."

"That sounds even better."

"Good. Now I have a much better idea of what type of policy to prepare for you. We have about five policies that fit the description of your needs as you've just told me. They vary in price, rate of cash value accumulation, duration of premium payments, and flexibility in the annuity section."

"Okay."

"Do you have any idea what amount of money you would like to spend each month on the premium?" Daphne asked.

"No. Haven't really thought about that."

"I see. You say you don't save a lot of money."

"No, I really don't save any."

"Tell me a bit about your budget. Do you have money left over after your expenses? Or are you finding yourself short at the end of each month?"

"Actually, my paycheck covers my expenses. When I have months that I have high commissions, I do quite well. I don't know why I don't save money. I eat out a lot. In fact, I really don't cook at all and I eat out all the time. That may be it."

"One benefit of that policy is, it has a variable premium that allows you to put in less if you need to. So you think you can afford to put away maybe $50 a month without feeling any real pain? That would probably mean eating out five or six times less often to cover that each month."

"I could afford maybe a little more than that. I can work a little extra harder and earn more commissions. But I'm not going to be good at trying to save on my own. If I know there's a minimum, I'm only going to pay the minimum."

"We can have it automatically drafted out of your checking account."

"Okay. That should work. Better yet, I'll pay an annual premium up front."

"Great! And you are sure you don't want me to prepare for you a specific printout of your policy, showing our current interest rate and a table of the cash value accumulation, assuming that rates remain steady? I can probably have that for you tomorrow."

"Interest rates are so volatile right now. I don't see how it could be assumed they would remain steady for any period of time. I do like the idea that there is a floor."

Daphne was seriously impressed. In her experience, few people understood anything of basic economics. Kate apparently understood floor-to-ceiling ratios of interest rates.

"You are so right," she said.

"And I really would like to get it settled tonight."

Still Daphne hesitated.

She would like to get the sale settled as soon as possible also. Kate Traval had all the makings of becoming a valued and lucrative client. Yet there was something ambiguous about this woman. She was leaving too much to chance. She was displaying an analytical intelligence accompanied by a strangely naive vulnerability.

These traits together confused Daphne. It was another red flag piled on top of several already having popped up.

Lots of green flags were still waving brightly as well.

Daphne had been asked to call Kate Traval by a third-party who told her that Kate was interested in buying life insurance. While this had happened before in the almost six years she had been selling insurance, it was a rare occurrence. This was the first anomaly.

That the third party was her fiancé who told her he was doing it at the behest of one of his fellow police officers, who was acquainted with the potential client, had caused her to totally relax her guard until she met Kate face to face.

Now several more factors were not adding up.

Kate Traval wanted life insurance but did not know how much she wanted or how much money she wanted to spend per month for the premium. Most people who decided to purchase insurance independent of an agent's influence had already made those decisions before they talked to the salesperson. They wanted to avoid the conventional sales pitch and just place an order.

Daphne was a bit frustrated at her own stalling. She was, after all, in the business of selling insurance and here was a person who was doing her best to buy a policy. The few shivers vibrating up and down her spine could just be pre-wedding jitters.

She found visions of her wedding popping up more and more as the date grew closer and closer.

It was a confusing phenomenon.

She had never been serious about a man before.

A contemplated wedding of her own had heretofore always been a fantasy.

Daphne was much more at home in the business world.

She took a deep breath and disciplined herself to focus on the task at hand. She had little to fear from selling this woman a policy in good faith.

Short of committing actual insurance fraud in collaboration with the client, there was very little liability assigned to an agent who was only following up on a requested sale.

If Kate had some ulterior motive for buying life insurance or someone was trying to coerce her into purchasing a policy, there was no way Daphne could be held responsible just because she experienced a little nervousness when she wrote the application.

No one would ever know if she did not say anything.

*Maybe I'm overreacting. Being around Peter so much has*

*made me suspicious of everything,* Daphne mused to herself. *If she can give me a concrete answer to my next question, I'm going to close the sale.*

"In order to go ahead and write the policy now, I need to know how much money you would want to go towards paying for death benefit versus how much you would want to go into the savings aspect of the policy."

If Kate could not coherently answer that question, Daphne had decided she was not going to write any insurance tonight.

"I want as much as possible to go into the savings aspect while still providing a reasonable death benefit."

Daphne adjusted her position again.

That was certainly a coherent answer and the most logical answer a healthy young woman who had no minor dependents and no husband should be expected to give.

Daphne's nervousness ebbed away.

"Two start at $10,000 and the other three start at $25,000. The cost is going to range from $25 a month for the cheapest one, which will give you very little savings and you would not be able to access it for five years, to $70 and up for the more expensive one, which would allow you to access your cash value in one year and give you a guaranteed rate of 4 percent minimum lifetime guarantee on the annuity portion of the cash value. The company is currently paying 12 percent."

"I'm not sure I want the most expensive but I do like the idea of the 12 percent and would like as much of my premium to go towards the 12 percent as possible."

Daphne dropped all of her inhibitions.

"Wonderful. Well, perhaps one of the two policies in the middle. Both have a $25,000 death benefit. The main difference is the percentage of the cash value of the life insurance that you can access. Now you can cash in the annuity at any time. There would be a front end load for the first three years."

"What is a front end load?" Kate asked.

"I'm sorry, I forgot for a moment you were not in the financial industry. A front end load is the penalty that you pay for making an early withdrawal or an early cash in."

"I see. Tell me, Ms. Martin, of those two particular policies, which one would you recommend for me?" Kate asked.

Daphne happily began the application while answering the question with more details about the policy. As she worked, she felt real gratitude for this sale.

*A true believer in life insurance. Rare but it happens*, thought Daphne, with relief. *That explains everything. Probably her parents had good policies. I hadn't thought of that.*

People who had benefited from a life insurance policy, especially after an unexpected death, frequently made excellent clients.

The waiter was bringing them their food. Fortunately, the table was spacious and Daphne was able to move over slightly and tend to the application form while Kate started her meal.

"I forgot to ask who your beneficiaries are going to be. You said your parents are deceased? Siblings?"

"Just my estate."

Daphne looked at her in surprise.

"I can change it later right?"

"Of course."

*Must be a man in the picture somewhere*, Daphne thought. *Married, probably, or she would go ahead and name him. Guess she and Jordan are only friends like he said, after all. He's probably fronting for her married boyfriend who's probably a décor client.*

And as she filled out Kate's insurance application, Daphne could not keep from smiling as she remembered completing another life insurance application just a short time ago for the client who was still in the process of changing her own life, Lieutenant Sinclair Peter Plate.

Chapter 26

When Plate got home, there was a message from Alice Willhouse on his recorder. He returned her call.

She wanted him to come by her house and although it was late and although he was off duty, and it was the middle of the night, and he needed sleep, she was the widow of his colleague, his fellow officer.

He did not even consider not going.

As he drove to the Willhouse home, he suddenly remembered his chief's request for Daphne to help out by quartering at least one policewoman for Willhouse's funeral.

He glanced at his watch and decided not to stop and call her. She was probably still with her client.

Plus, he wanted to see Alice Willhouse before it got much later.

The widow looked gaunt when she opened the door of her modest home to Plate.

Plate tried to express sympathy as best he could.

"The chief asked me if someone had a motive for murdering Timothy." Alice was nervously fixing some coffee.

Obviously that was the last thing she needed, for it looked as though she had not slept since her husband's death.

Plate did not criticize her. He accepted the coffee with thanks.

"He asked me that," she continued. "And I told him no."

"Yes, have you thought of something?"

"I didn't want to say anything to him. You were close to Timothy? I didn't know if you knew about Timothy's history as a police officer."

"I do."

*But not because I was close to him,* Plate reflected silently.

"That makes it a little easier. I think I may have found something but it doesn't really make sense."

"What is it?"

"It concerned someone close to Timothy. The funny thing

about this was that it was never mentioned. I mean, maybe Timothy knew, but he never told me. I have to speak in confidence."

"It will never go any farther," said Plate, wondering if Willhouse had a woman that he had never heard about or some other secret aspect of life.

"I've got a job and I'm going to work. Timothy didn't leave any personal life insurance. All I have is the departmental benefit, not much. Two year's salary. I'm going to try to keep the house."

Plate was trying to be patient.

He understood Alice's thoughts were disjointed and confused.

It was understandable.

"The thing is, this person has offered to help. So I don't want to say anything against this person," said Alice.

"But something has you concerned? About their motive?"

"No I- I'm sorry, Lieutenant. I should not have asked you to come over. I'm really extremely tired now and I need to go lie down."

"Of course, I understand." Plate rose quickly.

"Let me come by your office later. If I'm still bothered, well I'd appreciate you putting some time aside for me," she said.

She showed Plate to the door.

"Fine. I'll be in my office in the morning."

"You do understand I'm not going to be able to be in your wedding."

Plate had not even thought about that aspect of the situation.

"Of course not. You couldn't be expected to participate. We would have canceled it, but it being a movie-" He held out his hand in a helpless gesture.

"Don't give it another thought. I wouldn't take away from your wedding for anything. If I were not sure the movie guy can get a substitute for me, I would have stood with your bride anyway. Don't let this spoil things for you. Be joyous at your wedding. I had mine. It was wonderful and I will treasure its memories forever."

"If I could ask one question? About that day. I'll understand if you say no."

Alice swallowed hard. "Go ahead."

"Tim left before you got up? You did not know what time?"

"True. He was gone before I got up. I was irked he was going off fishing on one of his precious vacation days. I did not see him off."

Plate left then, after once more inadequately expressing his condolences.

Alice shut the door on him without responding.

Abruptly cut loose, both emotionally and physically, from the draining session with his colleague's widow, Plate was temporarily at a loss.

Driving away, Plate began debating whether he would try to meet up with Daphne again after her insurance sales appointment.

Although most of her evening appointments were wrapped up by 9 or 10 PM, occasionally they ran to 1 or 2 AM in the morning, especially if Daphne needed to do a little amateur psychological counseling to close the sale.

And sometimes she just liked to visit later if she and the clients hit it off well.

Plate was hoping that would be the case this time. He knew she was seeing Jordan's friend.

Jordan's gesture had given Plate a really good feeling. That Jordan had asked about Daphne when he found out that his friend was considering taking out life insurance was more than considerate.

He only wished somehow Daphne had been able to sell Timothy Willhouse additional life insurance.

He went over in his mind how that might have been accomplished before it was too late.

Never a more futile mental exercise.

Chapter 27

More unexpected camaraderie between Daphne and a member of the police department was taking place the next morning.

Plate held up his hands then dropped them to his side again.

His fiancée and his chief had become co-conspirators right before his eyes.

He and Chief Brecken stood behind Daphne as she sat at the chief's new computer.

In the day and age of computer technology, police departments of all sizes throughout the country were in various stages of converting their data from handwritten records or typed forms and manuscripts to computerized files.

A few were already as sophisticated in their data collection, coordination and organization as the FBI. A significant number had not yet even started the process. Most were in between, with their old files still in handwritten or typed form, but attempting to get all new incoming data into some type of computer system.

Sharing information had become even more complicated in this transitional period.

A simple query that used to produce a quick glance at an alphabetized file system now required someone to not only check older material but also go into the computer and find the newest updates and additional information.

Some computer systems could electronically talk to one another over the phone lines the way Daphne's general manager's system could access records from the nationwide insurance data bank.

The lack of completeness and sometimes accuracy of police data files caused information found in the insurance companies' databases to be not only faster but also more certain.

Not all police department computer systems were compatible with one another but insurance companies had long cooperated with each other.

Informally, unofficially, and somewhat secretively, Daphne targeted the insurance data bank she normally accessed at her manager's office. Without informing her general manager.

"No one will ever know from where you accessed the files, if you can just get in," Plate told Daphne.

Daphne's desire to be accepted by her fiancé's colleague overcame her instinctive hesitancy about the procedure.

She was wishing she could give the appearance of complicity without actually doing anything.

"Strictly speaking I'm not supposed to read about anyone that's not my insurance client," said Daphne. "Even then I need a signed permission slip."

"There you are," said Plate. "Mrs. Willhouse's signed permission allowing you to view insurance records of her husband."

"You stole this form from my desk!" Daphne exclaimed.

"I don't think you have any proof of that accusation."

"We don't usually look into records of dead people. It's too late to sell them life insurance," said Daphne.

"Suppose Timothy Willhouse took out life insurance that his wife didn't know about," suggested Plate.

"I don't suppose that's unheard of is it?" asked the chief.

"No," Daphne admitted. "In fact, it is quite common."

"Pull up the database. Here are more names to check. Focus on the Paulizas first," Plate directed impatiently, producing a list.

Daphne started typing at the keyboard.

While she was working, Plate and the chief stepped over to the side, talking softly as if their voices would interfere with the computer's functions.

"While we are waiting, here is more information gathered by good old-fashioned police work without the aid of computers. I got this out of Mrs. Pauliza, reluctantly, I might add."

Plate repeated the story about the barbecue grill.

"I think they're making all this up to confuse us. I don't believe the story about the grill," said the chief.

"Why make up stuff like this?" Plate asked.

"I don't know," Brecken admitted.

"Why not make up threatening letters or something that makes them look innocent?" Plate asked.

"I swear I don't know."

"And the information that we've gotten from our computer database on unsolved crimes?" Plate asked.

"Yes, here it is. Before they moved to Sand Waves, the Paulizas were victims, not criminals."

"Victims?" Plate asked.

Brecken shrugged. "Victims, that's the record. Already on the police database. You can see for yourself."

Plate read aloud from the file, paraphrasing and summarizing a detailed report. "Before they moved to Sand Waves, they lived in Houston. But before that, for two years 1969 and 1970, they lived in a small town in East Texas, where she was in a nurse trainee program at a private college. She had off campus housing because she was married, a rented old house in the town."

"A burglar broke into their house one afternoon," Brecken interjected.

" 'She and her husband were asleep. She was a night nurse trainee at the local hospital. He worked the night shift at a local oil company.' This report gives their life histories!"

"It is quite detailed on the crime but no follow up information, unfortunately. Pauliza attempted to overpower the attacker by hand but he was too slow. He was knocked out. He ended up in the hospital, treated and released. Mrs. Pauliza was seriously injured. She was hospitalized a month," Brecken said.

"That's a long time," said Daphne, rising from the desk chair.

"Anything?" Plate asked.

"It has only been an hour. The computer is working as hard as it can," said Daphne. "What have you two got?"

"I guess it's okay if she hears this confidential information," Brecken said sarcastically. The sarcasm emphasized the concern behind the statement rather than diminishing it.

"I am very discreet," said Daphne.

"I can vouch for that," said Plate.

"Well, you're soon to be married, so at least you won't be able to testify against one another." There was just the right amount of sarcasm in that statement to make its seriousness ambiguous.

Plate turned his attention back to the contents of the file rather than its dissemination. "So what you're saying is that we have to look at the Pauliza couple from the point of view that they're fine upstanding citizens."

"Just sharing what it says here on the report, I didn't write it."

"Go ahead, Chief," said Daphne.

"No assailant ever caught or identified. The details are all here. This police department has just gotten into the statewide computer system but there is little crime in this area normally, so they went ahead and entered data several years back to get their file large enough to qualify."

"Sounds like they hired a data processor," said Plate, not without jealousy.

Brecken ignored the comment.

"That explains the gun. That explains why Pauliza wanted a permit and why it was granted," Plate said.

"Yes and listen to this- 'distressed that he could not protect wife, husband of victim made verbal threats against assailant if latter ever found,' " Brecken relayed.

"That would be wonderful if 14 years ago Timothy Willhouse was a housebreaker. But he was on the other side, remember."

"Here's the rest of the data," Brecken said. "The Paulizas came to Houston to get higher paying jobs. They were burgled twice in Houston, where they lived in a less than desirable neighborhood to be closer to their workplaces. Both incidences were at night when they were at work. Both times, there was vandalism at the scene and property loss. So they saved enough money to move to the nice safe community of Sand Waves and bought a gun to keep under the bed. And became active gun club participants as well as active in civic affairs as well as supporters of the local police. Us."

"It does not make sense. All this seems to put Pauliza on our side, at least in his mind. Why would he kill a policeman?" Plate asked.

"Now as I see it, we've got two questions. Back to basics, why did Timothy climb to the balcony? Is Pauliza is telling the truth?" Brecken asked.

"Judging by this fact sheet, Pauliza was a loaded weapon waiting to go off at the next burglar who broke in on him," said Plate.

"But living in Sand Waves, he wouldn't be anticipating any burglaries," said Daphne.

Plate and Brecken laughed.

"You have been reading the advertisements again," said Plate.

"Oh, I forget," said Daphne. "I moved here under the illusion of real security. I had to fall in love with someone who shattered my rose colored glasses. At least, I'll soon have live-in security."

She and Plate exchanged a smile. He put his arm around her.

"It's not that I am not a fan of true love, but let's keep this businesslike, please," Brecken commented.

"I still find it hard to shake off the delusion that this is a crime-free area of the world." Daphne sighed deeply, moving away from Plate. "It is such a nice fantasy."

The computer started grinding. Daphne sat back down and started typing quickly. A sheet of paper popped out of the printer.

"Here it is. We found a match."

The computer had matched the names of Klaus and Donna Lewegz with Sarah Pauliza.

Chapter 28

Chief Brecken bit his lip as he read over the printout Daphne had given him.

"What is it?" asked Plate.

"Daphne, is there any more on the screen?" asked the chief.

"Yes, there are two pages. She's been doing this a long time," said Daphne.

She and Brecken exchanged places. He sat down at the computer. She stood beside Plate, holding the report in her hand.

"I certainly see now why you value the information you get from your special source here," said Brecken.

Daphne smiled. "I almost feel like I'm part of the team."

"Speaking of part of the team," said Plate. He had been waiting for such an opportunity to bring something up.

"Yes?" Daphne asked.

"Jordan asked me if it were possible for Kate Traval to be in the wedding party. I spoke to Wynter and there's no problem arranging that, unless you have an objection."

"Oh no. No way would I object. I like her. She's really nice."

"Good," said Plate.

The computer gave noisy signals that it was ready once again to receive directions so it could provide the output they desired.

"What is this database used for anyway?" Brecken asked.

"Primarily to make sure that people who are uninsurable do not slip by the insurance company safety nets," said Daphne.

"What exactly does that mean?" Brecken wanted to know.

"Most people applying for life insurance tend to tell the truth on the first application they fill out. It is actually human nature to give detailed answers when questions are asked about health. People are trained to do that from little up by their doctors. So along comes an insurance application asking all of these same questions that you get asked on your first initial doctor visit, or when changing doctors. People just automatically fill it out. A percentage of people have medical conditions that make them uninsurable. When they report those conditions to an insurance company then they are usually turned down for health and life insurance. They could be rated, that is charged a higher premium for life policies. On the other hand, if applying for health insurance, they might be accepted but the pre-existing condition not covered. The law doesn't permit us to exclude reasons for death in life insurance policies, except act of war, so someone with a life threatening medical condition will just be declined," said Daphne.

"Everyone that is declined goes into this database?"

"Everyone that applies goes into the data bank. Those that are declined for health reasons are separated in a special file and the reasons are noted. People think they can apply and be declined at one insurance company and go to another insurance company and try again."

"And if they do that?" Brecken asked.

"If they have been declined initially, they now know a second insurance company is not going to accept them if they tell the truth. Many people then lie about their health the second time they apply for insurance, thinking the second company won't know anything about the first company. But in every application there's a little disclosure paragraph that says the applicant is agreeing to be put in this database. Before computers, the company had to be suspicious about an individual applicant and write an inquiry letter to find out any information. Nowadays, names are routinely run through whenever anybody applies for insurance."

"So if I tell company B I have had a heart attack and they turned me down, then I go to company C and say I'm in perfect health, they're going to turn me down also?" Brecken asked.

"Yes," said Daphne.

"And that's because of the information they find in this database?" Brecken asked.

"Correct," said Daphne.

"That is a little scary. I would have thought you could not keep information about people like that, except for criminals like we do."

"Oh, yes. They can do it and they do," said Daphne.

"Why keep information on healthy people?" Brecken asked.

"Marketing. All these private insights can be useful when you're trying to close a sale," said Daphne.

"But don't you have to have people's permission to access this information?" Brecken asked.

"Not really. There's no law about any of this yet. It's all so new. My company's policy is that I need a person's permission to look for their information. I don't want to be in violation of my contract. So I follow their rules," said Daphne.

"She's right. They haven't passed any laws concerning these computer databases, which didn't exist years ago," said Plate.

"So what we have here then is a massive accumulation of information about anyone who's ever applied for a private insurance policy in the state of Texas," Brecken concluded.

"Actually, it is a nationwide data bank," said Daphne.

"And they keep records of all the physicals, the results and who did them?" Brecken asked.

"Right. That's in case there's ever any litigation about a specific policy. People slip through the cracks. If you lie on an application for life insurance, and you manage to survive for two years, a policy is good no matter what. That's our state law. Sometimes people with serious illnesses do not disclose their conditions, do not tell us about doctors they have seen, have no obvious symptoms and manage to pass the medical test, which isn't even administered unless it's a high face value death benefit. With health insurance, they almost always have to pass a physical. But some people with serious or even terminal illnesses still manage to get coverage. It becomes a problem if they die before the two-year period is up, or they start making health insurance claims," said Daphne.

"If they wait two years to make claims?" Brecken asked.

"No, it doesn't work that way with health insurance. If I lie on an application for health insurance about having cancer six years ago and I have a recurrence of cancer and start making claims on a new policy, that can constitute insurance fraud. Insurance companies don't usually prosecute criminally unless there's massive fraud or a tremendous amount of money involved. But they are within their rights to deny the claim, cancel the policy, and refund all premiums paid. If the client doesn't accept that and goes to court, the company can look up the records and have some evidence on their side as to who administered the physical, and possibly even call the tech to testify about what the client said during the process."

During Daphne's detailing the facets of the insurance databases, the computer started sputtering and clicking again. It issued forth more printed documents.

Not expecting any more results from the cross-referencing of the data they had submitted, the three people stared at the machine a full 30 seconds before Plate reached down and pulled the paper from the slot.

"Well," he said, after reading for several seconds. "A second match has come up. Other names that we did not anticipate had any connections."

"Who?" Daphne in Brecken spoke in unison.

Plate handed them the paper and they both read it together.

"Is there a fast way to find out if this is the same Elizabeth Lopez?" Plate asked.

"That is a very common name. We'll have to send off for a birth certificate," Brecken replied.

"Even if it is, the fact that she listed Emilio and Yolanda Cardioxa as her employers on a health insurance application doesn't mean she's done anything wrong. Does it?" Daphne asked.

"It means somewhere down the line we missed this in the investigation of Yolanda's death," said Plate. "Maybe they are not the same woman."

"This has to be the same woman," said Daphne.

"It's unclear. We cannot tell from this," said Brecken.

"We need a Photostat copy of the application. Is that possible"?

"I think you need a court order for that," said Plate.

"So if we can get this stuff on a computer, we can see it-there's no problem. But if we want a paper copy we can hold in our hand, we have to get a court order?" Brecken asked.

"That's about the size of it," said Plate.

"That's quite impressive results. We now know Sarah Pauliza did the physicals for Klaus and Donna Lewegz's life insurance applications and that Elizabeth Lopez may have once worked for Emilio and Yolanda Cardioxa," said Brecken.

"And also, I'd almost forgotten this," Daphne recalled. She reached for a result already buried under the latest paperwork in the printer's bin. "Timothy Willhouse only had the standard department life insurance. He never took out a private policy. His wife just gets twice the annual salary."

"That is not much," Plate commented.

"Standard, though," said Daphne. "For most jobs."

"It should be more for police officers," said Plate.

"Then fire fighters will want more. Next you know, the school teachers will want to be on the same level with us," said Brecken.

"Anybody can be a school teacher," said Daphne scornfully. "I could be a teacher. It takes somebody special to be a police officer."

She gave Plate a soft look.

"No chance Tim could have an old policy his wife does not know about? Before this database was constructed?" Plate asked.

"No, it would be here."

"I was hoping that was what his wife wanted to talk about. She is going to come by my office," Plate said.

"No, she's not," said Brecken. "She called me and said she would get back with us. I know she's been talking to you. But let me handle her from now on, would you? I have more experience with this and you need to focus on the investigation."

"Yes, Chief."

"You two focus on your wedding. Leave Alice Willhouse to me."

Chapter 29

"So you see why it's all that much more important that we go ahead with the wedding tomorrow the way Stark Wynter wants to stage it."

Plate did not yet understand that Daphne had dropped all objections when she saw the finished wedding dress.

She had never seen a garment so beautiful.

As a little girl, like millions of other little girls in the country, she had seen the movie, *The Sound of Music*. The bride in the movie wore a wedding gown in a scene that Daphne had never forgotten.

At the same time, she was playing with a Barbie doll wedding dress that was similarly styled.

Somehow, Stark Wynter's costume designer had come up with the perfect combination of those two dresses.

Those dresses were designed with tall women in mind and this gown was designed for a short person like Daphne. It gave her just the right balance, not insulting her stature by trying to make her look taller but rather enhancing her natural form without emphasizing her height. The material was exquisite. The style as beautiful as Wynter had described at their luncheon, which seemed like a long time ago.

The wedding might be eccentric. In the long run what really mattered except the overall experience and the pictures? And there would be a Hollywood film of this wedding. Daphne had seen the VHS tapes generated by the new industry of videography and most of them were just terrible, occasionally some quality shots came through, but most were blurred, or discolored, or jerky. And audio, if it existed, was unpredictable.

Daphne began to look forward to the Hollywood experience.

"Yes. I understand," she replied.

Still, there were drawbacks. She was expecting some bittersweet moments. No parents would be there. Initially all their siblings had cited excuses before Daphne and Plate could tell them why they were being invited to Sand Waves. They all had other important plans.

Now Darica would be on hand.

She seemed like an anomaly.

Grant Skaar's wife, Geralyn, was also going to be a bridesmaid. Officer Jordan's girlfriend, Kate Traval would round out Daphne's private entourage, replacing Alice Willhouse.

It was not the wedding Daphne had fantasized about as an adolescent. Yet she was determined to be happy with the people present rather than mourn for people absent. As the time had gone by, the realization had slowly dawned that somehow, without her actually telling him, Plate had perceived her need and fulfilled it for her.

She was pleasantly surprised to find Kate Traval was Jordan's girlfriend, dispelling her imaginings that Kate had a married lover.

*Maybe she was just cautious and not going to put him on her policy as a beneficiary until after the wedding.*

Daphne had already changed her beneficiary on her policy to Sinclair Peter Plate. And she knew for certain she was already his beneficiary.

*I'm glad we can trust each other completely from the beginning,* she thought.

Plate also had his groomsmen lined up. Randy Harriman, an old friend and former police officer, was going to take Willhouse's place. Jordan and Skaar would stand also with Plate.

Costumes were being arranged for the newcomers. One by one, the other participants in the movie had arrived. Wynter's wife, Regina, came to host the parties.

Stark Wynter had spared no expense in preparing for the crucial beginning of the movie. With the wedding being the most personnel oriented scene in the entire movie, Wynter was eager to get it over with. After it was successfully shot, most of the crew, actors and extras would be done and could go home to Hollywood. And the most temperamental person in the show could go back to Italy.

Wynter was patient and dedicated to his project. But he was ready to be done with Joanna Scarpartti and the trouble she brought, no matter the consequences.

163

Chapter 30

"I kill you all."

Princess Joanna screamed and stormed off the set.

The scene had been perfectly staged for the wedding sequence of *Murder as the Organist Plays*.

Daphne was in the 1940s style wedding dress. An extremely expensive black wig looked perfectly natural against her pale skin and the tulle veil so obscured her facial features that details of her countenance were imperceptible.

She could barely see past its denseness.

Few could discern her as well.

From a distance, it was hard to tell that she was not the Italian princess behind the layers of netting.

Darica had been deemed too tall to be the stand-in for the actress that was going to play Coria. She was relegated to being the least important bridesmaid, easier for her to be cut out of any scene that caused her height to come in focus.

Geralyn Skaar and Kate Traval were of average height so they went last. Kate was directed to stand next to Daphne until the actual ceremony started. Then Kate and Darica could switch places and Darica could act as Daphne's maid of honor.

Then after the vows were said, Darica and Kate needed to switch back for the march back down the aisle.

The extras hired to be in the movie were dressed in period 1940s bridesmaid's gowns identical to the real bridesmaids. Bridesmaid-extras already had fake blood smeared on their dresses. This saved a little money over the spurting fake blood capsules and insured the blood got exactly on the rose pink costumes where Stark Wynter wanted it.

He could use shots of the real bridesmaids in blood-free dresses to blend in, obscuring their faces.

The hairstyles and general overall appearances of the real bridesmaids were mimicked by the extras, Darica's height being the only problem they could not overcome.

The same identical plan was executed for the groomsmen.

Plate was wearing a 1940s style tuxedo as were Jordan, Skaar, and Randy Harriman.

As were the extras that were to alternate with them.

Only Jordan stood out as heavier and bulkier than the rest of the men.

Daphne and the bridesmaids had to go up sidesteps to get to the platform that mimicked a hotel balcony as was described in the book.

Plate and his groomsmen stood at the bottom of the staircase on a platform, surrounded by a multitude of flowers, the stand-in organist and the real minister.

It was rumored that the Austrian born star had indeed accepted the prime role of the preacher. Neither pastor that Daphne and Plate had recommended to perform the ceremony resembled him at all. Reverend Arthur Harriman was too short and Reverend Erick Skrale was too slender.

Stark Wynter had advertised for a look-alike clergyman.

Daphne was insisting on a minister. No justice of the peace would suffice.

Wynter was sure that one existed within the greater Houston-Galveston area who resembled the new star, at least enough to look like him from behind so that the shooting could start.

Regina Wynter found one at the last minute. No facial resemblance to the famous actor, but same muscular build, height, and coloration.

The show could go on.

Joanna's identical style bridal gown, made of cheaper material, was rigged with exploding capsules of fake blood that would burst when she pressed a trigger at the same time the stunt marksman fired his shot.

After important personages in Sand Waves were seated, the remainder of the chairs was filled with persons selected from the crowd of onlookers attired in the best and most authentic 1940s wedding guest type clothes.

A number of people had spent a great deal of time researching exactly what the upper class wedding guest wore in the 1940s. The immediate post-World War II era, which gave birth to the highly fashionable social structure of the 1950s, was still affected by the elegance of the 1930s.

Women who were seriously committed to being in the movie made sure to have their outfits completely match in every way in coloration and material, including gloves, hat, purse, and shoes. The most dedicated men discerned what time of day and in what type of weather the wedding was supposed to be held.

In 1946, different wedding start times still called for different types of suits in some of the higher echelons of society.

Their diligence paid off and to the dismay of many, the chairs were quickly filled with very authentic looking guests.

A number of latecomers and prominent Sand Waves residents, who had to be told they did not have the perfectly correct look for the shot, were already starting to complain.

If they would not agree to be off-camera spectators, Wynter's private on-the-set security politely asked them to leave.

There was already talk of lawsuits.

But this was the least of Stark Wynter's problems.

He stood off to the side, away from everyone else to watch. He had just begun to relax when disaster struck.

The organ music started.

All of them being trained dancers, going down the steep steps in high heels was no problem for the bridesmaid extras.

They floated down.

Daphne had some trouble making her way down the steps.

She was wearing low heels and she had a good sense of balance.

The dress was bulky but she managed that by clasping it with one arm, holding the bouquet with her other, and peering down beneath the tiers of tulle lace at her pointed toe shoes as she made each step. The veil was the problem. It was so dense that she could see only bright blurred lights, dancing flames against dark shadows.

She proceeded very slowly so as to reach Plate's side safely.

The minister began his preliminary speech in his very thick Austrian-German accent before starting the vows.

It was at this moment that they heard the blood-curdling yell from Joanna.

All attention had been focused on Plate and Daphne.

No one had noticed that Joanna had moved.

By this time Princess Joanna was at the top of the staircase, holding a dagger, just as in the original book's plot.

But not in the modernized script.

Once her scream had captured everybody's attention, she threw the dagger in Stark Wynter's direction and loudly declared in English-

"I kill you all!"

Wynter ducked just in time.

The stunned crowd stared at princess. Most of them were progressively deciphering at varying rates the four English words she managed as she took a deep breath and continued in Italian-

"Especially I kill Stark Wynter! I was told that I was in the lead role. I came all the way from Italy to do this book into a movie. I will not be killed in the first scene. Instead I will kill the no good rotten producer, Stark Wynter, who tricked me into this horrible situation in this dreadful terrible place where sand chokes you with its waves and the college students attack you to prove their manhood because they are so rich they have nothing else to do. I will kill everybody in this entire colony! In the entire state of Texas!"

She rushed down the steps. Down the aisle.

Dashing towards the stairwell that led to the third floor.

"Get after her," yelled Stark Wynter to the translator.

Elizabeth was on the front row, dressed in a very awkward costume that somewhat impeded her movement.

"Princess! Wait!" Elizabeth yelled.

Hampered in movement by her taffeta four gored flared skirt, she ripped off the matching peplum overskirt and tossed it aside, briskly striding towards the princess from the other end of the room.

With deft athletic movements foreign to her body type, Elizabeth caught up to Joanna.

The princess continued to scream in Italian to the translator as the stairwell door closed behind them.

The other actors, guests, extras, musicians, cinematographers and all other movie personnel were left waiting.

"Cut!" yelled an assistant director, belatedly.

"Go on with the vows," Plate directed the minister.

"I can't, until I receive instructions from Mr. or Mrs. Wynter, I don't know what to do."

Daphne ripped the wig and veil off her head.

Her blonde hair fell sloppily on her shoulders.

"I told you this was not going to work," she said angrily to Plate. "I'm going to change back into ordinary clothes. The dress may be beautiful but I feel like an idiot in this black wig and I can't see through this thick veil. I'm not wearing this again!"

Still clutching both headpieces, she pushed her way toward the isolated bathroom where she had changed previously with studio supervision. Her clothes were still there.

Once inside, her anger dampened a little as she recalled the events in that same little bathroom that had just taken place a few months ago. That had been a life-and-death situation and this was merely extreme aggravation.

Still, it was supposed to be her wedding.

Her mood darkened.

It was hard to get out of the dress. It had pearl buttons at the back of the neck that needed an extra pair of hands to help.

She was all alone in the restroom. She had to assume a very undignified position to reach the fasteners.

Daphne fumed as she hung the wedding dress on the door hook and got back into her pantsuit.

Meanwhile, Joanna completed her rush up to the third floor with Ms. Lopez still trailing behind her, imploring her to slow down her speech.

"What all did she say?" Stark was coming up behind the

translator, huffing a little as he climbed the stairs.

Ms. Lopez turned and looked down at him, standing several steps below her. The door slammed behind the princess and an audible lock clicked.

"She is very displeased with the fact that her character is killed off after the first main scene," said the translator. "I don't think she intends to work anymore today."

The understated translation caused Stark Wynter to smile in spite of the situation.

"I thought she knew the plot. Surely, she doesn't think that she could play the lead in the whole movie? The first movie I make at my new studios! How could she think that? Where did she get such an idea? She doesn't hardly speak English," said Stark Wynter.

"She has read a Spanish translation of *Murder as the Organist Plays*. The only scripted scene you gave her was her entrance in the wedding scene. The assistant director gave her instructions to die this morning. It was the first she knew," said Elizabeth Lopez.

"Damned book! How did she think she was going to play Elicia as written in the book?" Stark asked incredulously.

"I think she was under the impression that she was going to memorize her lines in English."

"But she's got a terrible accent. This character can't possibly have such an accent."

The translator reminded Stark Wynter that his primary proposed male star had a significant accent and had carried other movies in the same manner the princess had believed she would be carrying this one.

"The preacher can be German or Austrian or whatever. He can have an accent. He can be a recent immigrant. But not Elicia. She's part of the high society elite of East Texas. And the actress playing Coria is from Tyler. I can't have one sister with a thick Italian accent and the other speaking in an East Texas drawl!"

"If I may venture an opinion, I don't think those details are important to the princess."

"Look, you've got to go in there and get her back out here. I've got everybody here for this. Rescheduling will cost a fortune. And I've got that couple here that's really getting married."

The translator started back down the stairs and passed Stark Wynter as she spoke.

"I'm sorry. I'm afraid this is out of my job description."

Ms. Lopez continued down the stairs leaving Stark Wynter to pound on Joanna's door in frustration.

The translator came back out into the main room. She faced a large contingent of people looking to her for an explanation and directions.

She shrugged and started to walk around them.

When his fiancée stormed off, Plate had to choose whether to go after Daphne or remaining to keep an eye on suspects in Timothy Willhouse's death.

By now, the structure of the movie shot had totally dissolved and many people were moving in many different directions simultaneously in the huge room.

In her exit pathway, after brushing off Stark Wynter, Elizabeth Lopez headed directly down the aisle towards Plate.

He looked in the direction that Daphne had fled. It would take him in the wrong way but he took a step in that direction.

Then his dilemma was solved when Daphne returned to his side within moments, dressed in street clothes.

He caught her eye and she gave him a wry philosophical look, which involved twisting her mouth to one side. He relaxed.

The translator passed right by them.

Plate grabbed Elizabeth by the arm and asked for reassurance that the princess was secure on the third floor.

"Yes, Lieutenant. Unless Mr. Wynter kills her. Now please, may I go? I have a terrible headache. This day has been a complete disaster and I'm probably going to get fired."

"I couldn't agree with this lady more. I told you this wouldn't work out. I'm done with this." Daphne grabbed Plate by the arm.

She pulled him aside and started whispering.

"I saw something strange after our part was interrupted and

everybody was looking at the actress. I saw that woman talking to one of the husbands of one of the victims of the serial killer. It looked like an intimate conversation. Do they know each other?"

With a simple hand gesture, Plate bade the translator to continue on her way.

He kept her in his sights.

"Not that I know of," he said to Daphne. "Which one was it?"

"I don't know. I don't remember who was who. But I know it was one of them." Daphne was searching for any indication that he did not believe her and she was going to explode if she detected skepticism.

"Okay, let's talk about it later. Right now, Daphne, could you sort of follow Ms. Lopez and try to get a little bit of information from her about what's really going on with the princess?" Plate asked in a low voice. "If she catches you, use your charm."

"Shouldn't you be going up there to see about her highness's safety?" Daphne was somewhat mollified by being asked to help.

"We've taken care of the security breach that let the college students get in. She is safe as long as she's locked up on the third floor. I have some other people I want to talk to. Don't worry about the wedding. We will work something out."

He kissed her quickly.

She handed him the wig and veil.

Refocused, Daphne went after Ms. Lopez and Plate started looking for some of the people that he had been surprised to see when he had arrived for the event.

He turned to find the chief standing directly behind him.

"Plate," said Chief Brecken. He was obviously on his way to the exit.

"Yes, Chief? Is there someone specific you'd like me to check up on?"

"Since you obviously won't be having a wedding or reception today, you can go ahead and pick up Shiameto at the airport and I can go home."

Mr. Shiameto was scheduled to arrive in the middle of the

night at Houston Intercontinental. With Plate occupied with the wedding, Skaar continuing security for the princess, and Jordan driving only minimally due to his ankle, Brecken had planned to meet the plane.

"Yes, Chief."

"Good things come out of everything," the chief observed and took his leave.

Plate sat down in one of the guest chairs as more people swarmed around. He was already dead tired. But his respite was not for the purpose of resting.

He placed the wig and the veil on the chair beside him.

He pulled out his notebook and wrote down the names of everyone pertinent who had been at the movie set.

Several unlikely people had somehow become involved in the shooting of this scene. He wanted to know why and how they had managed it.

Many were still on the premises.

He was trying not to be judgmental but there were too many grieving spouses, recently bereft of their significant others, seeking the entertainment limelight.

Alice Willhouse, after dropping out of the actual wedding party, came at the last minute as a guest-extra. Her costume, being minimal, she was almost kept out until Brecken spotted her and intervened.

Mrs. Brecken had decided not to come, so Alice had sat with the chief.

Emilio Cardioxa had been in the crowd and had a rather prominent seat in the middle of the congregation despite his suit not exactly being 1940s era.

Klaus Lewegz had apparently spared no expense to make sure that he was in a good enough costume to be placed near the front. He wound up seated conspicuously next to Emilio Cardioxa, on the latter's left.

Both men appeared agitated to be near the other.

One of the latter two men had to be the person Daphne saw

talking to Elizabeth Lopez.

Presumably, it was Cardioxa. If the data was correct that she once worked for him.

However, it was a common name.

Maybe they were just making small talk.

Elisabeth Morgan had spoken to him also.

It was just too much of a coincidence.

Elisabeth Morgan's maiden name was Lopez.

The Photostat of the handwritten application in the file was slightly blurred. The 's' might have been a 'z'. Or the reverse.

They were still not one hundred percent sure.

It had been some time since Klaus Lewegz's wife had been killed and perhaps his demeanor was not still of a deep grief, more like a desire for revenge.

Maybe he just wanted to be in a movie.

That might also be able to be said of Elisabeth Morgan.

Elisabeth Morgan was not grieving.

She had no connection to the Zopev case as far as Plate knew. But he had seen her in earnest conversation with Klaus Lewegz before the seating began and she had sat to his left in the chairs.

On purpose. Or had an assistant director placed her there?

Klaus had deliberately turned his back towards Cardioxa and spent much of the event with his attention on Elisabeth.

And Jordan and his girlfriend, Skaar and his wife had been expected to be there, as was Chief Brecken.

But with Mrs. Brecken, not Alice Willhouse.

Plate reflected that Mrs. Brecken was the only person connected with the police department in Sand Waves not there.

This was an exaggeration, of course.

But he felt like too many people he knew personally were involved in this event, wide open to the general public in the area.

He now perceived Stark Wynter had set no limit on the number of people allowed behind the gates for this venture.

Anyone sending in a card had achieved admittance.

There were so many people there involved either directly or

on the periphery of the Zopev trial and Willhouse murder that Plate would not have been surprised to see Eduardo and Sarah Pauliza in the crowd.

After his observations now, he was sure they were not.

In the exodus as the set was shutting down, he looked around to see if there were any more familiar faces.

The place was emptying rapidly. By now most people had already gone.

Those who had already left, he was planning to track down and ask them to explain their presence.

His blood pressure rose as he noticed another familiar face.

One of the college students who had attempted to make the princess part of their fraternity hazing experience.

Out on bail, he had the right to come just like anybody else who had an entry card. He had undoubtedly gotten a costume as an extra.

Plate was about to start in the direction of the culprit when another man intercepted him and angrily gestured in a manner that indicated that if the student did not leave immediately, he would face unpleasant physical consequences.

The college student was out the door before Plate could blink twice.

Plate eyed the aggressor, a dark young man with a large nose and thick eyebrows. He was dressed in the costume of a groomsman.

This man was also quickly exiting.

*One of Stark Wynter's people?* Plate wondered. Weary, he felt grateful for the help. Guilty for not taking care of the student himself. But more grateful than guilty.

He looked around for the producer.

He needed to get rid of the wig and the veil so he could continue with his job.

Chapter 31

Coming back down after a futile attempt to reason with the princess, Stark Wynter called off the shooting and rescheduled it for Tuesday.

This would give the producer four days to win over his star before he would have to scrap her and look around for another actress.

He planned to wave the magical name of the proposed male star, who was so close to signing it was breathtaking. Being in a movie with him would set up her career for life.

Plus, he had the weapon of potential deportation if the princess was not legitimately employed.

Wynter knew this was weak.

She could easily get another job doing something, with all the publicity surrounding her.

His final resort would be to offer her lots more money.

He figured that would do it, if nothing else.

But he was first going to try the less expensive tactics.

He informed Plate promptly of this decision, imploring him to get Daphne to understand and for them come back and try again.

The murder of Timothy Willhouse was somehow connected to all of this movie making, Plate now believed.

Plate reassured Wynter.

They would be back.

"Where is she? Where did she go?" Wynter asked anxiously, looking around, still envisioning Daphne with dark hair in the wedding dress.

"My fiancée was just a little concerned."

He handed Wynter the wig and the veil.

Wynter was still somewhat shell shocked.

"I'm going to fire the prop guy that let her have that dagger! And my marksman has a contract for another film that starts Monday!"

"I wish you would try to keep the same personnel if we are going to try this again."

"Oh, of course I will. Just frustration talking. I can get him back for one day. Professional courtesy from his new producer. We do it for each other. Don't worry, Lieutenant. We're going to see to it that you get married, no matter what. I had my assistant director contact the Marriott to explain that we're not coming today and we will be rescheduling."

"I appreciate that." Plate said.

He was bemused by the idea that the movie producer did not think he and Daphne could manage a wedding without his supervision.

*He must think all public events require a producer and director along with actors and actresses in the side roles*, Plate reflected.

"Daphne is very understanding about things like that," Plate replied. "She did change out of her dress." *And what did she do with it?* Plate suddenly wondered to himself.

"Where did she go?" Wynter looked baffled. He regarded the items in his hand as if seeing them for the first time.

Plate's simple reassurance that he and Daphne would continue to cooperate in the project was not the reaction Stark Wynter normally experienced from temperamental actors and actresses when things went wrong.

He was waiting for the opportunity to get more reassurance and see what type of compensation was going to be demanded by Plate.

Regina Wynter appeared at that moment and graciously took the wig and veil off his hands.

"She, ah- went to take the dress off," Plate said, believing Wynter had not understood.

"The dress! I've got to go back and make sure that wild female didn't release the blood pellets and ruin her dress!" He whirled. "If so I will have to have the one your girlfriend has back!"

The producer director dashed off.

"I will get him calmed down," said Regina Wynter, clutching the headpieces. "Please let your fiancée know we may need the dress back." She strode off after her husband.

*Then you are going to have a problem,* Plate reflected with some amusement.

Then his mood became somber again. He had forgotten to ask about the groomsman acting like a security guard.

At least the college student was gone.

Still assessing the overall situation, Plate remained where he was.

He continued to scan the dwindling group.

After telling her to trail Ms. Lopez, Plate lost track of Daphne in the crowd.

He figured she might have left the building. If so, she could get home all right.

He was technically at work and on the clock.

As were officers Jordan and Skaar. The latter was already resuming his post as the princess' bodyguard.

Skaar was already back in uniform. He had not needed to be told his duty. Mrs. Skaar discreetly departed.

Jordan, still in his tuxedo, took this inopportune moment to intercept Plate and formally introduce his girlfriend, Kate Traval.

She generously thanked Plate for his part in getting Daphne to agree for her to be a bridesmaid.

"I finally get to meet you at last," Plate said as he shook hands with Kate. "Sorry this couldn't have been a normal wedding party experience. We will all get together and celebrate after it's all over."

"I hope she and I can get to be friends," Kate was saying about Daphne. "She certainly is a very knowledgeable insurance agent. I may need to change my beneficiary in the future." Kate looked shyly at Jordan. "Ed says he's not the marrying kind, but..."

Jordan put his arm around Kate and winked at Plate. "I've never said any such of a thing, have I, Lieutenant?"

"Of course not," Plate said loyally.

"It's just that so soon after Tim's death..." Jordan looked at the ground.

Plate nodded. "I understand. Had the circumstances been

different, Daphne and I would have postponed our wedding."

"Oh, I wasn't implying any criticism of that, Lieutenant," said Jordan hastily. "I know how this was planned before Tim died, and in conjunction with this movie. You could not be expected to do anything else but go ahead. I was just saying, Kate and I have not made definite plans yet."

"And we are in no rush," said Kate firmly.

Plate met her eyes as she made that statement. They belied the comment.

"No rush at all," said Jordan, with a much less conflicting look in his eyes.

"Daphne and I are not exactly rushing," Plate paused, thinking, *actually, that is just what we are doing.*

"Oh, no. I didn't mean that," said Jordan. "I know what the chief has been saying but I believe in love at first sight."

He emphasized that by kissing Kate noisily. She beamed.

"I have to find that dress," Plate said worriedly. "If Daphne loses that dress she will never cooperate with me on anything again."

"I saw her come out of a restroom in ordinary clothes," said Kate.

"Do you know which one?"

"Yes, I think so."

"Maybe, Miss - ah Kate," said the lieutenant hesitantly. "You could get Mrs. Plate- eh, Ms. Martin's dress for her? Could you go in there and get the dress. She must've left it there."

"What do you want her to do with it, Lieutenant?" Jordan asked.

"Well, I can take it home with me, if the rest of you have other duties," Kate began. "I came here in a separate car as Ed said he might have to work later. I'm not even going to change out of this costume. I'm going straight home. I'll just take it with me."

"Wonderful. Thank you."

Plate promised to retrieve it as soon as possible.

Jordan grabbed Kate and drew her close to him.

"That's my girl. Always trying to help out."

178

Plate nodded and left the couple then. Jordan was taking a long time saying goodbye.

*Doesn't want to get back to the station and get to work*, Plate thought uncharitably.

He said a quick prayer that once Jordan left, Kate would take care of the dress.

Then he let it go. He had no time to dwell on it.

*Worse case, Daphne can buy another dress*, was his last thought about the bridal gown.

Plate spotted Elisabeth Morgan as she was exiting the mansion.

As he followed her outside, he saw the yard was still quite crowded. He pushed a few other people aside to catch up with her.

"Lieutenant," said Elisabeth, when she saw him. "I want to congratulate you. I didn't realize you were the real groom in all this."

"Yes, I am," said Plate.

"Then, it is your ancestor this movie is about?"

Plate laughed. "Not exactly."

People walked beyond the mansion's grounds, heading towards their cars parked on the sidestreets.

Both the policeman and the witness to Willhouse's murder were distracted from their conversation by the extraordinary number of cars lining the avenue.

Wynter had gone through reams of paperwork to get permission to allow the exclusive neighborhood to become packed with people for this commercial venture.

The Colony Federation Board had reluctantly gone along with the special use permit, mainly because they were all planning to be extras in the scene.

Wisely, Stark had requested a month long permit, so the delay was not going to be a problem in that respect. However, he had only arranged transportation shuttles for the day the scene was to be shot.

Even with shuttles available, the street was so choked full of cars, non-participating residents were having trouble moving around within their neighborhood.

"I'm not going to able to come back, so I have missed my big chance at fame," Elisabeth said with a laugh.

"I think there were numerous people turned away today," said Plate. "I got here at 4 AM. At first it was only a trickle. But by 6, I was hearing anguished cries of those arriving too late to get a seat as a guest extra."

"I'm told we'll be paid for today anyway. I did buy some antique clothes for this which I don't have any other use for. Maybe I'll get enough to cover that expense," said Elisabeth, stopping beside a gray Buick. "This is my car here."

"Since it has been a while since we talked, is there anything else you have thought of that you saw that day? The day of the shooting."

Elisabeth looked thoughtful. She lit a cigarette.

"No, but I saw something today that I thought was strange. When all eyes were on you and your fiancée, just before the tirade, I saw the actress heavily involved in a passionate kiss with a groomsman."

"Say that again."

Elisabeth Morgan repeated what she had just told him.

"Could you identify which one it was?"

"All I could see was his back. But they were wearing those distinctive 1940s style tuxedos. I'm pretty sure they were the only people here dressed in those specific costumes. I suppose I could be wrong about that?"

"No, no. I don't think you're wrong about that. Thank you so much for your information. Also, are you acquainted with Klaus Lewegz?"

"That's an odd question. As a matter of fact, he was the gentleman sitting next to me. I just met him today. I did recognize him from the TV new casts. I was surprised at how pleasant he is. Very nice man."

"Again, thank you so much for your information."

"No problem, Lieutenant. You know where to find me if you want to talk to me again."

"One more thing."

Plate pulled out the small puppet Sarah Pauliza had given him from one of the generously sized 1940s style pants pockets in his tux.

She examined it with interest.

"Too old and fragile to be of use to me, I'm afraid."

"What would it be useful for then?"

"I don't know. A collector might want it."

"Even though it is damaged?"

"It is?"

"Yes, a little piece is broken off and it's slightly scorched at the break." Plate showed her under the puppet's clothes. "Where would I normally find something like this?"

"I don't know. A museum? Antique shop? I really don't know. I am just guessing. I buy new puppets by mail order from a shop in California. They break fast enough. I don't need any old broken ones to mend."

"Thanks again for all your information."

"No problem." Elisabeth Morgan extinguished her cigarette and entered her car. Plate left her and headed towards his. It had started to rain again.

There were thousands of antique shops and hundreds of museums in the greater Houston-Galveston area. Not to mention in the surrounding countryside.

It would be near impossible to find the origin of the puppet.

He had forgotten he was dead tired.

His eyes closed involuntarily even as he started his engine.

The effect of less than fifteen hours sleep in the past four days.

Plate decided he had better take a few hours off if he was going to be spending the middle of the night at the airport.

He needed rest.

He started home to his apartment, with the notion of taking a nap.

As he drove, his mind wandered as showers and mist surrounded him.

Soon he found himself back on Harbor Shadows.

The rain was pouring down.

It was dusk now.

His headlights shining into the rain bouncing off the pavement caused the droplets to look like little sparks on the street. Popping like little firecrackers.

He parked in front of the Pauliza home.

The rain came down hard.

He did not think the couple living there could possibly see his car even if they were awake and were looking out their windows.

Or if they saw the car, they could not see who was inside.

Lights were on downstairs.

Plate saw the lights flicker behind shears through the rain.

He blinked several times, wondering if his fatigue was producing an optical illusion.

The rain let up for a moment just as another car was passing in the opposite direction.

It came to a stop just before Plate's vehicle, whirled quickly into one of the driveways, sat for a minute and the driver revved his engine.

Smoke from the exhaust pipe competed with the moisture for space in the atmosphere.

Smoke won, rising unimpeded as the rain diminished.

The car backed out onto the street and roared off in the opposite direction, leaving more exhaust that lingered in front of the glowing lights in the Pauliza's windows for just an instant.

Plate abandoned all thoughts of trying to talk to the Paulizas right now.

He had seen all he needed to see.

He was wide awake.

He needed to talk to Daphne.

Daphne!

Belatedly he remembered she was shadowing Elizabeth Lopez for him.

She was probably still at the Wynter compound.

He had blatantly ignored the fact that Daphne was not a

policewoman.

He had sent her on an errand that should be reserved for law enforcement officers.

And he had done it for a selfish reason. To placate her and turn her attention away from her frustration about wedding situation.

Now she was probably to the point where she did not know what to do next.

At best, she was still just watching Elizabeth Lopez unobserved.

At worst, she had confronted the translator and was possibly in some type of danger.

Whatever was happening, he was sure she was waiting for him to come and resolve the situation, tell her what to do.

Plate sped back towards the gates of Sand Waves.

It was turning dark.

He passed easily through the several layers of security and bounded up the stairwell to the third floor.

The only light shining made a horizontal line under Joanna's door.

He banged on the bedroom door.

Ms. Lopez let him in with a cryptic smile.

Breathless, he walked into the large bedroom where he once encountered Amelia Mattworks making tea.

He saw the princess sitting at the same table.

Sitting with Joanna Scarpartti was Daphne Martin.

The Italian princess was filling out a life insurance application.

Chapter 32

"In addition to the $5 million of face value life insurance, you're also getting interest-bearing annuity worth-"

"Daphne! What are you doing here? What's going on?"

The princess and Daphne looked up from the paper-strewn table at the same time. Joanna reacted to Plate's unexpected presence before Daphne had a chance.

"If danger to my life comes true," she shouted in broken English. "Your American company will much pay. Big time. Big!"

The Italian actress grabbed the life insurance application form and shook it at the officer. Daphne hastily took it from her and smoothed it out before it became too wrinkled.

The company frowned on carelessly handled paperwork. They expected all documents to be pristine.

"Daphne!" Plate ignored the princess' gesticulations and stood next to Daphne's chair.

"Don't get huffy. The princess needed some life insurance."

"She's from Italy! How can it be legal for you to sell her life insurance?" Plate did not like the idea that anyone might find out the Joanna's life was insured for $5 million.

"I can sell life insurance to anybody from anywhere in the world," Daphne declared.

"How is that possible? How is that legal?"

"The last time this discussion came up, I explained to you. I can sell insurance to anybody, including anybody from any alien planet, so long as we are in the state of Texas. That is providing the alien is a human. I can't insure other life forms or animals."

Plate ignored Daphne's dig at his penchant for science fiction novels.

"How can she pay the premiums? In lira?"

"Have you never heard of foreign exchange markets for currencies? She merely has to get her bank to convert her money into American funds and send it in."

"Your company will send her a bill in Italy?"

"My company will send a bill to the moon if necessary. I do know my job. This is a perfectly legitimate life insurance policy. She has just paid me. In American dollars. That makes the contract legally binding. For the company as well as her." Daphne held up some cash and waved it at him. "All she has to do is take a physical and that's only because it's such a large amount. We are legally obliged to insure her if she passes the physical."

"Her death benefit is not bound yet?"

*Maybe there is a way to stop this,* he thought.

"It is not payable until she passes the physical, but this is a legal contract. It's a gray area. That's why we try to get physicals done as soon as possible."

"I cannot allow some strange medical technician to come in here and do a physical."

"Peter, I am a licensed agent and you cannot stop a legitimate business transaction."

"Don't call me Peter in front of other people," he warned in a lower voice.

"She doesn't speak English. Now–"

"That's another point. It might be said that she doesn't understand what she's buying."

"I understand thing!" said the princess, in English because she recognized the word 'understand'.

She continued in her native language with both Plate and Daphne staring at her. "I understand that if you, Mr. Police Officer, allow me to die at the hands of those who would have my body torn from limb to limb, your American insurance company will pay millions and they will have your head on the platter as revenge."

Not understanding a word of this, Daphne and Plate looked at each other.

"The translator was here until just a second ago," said Daphne.

They looked around. Sure enough, Elizabeth Lopez had stepped out of the room.

"She probably just stepped out to go the restroom or over to her bedroom down the hall," said Plate.

"Apparently, they're going to clear out another bedroom up here for a policewoman? That's what I understood," said Daphne.

"Yes, the county is sending somebody," Plate confirmed.

"So you think she is in danger."

"Let's not discuss it here."

"Okay. Anyway, Elizabeth Lopez was here earlier. She was here when I explained everything very carefully. The translator related in detail. The princess understands exactly what she's doing."

"Si! Si! Understand!" yelled the princess.

"Now, you cannot prevent an authorized medical technician from giving the princess a physical," Daphne continued. "You can be present if you want to. All they are going to do is take her blood pressure and ask a few questions. I warn you, my company will sue the police department if you try to interfere. This is a lot of money for them and a big commission for me. The biggest I've ever had."

The princess was watching the couple in some confusion at first, catching only a few words that she had learned in English as they dickered.

Plate indicated subtly to Daphne to stop talking about the translator. Even if the princess did not understand, he did not yet want Daphne telling him what, if anything, she had observed when following Elizabeth.

Daphne also subtly indicated she understood.

Something in their mannerisms gave them away and Joanna suddenly started to laugh.

"Ah ha! Amoré!" she said, and clapped her hands.

Daphne and Plate looked at her guiltily, then looked at each other, trying not to smile.

"Princess, can you not see how this could be construed as a conflict of interest?" Plate asked, in spite of knowing that she did not understand.

The translator picked that moment to enter the room.

"Nonsense," said Daphne. "It would only be a conflict of interest if she makes one of us the beneficiary. If it's all that important to you, I can assign the commission to some other agent."

The translator conveyed to the princess the idea that Plate feared Daphne was somehow taking advantage of her due to the relationship Daphne had with Plate.

"You can transfer the commission?" Plate asked Daphne.

"Yes, I can. It's my money. I could do anything I want with it. Or I could give it all to charity."

"How much money is it?"

Joanna laughed again as she grasped the translator's message.

"I've never heard anything so stupid in my life," said the princess in Italian. "In my country taking advantage of a situation like this would be considered brilliant. You would be crazy not to."

The translator waited until Daphne had finished whispering in Plate's ear before repeating what the princess had said in English.

The princess spoke up in Italian again at the same time.

"If you deny me the right to take out this valuable insurance policy, and then I am violently murdered, my family will not only sue you for everything you have, they will come over and demand satisfaction. There will be a vendetta between us for all of eternity."

Plate turned white.

"How much did you say?" he asked Daphne, with incredulity.

Daphne whispered in his ear again.

"That's compared to maybe $17.00 a month I will get off of Kate Traval's policy. I appreciate your referrals but I cannot live on them," she continued in a normal volume.

"Officer." The translator tapped him on the shoulder. "The princess is insisting on her legal right to take out the insurance policy. She is threatening legal action if she is denied the policy."

Still quite pale, Plate looked at all three women in turn.

Daphne looked smug.

The princess looked hostile.

The translator looked anxious.

"There will need to be a police presence when the physical exam is made," he said weakly.

The translator conveyed this and Joanna nodded.

Plate led Daphne to the door. "Let me know as soon as the

physical is scheduled."

"I take it you need to talk to the princess in private?" asked Daphne.

The translator started to talk to the princess. Plate held up his hand. "Could you give me a moment before you speak to her?" he asked, then turned back to Daphne.

"And about the commission?" Daphne asked.

"We'll talk about it later," he said softly. "Something can probably be worked out."

"We're not married yet."

"I know. That's what I mean. If you might have to give some of it to charity or something just for appearance's sake. Or what was the second-biggest commission you've ever gotten? Maybe give the difference to charity."

"Okay. No problem."

"I do need you to leave now." He bent down and kissed her.

"E ' storia d' amoré!" They heard the princess happily exclaim.

"But before you go, just what was your second-biggest commission?"

"It was a long time ago. When I first went off salary and onto straight commission, a friend in Austin, who I have mentioned previously, took out a big policy."

"Okay. That will probably be the solution. Go now, I have work to do."

"You coming over after?" Daphne asked.

"No. I have to go to Houston Intercontinental Airport to pick up the Japanese visitor."

"Airport? Really? Could you call me when you get there? You might could do me a favor and save someone an expensive taxi ride."

"Okay, I will. Go home now. Put that money in a safe place."

"I'm getting this to my office safe right away," said Daphne, clutching the cash and the paperwork as she slipped out the door.

"You needed to talk with the princess?" The translator repeated her question to Plate after Daphne left.

"Actually, no. Ms. Lopez. I need to talk to you."

Chapter 33

"I thought your girlfriend was following me. When I confronted her, she found the pretext that she was here to sell the princess life insurance. Since the princess probably does need life insurance, I decided to go along with that."

"Are you insinuating that my fiancée has done something wrong?" Plate asked.

"I never seriously thought about it from an ethical standpoint. She acts as if she is in the employ of the police department. But we will let that pass. What was it that you wanted to see me about?"

"Just a few questions. And before we start officially, do you by any chance, translate between English and Japanese?" Plate asked.

"Spanish is my first language. English, my second. Italian is my third. I also speak a little Japanese. Very little though. I am not qualified to translate Japanese. Sorry, I cannot help you," said Elizabeth.

"It was just a thought. I am sure we won't have any trouble finding someone. It would have just been convenient since you are already here."

"Again, I apologize for inconveniencing you."

"No. Not at all. I'm very impressed. I wish I could speak a foreign language. I took French in high school. And promptly forgot it all soon as I graduated. Spanish is the language needed in this area of the country. Why all my Texas high school offered was French, I have no idea."

"Until recently it was the international language. Especially of tourism and business. English has overtaken it, I am afraid. Some of my colleagues who only translate French to English and back are having a hard time getting jobs these days."

"I'm sure that's more a result of supply and demand in this economic downturn," said Plate, feeling inwardly grateful for Daphne's impromptu economic lessons that occasionally burst forth in the middle of ordinary conversation. Despite having a bachelor's degree in criminology and several hours accumulated towards a master's in the same field, he felt uneducated in the presence of this mistress of languages.

Quoting a little economic theory caused him to rise in her estimation. He could see it in her facial expression.

"Quite so. I do think being able to translate any language is going to be an excellent guarantee of employment in the future. Once we get past the rough spots, my Français speaking friends will do well," said Elizabeth.

"That's part of what I wanted to talk to you about today."

"Indeed?"

"You've done some private translating in the past between individuals in romantic situations who did not speak the same language?" Plate inquired.

"Yes. In these difficult times I have sometimes had to resort to that type of job when I cannot get commercial or governmental work."

"Did you translate for a couple named Emilio and Yolanda Cardioxa during their courtship and shortly after they were married."

Ms. Lopez was very good at stifling all of her body language so that it did not interfere with her verbal translations.

Lieutenant Plate was better at detecting near imperceptible movements that indicated guilt or innocence when faced with an unexpected or feared question.

"Yes. I do recall that couple. It was a very short-lived job."

"Are you aware of the circumstances of the recent trial of Castroe Zopev? Surely you knew Mrs. Emilio Cardioxa was the victim?"

"I have been extremely busy with the princess and Mr. Wynter and trying to deal with all these volatile demanding movie personality people. I did not really follow the trial."

"Weren't you still working for Emilio Cardioxa the time of Yolanda Cardioxa's death?"

"I had quit several months prior to her killing."

"I see. So before her death, Mrs. Cardioxa and her husband had learned one another's language or learned to communicate in

English? English is not the first language of either one of them is it?"

She stiffened more visibly.

"Mrs. Cardioxa's native language was Spanish, same as mine. Mr. Emilio Cardioxa speaks fluent English so we dealt only with English and Spanish," Elizabeth said.

"Then you don't speak his native language, which is? I forget. Which language was his native language?" Plate asked.

"I do not recall, Lieutenant."

"You don't recall?"

"Yes. No. It was an obscure Eastern European dialect and since I did not speak it at all, it never came up."

"I see. I was wondering if you have had any contact with Mr. Emilio Cardioxa since his wife's death?"

"Absolutely none at all."

"Are you personally acquainted with Klaus Lewegz?"

"No. I have never met the man."

"But you know who I'm talking about?"

"Certainly. I read the newspapers. I do not know him. Now if you will excuse me, I told you earlier I have a terrific headache from all of this. Your girlfriend has landed a plum life insurance policy with a high commission. I am sure you two have reason to celebrate. My tenure with Mr. Wynter ends very soon. Despite his having unexpectedly asked me to stay on if Joanna's role is not cut quite as short as he had anticipated, I have no intentions of doing so. I have another job lined up that will take me to Washington D.C. for a while. Now that you know pretty much everything there is to know about my life and career, I would appreciate it if you do not bother me again."

"I apologize if I've given any offense, Ms. Lopez. I can't promise I won't be speaking with you again."

Plate left, hostility still hanging in the air as he walked down the stairwell.

Back on the road, he got a bite to eat on the way from a fast food restaurant on the highway.

He was headed to Houston Intercontinental Airport, known for some reason by the jumbled anagram IAH.

191

Chapter 34

"It is so easy to get the letters mixed up. So I speak so little English, and speak it so very poorly," said Mr. Shiameto, not sounding like he spoke English badly at all, "that I have brought my own translator. Mr. Ito."

The Japanese translator, even thinner and younger than Mr. Shiameto himself, bowed.

Plate returned the formality.

"I hope it's not a problem. But there's another flight due in about ten minutes and I need to give a ride to a person coming in on that plane."

"Not at all, certainly no trouble," said Mr. Shiameto, after his translator detailed Plate's statement in Japanese.

"I'm looking for a Dan Daniels," Plate showed his badge to the attendant preparing to welcome exiting passengers off the Southwest flight from Dallas.

"Yes, sir."

"He's about six feet tall. White male, brown hair, about 200 pounds. Possibly dressed in a business suit, or a sport shirt and blazer. About 28 to 30 years old."

The flight attendant's heart began to pound. She had never been in on an arrest before.

"What has he done?" she whispered to Plate.

"I'm not sure. But I think he is some kind of shoe salesman."

"Oh." *Must be code for some criminal activity they don't want publicized,* the flight attendant thought.

She stepped up to the ramp and started visually scouring the passengers as they stepped out of the long tube into the lighted spacious waiting area.

"Mr. Daniels? Looking for a Dan Daniels? You have a party waiting," she called loudly in a professional voice. Although she had no placard to hold up, her hands assumed that position unconsciously as she searched each possible face for a response.

"I'm Dan Daniels," called a man wearing a brownish reddish

business suit with a straight narrow tie. He was holding a briefcase with one hand and waving at her with another.

She caught her breath. She had forgotten to ask the police officer what to do next.

Plate made a reply gesture and walked away from the Japanese men in the direction of the waving well-dressed man.

"Mr. Daniels?" he called. "Daphne sent me. I'm- her friend, Lieutenant Plate."

"Oh, of course!" Dan Daniels smiled happily. "She didn't tell me you were going to meet me. I was expecting to have to get a cab."

The two men shook hands. The flight attendant absorbed this and slinked away back to her desk, feeling used.

Neither man bothered to thank her as they walked back towards the two Japanese gentlemen.

"It was a happy coincidence that I was going to be here at the airport anyway," Plate admitted to Dan Daniels. "I was picking up these gentlemen in the course of my duties."

Plate introduced all three men, hoping he was getting their names right.

Greetings were exchanged as if somebody whom they had all known for years had introduced them.

"Where am I taking you, Mr. Daniels?" said Plate, as they started towards the luggage collection area.

"Just Dan. Please. I'm staying at a small motel just outside of Sand Waves. As close as I can get to the place, since there's no hotel or motel in the colony."

"That's correct. I know the spot. It's not the greatest luxury place but they do provide a bed."

Mr. Ito whispered something to Mr. Shiameto in Japanese. Mr. Shiameto replied with a short sentence, then addressed Plate.

"It is my understanding that my associate and I are staying with man named Mr. Stark Wynter?"

"That's correct. He has several guest cottages on his property. The police department is- uh- assisting Mr. Wynter with his project in Sand Waves and he is returning the favor by letting the two of you stay there. We do have a guest house available but it is out of the way and security is very tight at Mr. Wynter's estate right now."

Plate let his mind slip back to the last time the department had utilized the tiny guest cottage they maintained hidden on the green belt. He had experienced an encounter there he was unlikely to ever forget.

"I hope it is not an imposition on Mr. Wynter that I have brought my translator," said Mr. Shiameto. "I had engaged him before I knew the circumstances that caused Sand Waves to be without adequate accommodations."

"I'm sure it won't be a problem. Sand Waves is not prepared for temporary visitors. It's crazy but that's the way it is. Staying on Mr. Wynter's estate is the best possible scenario for you right now. We have one of our officers, Grant Skaar, also residing on the premises. And the way things are going, I'm liable to be there soon. The cottages are very nice with plenty of room for both of you."

Dan Daniels looked a little jealous as they were collecting the luggage. Plate suddenly recalled how unpopular Japanese people were in the United States right now. Their booming economy in the face of America's recession, easily overlooked in the booming Houston area, and Japanese propensity to buy American property, taking over American businesses, was causing controversy.

Many in the older generation recalled the hard days of World War II, wartime atrocities in Asia, and were less than pleased to see the Japanese gaining prominence and respect in the world of American business and real estate.

Considering all that had happened since the first of the year, Plate did not feel like he was being a little paranoid to wonder if Dan Daniels harbored any ill feelings towards the Japanese.

A wild thought that Daphne's ex-brother-in-law was in town to assassinate the royal relative of Hirohito crossed his mind.

He felt terror for a split second.

The supposed shoe salesman was smiling and happily chatting with the two foreigners about the upcoming movie scene that was going to include the wedding of Plate and Daphne.

"I was so pleased the first one was canceled and it was rescheduled," Daniels was telling Shiameto. "I was unable to make it in time. I was flying in tonight in hopes of getting to the Marriott in time for the reception. My plane was delayed to these wee hours of the morning so that wasn't even going to be possible, but I thought I would come on anyway. Nonrefundable ticket. Plus, I hoped maybe there would be some more partying the next day. But then apparently the whole thing's been canceled?"

"Yes, that's right. We anticipate it will be rescheduled."

"Well, I've got a week's vacation. If they don't take too long in rescheduling, I'll get to come."

Mr. Shiameto spoke to his translator.

"This was to be your wedding night, Lieutenant?" Mr. Ito asked Plate, astonishment in his voice. "We would never have dreamed of imposing on you this way if we had known that."

Mr. Shiameto indicated agreement.

"If the- it's complicated- however, had the event Mr. Daniels is referring to not been aborted, another officer would've come here to meet you."

"Indeed may we offer our congratulations and regret we did not bring gifts."

"Oh, that would no way be necessary. It was not going to be a traditional type wedding. Might happen Tuesday."

As they carted the luggage to Plate's car, Plate had to spend even more time trying to explain to the Japanese visitors about how he and Daphne would be united in marriage within a movie.

Dan Daniels sat quietly in the front passenger seat as Plate talked over his shoulder to the two men in the backseat.

Plate was trying to find out exactly why they were in Sand Waves and exactly what they expected but they were being very vague.

"Mr. Daniels?" Mr. Ito addressed Dan out of politeness, since Dan was being left out of the conversation. And to try to distract Plate. "Mr. Daniels, so sorry I did not catch. What is your business?"

"I work for the telephone company."

"I thought you were a shoe salesman," Plate said.

"That's what I did when I got out of college. Well, dropped out of college was the way it went. Darica wanted to get married and one of us had to work," said Dan.

"Now you work for the phone company? What section?" inquired the senior Japanese man.

"Section? Oh, you mean which department. I'm in security."

"Most interested."

Plate was suddenly interested, too.

"Need for security very great at telephone company?"

"It's growing," Dan admitted. "It's been an epidemic the last few years. People hacking into the lines and making long distance phone calls."

"Is difficult to do that, no?"

"Unfortunately it's quite simple. An amateur can do it. People can now buy alligator clips at Radio Shack," said Dan.

"What are alligator clips?" Plate asked.

"They are called alligator clips because when you squeeze them open they looked like the teeth inside an alligator's mouth."

"How do those work?" Mr. Shiameto asked.

Dan Daniels proceeded to tell.

"Find the outside phone line, easiest place to access is an apartment complex or in a city high rise. You can get access to all the phone lines in the building's telephone multipoint terminal."

"Why wouldn't that be locked up?" Plate asked.

"Well, some are in behind a locked door. But in some large buildings they are not," said Dan.

"That sounds irresponsible," said Plate.

"Tell us more, please," requested Mr. Shiameto.

"You connect two alligator clips onto to two connection points in the terminal, which allows you to steal from anybody in the building. Sort of like jump-starting a battery. Instead of positive and negative, you have tip and ring. Those terms actually come from the old switchboards dating back from the 1900s and still used into the 1960s. Back then, you had the tip of the plug and there was a metal ring that was further back. Both of those had to be connected for the current to run through and the phone to work. I know a little phone company history."

"I see," said Mr. Shiameto. "And today? What about thieves?"

"Now you have these two wires named tip and ring. The thieves cut the cord open, separate those wires and splice in their wire and make it look like it's supposed to be there. They connect to their apartment or office and they are in business of stealing long-distance."

"You take down these criminal apparatuses?" the translator asked Dan Daniels.

"My job is more to detect. I do a lot of listening in on telephone conversations," said Dan.

"Indeed?" Plate commented.

"Interesting but not so much as your wedding, Lieutenant," said Mr. Shiameto.

By the time he had dropped Dan Daniels off at his motel and had gotten the Asian men to their guest cottage, Plate still was not sure that the latter two men quite understood what was going on with the movie wedding combo activity.

But the Japanese had learned all there was to know about how to tap into a phone line and make a criminal long-distance phone call.

And Plate had been, at first vaguely suspicious, then certain, someone had followed him to the airport, to the motel where he deposited Dan Daniels, then back to Sand Waves until he entered the gates with the Japanese visitors.

When he exited the gates on the way to his apartment, no one followed. He was all alone.

Deciding whoever had been following was interested in Daniels, he reflecting on the illusion of privacy on the telephone line.

And other illusions of modern-day life in the 1980s.

He wondered how unaware he truly was in this world.

Chapter 35

It was Saturday afternoon before Plate and Daphne had a chance to catch their breath and discuss their predicament.

"There's no way we can be legally married. We didn't finish our vows," Daphne insisted.

"It has more to do with the signature on the marriage license. We may be actually married if the preacher signed a license," said Plate.

"He didn't give me the license. Did he give it to you?" Daphne asked.

"No."

"They must still have it."

"I will try to call Stark Wynter and find out something."

"Meanwhile, I don't think we can consider that we're married."

"I agree," said Plate.

"I have to face my family, you know."

"Okay. It's settled. We will not be married until after Tuesday. After the scene is done and completed. Speaking of family, where is your sister?"

"Darica is out trying to get some kind of interview. I think she's going to write a story on the upcoming 1984 primary elections."

Sand Waves resident Forrest Pointpar was expected to win nomination for a congressional seat.

Grace York, the former resident of the home being used as the movie location, was expected to gain a nomination for the US Senate.

"That would be a good avenue for Darica to pursue right now," Plate said approvingly.

"I told her no way she's going to get into Willhouse's funeral."

"I don't know I'm even going to be able to get you in. It is going to be so crowded."

"That's okay. I didn't really know him."

"You know, Daphne, I really didn't know him either. I worked with him for years and I took a strong interest in him professionally. But I've always been wrapped up in my own personal life. I have my parents and brother and sisters, their families, all of whom I don't get to see often enough. I just never really have taken the time to get to know any of my coworkers personally. I suppose I know Robert Brecken fairly well. But it's still all work. He has a wife and children. No personal time for coworkers," said Plate.

"I've never really had a work environment where we worked as a team. On all the TV shows, people they work with are sort of like a second family," said Daphne.

"That's TV shows. In real life, people you work with are just people you work with. Family is family."

"I suppose I have been kind of looking forward to being part of your work group socially in our marriage."

"I'm not sure we have a social group. In fact, I know we don't. Don't really even have a Christmas party. Just extra food usually. And an office tree. Betty Brecken comes in and puts one up."

"Still there's the potential. And you have a bond. Look at all of these police officers coming for the funeral."

"That reminds me. Most are going to arrive Tuesday night."

"Tuesday night?" Daphne complained.

"I know. It can't be helped. Timothy's funeral is very early Thursday morning. The vigil is Wednesday night. Many want to come for that since they're not going to actually get inside the chapel next day."

"There is no bed in the other bedroom. I use it for storage."

"Kate Traval is taking two in just a small apartment in Galveston."

"She lives in Galveston?" Daphne frowned, confused. "She didn't give me a Galveston address when she applied for insurance."

"Maybe she's moved. She said she was selling her house."

"Selling her house? She did not mention that to me."

"Is that pertinent to applying for life insurance?"

"Well no, not really. But it's not something people usually leave out when they're talking."

"Anyway. What about accommodating a policewoman?"

"I can't," Daphne said. "Darica has the guest room."

"Can't you convince Darica to leave after the wedding?"

"She didn't even know about the wedding before she showed up. I asked my parents not to tell her or Scott. And I'm sure they did not betray me. She is sticking to her story about coming for the funeral of Willhouse."

Plate had conceded that the idea of staging their wedding in conjunction with the movie scene had turned into a disaster.

But there was too much to be gained by not backing out.

The links to the investigations were a crucial factor.

And he and Daphne had signed contracts with Stark Wynter.

Plate had warned Stark Wynter, that contract or no contract, Daphne, he, and other members of the police department would no longer participate if the shot was not finalized on the next try.

Stark vowed the wedding would happen no matter what.

Plate was no longer concerned with the wedding details, more about how he could use the event to help further the investigation into Timothy Willhouse's death.

With the delay in the shooting caused by the temperamental princess, the scene was now scheduled to be shot just two days before Timothy Willhouse's funeral.

The looming somber event now overshadowed the celebratory one. Plate tried to get this attitude permeated in Daphne's mind.

"I promised Chief Brecken you could accommodate at least one policewoman, possibly two. He knows you live in a large house for a single woman."

"How judgmental! I use every facet of my house, thank you. I cannot imagine living anywhere smaller. My apartment was bursting with paperwork when I lived there and had no separate section for an office."

"Never mind the past. You live in a 2100 square feet home with three bedrooms and an extra room that is legally a fourth bedroom. All that space for just you and one small cat," said Plate.

"Catherine is a medium-sized cat."

"Daphne! Jeanne! Be serious! I need you to do this for me!" Plate exclaimed.

"Even if I rented a bedroom suit for my third bedroom, where would I go with all the stuff in there?" Daphne asked.

"I can help you put it all in the garage. You'll just have to leave your car out for a short time."

Daphne sighed. "Okay. I will call the rental furniture company first thing in the morning. But just one policewoman. I cannot throw my sister out, much as I would like to."

"Good, it's decided. We go through with this wedding, no matter what, on Tuesday."

"Oh no! I left the dress!" Daphne exclaimed in sudden distress. "I forgot about it. What happened to it? Do you know?"

"That was taken care of. Kate Traval has it. She took it to her place."

"That was nice of her."

"I think she's going to be good for Jordan. He's never struck me as a happy person."

"Since she is more or less one of my bridesmaids, maybe I get to be a bridesmaid for her," Daphne said happily. "I've never been a bridesmaid."

"No?"

"No. No one has ever asked me."

"They didn't want a bridesmaid more beautiful than themselves," said Plate.

Chapter 36

Daphne got her morning paper on Sundays fairly early.

If she did not, a neighbor would inevitably steal it, one of many whose credit card debts precluded their ability to pay their monthly newspaper subscription fees. All the good discount coupons came on Sunday, so it was that paper that was prized the most.

Daphne knew at least two neighbors living on her street prowled about early until they found a paper to lift. One was only a few doors down from her and the only way to keep him from getting to hers first was to make sure that she got there ahead of him.

She was still half asleep when she stumbled back into her den and flopped down on the couch. With so much going on, she barely had time to read the paper recently.

Having patrolled the interior perimeter of the house most of the night, Catherine saw a good opportunity and climbed up next to her mistress and settled in for a dawn catnap.

Rather than risk disturbing the feline, Daphne decided to just stay there. She unrolled the paper.

A banner headline with several color photos underneath on the left greeted her. The layout looked like a combination of yearbook pictures and bridal setting shots, and had a secondary smaller size headline on the right with a byline underneath.

***Why a Serial Killer Goes Free-*** read the banner headline
- *A daring exposé of inadequate prosecutorial response to the murder of innocent women in clusters-* ran the secondary headline.
*'By Darica Daniels'-* read the byline.

"Oh no," Daphne moaned, and sat up so quickly that the cat got mad and ran down the hall.

Daphne glanced after the animal, wishing she could run down the hall and hide along with her.

She held the newspaper up and focused her eyes to read.

Houston- Since the days of Jack the Ripper the

victims of male serial killers are invariably profiled as either deserving, provoking, or meeting their fate due to the severe ignorance of their sex. The truth could not be more incompatible with those theories. This article takes an in-depth look into the investigations of several sets of serial killings over the years including the recent spate of murders attributed to the recently acquitted Castroe Zopev. That Zopev is the prime suspect in these killings, and has only ever been arrested once and was found not guilty, is a prime example of how mostly male investigators have allowed their own prejudices and stereotypes of women to blind them to the true nature of the crimes which take the lives of a multitude of female victims- *continued on page 15*

Daphne did not want to turn to page 15. She did take a quick peek and saw that Darica's prose covered the entire page with the facing page full of more pictures, these in black and white.

She quickly shut the paper.

After a moment, curiosity getting the better of her, she took a good look at the colored pictures on the front. Darica had undoubtedly gone to a great deal of research to find old color photos of numerous persons connected with serial killer cases over the past few years. Most reproduced well, even though some of the hues were faded.

The photos were an eclectic mix of law officers, prosecutors, victims, and suspected killers that caught the eye.

Daphne forgot her aggravation for a moment and studied them to see if she recognized any of the names printed under them. It did occur to her that although she knew exactly what Castroe Zopev looked like and had a good idea how other famous serial killers appeared in file photos, this was the first time she had seen any clear images of victims during happier times in their lives.

Darica's feature covered a wide range so only a couple of the names were familiar. Yolanda Cardioxa was there, being the most recent newsworthy dead woman. A photo of her taken at her bridal sitting was sharp and bright. A more faded late 1960s high school photo of a young girl with a light brown bouffant hairstyle and a salmon pink colored sweater was identified as Sally Monroe. Compared to most of the other pictures, it looked more dated. It struck Daphne how styles had changed since the late 1960s. The perfectly coiffed hairstyles and dark rimmed glasses had given way to the hippie flower-child stray hair images of the 1970s. Finally in the early 1980s women dressed elegantly again, and if not fixing their hair, at least wore decent haircuts with simple styles, as so many of them went into the workforce and their careers demanded professional outfits and a well-groomed appearance to compete with cleanshaven men in suits.

Daphne wondered about the nice looking girl with the prim sweater and teased hair and glasses.

She had lived long enough to see styles get sloppy but had died before women looked nice again. Before contact lenses became common place.

Daphne felt sad for her.

The phone rang shrilly.

Although there was no possible way to tell who was calling, Daphne looked at the jingling machine and knew without a doubt that it was her fiancé.

"Is your sister up yet? I need to speak with her immediately."

Plate did not even say hello.

"I'll go see. If she's not up I will get her butt up."

"I'm coming over," he said crisply. He hung up.

Daphne did recall Darica's reaction to the glass of cold water splashed in her face with a great deal of pleasure for a long time to come.


"I see you're on your way to work." Daphne was commenting on Plate's uniform as she greeted him.

Darica was seated at Daphne's dinette table, sipping a Coke.

"If I still have a job!" Plate angrily tossed his copy of the front section of the *Chronicle* on the table.

"Have you read my story? Don't judge it until you read it."

"I haven't had time to read it," Plate admitted.

"Peter, I have read it and it really doesn't say much." Daphne went behind the tabletop bar into the kitchen section of the room.

"Thanks a lot!" said Darica, setting her Coke down on the table hard. Several drops splashed out the small opening.

"I'm not saying it's not well written, Darica. But there's nothing new in it." Daphne pulled out a frying pan and set it on a stove burner.

Plate set down at the table. He opened the paper and read.

"Would you like some breakfast?" Daphne asked.

"No, I can't stay," Plate said. "I mainly came by because I knew I was going to be asked about this. I am going to be asked if I talked to the writer about it, if I knew about it, and if the writer knows anything that she didn't put in the story and should tell the police."

"I can answer no to that last question. And if necessary, I will swear to anyone interested that I did not talk to you, or even Daphne, about the story."

"And who did you talk to?" Plate asked without expectation.

"A confidential source," said Darica, fingering a business card from Klaus Lewegz surreptitiously in her pocket.

Plate finished the article. It did seem to be a simple feminist argument that if a female serial killer were going after men, the police would do more to get the culprit off the street.

"So what did you think?" Darica asked lightly. She was watching his face for reactions as he read.

"I have no official opinion." He folded the paper back into its normal position and drummed his fingers across the photos on the front page.

"I can scramble some eggs in just a couple of minutes," Daphne said.

She was in the small square kitchen that was divided from the dinette by a table height counter which stopped just short enough to leave a standard interior door-width passage. Just wide enough for the built-in oven's door to open. The cabinet above the electric oven held a built-in microwave.

The open-air stovetop was on the counter behind the bar. The split height counter had a backsplash rising for the stovetop, with the taller counter facing the den, dividing the living area from the kitchen.

Plate rose from the table.

"I have something else I need for you to take care of for me."

He walked quickly around the bar and stepped up on the foyer and went out the front door. The two sisters did not have time to react before he returned.

He placed a large black container on the tiled foyer.

"The apartment manager is coming to inspect to see if I get my deposit back tomorrow. Therefore, this cannot be found there."

He opened the door of the container and a large black tomcat cautiously crept out.

As if by magic, for she had not been seen since her earlier temper tantrum, Catherine appeared in the den.

"Plate!" Daphne protested. "You can't just let him out like that."

Before she had finished speaking, the two felines were within inches of one another.

Both crouched close to the carpet.

Both tails twitched rapidly.

It was her territory. Catherine felt obliged to strike first.

She hissed, drew back, spit.

Then she raised a front paw, allowing it to hover in the air a split second before it came down on the tomcat's ear.

In a matter of seconds, both cats and both women were screaming at the same time.

The cats assumed a paws-on position, rolling on the floor.

Plate stood on the foyer and folded his arms.

"Vandal! Stop that," he said loudly. "Cats! Both of you! Behave yourselves!"

"What are you going to do? Put them in jail?" Darica asked.

Frantically, Daphne ran to the kitchen cupboard. She pulled out two cans of cat food from the cupboard, tossing one to Darica.

"What you want me to do?" Darica asked, catching the can instinctively.

"Open it. Then get behind them. Stand in the hallway!"

Daphne pulled the top off one can and got down on her knees.

"Do what I'm doing! Try not to get any cat food on the carpet. You lure one towards the garage. I'll lure one into the kitchen."

Both cats had tussled and rolled long enough. Never losing eye contact, they separated and backed off, preparing for a second attack.

Plate observed both sisters now down on the floor, calling 'kitty kitty kitty' on their knees, feet pointed in opposite directions.

"Oh, this is nonsense!"

He stepped between the cats and grabbed Vandal by the back of the neck. Holding the tomcat in the paralyzing grip that rendered it helpless without harming it, Plate lifted the animal up in the air.

"Don't hurt him," Daphne cried.

Plate looked down at Daphne and Darica on the floor.

"I think I am the one in danger here," said Plate.

Ignoring Darica's entreaties and the smell of the cat food, Catherine fled to Daphne's bedroom.

"Put Vandal in the garage." Daphne struggled to her feet. She put the cat food on the bar. "Let me close the cat door so he can't get back in the house."

"What cat door?" Darica asked. "Which door is it in? I've never seen it."

"It is in the wall between my third bedroom and the garage so that Catherine can come in and out when she wants to, but can be restricted to that bedroom only, if I shut the door going into the hall."

"What? You had a carpenter cut a hole in your wall? For the cat! How much did that cost? What a spoiled cat!"

Darica was on her knees, holding the liquidy animal food as if it were a lit candle she feared would flame out.

"Darica, take your can of cat food and go after Catherine," Daphne directed. "Stop worrying about how I spend my money."

"That's easier said than done." Darica balanced the can precariously as she rolled on one side. Before the taller woman could finish getting up, Daphne stepped over Darica to get by her.

The can of cat food wavered in Darica's hand, but did not fall.

"You might help!" Darica yelled at Plate.

Plate nodded at the black bundle clutched paralyzed in his hands. "I don't quite see how," he replied. "I have a time bomb here."

Daphne sprinted across the house to block the cat door.

Still holding the solid black animal by the neck, Plate decided to wait until Darica got out of the way before he proceeded.

Putting his hand under the animal's behind to brace it, he turned the cat slightly and looked it in the face.

Vandal had all four paws extended frozen in the air, his tail drooping down. The feline's eyes stared straight ahead with a glazed look, but its mouth was open, revealing long sharp white teeth that were ready to create puncture wounds as soon as Plate released him.

Darica went to the bedroom, calling Catherine sweetly.

"Think you're tough?" Plate said to the tomcat. "I have dealt with murderers, thieves, drug addicts, and rapists."

Despite his predicament, the cat managed a low guttural sound from within.

Plate quickly turned the cat away so their eyes no longer met.

"It's all right, kitty," Daphne cooed from the laundry room. "Don't be scared, Vandal. It's okay."

Vandal did not agree.

Holding Vandal at arm's length, Plate trotted down the hall, through the laundry room. Daphne opened the door into the garage.

He tossed the cat firmly. The feline landed two feet away.

Vandal alighted on four paws, turned, hissed, and started coming at Plate.

Plate quickly shut the door, stepping away, dusting his palms.

Darica came out of the bedroom, nearly colliding with Daphne and Plate as they came back into the den.

"That could have been handled better," Daphne said.

"They're simply going to have to get used to each other." Plate went to the kitchen sink to wash his hands.

"Your female cat is traumatized and hiding under your bed. She won't come out," Darica reported. "I put the can of cat food at the foot of the bed."

"You didn't get any on the carpet?" Daphne asked anxiously.

"No," Darica replied.

"But she's liable to make a mess if she starts eating it. I better go get it. Peter, you might want to take that other can out to the garage. There's some dry cat food out there but I don't know how much. You need to go talk to Vandal and calm him down."

"The cat is fine. I don't have time to go talk to him. I have to go explain to my boss why my future sister-in-law is writing front page stories about legal cases I'm involved in."

"Chief Brecken can wait. You should go to your cat," said Daphne.

"I have to choose between keeping my job or consoling a cat?"

*Nothing like those two choices for a pleasant day*, Plate thought silently.

"You said this was not your case," Daphne reminded him.

"It's not. Nevertheless, believe me, the subject will be brought up. In fact, I'm sure the conversation has already started without me."

"So you just brought this cat over and you're dumping it on Daphne and telling her that she's got to take care of it and make her cat like it," Darica observed.

"I'll be back as soon as I can. Surely in the meantime I can count on you, Daphne, being a cat expert, to placate the tomcat."

"He's bound to be scared out there. He doesn't know me."

"He didn't know me either when I got him. I told him it was me or the pound. He got the message."

"Oh, I'm sure he did. He's going to think you abandoned him."

"Like I said, my apartment manager's going to inspect the premises. If he finds the cat there, he will call animal control."

Catherine crept back around the wall that divided Daphne's master bedroom from her den. She looked warily all around her, sniffing before she took each step.

"See, Catherine's okay. Now I have to go to work. Being late isn't going to help me with the situation."

Plate left.

Daphne retrieved Catherine's can of cat food from the bedroom and made a spot for it on the vinyl dinette floor. She started looking for a box to use for litter.

"See what I told you," Darica said. "That's the way men are. No feelings. No consideration. No planning. They want to dump all their problems in your lap and you find a solution for them. Their time is always more valuable than yours. Their job is always more important. They expect you to take care of their little messes. But if you have a problem, just try to get them to help you out."

"All right, Darica. I concede that men in general are inconsiderate. I acknowledge that Peter is a man, therefore he falls under that generalization. But right now I have to worry that these cats. Can YOU help me out? All my cat litter is in the garage and I don't want to leave Catherine right now."

"I'll go out in the garage and get the litter," Darica said. "And I will talk to the tomcat."

"Thank you," said Daphne.

"Even though it is another damn male," Darica muttered under her breath.

At the police station, Chief Brecken had already scrutinized Darica's reporting.

"None of her information is inaccurate," Brecken said.

"I only glanced at it. But I noticed one thing no one has mentioned before," said Plate.

"Right. The husband of the first victim had been a cop. But before his wife is killed, he passed the bar."

"Why do you think that slipped past everyone?"

"Good question."

"Is it important?"

"It could give some clue as to Zopev's motivation. As to how it helps us in the long run, I don't have a clue."

"These journalists can retell the stories in dozens of different ways but if there's no hard evidence, we are wasting our time reading what they write."

As if in hopes of proving that statement untrue, the two men spread the two identical newspapers on the chief's desk. Brecken opened one to the jump page, placing the other's front page adjacent.

The recent practice of putting color pictures on the front page had become routine for the *Chronicle*. They contrasted sharply with the dull black and white pictures on the inside section.

Plate and Brecken bent over and stared at the newsprint for several seconds before almost simultaneously coming to the same realization.

"We were so busy spying into computer databases that we failed to observe the hard evidence in front of us," Brecken said.

"The pictures?"

"The pictures."

A sailboat rocked gently in the rain. Tied up at the pier, its occupant was thinking about setting sail.

Klaus Lewegz also had reacted to Darica's newspaper article.

And had reached a decision.

Life, as he lived it now, could not go on.

He was going to make a change.

And it was going to be soon.

From his boat phone, he dialed a phone number in Sand Waves and a woman answered.

"Elisabeth, I need to see you now," he said.

"That sounds ominous. Like an ultimatum."

"It's now or never for me. I'm sorry. I wish I could be different."

"It's all right," she reassured him. "Actually, I have been waiting for your call. I am ready to go whenever you say."

"Monday? Tuesday? There is that movie scene to do again. I was there the first time. It will look suspicious if I don't go back."

"Tuesday it is. We can leave after," she replied.

"I want to get as far away as possible."

"I have a passport. I'm ready."

"Tuesday it is," he said with satisfaction.

Chapter 37

"Haven't you done enough damage?" Daphne asked.

After a great deal of petting, distributing kitty treats, and soothing talk, both cats had calmed down.

Completely separated by wood and sheetrock, they had arrived at a peaceful but divided existence.

Vandal had taken over the garage.

Daphne had made a litter box for Catherine and placed it in her master bathroom.

"Whatever made you decide to get white carpet all through the house," criticized Darica.

"There's vinyl in the kitchen. And the Italian tile on the foyer."

"You can hardly keep a litter box in the kitchen. And the foyer is not a good place either."

"The house came with carpet in the bathrooms. I never thought about asking them to change that. I wanted white carpet in the den. I only got one choice. The same carpet throughout the house."

"You got a different wallpaper in the kitchen, and it's different in each bathroom."

"I had a choice of three wallpapers. They didn't have to be the same."

"Must be nice. Apartments don't give you any choices at all."

"I'm going to see about having a little remodeling done."

"Remodeling? This is a practically brand new house."

"I was planning on having a few things done before Peter moves in. It will be an adjustment for me. Having to share my space."

"I live in a little 500 square feet apartment. You've a 2100 square feet house and you're worried about sharing your space?"

"Let's not get into that. Let's get back to the damage that you did and how you now have the gall to ask me to do something that could cause more trouble."

"How did I do any damage? I wrote the story from a historical perspective. It was a freelance piece. I had no idea the *Chronicle* planned to put it on the front page. Now, about this Japanese VIP- "

"No!" Daphne snapped.

"I know Plate picked him up the airport. My contact says not only did he pick up Shiameto but another Japanese guy and a white guy. He ditched the white guy at a cheap motel. Then took the Japanese behind the gates. My contact couldn't get any further," said Darica.

"Your contact? You are having Peter followed? Why don't you just follow him yourself?" Daphne asked.

"Because he would see me. Look, I'm just using one of the college kids. He thinks he is Sherlock Holmes and he's making a few spare bucks. He's planning to be a private detective someday. He's getting a little training. Help me out here. I know you can get behind the gates of Sand Waves."

"Whatever happened to our agreement that we kept our professional lives separate?" Daphne asked.

"Am I asking you to do anything with any of your clients? You have not insured this Japanese guy, have you?"

"Never even met him."

"So that's my point."

"I know our agreement was professional and about clients. But I'm going to marry Peter. You can't have people following him. He is a client also. He bought insurance from me. So technically, he falls within the realm of our agreement."

"He bought insurance from you? Isn't that unethical?"

"Not unless I kill him," said Daphne impatiently. "Insurance agents start selling with their families most of the time. I never try to sell any of y'all any insurance when I started out, but most agents start with their families."

"Is that true? Why didn't you ask any of us?"

"Mom and Dad were upset that I was becoming an insurance agent instead of a school teacher or secretary or something like that. I didn't want to antagonize your new husband. And I knew better than to ask Scott."

"Yeah, I can see that."

Darica and Daphne contemplated their elder brother for a few moments.

"There but for the grace of God, go I," said Daphne.

"Right. Me, too," Darica concurred.

Then both took a respite to Daphne's kitchen to get a Coke and some aspirin.

"Plate bought insurance from you?" Darica repeated, after swallowing her pills.

"Yes." Daphne debated on telling her sister about the sweet and surprising way Plate had proposed.

She decided Darica did not deserve to share in the joy of that moment.

"Will he make you the beneficiary when you are married?"

"I'm already the beneficiary."

"How much did he take out?"

"That's privileged information and none of your business."

"He can always change the beneficiary. Can't he? Without your knowledge."

"Darica! He's not some kind of con artist or criminal! He is on the other side of all of that. He doesn't have some ulterior motive for marrying me. What could it possibly be?"

Darica contemplated this for a moment. She could think of several right off the top of her head. Daphne was much better off, owned a house, made more money, probably had savings in the bank.

He would be moving from a tiny little apartment into a very nice home.

Daphne also had a better car.

And then there was sex. Like most men, he probably wanted children, somebody to raise them, somebody to keep house for him.

Now he would have a house...

"You can't think of anything, can you?" Daphne asked smugly.

"It was ethical? If he dies, you get the money?"

"Yes! Ethics! Hell! Whatever happened to right and wrong?"

"Let's make a deal," said Darica, assuming Daphne had asked a rhetorical question. "Do me this one favor. Get me an interview with the Japanese and I will treat your relationship with this police officer with the same respect that I treat your relationship with your clients."

Daphne was silent.

"What harm can come of it? All I'm asking for- you get me in front of this guy. He's perfectly at liberty not to talk to me. I don't even know that he speaks English. Just like you need to get in front of people to try to make a sale, just like if you don't have anybody that will listen to your sales pitch, you can't possibly do your job, if I can't get in front of the people that I need to interview or get information from, I can't do my job. All I am asking for is a chance," said Darica.

"It's been hard for me to win the privilege of being able to go behind the gates whenever I need to," said Daphne.

"I know that. That's a good point. You know, this is America. What gives these people the right to wall themselves off from everybody else? Why did they have the right to put up fences around entire neighborhoods and not let anybody in on public streets?"

"I don't know. Private property rights?"

Daphne was not very interested in politics and, if it did not concern insurance, she paid little attention to what was going on in the U.S. Congress or the Texas Legislature.

"Money, it's all about money," Darica said.

"Well, they have the money to put up the gates and to hire people to keep other people out. I imagine the roads in the neighborhood behind the gates are technically privately owned or something. I don't know."

*I don't really care,* thought Daphne with exasperation.

"All I'm asking is one trip in. I'll never ask again, I promise. This feature story on the front page of the *Chronicle* is big for me. I am going to do a very sympathetic story about Officer Willhouse's death, which I know I'm going to be able to sell. Add in a scoop interview with the mysterious foreign visitor and I just might be able to make it without having to go back to work at those crappy little newspapers. They don't pay anything and don't give any recognition and want to tell me how to write."

"Okay. I get the point. You know, we have to get back inside the Stark Wynter estate."

"Yes, I know. I'll be grateful forever."

"I suppose I can say I have come to check on something about the wedding, if anything's been changed on the set since last time or something."

"That's brilliant! You have a copy of the script?" Darica asked.

"No. But I've a book! They are basing the set design on it."

"We will take a copy with us. Make like we're comparing."

"Just this one time," warned Daphne. "And, from now on, if you ever have my fiancé- my soon-to-be husband- followed again, that's it. We are done. I will never speak to you again."

Darica felt a chill in her heart at the look in Daphne's eyes.

"Done. And promised! He'll just be my brother-in-law. I won't ever think about him being a cop ever again. After the wedding."

Daphne unfolded her arms. Darica held her hand out. "Deal?"

"Deal." Daphne solemnly shook hands with her sister. "Let's go. No time like the present. I have Wynter's private number. I'll call and tell him I need to come by and see the set this afternoon. With my sister. He's scared I'll call this all off. He won't dare not let us in."

Upon arrival, the sisters quickly made their way through the house. They had slipped out the back door and across the yard. They knocked on the door of Mr. Shiameto's cottage, easily distinguished by colorful wind chimes fluttering in the breeze. Grant Skaar's porch had accumulated home-style clutter. Stark Wynter's abode had expensive custom made lawn furniture. The other cottage was empty.

Neither Wynter nor Skaar had seen anything unusual about Daphne and her sister touring the set. Another county official now stationed at the compound, a female officer, was up on the third floor with the princess. She was routinely informed.

Mr. Shiameto and his translator had no trouble accepting the rather lame explanation Daphne and Darica came up with for knocking on their door.

Daphne introduced herself as the bride in the movie being made on the compound, Plate's fiancée, and an insurance agent, causing some confusion. Darica was easier to comprehend.

Darica said she was doing a feature on Japanese and American relations in the 1980s, a good pretext for asking prying questions.

Mr. Shiameto seemed to speak very little English and directed almost every inquiry to his translator who seemed singularly unable to think of things to say, despite speaking English very well.

It was like a cross examination of a hostile witness in a *Perry Mason* show.

Darica gave up after about 30 minutes.

Daphne likewise was thwarted in any attempt to sell the two men life insurance. They both assured her that the insurance provided by their company, (which they were extremely vague about the nature of its business), was a more than adequate for their needs.

The sisters could almost believe they were just wealthy Japanese businessmen in Sand Waves for business reasons.

Still, the Japanese gentlemen were charming and Daphne thought that it was the height of rudeness that they had not been invited to join in the wedding festivities.

So she corrected that oversight.

"Just right across the yard." Daphne stepped out on the porch of the cottage with Mr. Shiameto. "They are going to shoot the wedding scene day after tomorrow. I am surprised nobody invited you. It could be because it was supposed to have happened last week and it didn't come off. You hadn't got here yet and probably nobody thought about it."

Mr. Ito repeated the comment to his boss.

Mr. Shiameto replied in Japanese.

The translator answered in English. "Mr. Shiameto is most honored by your invitation and he will be happy to attend."

"You too, of course," said Daphne.

"Thank you," said the translator. He bowed.

"You don't think it could possibly be because the wedding is set in the 1940s and they are Japanese?" Darica said in a half whisper.

The translator started to speak.

"Don't translate that," Daphne said hurriedly and waved her hand at the man. She then whispered to Darica, "I don't care if they are Japanese. I am the bride and I can invite them to the wedding if I want to. Stark Wynter can just manipulate the shots around them."

"Please be sure to come," Darica said loudly, thinking, *maybe I'll get some shots of them in the wedding guest congregation that I can use later if the movie is a success.*

"We be there," said Mr. Shiameto in English. "Front. Center. Will take pictures!"

Darica shifted. She had a mission she had not confided to Daphne.

She was waiting for a chance.

Darica had every intention of surreptitiously slipping a camera into the event.

There had been such a rush to get her a dress and get her part integrated into the scene that she had neglected to accomplish anything like that the first time.

She was still kicking herself that she did not get some pictures of the princess having her temper tantrum.

This time Darica intended to be prepared.

She was grateful for a second chance.

Making small talk, the Japanese men were relating details of a meeting with the princess and her translator.

"A most enjoyable afternoon of tea was provided by Her Royal Highness and her translator yesterday," said Mr. Ito. "She brought her boyfriend, the one playing a groomsman and they were kissing throughout the teaparty. A little annoying. But I was able to enjoy some professional talk with Ms. Lopez about our mutual profession. Her Japanese being most advanced."

"How interesting," said Darica, bored.

"Actually it is not the place of the actress to invite anybody to the wedding. She doesn't have that authority," said Daphne, not much interested in the communications between translators either.

"Movie? Wedding?" Mr. Shiameto still did not seem to fully understand.

"Here! Let me show you this. Darica, get that copy of the old book out of your satchel."

Darica complied. She then indicated she needed to use the facilities, demurring to inconvenience the two men.

She would go back to the mansion and find a restroom.

She had picked the ideal spot to stash a camera bag where she could retrieve it discreetly after her part in the wedding was over.

She slipped back to the house to accomplish this.

Daphne focused the attention of the men on the book.

*Murder as the Organist Plays* had been resurrected and reprinted in light of the movie to come.

Daphne explained to Mr. Ito that this was the book that was going to be made into a movie. The wedding scene was going to be shot at the same time a real ceremony was going to be performed.

"Very cool," said the translator.

"You wed lawyer?" Mr. Shiameto asked in broken English after Mr. Ito told him about the wedding described in the book.

"No," Daphne said. "That's just the book. I am married to- will be married to a policeman."

She opened it to the section that described how Jenny Plate felt about her undercover lawman going off to both the sexual and mortal dangers of his job.

*"There is a nice desk labeled Lieutenant Plate waiting for me." He did his best to sound convincing. He could be very good at it. "No one will ever summon me by my surname again. Everyone will call me by the title that befits my rank and position."*

*"I'll believe that when it happens," Jenny had said.*

*He knew that the most Jenny hoped far was a small cottage in a respectable section of town with a semblance of normalcy and respectability. She dreamed of the opportunity to take her family to church, grow it in a Middle America Christian community with her husband at her side.*

After hearing the translator read the passage, Mr. Shiameto nodded a little sadly and said once more to Daphne in English.

"So you wed policeman?"

"Yes." Daphne nodded emphatically.

He shook his head and smiled at the same time.

"Hard life," he said in English. "My wife have much tolerance, much concern."

"Yes," Daphne said, thinking of Alice Willhouse.

"Could read more from book, please? Now, translator."

Scowling at his boss, Mr. Ito obediently read a section about Daphne's fiancé's great-grandfather and his wife in 1904...

*"I have a plan. I shall enhance our position in society through this case, one way or another. They say no man can resist Elicia Ellagin's beauty. I'm going to behave as if I am entranced by her." He laughed. "It will be the best con of my career."*

*"Your specialty." Jenny knew her husband had more than once used his charms on the opposite sex to smooth the way in his job. She had taught herself to ignore the means if the ends were indeed justified and he came home alive.*

*"So remember, if there is gossip, I am just playacting. Just don't give me another thought until Monday. Goodbye. I love you." He had rang off then. He wanted to get to the Ellagin house before the abortive wedding entourage arrived. He knew a shortcut. All he needed was a good horse.*

*Jenny wondered after he hung up if he knew just how much she loved him. She wondered when, or if, she would ever see him again.*

*Making sure the child was settled, she took out her Bible, clasped it to her breast, and bowed her head in prayer for her husband's safety.*

The translator's tone was monotonous but Mr. Shiameto mentally heard the prose in Daphne's voice, with all the emotions that went with every word.

Chapter 38

Darica returned from her mission.

She was clearly ready to depart.

Daphne handed Mr. Ito the copy of *Murder as the Organist Plays*.

"Keep it as my gift," she said. "I apologize I only have one. And here are wedding programs and invitations with my notation that you are my guests. That will let you bypass the costume selection process."

Daphne had only given out a few of her share of the invitations, to the Harrimans, Skrales, and a few clients. One other to Dan Daniels.

"Thank you so much," said Mr. Ito. "We will share this lovely gift. I will read to Mr. Shiameto later. He has much on his mind now. Please excuse us now."

Mr. Shiameto was looking preoccupied and tired.

"Tell him it ought to be an enjoyable show. Stress relief," said Daphne.

"Don't worry. We will be there on the strength of your invitation."

The translator seemed to have everything down pat.

The sisters took their leave.

"Maybe a romance brewing between Mr. Ito and the translator that goes with the princess?" Daphne speculated as they left.

"That was pretty much a waste of time. Translator romances don't make news."

"I can hardly be held responsible for that. You do intend to stick to our agreement?"

"Yes. I do."

Daphne relaxed.

Darica may have felt the trip was a waste of time.

Daphne was very glad they had gone.

Even if she did not sell any insurance, it was a Sunday evening well spent if it got Darica off Plate's back.

The sisters spent the remainder of the weekend working on making positive progress in the new relationship between Vandal and Catherine.

Monday morning Sarah Pauliza arrived at the compound to give Joanna the required physical for her life insurance policy.

Plate was under strict orders not to speak with her concerning the death of Willhouse.

Nevertheless, he had manipulated a few strings to make sure that she was the EMT assigned to do Joanna's physical for her life insurance.

That took no small maneuver as he had to make sure that Sarah's schedule was altered to the point that she had the day off. For that, he had to call in a few favors at the Sand Waves medical facility where she worked.

The second part, getting the insurance company to coordinate with the temp agency to assign Sarah the job, was much easier, but still involved some diplomacy and authoritative socializing.

He then relieved Grant Skaar from his duties for a time so the younger officer had a chance to go home to his wife.

Thus, Plate appeared behind the oval glass in the front door for Sarah Pauliza to see immediately when she arrived.

Sarah turned pale when she saw the police officer.

Forbidden to speak at the cost of his job, Plate nevertheless thought it would be a valuable interaction just to watch Sarah's reaction to his presence and observe her body language as she conducted the basic physical for the princess.

He opened the door for the nurse without any words passing between them and showed her up to the room where the princess was waiting.

Elizabeth was also there to translate.

The tension in the room was thick as butter.

Only Joanna seemed happily unaware of the anxiety and hostility vibrating between the three people with her in the small foyer-like hall on the third floor.

It was obvious that only years of experience and competency at her job allowed Sarah Pauliza to perform the simple tasks of taking the Joanna's blood pressure and temperature while asking routine medical questions, without literally shaking.

She did stutter several times over simple questions she undoubtedly could normally recite in her sleep.

Elizabeth translated with cold cordiality.

Joanna answered each question with extreme positivism or vehement denial.

Despite the ease of the procedure, the nurse swayed a couple of times and Plate half moved towards her once, sure she was going to faint.

She recovered and stepped as far from him as possible.

Such extreme anxiety puzzled Plate.

The couple had the upper hand in the situation. All evidence, not just most of the evidence, but all of the evidence, indicated that on that rainy morning just six days ago Timothy Willhouse cracked. As a result he trespassed at the Paulizas house, climbed up to the balcony of their bedroom, broke open their French doors and invaded their home, screaming like a madman, apparently motivated by the belief that Eduardo had deliberately lied at the Zopev trial resulting in a killer going free.

Plate was one of the few in authority who even allowed for the possibility that Pauliza had lied. And he was keeping that opinion to himself.

The district attorney still had investigators trying their best to find evidence that the furniture mover committed perjury when he gave Zopev an alibi.

Getting the serial killer was still a priority.

But they were no longer even investigating the circumstances surrounding Willhouse's death.

Lawyers for all the official entities vulnerable to the lawsuit were plotting strategy to reduce the damages as much as possible when the expected legal onslaught came from the Pauliza couple.

Despite the fact that Timothy Willhouse had paid for his

aberrant behavior with his life, attorneys for hire were lining up at the Pauliza's front door offering to represent them for a contingency fee when they filed suit against the colony, the police department, and probably even Chief Brecken, just because Willhouse was under his command. Technically, Willhouse was also under Plate's command and they could add his name to the lawsuit if they wanted.

So far, no suit had been filed.

Everyone was wondering what they were waiting for.

Plate wanted very much to ask. But he could not.

As she completed her duties, Sarah Pauliza took leave of the princess and the translator, allowing Lieutenant Plate to escort her down the stairs.

No words had yet passed between them.

Before they neared the bottom of their heretofore silent descent, she stopped and turned to face him.

"I want to express my sorrow at the death of the police officer."

She said the words in a hushed whispered tone of voice as if she was admitting something that she dared not speak loudly.

Her words were hesitant and slow, obviously rehearsed, and delivered with a great deal of stress.

Yet for a brief second when their eyes met, Plate was sure he saw sincerity.

"Thank you." He spoke with simple clarity.

Sarah turned and continued down the stairs. She did not reply to his bidding her a good day as she exited.

*I am missing something about all of this,* he thought, as he watched her leave.

Her demeanor, attitude, and words painted a completely different picture in his mind than his previous conception of the situation.

He desperately wished he could talk to her one more time, now that his emotions were more under control, and there was a little bit more distance from the events that cost Willhouse his life.

He had to think of a way. But nothing came to mind as he

ascended the stairs.

Elizabeth Lopez stepped out for a break as soon as he returned to the princess.

"I insured now," said the princess happily in thickly accented English. "You allow me die, they pay big $5 million."

Plate knew the company would have to process the results of the physical before the policy was officially issued. But he had also learned enough from Daphne to know that if the princess died before the paperwork was printed, and it could be shown that the physical was valid and had good results, someone indeed would be $5 million richer if anything happened to Joanna.

He knew that she didn't understand that the threat of an insurance company having to pay a sizable claim had no effect whatsoever on the quality of security his department was going to provide for her.

This was America.

The police were beyond the reach of life insurance companies' wrath even if constabulary carelessness caused a rich corporation to have to pay out a sizable death benefit.

He smiled back at the princess and nodded.

If this policy gave her a little peace of mind, he was not going to try to take it away from her.

He did not have the language skills to do that without translation anyway.

And the translator was silent.

Chapter 39

With Elizabeth Lopez's grudging assistance, Joanna had earlier denied kissing anyone, especially any one of the groomsmen-extras, as Elisabeth Morgan had reported to Plate the day of the botched ceremony.

Police were still trying to get details on the groomsmen-extras. Stark Wynter's lack of attention to details about his personnel was causing a delay in accessing the information. His studio had issued them expense account credit cards for the trip to Texas. They were scattered in hotels throughout the Houston-Galveston area. Studio personnel in California were not keeping track of them. Compiling information on their backgrounds was not a high priority for Wynter's employees in the sunshine state.

Faxing the information to Texas, even less.

The groomsmen-extras were all supposed to be returning for the next scene attempt tomorrow.

Plans were to intercept them all at that time and find out exactly who they were.

*Why would Elisabeth Morgan make something like that up?* Plate wondered. *And if she did fabricate a story about Joanna and an extra, what does that mean about the story she told about Willhouse's death? And what about her and Klaus Lewegz?*

If circumstances changed and they needed her to be a reliable witness for any reason, the princess disputing her story concerning the interaction with the groomsman-extra could be real trouble.

Going against every possible type of policy and the rules of police procedure, Plate had not yet reported or written down Elisabeth Morgan's disclosure. Or what he had seen himself.

And he still had the puppet.

He was not sure what to do about either dilemma.

Joanna interrupted Plate's worries by tapping on his shoulder and pointed to a clock on the wall. Plate indicated to the princess that he was leaving and pointed to the phone.

She understood by his gestures that she could call him if she needed and waved him away.

He called Skaar from the downstairs phone in the den. Time for the patrolman's break to end.

"Get accurate, confirmed information about the identities of the groomsmen-extras from Hollywood immediately, one way or another," Plate directed Skaar. "I don't care if you have to fly out there. Just keep in mind the department will not reimburse airfare."

Plate took the rest of the day off. Tomorrow was the wedding. He would not be prevented from spending this evening with Daphne.

It was already unclear what they were going to do Tuesday evening. He did not want to spend his wedding night with Daphne at their house with her sister in one extra bedroom and a policewoman guest in the other.

Two visiting male officers were expected at his place soon.

Plate was going to discuss an idea with Daphne that they go off to a hotel and just leave their residences in the hands of strangers.

He had a feeling Daphne was not going to go for that.

He did not much like the idea himself.

So he was going over to her house tonight, their last unmarried night, to discuss what they were going to do for a wedding night. If not Tuesday their next opportunity would be the eve of the funeral.

It sounded like it was going to be a stressful conversation.

He decided not to tackle it until after a nap.

Back at his apartment, Plate resisted temptation to pick up his sci-fi book. He wanted to reread Darica Daniel's article.

He had the feeling she had picked up inadvertently something that he had missed.

Several times he had gone over everything again in his mind in chronological order as if it were a movie.

In almost every scene he felt like he was missing a piece of the plot in this show.

However, he could not figure out what.

He placed a quick call to Daphne's house.

Darica took the phone from her sister reluctantly when she found out who was asking for her.

"Where exactly did you get the photo of Sally Monroe? Did you find her high school yearbook?" Plate asked.

Expecting another scolding, Darica was a bit caught off-guard by her future brother-in-law's professionalism.

"No. I found a single picture in an old police file. No name or anything on it even. It could have been anyone connected with the case. No notation about who it was. The only way I know it was Sally Monroe was it had appeared previously in black and white in the local newspaper, in the town where she died, with her name under it as the caption. Along with a little short piece about her death."

"Do you have a copy of that story?" Plate asked.

"I have a copy printed from microfiche. The picture is awful and the copy is hardly readable but it's definitely the same picture. It was a great find to actually get ahold of the original. Back then a cop must have lent it to the local newspaper to run. Then the paper gave it back. A true miracle all the way around. Especially since that newspaper is out of business now and all of their files were trashed."

Plate doubted the newspaper had voluntarily returned the picture. Most likely, some enterprising police officer had followed up and retrieved it. Then he or some clerk had put it back in the file without noting the name.

"Could I see your copy of the newspaper story? If it's that bad, probably a copy of what you've got would not be decipherable at all. It would save me a lot of trouble over having to track it down myself. I would appreciate it."

"Definitely you could not read a copy of a copy of this. I'll let you borrow my copy if you promise to give it back."

Plate made the vow, not seeing any other way to get what he wanted expediently.

He asked to speak to Daphne again.

"Can you get rid of Darica this evening? I would like us to spend the evening before our wedding together."

"I will get rid of her if I have to kill her," Daphne promised.

Then he threw the phone off the hook, cut his pager off, grabbed his sci-fi book, and began his long-awaited nap.

Chapter 40

"I'm so happy we are going to spend the whole day together," she had said in response to his middle-of-the-night phone call the previous night. "I was afraid you'd be busy before the big day tomorrow."

"I'll pick you up. We can spend the morning on the boat and go to the movies."

"What's showing?"

"I thought we would see *Something Wicked this Way Comes*."

"Sounds wonderful. Just let me get a couple more hours sleep and I'll be fresh as a daisy. You know the event tomorrow would be the perfect occasion to announce our engagement."

"I still feel we are stretching it just a little bit."

"I think everything is going fine," the woman said.

"I think it gets us a little further along to where we want to be. Now you have got to get everything prepared for tomorrow."

"You do want me to do you proud?"

"I do."

"I am going to do you proud."

She had no idea it would be her last chance.

They followed through with their plans. They spent the day on the water.

For once it stopped raining long enough for a good sail. They went to a matinée, then called it an afternoon.

She wanted to get a good rest so she would look her on best Tuesday morning.

He did not go home. It was dark now. Most of the city would soon go to bed.

He drove down to the beach. Empty on a Monday night.

He parked his car and watched the waves for a long time, planning to see the sun come up over the water.

Then he turned his interior lights on and reached in the backseat, pulling a copy of the Sunday *Chronicle* from under a pile of paper bags from the grocery store.

He read the story again.

He looked at the pictures again.

He gazed back at the ocean and cut the interior lights back off. Tears came to his eyes.

She had seen it in the newspaper. Somehow.

A simple comment she had made had given her perception away.

And had he not put her in a position to where the full truth was staring her in the face if she just looked?

It was his fault.

And he knew it.

She did not see the full implications. But she was a sharp and intelligent professional woman of the 1980s.

Sooner or later, she would figure it out.

There had been a contingency plan all along.

The irony was the plan was not directed at her but at the other danger.

The other person in a vulnerable position because she might delineate or guess too much. But she had remained ignorant.

How ironic.

The contingency plan was conceived in the first place in case his partner's woman became a problem.

He had blackmail leverage to make the lowlife do whatever was needed.

And no matter how much the SOB loved the woman, his partner loved himself even more, and if she had become a danger and his partner had to choose, the SOB would have chosen self-preservation without blackmail.

His partner was nothing but a worm.

The lowest kind of low life.

But his partner's woman was sophisticated and discreet. She had been an aid rather than a problem.

And the man in the car watching the waves had successfully concealed his identity from her, so the lowlife was going to get to keep her.

For the rest of his low life.

Which would necessarily be a little longer.

The better woman was the danger. It was just another sick irony in this sick world.

Briefly, he considered throwing his cigarette down in the sand, opening the car door, and running through the rain cooled wind directly into the sea.

However, it would leave too much unfinished.

The guilty would go free.

*Better an innocent die than the guilty go free.*

The tears in his eyes did not fall. Rather they just dried in place, leaving only a burning sensation.

No release.

He started the car and drove to the phone booth.

The relief in the lowlife's voice when the explanation of what had to be done filtered through the phone lines, repeated several times, for the lowlife got emotional.

So the lowlife had feared for his soul mate.

Another irony.

The desire of the lowlife for the woman who was safe made it much easier to blackmail him into action.

Much easier to do what had to be done.

A short time later, the caller was back at the beach.

Plans were now in place.

While on his hated mission, necessary to finalize his plans, necessary to secure his future, he had missed the sunrise.

Waves were crashing toward the shore.

He recalled the film about the Great Storm.

How the destruction had spared no one.

How the winds had swept the innocent with the guilty.

As soon as all this was over he was going to go see that movie one more time.

It sometimes gave him a kind of peace for a short time.

Such massive death and destruction dwarfed his own pitiful actions.

Chapter 41

Darica did not mind going solo to a movie Monday night. She had already gotten enough response concerning her feature story making the front page that she felt she well deserved an evening off. She made plans to attend the late night showing.

Plate and Daphne also stole some time alone in the early evening by making a short trip to Galveston to get Daphne's wedding dress back from Kate.

"I'm so excited about tomorrow," said Kate, as she met them at her apartment complex. "I would've brought the dress to you but I've been so busy. I'm sorry you had come all this way."

"I guess I didn't realize you actually had to go into an office every day," said Daphne.

Although it was still early, Kate looked as if she were ready for bed. She extinguished a cigarette burning in an ashtray.

"Yes, we're expected to work an eight hour day. Then any extra time we spend on the job with the client after hours, and most of our clients need to spend time with us after hours, we get comp time off. But we have to report in every morning regardless. Very tiring."

"My setup is entirely different," Daphne said. She added to herself silently, *thank goodness, I don't have any office hours.*

"The more time I spend in the office," said Plate, glancing around at the small one-bedroom efficiency apartment, "the more my boss thinks I'm not working. You live alone here?"

"Yes, I do. Quite alone. The dress is in the closet."

Daphne was surprised at the tiny one bedroom apartment that only had a half-wall divider between the sleeping quarters in the kitchen. She would have thought Kate could have afforded better.

"I do appreciate your taking care of it for me. There was such chaos when that Italian actress decided to throw a temper tantrum."

"It must've been awful for you. But I have to admit I'm going to enjoy getting to do it a second time," said Kate.

"It was awful," said Plate.

"This time I'm going to get to be in the actual movie for sure."

"Really?" Daphne was impressed.

"Yes, Stark Wynter called me last night. One of the extras is sick. I look so much like them, he wanted to know would I go ahead and continue on in the scene when they start shooting the movie."

"That's wonderful!"

"Grant is getting to stay in for the movie as well," Plate said. "One of the male groomsmen-extras quit. They're going to pay him."

"Are they going to pay you?" Daphne asked.

"Yes, but that's not the important part. I am so excited. I knew I had a chance to be in the movie if they sort of accidentally used a scene with me in it. But this means I really will be in the movie for sure. I put your dress in this garment bag and it should be still in pristine condition. I took very good care of it."

"I'm so grateful."

"It is an incredibly beautiful dress."

As Daphne went after the dress, Plate was glancing at a photo album that was flipped open on a TV tray functioning as a nightstand.

"Oh, those are just some old pictures," said Kate. She picked up the photo album and closed it before Plate could turn a page. "Might be a few embarrassing shots in there."

"Do you enjoy living so close to the beach?" Daphne asked.

"Yes. The house I own in Sand Waves is close to the colony's section of the beach. I knew I'd regret not being close to the water."

"Any offers on your house?" Daphne asked.

"No. Well, yes. But not good ones. Say, I don't really want to rush you two off, but I have a lot to do tonight."

"Of course, we understand," Plate said.

Plate and Daphne walked the short distance from the front door of the apartment to the parking lot.

"So looking forward to tomorrow," Kate repeated, calling from the apartment's balcony.

"She didn't tell me she smoked when she applied for life insurance. I didn't directly ask her. I let people fill out the routine sections themselves sometimes. She checked nonsmoker. I'm sure."

"Make a difference?"

"No. Not unless there is a medical condition accompanying the habit. Some companies give a discount for nonsmokers. We don't. It's just the idea. Technically she lied on the app."

"Serious problem?"

"No, it would be put down as an oversight, unless she dies of lung cancer or emphysema within the next two years. Most unlikely."

"Forget it then. Let's stop thinking about work things and think about wedding things."

"Have I ever shown you the wedding pictures of Darica and Dan Daniels?" Daphne asked Plate, as they started down the highway.

"No."

"Darica wanted them destroyed. But Mom couldn't bear to do it. She gave the album to me and I was supposed to do it. But I could not stand to. I have got them hidden in my attic. "

"Show them to me tonight before she gets back from the movies. What was she going to see? Did she say?"

"I think something called *Valley Girl*."

"Oh. Must be a historical feature about California."

Arriving home, Plate moved some of Daphne's den furniture out of the way so he could pull down her disappearing staircase.

Daphne only had to go partway up the staircase to get the wedding album. As she brushed the dust off, she listened to Plate's suggestion concerning their activities Tuesday night.

"I don't see how we can possibly do that." Daphne was responding to Plate's thought about getting a hotel room.

"I just wanted to make sure you would not be disappointed if we didn't have a wedding night. It's just that I don't think I can. Well, Darica will still be here and the policewoman that is coming from New Mexico to attend Tim's funeral will be here."

"I'm really not thinking of this as our real wedding night. So I think we're better off waiting until Friday. They'll all be gone then."

"I've already contacted the moving company. Friday's the day that they're going to be moving my stuff."

"We need to think about having the reception for the family sometime in the near future and then take a real honeymoon."

"I agree. But there's only one real wedding night."

"I know. We haven't really discussed it, other than we agreed to wait after last time. Suppose we make it later? Has that been that much of a sacrifice for you?"

"What do you think?" He put his arms around her and held her close.

She pulled away from him, sat down on the couch and opened up Darica's wedding album on her coffee table, recalling Darica's initial reaction to the news of her engagement.

"Don't be coy. I know I've never said. But surely, you have figured it out by now. There's never been anyone else for me." The album contained mostly eight-by-tens and five-by-sevens. The bright spring colors at the outdoor wedding reception offered such hope and pleasantness that for a few moments neither Plate nor Daphne could take their eyes off the photos.

Daphne slowly turned the pages as they kept talking.

"Have to admit," he said softly. "It was sort of my hope."

"You will be. So there. I've been a social failure for years. Any contemporary women's magazine will tell you that."

"I don't see it that way. I don't read women's magazines. And I imagine you had plenty of opportunity."

"There's opportunity. And there's opportunity."

"That's very true."

Daphne did not reply.

"One woman once told me one time that it's unfair that men can usually tell if a woman is a virgin but the reverse is not true."

"I don't think any of it is true," Daphne said. "Women can fake it. At least that's what all the books say."

"I wouldn't know."

"So I will be your first virgin?" Daphne asked, trying to strike a light tone, but failing.

"That's not what I said."

"Surely you're not going to tell me you are inexperienced. Not with your reputation."

"Define experience."

Daphne closed the wedding album.

Plate walked a short distance away, folded his arms, and gave her a sly look.

Daphne stared at him. "Will it be your first time?"

That question seemed clear enough.

"Let me ask you this. Suppose I found myself in a situation where I either, well, you know, or my cover was blown and I would be killed. What would you have me do?"

"You mean?"

"Just hypothetical."

"What are you telling me?"

"I'm telling nothing. Just a hypothetical situation."

"So I'll never know."

"Cannot you just take my word for it that you will be my first time to make love, real love, and let all other physical aspects of the situation go?"

"It's sort of not fair that you know about me," Daphne said.

"Do I? Sometimes I feel you don't completely belong to me."

"Odd that you should put it that way."

"You might feel you have to present yourself that way to me, After all you are 27 and maybe you think I expect it of you one way or another."

"It's all about trust, isn't it?" Daphne asked.

"Yes. So you may never know all about me. Or I about you."

Sitting in Daphne's den, they held each other.

"The answer to your question is, I would not have you killed for any reason," she said. "Or harmed in any way."

Plate opened up Darica's wedding album again.

"It seemed like a good idea when Stark Wynter proposed it. But I should have told him no."

"What seemed like a good idea?" Daphne asked.

"It seemed so simple. We wanted to get married. You wanted a big wedding with a beautiful dress and lots of people. All we had to do was show up and follow directions and we got all of that for free. No hassle." He laughed.

"See, you thought it was a good idea because you're a man and you didn't want to go through the process. The process is part of it all. All the planning. All the stress. All the mess. And then it just comes together."

"Is that the way Darica's and Dan's was?"

"Pretty much."

"And you want a wedding like they had?"

"Not exactly. Theirs was a little simple for me. And it was an outdoor wedding reception at home. I wanted a church ceremony like they had. But not that type of a reception. I want a party."

"I'm sorry. Forgive me. I will try to be more considerate in the future."

"It is not entirely your fault. I was not totally opposed to it. In the end, I went along with it. I didn't have to."

"Tomorrow, it will all be over."

"No, that's what really bothers me about this wedding. It seems inextricably linked to a funeral."

"I know. I'm sorry about that, too. But I don't know what to do about it."

"Yes. There is no way I can blame you for that. I could better blame the Italian actress princess, whatever she is."

"Why blame her? She's just a kid."

"She should have stayed home if she didn't want to marry the Arab. Just say so and not run away."

"I think it's a little more complicated than that with her."

"But you're right. She is young."

"I'd say about more than a decade younger than us."

"You know what Arthur Harriman said when I told him we were getting married?"

"No, what?" Plate asked.

"An old bachelor marrying an old spinster."

They both had a good laugh.

Neither denied that it was true.

Chapter 42

The visitor from Japan felt honored to have been invited to the wedding although he did not know the bride or groom. He found being on the movie set exciting.

To better be prepared, Mr. Shiameto had procured a written translation in Japanese of the pertinent scene in the book.

After studying it, he and the translator had gone in search of expensive 1900s formal suits. Fortunately they had found an antique clothing shop.

Mr. Shiameto had the translated scene with him along with the ceremony program and invitation.

He glanced over them again. His companion was at his side and whispered the answer whenever Mr. Shiameto asked a question.

In his methodical mind, the success of the wedding scene depended on how closely it followed the scene written in 1904-

*With great anticipation, the glittering guests awaited the momentary approach of the bride. The orchestra music started. The guests were hushed. All eyes rose, scanning up the grand staircase.*

*On the balcony the first of the bridesmaides appeared. Behind her were six more ladies all gowned in rose pink. The sound of keys tapped and the organ music accelerated as they marched down in perfect time. Behind them now came a lovely preview of the great beauty yet to come...*

*...few gazes followed these women during their laborious procession... No one wanted to miss a moment of the splendored Elicia on her wedding day.*

*Even the organist, his hands raised into the air above the keyboard, paused a moment and there was a rush of silence, but the music break lasted only for a second and the notes started again.*

*The bridesmaides finally finished their journey, the maide of honor taking a particularly long time, obviously relishing her moment as center of attraction. Again, the organist paused dramatically. Then like a man possessed, he wrung the notes from the organ one at a time- here – comes – the – bride – ...*

He sat straight in his seat looking over the real wedding program that outlined Daphne and Sinclair's ceremony, putting it in his pocket when the music indicated the procession was starting.

The bridesmaids did indeed come down slowly as described in the book.

However, the bridesmaids seemed to be dressed in much more modern costumes than the book called for, although not contemporary.

The organ music was just mediocre.

Cued by the music, everyone stood up for the entrance of the bride.

She was certainly a disappointment.

Her dress was enchanting.

Her veil was overdone.

Mr. Shiameto frowned. He recalled Daphne as a blonde.

The book bride was supposed to be black haired. This bride's hair was pulled back so that hardly any of it was visible.

He was sure he saw blonde peeking out from that thick veil.

He frowned more deeply. He could not get a good view of the face of the groom either. Was this the real wedding or the movie shooting? He thought he had understood where he was supposed to be but what if...?

"We are gathered here today to join this man and this woman in holy matrimony," the preacher began. Now seeing only the back of their heads, Mr. Shiameto let his mind wander during the preacher's pre-vows message. He recalled the informal way he had been invited. Then the wedding vows began and Mr. Shiameto's ears perked up.

"Repeat after me," the preacher was saying. "I, Peter, take thee, Jeanne, to be my lawfully wedded wife."

"I, Peter, take thee, Jeanne, to be my lawfully wedded wife..."

Mr. Shiameto frantically felt his coat pocket. He was vaguely aware of a smattering of murmurs throughout the crowd. As he pulled the program back out and reached to adjust his glasses, the bride was saying her vows.

He pointed frantically to Mr. Ito when the minister began the interactive part of the vows.

"I, Jeanne, take thee, Peter, to be my lawfully wedded husband."

The translator shrugged.

*"The wedding of Daphne Martin and Sinclair Plate"* was the clear title on the program.

Mr. Shiameto opened it up and scoured the interior for any mention of anyone named Peter or Jeanne.

Surely, there could not be two staged weddings for movies at the same time in the same colony. That was absurd.

But Mr. Shiameto was a stranger in a foreign country whose language he could not read and write perfectly. He had been invited to the wedding by a young woman he did not formally know. She had dropped uninvited into his temporary abode with an obvious journalist at her side.

Perhaps they had been impostors.

Maybe he had been tricked.

A practical joke. Or worse.

Mr. Shiameto and Mr. Ito had both noted strange reactions to their arrival at the event and some reluctance on the part of the usher to seat them in spite of the notes from the bride on their hand written invitations.

He felt a lost traveler's panic rising.

"That's her first name and his middle name," he heard someone whisper. "I don't think I've ever heard anybody call either one of them by those names."

Although Mr. Shiameto understood and caught the whisperer's meaning, the translator clarified.

"Secret names now revealed as part of ceremony," said Mr. Ito. "Must be confusing American custom."

Mr. Shiameto relaxed and put the program away and started listening again to the ceremony.

He was at the right wedding after all.

Chapter 43

Daphne and Plate faced the audience. The minister announced with his thick German accent. 'Mr. and Mrs. Plate'.

Stark Wynter popped out of the audience in his 1940s style tuxedo and took the microphone from the minister.

"Now, Ladies and Gentlemen, we will now restage the wedding with the stars of our movie. Please be seated. Pretend you are witnessing the beginning of the wedding. Keep your eyes on the actors and actresses. We will be recording facial expressions and following my directions will help you have a better chance of actually getting in the movie as a close-up cameo. Just react as you would normally react any wedding, perhaps paying a little bit stricter attention.

"Do not be alarmed by any violence you witness. It is only pretend. Try to react as you would to real violence but please no hysterics or loud noises from the audience.

"We will be adding in those sound effects later."

Stark Wynter also warned the crowd not to impede the marksman's movements.

"Act fearful. Get out of his way. If you see that you are in his path, jump aside. He needs to make a quick escape. Remain seated, or otherwise in place, until you hear me shout 'cut'.

"Now just relax and enjoy the show. After we have cleared the set, all the guests of Mr. and Mrs. Plate can go onto their wedding reception. Actors, extras, and crew- report to me in the den by the fireplace. We will regroup for any outtakes."

Plate, Daphne, Darica, Jordan, and Geralyn Skaar moved off to the mansion's foyer where, due to lack of complete walls, they could still see the scene being shot but would not risk being in the camera range.

Chief Brecken said goodbye and left. He had stood as a groomsman this time as Randy Harriman had not been able to make the second attempt at the wedding scene.

Alice Willhouse, preparing for her husband's funeral day after next, also had not come. Mrs. Brecken had remained with her.

The chief likewise felt his presence was no longer required.

Brecken felt the need to get back to work as soon as possible. He could celebrate Plate's marriage some other time.

As planned, Skaar remained on the actual set as a groomsman, replacing the groomsman-extra who had quit after the first dry run.

"Rather than replace him with a professional, Stark Wynter so liked the way Grant looked in his 1940s tuxedo, he retained Grant as an extra," Geralyn said proudly.

"We know," said Darica, somewhat rudely.

"Not only is he getting his regular pay, extra security pay for guarding the princess, he is now going to get pay as a Hollywood extra on top of that," Geralyn continued.

"Likewise, Kate has been asked to remain as a bridesmaid in the shot when one of the bridesmaids bailed," Jordan said softly, not invoking his usual bragging tone. "She had not known long in advance. She was so excited when she called me about it."

"Afraid you will lose her to Hollywood?" Plate asked.

Jordan did not reply. He did look a little sad.

The group ceased talking. Music indicated the show was about to start.

Wynter was extremely grateful that both Kate and Skaar looked enough like the general appearance of the groomsmen and bridesmaids that it was going to be possible to use them. In fact, Stark was already thinking of ways to splice the film where scenes with them in the actual wedding would show up next to the reenactment in the movie.

*Everything is working out so much better than the first time we had tried to stage this wedding scene. It is almost worth the additional money it is costing to do it again,* Stark Wynter thought.

He did note something vaguely odd about the extras seated as the congregation.

His assistants had been thoroughly educated in 1940s wedding guest attire. He was confident they had chosen well. Still, as he briefly surveyed the crowd, a couple of the guests seemed out of place.

His primary focus had to be the wedding party so he decided to worry about the congregation later. During the editing procedure, it would be easy to remove any anomalies.

Before yelling 'action', Stark Wynter meticulously adjusted the entire group for height. He placed Joanna exactly where he wanted her on the staircase.

Fetching her camera from where she had stashed it in the foyer, Darica aimed it at the stage set, planning to sneak in a few shots without a flash while the scene was filming.

The music was a false cue. Wynter was not ready yet. Conversation resumed.

"Will you really be able to sell these for money?" Jordan asked Darica, bending over slightly and keeping his voice low.

"If I can get a clear shot." Darica suddenly gasped.

"What?" Daphne asked with a little mild alarm.

"One of the groomsmen, the one second from the left, the producer just moved him over two spaces," Darica said to Jordan. "I recognize him."

"From where?" Jordan asked.

"Who is he?" Plate asked, overhearing.

"I don't remember his name but I've seen him in press packs before."

"Think," said Jordan. "Try to remember where you've seen him."

"You are sure he's a journalist? Was he here the first time?" Plate asked.

"Positive. But I can't place him. I don't remember him being here the first time. Maybe I missed him. I was rushed and flustered that first time."

"Maybe he's just here trying to get a story. Wynter may even know about him. He might be on the payroll, part of publicity," suggested Jordan.

"That sounds a bit strange," said Daphne.

"I can't very well check him out right now," said Plate. "Stark Wynter was supposed to report any changes of personnel. Skaar was supposed to get the information about them."

"Certainly everyone here was screened before they came into the building?" asked Geralyn, nervously watching her husband on the stage.

"We screened all the guests, all the local people and not so local people, who showed up to be in the congregation," said Jordan.

"It was Wynter's responsibility to check his own people. He's got his own private security, I expect. We're just paid supplements. Other than the college students involved in the hazing, there's been no evidence of any real threat to this actress. I think I know this guy," said Plate. "I'm not so sure all of it was not for the publicity anyway."

Diverted from thoughts of his wedding ceremony, his mind back on the job, Plate scoured the faces of the congregation as well as the lineup of the bridesmaids and groomsmen.

"Does your camera have a zoom lens?" Plate asked Darica.

"Of course," said Darica.

She handed Plate the camera and fixed the lens for him. He repeated his scrutiny of the crowd, getting a much better view.

"If you see an interesting shot, push this button," Darica directed.

Plate saw several.

"Where is Elizabeth Lopez? She was front and center at the first run-through last week. She had an elaborate costume," Plate said.

"I remember that. I don't see her anywhere," Daphne commented.

"On the other hand, Elisabeth Morgan told me she would not be back. But there she is," said Plate. "With Klaus Lewegz."

"One of the county men has been keeping tabs on her since we were all busy with this," Jordan said. "The chief had me put that call in myself."

"This was a mistake," said Plate. "All of this was a mistake. We should have stayed out of this movie and stuck to our jobs. Had a normal wedding."

Daphne reached and pulled Plate close to her. She whispered something in his ear to the effect that she was not one to say she told him so.

"Yes, you are," Plate replied.

"This is not a good time for you two to get lovey-dovey," said Darica.

"We just got married!" Daphne protested.

"I'm really nervous. It's coming back to me where I've seen that guy. I think it was when I went to cover that story in the Middle East," said Darica.

"If he has been in the Middle East, maybe I'm wrong," said Plate, with concern.

The music struck up then, distracting them before Plate could decide what to do about Darica's alarming statement. The bridesmaids finally began their descent and the princess appeared at the top of the staircase that went nowhere.

No one but the producer-director had noticed the marksman was late. Wynter, watching for him for the last 15 minutes, was relieved when, carrying a long rifle, he dashed to his spot on the fake balcony built just a few feet off the floor on the far wall.

*Hell, he is not in costume, like I told him to be,* Wynter fumed. *Well, he's just missed his chance to be on the screen or ever work stunts for me again. I'm only paying him stunt wages, no extra money. I'll see how he likes that!*

Wynter was at least relieved the shooter had arrived. The producer-director turned his attention back to the focus of the scene. The first attempt at the scene several days ago had never gotten that far but this one was almost done.

*Damnation!*

Too late to halt the beginning movements, Stark Wynter realized what was wrong with the congregation.

This was a wedding scene set in conservative East Texas in 1946, but there were two elaborately attired Japanese guests prominent in the center section, just as if World War II had never happened.

Chapter 44

The music changed to *Here Comes the Bride* and, with the bridesmaids almost to the bottom of the staircase, Joanna made her first step down.

She was carrying a bouquet.

No dagger in sight.

Joanna went over it in her mind. It might be her only scene but she was going to do it right this time.

On a musical note from the organist, the stuntman was to fire the shot, then race through the crowd to make his getaway.

The music started on time.

She noted the marksman assuming his place at the last minute.

Ready!

Perfectly on cue, the shot was fired.

The princess activated the fake blood pellets on the wedding dress and fell down the steps in a graceful heap.

The crowd reacted admirably, with subdued horror and shock, just as Stark Wynter had asked them to do.

The shooter, holding his long rifle, made a quick getaway. He was so fast he was little more than a blur. Everyone watched his athletic graceful movements with awe.

"Cut! Cut! CUT!" The director was yelling angrily. The crowd momentarily turned their attention from the Italian actress and the now vanished assassin, to Stark Wynter's dramatic gestures.

"What did they do wrong?" Daphne asked.

The crowd was wondering likewise.

"Young lady, what do you think you are DOING?" Wynter's words and gestures were directed towards the lower left of the staircase. The eyes of the crowd followed him as he started in that direction.

One man sprang from the guests and started trying to make his way towards the sidewall, towards the real wedding party spectators.

From their vantage point to the side, the two sisters and the two police officers were dimly aware of what they were looking at.

Darica's attention turned to the man coming at them. She ran in his direction, her camera already aimed.

"Geralyn!" Grant left the other groomsmen-extras and started towards his wife. He waved his arms at her. Geralyn Skaar started making her way to meet her husband.

Plate, Jordan, and Daphne looked in a different direction.

One of the bridesmaids, settled in a folded position on the bottom step, had Stark Wynter's attention.

"Only the bride is supposed to get shot, didn't you understand THAT?" yelled Wynter, moving aggressively toward the offending extra. "It's NOT going to get you a bigger part. I know it may look dramatic but I can't have these kinds of theatrics on a movie set!"

Jordan thrust his way onto the set, pushing everybody aside, making a straight line for the huddled bridesmaid, actually reaching her before Stark Wynter.

"It's Kate!" Daphne said.

"Oh my God!" Plate sprang into the crowd, following in Jordan's path. Skaar met his wife halfway and directed her to find a small enclosed room and lock herself in. He joined his coworkers.

Most of the other guest-extras were still unaware that Kate's collapse, and reactions to it, were not part of the show.

Darica was rapidly shooting pictures and remembered to turn on her flash halfway through her roll of film. The advancing wedding guest passed Daphne and reached Darica before he stopped.

He put his hand on her shoulder.

Darica turned and stared at him for a moment. She suppressed an urge to strike him, instead enlisting his help in carrying her bag with her lenses and extra film, so both of her arms were free to better handle the camera.

He shadowed her as she continued working.

"Get an ambulance. Kate's been shot!" Jordan yelled just as Plate reached him. The crowd, having already spent their hysterics on the fake scene, was still abnormally quiet.

Only Princess Joanna rose from the floor and started to scream, her fake blood on the wedding dress more visible than the real blood on the fallen bridesmaid. One of the groomsmen-extras detached himself from the others, ran over to her, grabbed her and shook her. She clasped onto him, sobbing more quietly then.

Still in her unstained wedding dress, which would have made quick movement difficult, Daphne held back, watching. The picture before her was so surreal that it became uppermost in her mind that she needed to make sure she got neither fake nor real blood on her gown.

*That groomsman consoling the princess is the one Darica was talking about,* she thought, with confusion.

Across the room from Daphne now, Plate was watching the same groomsman-extra out of the corner of his eye and having his own thoughts. *It's the one that was acting like a bodyguard last time. The one who threw out the college student,* he thought, with awkwardness.

He was right.

Stark Wynter abruptly halted his tirade. He ran to the phone in the mansion's adjacent den to call an ambulance.

"She's dead," Plate said softly to Skaar. They had both reached Jordan's side. Jordan was still holding Kate and talking to her. "Grant, go after the shooter. I will contact the chief and tell him what's happened."

Plate went to the princess and the groomsman, who had taken a hold of her. The dark man reluctantly let go and stepped back. She patted his shoulder and spoke to him calmly in Italian, clearly calling him by name. Fabrizio. He stepped farther away. She gave a thumbs up signal to Plate that was both poignant and ironic.

*Fabrizio is in the country illegally,* flashed through Plate's mind randomly. He also noted that Joanna was quite brave to stand exposed before them all. And so calm around Fabrizio.

*She's protecting him at the same time he's protecting her.*

The probably-illegal groomsman was hovering near, looking very much like a bodyguard. Sent perhaps from her father in Sicily?

Only a bodyguard would have behaved as he did.

A bodyguard or a lover.

Chapter 45

Plate stepped above the princess and addressed the crowd.

"Ladies and gentlemen! Please remain calm and stay where you are. Help will be on the way shortly. Will everyone please make way for the ambulance personnel when they arrive? Otherwise, please remain in the building. It might be dangerous to go outside right now. If you have a seat, please take it."

Princess Joanna was the only person who had no spot on the ground floor assigned to her except her death scene location at the bottom of the stairs. She looked at the police officer for direction. Then back at the groomsman she had addressed as Fabrizio, still near her. He had not taken his eyes off her.

He motioned for her to come to him.

Misunderstanding, Joanna backed up several steps. Her movement made her a perfect target if there was a second shooter.

Fabrizio jumped up the steps to stand in front of her.

Noticing this out of the corner of his eye, Plate felt no alarm at the performer's action.

"Again, I repeat, help is on its way," he called loudly to the crowd.

Joanna and Fabrizio, now just below Plate, embraced openly.

Stark Wynter bounded beyond his younger employees, joining Plate on the staircase.

"The girl is dead," Plate whispered to Wynter. "But I would like to conceal that fact until we at least get her body out of here. I need to meet the EMTs to give them instructions as soon as they come through the door. Skaar has gone after the shooter. Can I count on you for crowd control at least temporarily? I need also to call the chief."

"I already called him on his car phone," said Wynter. "He's on his way back. He said to tell you to call the county. He's having reception problems. But I got through."

Plate had completely forgotten the chief now had a car phone. "Thanks," he told Wynter.

"Your other officer?" Wynter indicated Jordan confusedly.

"She was his girlfriend."

"Oh no."

"Just leave him be. EMTs should be here in just a few minutes."

"Illustri agente di polizia?"

Joanna had not heretofore so politely addressed Plate.

She pushed gently at her protector. He reluctantly detached from her. Avoiding all eye contact, Fabrizio skipped down the steps.

"Who is that?" Plate asked, with a ghost of a smile.

"You suppose to know. You detective." She also smiled faintly.

Plate did not want to deal with Fabrizio right now. He was fairly certain the dark skinned man was a friend, not an enemy.

Plate took Joanna by the arm and led her down the steps. The groomsman-extra had moved even farther away but was still eyeing them warily.

"I want you to go up to your apartment. Activate all the security. Do you understand? Where is your translator? Where is Elizabeth Lopez?"

"I understand. I do not know where she go. She makes trip to see her lover very much. I go third floor, push secure buttons?"

"Right, the security buttons, all the buttons."

Plate somberly led the princess to the enclosed third-floor stairwell.

"No elevator lift?"

"Dangerous," said Plate.

She understood.

It would take more time to ascend steps in the bridal dress but as soon as Joanna entered the stairwell, the security system activated, locking its door. She was as safe as she could possibly be.

Unless someone was waiting up there for her.

This thought sent a cold chill down Plate's spine as soon as the door was locked. It could not be possible. The female county officer was up there, just in case. He felt pulled into different directions. He needed to phone the county officer and he needed to meet the EMTs as soon as possible once they arrived.

He was considering the merits of pulling Jordan away from his girlfriend, his condition notwithstanding, and asking him for help.

Mercifully, it was not necessary. The EMTs arrived at the door.

They were professionals and it only took a short consultation for Plate to explain what he wanted.

As they went towards the body, he went towards the den phone, recalling how he had used it before in a very different type of an emergency.

To his immense relief, the county officer confirmed that the princess had arrived on the third floor  and was safe.

Plate turned his attention back to the wedding set scene.

It had turned into chaos. But with the princess safe, and Kate Traval's body being removed, he felt like he had it more under control.

He stopped Darica from taking pictures and confiscated her film. She was surprisingly cooperative about this but he did not have time to analyze her uncharacteristic response.

Daphne was still standing to the side in the wedding dress. It occurred to him as much she loved the dress, he needed to get her out of it before she could possibly be of any help to him. He went over to her.

"Go change out of your dress."

"My clothes are upstairs. They moved my changing station to a bedroom this time."

"On the third floor?" Plate asked.

"No, we dressed on the second."

"All of the women? Including Kate?"

"Everyone, except the princess."

Plate escorted Daphne out of the room down the foyer into the open staircase that went to the second floor. "Go up there and change but don't touch anything except your own clothes."

"Can I bring it back down? They gave me a garment bag for the dress this time."

"No, but you don't have to leave the dress there either. That room is going to be torn apart for evidence. It wasn't in there at the time of the shooting so there's no reason for it to be left there. You can give them your clothes later if necessary."

This was not exactly procedure. Plate knew that if that wedding dress was tied up as evidence Daphne would never forgive him.

Plate recalled the room in the west wing once occupied by Corina Skrale. The famous singer, temporarily residing in Europe, still had possessions there. She and her husband and Daphne and Plate were friends although they moved in different social circles and rarely saw each other.

What seemed like a long time ago, but was only months, Daphne had been in that area of the house with Corina.

He reminded her of that.

She agreed it was the perfect solution for the dress.

Nothing in that area of the house could be considered evidence. No one would dare bother Corina Skrale's possessions without a court order.

"Take it there," he said. "I'll see to it you get it back later. I just can't let you leave the premises with it right now."

That he understood her concern for the dress in the middle of this tragedy made her love him deeper. She followed his instructions.

He turned to find Chief Brecken had arrived, along with county personnel who had taken over controlling the crowd from Stark Wynter. Brecken had reached the county.

Plate located Geralyn Skaar and told her it was safe to come out.

The shooter was long gone. He had made the escape Stark Wynter planned and had kept going.

The gates to the enclosed section of Sand Waves had been opened for the day to allow the public to access the movie set.

The killer was out of the colony, into the vast millions populating the nearby cities before anyone realized what happened.

Jordan left with the EMTs.

*Surely by now they have told him Kate Traval is dead, if he has not already realized it, and are probably treating him for shock,*

Plate was thinking. Stark Wynter returned and stood near Brecken.

"What happened?" The chief was more than pale.

"Is it possible the stuntman you hired actually did the shooting or do we have an impostor shooter?" Plate addressed Wynter.

"I couldn't get the original marksman back after the temper tantrum Joanna had that ruined the first take. This new man was highly recommended. But I did not know him. I never talked to him except over the phone. He was late and was let in without any verification of his identity. I am so sorry," said Stark Wynter.

"Get the address of his hotel and send somebody from the county there," said Brecken. He was shaken. This was going to taint him, he feared.

"Could somebody else have somehow taken his place without anybody noticing?" Plate asked.

"Yes, he was alone on that balcony perch. He was supposed to fire the shot, drop the gun, leap over the crowd, and get away."

"Whoever fired the shot did exactly that. They leapt over the crowd and got away. They kept the gun though," said Brecken.

"Did you have any other last minute changes in personnel that you didn't report to us?" Plate asked.

"Yes. I- I didn't report that one of the groomsmen was replaced at the last minute. I'm so sorry, Lieutenant. I wanted nothing to delay this scene today. He presented credentials that indicated he was in the Screen Extra's Guild."

"I need to know immediately who he is," Plate said.

"The young lady is really dead?" Stark Wynter asked.

"Is it truly Jordan's girlfriend, Kate Traval?" Chief Brecken asked, still in denial.

"Yes, Mr. Wynter. The victim is deceased. Chief, without a doubt it was Kate Traval."

"They were after the princess?"

The chief and Stark Wynter expressed this thought almost simultaneously.

"If they were after the princess, they were an absolutely terrible shot. She wasn't anywhere near the bridesmaid. And she was a clear target on the steps, coming down them solo."

"We do have to consider the possibility it was one of those college students. That he was a bad shot," said Wynter.

"I also have to consider the possibility that one of my officers might've been the target. He was actually nearer the person struck than the princess. Although again, not that near," Plate said.

The killer would also have had to be a terrible shot if he had been after Grant Skaar.

Daphne came down in her street clothes. Brecken shook his head.

"Congratulations, Mrs. Plate. Hope you're not superstitious about how your marriage starts out," he said.

Daphne did not reply.

There did not seem to be anything to say.

"Okay, let's get these people processed, get the forensics people in here, and hope to God that Grant Skaar comes back with some kind of positive result," said Brecken.

"If it's any consolation," said Plate. "Not only do we have it all in a movie, a journalist was taking some illicit photos while it was going down. I've got the film."

"That could be a break. Maybe he caught him on camera. Get it developed."

"She. A female journalist. We can only hope she is a good shot," said Plate.

Chapter 46

Stark Wynter went to call the Marriott once again to cancel the planned wedding reception. This time he told the hotel manager it would not be rescheduled.

"If Mr. Shiameto can be of help, gentlemen, he is at your disposal," said Mr. Ito.

Plate and the chief turned to face the two Asian men who quietly came up behind them.

Mr. Shiameto was holding out a badge in one hand and retrieving a paper from his coat pocket with the other.

"You are police?" Brecken asked.

"So sorry. Could not reveal purpose of visit at that point. But now in face of tragedy must show true self."

Shiameto waved away the translator. He went off to a corner.

"Translator for show. Mr. Ito actually very junior police officer who speak English fluently. So get free trip to America. Sorry again for deception. I send him right back to Japan on next plane. He is not needed, although my English much less than perfect."

"You're not a member of the Emperor's royal family?" Plate asked.

Mr. Shiameto laughed with true amusement in spite of the circumstances.

It dawned on both Plate and Brecken at the same time that they would hardly have been chosen to receive a member of the royal family of Japan, as federal authorities had insinuated. They had been conned into providing security at the expense of their department.

They had fallen into a trap of egoism

"Was best plan for my security and this was location I needed to be. I am here on investigation connected to the recent trial which ended in a quitter- no- sorry, word is acquittal."

"You're investigating Zopev?" Brecken asked.

"Sorry no. Investigation concern husband of a victim. Emilio Cardioxa. Not his real name."

"I think you had better come to the station and tell us all."

"Yes indeed. I come at your earliest convenience. However, I may have something to help you right now with this tragedy. Of which I have no connection except having been invited to witness by your lovely bride."

Mr. Shiameto held out a small round disc with interlocking edges.

"My humble contribution to investigation. Was so much enjoying the ceremony I could not help but snap a few. Maybe I catch something."

Plate took disc and put it in his pocket. "Thank you! How did you get a camera by security? Where is your camera? I don't see it."

Mr. Shiameto pulled a small four-by-five almost completely flat object from his coat pocket. He pushed a button and a round disc ejected from its side.

"Current experimental Japanese camera on loan to law enforcement. Called disc camera."

Brecken took the camera and turned it over in his hand. "It looks like a cigarette case."

"This disc looks like one of those picture wheels you put in those toy master viewers. It's not much bigger than a 110. How could it take any decent pictures in this type of the setting without a flash?"

"You will find pictures from this camera extremely good quality, very positive. Best of the best."

"How do we get this disc developed?"

"Oh." Mr. Shiameto reached inside of his coat pocket and pulled out a business card. "This company will be most helpful."

Plate took the card and looked at it. It had an address in a Sand Waves strip center, a local phone number, some Asian characters, a drawing of a camera, and the name Perkins Photographics.

"Company also quality develops 35 millimeter film taken by young lady in bridesmaid's dress. Reasonable price, also."

"That would be the journalist I was telling you about," Plate explained to Brecken.

"In a bridesmaid's dress?" Brecken asked, with a frown.

"I will tell you about her later," Plate said.

Chapter 47

"Why was your identity withheld from us?" Chief Brecken was questioning Shiameto. "We cooperated fully last year."

"I didn't know anything about it at all," said Plate.

"The feds chose somebody else to be the operative. I would have picked you, Plate. But they wanted somebody with heavier military experience than you have had. And it was a bonus that he had a boat," said Brecken.

"All would have been revealed if anything had come out of the operation that involved your officer," said Mr. Shiameto. "As it was, the operation drew a blank, as you say. There was no reason for any further communication."

"We still don't have any evidence that Cardioxa has done anything wrong?" Plate asked.

"We also investigated Eduardo Pauliza and found no reason to question his veracity," Mr. Shiameto continued.

"That's why you came to America?" Brecken asked.

"Yes, to continue investigation in secret of our agent Cardioxa."

"That, of course, is not his real name?" Plate speculated.

"Of course not."

"And his dealings in the past notwithstanding, our investigation indicates that if alleged serial killer Zopev did not kill Yolanda, the only possible killer could be Cardioxa."

"That's what we think, too," said Plate.

"Alas, there still seems to be no evidence," said Mr. Shiameto.

"So the marriage of Yolanda and Cardioxa was a marriage of convenience of international espionage agents?" Brecken asked.

"Not exactly. The wife's father was in employ of government of Mexico. Mexico and government of Japan, loyal allies. Emilio meets Yolanda in due course. They decide to marry. Most convenient for everyone," said the Japanese agent.

"She was not an agent?" asked Plate.

"A lovely lady, with powerful family members. It seemed like a wonderful idea. She would provide information from unexpected sources, we hoped. Emilio was excellent agent. Served for years. Dual citizen of both our countries, he served in Vietnam. Sharpshooter. We considered him too smart to shoot his own wife. We thought he would hire local a thug, with no agency ties, to do it."

"He does not look Asian," Brecken commented.

"One of many great benefits of his service. An Asian man looking Latin more than normal. Discrepancy in ancestry perhaps. Who knows? Not relevant to his service."

"He is fluent in Japanese?" Plate asked.

"Of course. His first language."

"So to sum it up, your agency suspected Cardioxa, for some reason, was plotting to do away with his wife," said Plate.

"We had a tip. It was hearsay. Very much, we did not want to believe it. To launch our own investigation openly would have caused bad blood if, as we hoped, as you say, there was nothing to it. Just some incompatibility between the couple that leaked out."

"So you set up a sting in which one of our officers posed as a hitman seeking work?" Plate continued.

"Not brilliant. But could have been most effective. We set up a situation where they become pals. Nice coincidence that both have sailboats. So we got your officer an upgrade in his dock slip position."

"That was a bonus for Jordan. The assignment was not without risk. He got to have an in-the-water boat slip at the marina Cardioxa used. It's almost $400 a month for a space there. Of course, on a police officer's salary he couldn't afford that. You recall he had to keep the boat in dry dock and bring it out and launch it every time he wanted to go out. A real headache," said Brecken.

"So it's arranged that he got a dock space near Cardioxa and the trap was set," Plate concluded.

"And Officer Jordan reported that there was no evidence that Cardioxa had anything but good intentions toward his wife," said Mr. Shiameto. "Jordan still forbidden to speak of this. National security."

"Nothing suspicious happened at all?" Plate asked.

"Only that shortly after that Cardioxa moved his craft to a

different marina," said Mr. Shiameto.

"That is hardly a suspicious action. Boat owners move their boats around all the time in search of a better spot and or a cheaper slip rental," said Plate.

"So you see, Plate, that's why I discounted your remarks about Jordan being able to afford the boat," said Brecken.

"I do see. And when the feds stopped paying the dock rent?"

"They paid it a year in advance, Jordan told me that at the end of the year, which was just about up, he was going to give up his apartment and move onto the boat," said Brecken.

"With his girlfriend?" Plate asked.

"He would never tell me that. You know how I feel about officers in unmarried relationships living together," said Brecken.

"Yes, that has been on my mind lately. Of course, back then his relationship with Kate might not have been so serious. We might not have even known her at that time. Do we know any details about that?" Plate asked.

"I was hoping you could tell me," said Brecken.

"What else do we know about his dealings with Cardioxa?" Plate asked.

"Your officer performed most professionally," Mr. Shiameto reminded them. "No blame could be attached to him that Cardioxa did not take the bait but, it appears, did later kill his wife."

"Jordan didn't have any experience doing anything like that," said Plate.

"True. And Emilio was experienced," said Mr. Shiameto.

"Is he really a lawyer?" Plate asked.

"Lawyer in Japan. Pretend lawyer in America."

"So up until now, he's been protected by the feds?" Plate said.

"With the idea that his wife was murdered by the serial killer. With the idea that Eduardo Pauliza was somehow manipulated or corrupted into giving the alibi," said Brecken.

"So what happens now?" Plate asked.

"I must go back to Japan and report that we can no longer count Emilio as one of our best agents. No more protection for him."

"We have no evidence against him," said Brecken.

"We do have one piece of evidence against him."

Brecken slightly shook his head at Plate. Plate knew that Brecken did not want him to mention Elizabeth Lopez's connection to Cardioxa yet. They were not sure yet if the name belonged to the woman they knew.

"How so?" asked Mr. Shiameto.

"He did not show up today," said Plate.

"Disappeared?" The Japanese agent seemed truly surprised.

"He was supposed to have been an extra in the movie scene," said Plate. "I kept a list of everybody connected to the- to all the cases going on right now- who were at the first attempt to shoot the scene. Everyone in attendance the first time came back a second time except Alice Willhouse, understandably, Elizabeth Lopez, and Cardioxa."

"We investigated Elizabeth Lopez at the time of Yolanda's death and found nothing," said the Japanese man.

"As you said, Cardioxa is a well-trained agent," said Plate.

"Any other discrepancy?" Mr. Shiameto asked.

"One person was back that had said she would not be. Elisabeth Morgan. She probably just changed her mind."

"You suspect this Elisabeth Morgan?" Brecken suggested.

"I don't think so," said Plate. "She told me quite spontaneously that she was not going to be at the second event, right when the first one was called off. She would hardly have done that if she was worried about calling attention to a future absence. And she gave me some other information that has turned out to be good."

"Could I inquire about the nature of that information?"

"Yes, Mr. Shiameto. She pointed out to me the Italian journalist boyfriend of the princess. We didn't know who he was at the time. But he has slipped into the country illegally, apparently in an attempt to get close to the princess again. His name is Fabrizio, but we're not sure if that is his first or last name."

"This man not sent by Egyptian lover?" Mr. Shiameto asked.

The Japanese Secret Service may care nothing about the Joanna's romantic exploits but her lovelife had captured the imagination of everyone, including Mr. Shiameto.

"No. That was Kareem Makikz, also faking his way in as a groomsman-extra after failing to set up an embarrassing incident with two college boys. He was at the first wedding attempt. Joanna identified him to Fabrizio and the Italian dealt with him. Our sources indicate the Arab prince then washed his hands of Her Royal Highness after the first wedding attempt. Two groomsmen-extras did not return for the second shooting. Kareem disappeared and another legitimate extra quit. One was replaced by an uninvolved professional. The other was replaced by Skaar.

"And the fate of the college students who caused such confusion?" asked Mr. Shiameto.

"Due to Stark Wynter's influence, the charges will be dropped against the two college students," said Plate.

"So there's nothing more to be done," said Brecken. "This is a total disaster. We don't have enough evidence to arrest Cardioxa. We don't know where he is. We don't know where Zopev is. Our hands are tied by our lawyers, so we can't question Eduardo Pauliza. Could you question Pauliza? When are you are leaving?"

"We are satisfied Mr. Pauliza is truthful," replied Mr. Shiameto, without revealing just when he had spoken to the furniture mover.

"Then you are going back to Japan empty handed? A wasted trip?" Plate asked.

"Not completely. I do have the honor of having my visit extended so that I may represent my country at the funeral of your officer," said Mr. Shiameto.

And he bowed.

Chapter 48

Daphne hesitated.

She had heard tales about how insurance agents used to go into a neighborhood and just knock on all the doors to try to get sales. The practice had almost completely died with the advent of dependable telephone systems. Modern phone technology had given rise to the era where virtually every residence in America had at least a partyline phone. It was no longer necessary to pound a beat to reach people. Being time-consuming and unpredictable in its productivity, most door-to-door solicitation had fallen by the wayside, at least in the life insurance business.

Daphne felt like ghosts of hundreds of insurance agents of the past were surrounding her as she walked to this front door of a house where no one was expecting her.

She was not sure if the spirits of the agents of bygone years were protecting her, or just watching out of curiosity.

She shook herself and raised her arm to knock on the door.

There was a lighter spot in the paint that disclosed by its outline that there had once been a doorbell, roughly removed.

Before she could complete her knock, the door opened before her.

Not much taller than her, Eduardo Pauliza gazed at her dispassionately.

"Hi my name is Daphne Martin I am an agent with Finest Southland Life Insurance Company I happened to be calling on homes in the neighborhood and was hoping you would let me show you our company's latest life insurance product-"

Daphne spoke all those words without any punctuation whatsoever before she was politely interrupted.

"Come in, Ms. Martin," said Eduardo. He stepped back to let her enter the house. Sarah was standing just beyond Daphne's original view. The nurse came forward now. Even shorter than her husband, she stood eye-to-eye with Daphne.

"We know who you are, Ms. Martin. Your picture was in the

local paper with the Lieutenant. Are you here on his behalf?"

"No. I, I- ah- actually am a life insurance agent. But now that you mention it, there are some things that my fiancé and I have wondered about."

They looked at her blankly.

Daphne detected some fear behind their gazes.

"My fiancé- and his colleagues- are- are human beings. Really good people- who have lost their friend..."

Eduardo turned away. Tears came to Sarah's eyes.

"They just want to know if there's anything you can tell them that can help them understand what happened. Lieutenant Plate doesn't want to harass you or cause you any type of anxiety or embarrassment. So, yes, I am sort of here on his behalf."

"And, of course, he has instructions not to talk to us in case we might decide to sue the police department," said Eduardo.

"Something like that."

"I want to talk to her, Ed. I need peace of mind over all this," said Sarah.

"Come in Ms. Martin and have a seat," said Eduardo. "I am glad you came. I don't even say we're not interested in some life insurance."

"Anything I can do to help," said Daphne, stepping quickly through the doorway into their den.

She placed her briefcase on the Pauliza's coffee table and opened it.

Life insurance was the only peace of mind she knew how to offer.

She felt both competent and inadequate at the same time.

# Chapter 49

"You went WHERE and did WHAT?"

"It was- was just an idea I had. I didn't plan to actually sell them life insurance."

"Daphne!"

"But after we finished talking, they wanted to buy policies. They are both terribly underinsured at their jobs." Daphne was simultaneously trying to watch his face and get a glimpse of a package he was holding slightly behind his left arm.

"Jeanne Daphne!"

"But it paid off!" she exclaimed hastily. "Sarah Pauliza told me a few things."

Plate felt his hostility start to fade. "About Timothy Willhouse's death?"

"No. About the time she was attacked years ago. 1969 actually. And what all she went through. It was something that had been bothering her all along for all of this. But her husband was under such attack for alibiing Zopev and then there was the shooting. She's been really scared."

"Daphne, I am not following you at all. Scared? What the hell did she say?"

"Sarah remembered after all this time. I am telling you this unofficially. But of course, you can go back and find records I am sure. That's what she is scared to death is going to happen."

"Find records of what? What could she be scared of?"

"Timothy Willhouse was the investigating officer back in 1969 when she was assaulted in Wilding Falls."

Plate was stunned. "The report said the department's chief was the investigating officer. It was signed by the chief."

"She was sure. There were only three police officers in the town, she said. The chief, Willhouse, and an officer she never met."

"I didn't find any record of anything like that. Tim must've been right out of the police academy. All the paperwork I saw from that town was signed off by his superior."

While many large city departments had their own academy and hired people first, then sending them to the academy at the department's expense, most small communities could not afford such recruitment policies. So persons wanting to be police officers could go to a private or public community college that offered an accredited course leading to a Texas peace officer's license. Such students paid for their own training and then applied for jobs. This was also a good route to take to get into the private security business, as it was possible to fulfill the required on-the-job training by volunteering as reserve officers.

Plate had gone to a private academy after his service in the military. Sand Waves Police Department hired both graduates of private academies and veterans of other departments. The colony did not reimburse any training expenses obtained prior to hiring. If they hired somebody fresh out of an academy, the rookie was subject to 90 days of on-the-job training, usually provided by Chief Brecken, sometimes by Plate, before the new hire was let out into the field on his own.

The myth of patrolmen always riding in pairs came from movies and TV shows. Most departments did not have the budget to double up officers in patrol cars unless there was a specific reason to do so for a temporary period.

Officer Willhouse had taken the same route to a badge as Plate. But whereas Chief Brecken had given Plate 90 days of intense on-the-job training, Willhouse came with prior experience from other departments.

After a brief few days of observation, he began patrolling on his own in the Sand Waves community.

The period in Willhouse's career when he would have encountered Sarah Pauliza possibly explained why his name was not on the report.

"She was sure it was the same man," said Daphne.

"It could make sense if he was still a trainee. Did something go wrong?" Plate asked.

"She didn't really remember him that well. Then she read

Darica's story about Zopev. It clicked. Darica used an old photo of Willhouse that she got from one of his previous jobs. He looked a lot younger of course, thinner, and with 1970s style hair and mustache. Sarah recognized him. Naturally she was terrified that the investigation would be reopened and her husband ultimately blamed after all," said Daphne.

"Even if this is true, why would Willhouse being the investigating officer on the old assault case give Eduardo a motive to kill him?" Plate asked.

"Sarah wasn't sure of the details. Officer Willhouse told her back in 1969 they had a good idea who had assaulted her and an arrest was imminent. Then she didn't hear anything back for months. Meanwhile they moved to Houston. Time slipped by. Five years later she finally contacted the police department and was told Willhouse had moved on to a different job. So had the police chief. In fact, all three positions were now filled by men who knew nothing about her case except what they had read in the reports. When she pestered them a little bit, they told her the lack of an arrest had something to do with how previous officer had handled the assault case and that she need not expect that the perpetrator would ever be arrested."

"I didn't find any records of anything like that," Plate repeated.

"Could the records have been doctored?" Daphne asked.

"Doctored? Unlikely." He paused. "More likely just buried. Buried under mounds of other paperwork. Which would mean I didn't dig deep enough."

"There's no reason for her to tell you- I mean tell me, knowing I would tell you- which I was upfront about that- anything like that if it wasn't true."

"No, quite the opposite."

Plate was silent for a short time.

"Anything else?" he finally asked.

"Just that they each bought a $10,000 policy."

"You know, Brecken finds out about this he is going to fire me."

"I will not tell him if you don't. It's confidential information anyway. I shouldn't even be telling you," said Daphne.

"Let's hope neither one of them die anytime soon," said Plate.

"Mr. Pauliza's recent chest pains were stress induced, his doctor told him. They reported they are both in excellent health."

"That doesn't seem to help anybody around here."

*He does have a point*, Daphne thought wryly.

"Since you've been taking matters into your own hands. I've been doing the same," he said.

He picked up the package.

"A present for me?" Daphne asked.

"In a way."

Plate went over to Daphne's computer and started disassembling it.

"Hey!" Daphne protested.

"I've got your computer a modem," he said. "So it can talk to other computers. It won't be lonely anymore. Now which phone plug can I use to set it up? You not giving me any trouble about this will possibly cause me to overlook any unethical behavior you've exhibited recently."

"You know, it's not too late to call off the wedding," said Daphne. "There's an extra phone jack over near the fireplace. It's hard to see. Look behind the potted plant. I guess my computer will be back on the hearth again. No fires in the fireplace anymore."

"Soon be summer." He relocated and connected the computer.

Daphne was once again looking over files from the insurance company national data bank. She gaped at the result.

"How could we have missed this?" Daphne asked.

"We were busy. And distracted by what we thought was inflammatory information about Sarah Pauliza working as an EMT and doing the physicals for Emilio and Yolanda's insurance policies. So when we found out Elizabeth Lopez worked for the Cardioxas, we thought we had everything. That is an old trap you fall into when you're doing investigations. You stop when you think you have everything you wanted to find. Can possibly find. But that is wrong. There is always more."

Chapter 50

It had been almost a week and a half since Timothy Willhouse had met his death on the balcony of the Pauliza home.

He was finally being buried.

The best of 1980s crime forensic technology had scrutinized the scene where he died, the home where he lived, his office, his vehicles, and his corpse.

His motivation for climbing to the Pauliza balcony was still a mystery.

It was another rainy day in Sand Waves.

The small chapel was standing room only. Hundreds of police came from all over the country. Most stood out in the rain to honor a man they had never met simply because he was one of their own.

Daphne's guest, staying in her bedroom with the rented furniture, had been extremely polite and formal, distant and subdued.

Darica had been placated with an invitation to the graveside service. As there were no cemeteries in Sand Waves, Officer Willhouse had to be buried elsewhere.

His widow purchased a small single plot near the bay.

He had been on his way to go to Galveston to go fishing when he had been killed. With no ties to the area, only married to Timothy Willhouse a few weeks, his widow had enough foresight to realize she would move on with her life. She was only 23 years old. In years to come, Timothy would only be a cherished memory.

She was not interested in a convenient grave to visit. Rather she chose a place she thought he would like to be if he was still alive.

His parents, Wisconsin residents, also cared little what part of Texas would hold their son's grave. They were appreciative of the fact that their daughter-in-law of such a short time had chosen a place they would be able to visit and choose between staying at a hotel or an RV park. Already in their 60s, with five other children and 11 grandchildren, they also knew their visits to his grave would be rare.

It was a relief to all of the police when the part of the funeral taking place in Sand Waves was over and they were able to move out onto the fast riding freeways connecting Houston and Galveston.

There they were able to pick up a little speed and shake off the claustrophobia they felt during the time they and their vehicles choked the arteries of the command design colony.

There was no press at the actual funeral and Darica was one of the few journalists allowed into the cemetery.

The consequences of her front page story notwithstanding, she commanded a new respect in her profession. Plate understood her well enough to know that if she had been denied entry, there would have been no vicious retaliatory story as they were expecting from a few reporters who skirted the periphery of ethical journalism.

Daphne had threatened Darica with her life if she wrote anything at all about the killing of Kate Traval. Legally Darica was a witness in that case and possibly subject to judicial action if she did.

She feared the consequences of the law less than her sister's anger. She had nothing to tell yet anyway.

The Hollywood shooter had disappeared on arrival at IAH.

His impostor had vanished as well.

Coverage of the new death eclipsed the officer's funeral.

Daphne stayed home. She was not yet Plate's wife.

She did not really want to go to the funeral of a police officer just days before she was supposed to marry one. She and Plate, in consultation with Chief Brecken, decided she would not go.

If there were any negative comments about it later, it would be presented in the light that it was a sacrifice for her not to go. A sacrifice she made so that one more police officer coming from far away could have a space in the chapel. Daphne was of the opinion that no one would even notice she was not there.

Darica told Daphne she was going to be spending the entire day out in the field. After the funeral she was planning meetings with various editors, her anonymous source, and the amateur private eye student she employed.

She left the latter two identities in a sealed envelope with Daphne, instructing her not to open it unless she met with misadventure. She also left prints from the film Dan had smuggled from the murder scene. She took her own set with her to peddle.

Daphne once again had her home to herself.

Catherine and Vandal came out of hiding and almost seemed at peace with one another as the overcrowding of humans diminished in the household.

Daphne was going to put her time to good use. The police had all been so busy, not one of them had been able to sit down and give all the important pieces of evidence undivided and prolonged attention.

While Officer Willhouse was being buried, Daphne had both the time and the space.

She opened up her formal living-dining room. Previously visible from the den and foyer, the formals were closed off with newly constructed walls and two sets of bifold doors. A local construction company had done the job in four hours the previous day.

The two cats could now be kept out of those areas. Catherine was trained not to go in there and disturb anything but Vandal was not. He had enjoyed free roam of the Wakefield mansion, and was used to climbing on furniture. While he was careful making his way around breakable objects, his long fluffy tail sometimes brushed the wrong way. The immensely rich Wakefield had just replaced anything ever broken, but almost everything Daphne owned had sentimental value. She could see she was not going to be able to train Vandal quickly. It was just simpler to have the walls put up.

Now she went behind those walls, shutting the cats out, leaving them on their own for the first time together.

She figured she could hear any discord with no problem.

With one ear listening for catfight sounds, she spread out all the developed photographs on the table.

There were few photographs taken of the abortive first attempt at filming the wedding scene.

Fortunately the second time Darica and Mr. Shiameto took surreptitious pictures. When Darica confessed that Dan had smuggled out a roll of film for her, Daphne's first reaction had been anger. Then Plate had given her a copy of the disc taken by the Japanese policeman and the film he had taken from Darica to analyze.

So it did not seem to matter if she had Darica's smuggled pictures also.

Plate told her that getting pictures developed at one-hour photo shops took a lot less time than sending them to police labs which could take days, even weeks to process them.

The difference in quality between the two cameras was striking.

Every minute detail was clearly visible in the Japanese agent's photos.

Darica's pictures were good. She had the better vantage point. But she had to stop and focus every time. And about a third were unexposed. Before she remembered to turn on the flash, the only photos that developed where those she simultaneously snapped in coordination with the movie lights. Occasionally she missed.

Unfortunately, Mr. Shiameto was stuck in the audience and could only shoot pictures from a fixed location.

Darica had moved around all over the place.

Daphne brought her smallest TV from the guest bedroom and set it up on her dining room table. It had a built-in VCR. There was no cable connection in that part of the house but she did not need the TV connected to the cable to watch tapes.

Plate had also let her have a copy of the movie picture shot on both occasions. Stark Wynter had rushed the motion picture shots and made a VHS copy for Plate at his discreet request.

The VCR remote control had a fairly short cord. She pulled her chair close to the machine. She wanted to be able to pause the tapes and compare what she saw on the screen with the still pictures that she had right beside her.

She had a list of names to watch for.

She turned on the device and started watching.

Chapter 51

"Why do you want me to do this research? You know I'll write a story about it if I find anything," Darica said to Daphne.

Darica had returned to Daphne's house after the service. The New Mexico policewoman had gone home so the sisters were alone together.

"Because you can do it free and fast. I have to go to the library and search through hundreds of microfiche slides. You can contact some of your friends in your profession and ask them as a favor to let you see their files," said Daphne.

"Then they're all going to be writing stories about it."

"I don't care. Just get it done. You should want to make up for all the deviousness you've pulled in the past few weeks."

"I'm just doing my job. If I were to behave in any other way it would be the same thing as you turning down people who want to come and buy insurance from you."

"Don't argue. Just do it before you leave."

Darica was going back to Dallas later that night to accept her offers. She had several contacts wanting her to do feature stories. They were offering her quite a bit of money for the photos she had shot during the crime.

She placed duplicate prints in an envelope with Plate's name on them. She delayed her departure long enough to do as Daphne requested. She called in favors from reporters at two area papers and delivered copies of pertinent documents to Daphne before she left.

Daphne was still going over the black and white copies of the news stories that Darica had dug up concerning Officer K. Fondrem when Plate arrived, tired and exhausted from the long ordeal of burying Timothy Willhouse.

They were more informative than all the recent photos and movies.

After he took a shower and changed clothes, Plate was ready to talk about the entire situation.

"Your sister's gone?"

"Yes. She did help us out a little bit before she left."

"What's bothering you then?" Plate asked.

"The information she gives me leads to a very difficult conclusion. I'm not sure we're ready to deal with it," said Daphne.

"We don't have any choice if it reveals the identity of the killer."

"It does not necessarily reveal that. It just points in the direction of someone. And it may be perfectly innocent."

"All right to let me tell you what I have figured out first?"

"Okay," said Daphne.

"I told Brecken his two questions were not the questions to ask at all. He had asked- Why would Pauliza kill a policeman? Why did Timothy climb to the balcony? Is Pauliza is telling the truth?"

"That's three questions."

"They were all the wrong questions."

"What were the right ones?"

"Illusion or not. That's the question? And Jordan and I collided when we moved too slow."

"You're not making any sense, Peter."

"I know it. None of this makes any sense."

"What are you trying to say?"

"Daphne, I know how Timothy Willhouse was killed."

"All right?"

"What we have here is like I said."

"Like what?" Daphne asked.

"A puppeteer. Someone who knew both Pauliza and Willhouse, who knew their backgrounds, knew they moved too slow."

"I don't understand," said Daphne.

"Each felt they had failed once before to protect another by acting too slow. Each suffered serious consequences due to their hesitation. Willhouse lost a fellow officer who died in a fire that he watched. And he may have felt some responsibility for Zopev being on the streets and killing so many people. Pauliza's wife was attacked."

"What are you saying?"

"Okay. Here are two men who are not going to let such a thing happen again. Pauliza had a loaded gun under his bed ready to fire on anyone violating his home. Someone knew that. It was as simple as pie to get Willhouse killed if he could be induced to break into that house," said Plate.

"Okay, I'll buy that. But how?" Daphne asked.

"Listen, Daphne, what did Mrs. Pauliza say Tim said when he burst into the bedroom?" Plate asked.

"Liar. He called Pauliza a liar because of the testimony that Pauliza gave in the Zopev case. Willhouse believed Pauliza had been paid for that alibi."

"No! Mrs. Pauliza said she thought he said 'liar'. She was pretty sure. It sounded like liar and in the context that was the only word that halfway made sense. After all, 'crier' wouldn't have made any sense. Or sire, or dire, and so on. But what consonant have I not used?"

"Fire!" said Daphne, her eyes lighting up with understanding.

"But 'fire' would not have made sense either. It would have to have been 'don't fire'. Tim wouldn't have burst in and yelled fire unless-"

Daphne's mouth flew open.

"Unless he thought the house was on fire!" she exclaimed.

"He thought the house was on fire," said Plate softly.

"Mrs. Pauliza heard right the first time. She thought she heard 'fire'."

"She told me in plain English. But I did not understand. She paraphrased, saying a lunatic had burst in and said 'shoot me'. Upon learning who he was, she came to the conclusion Tim would not have said 'shoot' because, of course, no sane man would tell anyone to shoot him. She used the word 'shoot' in talking to me. It sounded absurd. I thought she was making it up."

"But what she actually heard was 'fire'."

"Yes. She saw her husband with a loaded gun. She saw and heard Tim yelling 'fire'. When she found out that Tim was a police officer, not a burglar, she decided the word could not have been 'fire' because she did not hear the word 'don't' in front of it. She didn't hear 'don't, stop, no', any type of negative before the word 'fire'. Because no such word was said," said Plate.

"She converted the word in her mind," said Daphne. "From fire to liar."

"If Tim thought the house was on fire, does that explain everything?"

"Yes. Most everything. Remember, Mrs. Pauliza said she didn't believe Tim ever saw the gun. She feared he was a lunatic. Tim would have had two seconds to put it all together and realize that he had been duped by someone. Timothy Willhouse was not that quick. No, someone convinced him that the house was on fire. Convinced him so fast that he didn't take time to stop and think."

"And the lights downstairs gave the illusion of fire behind those sheers," said Daphne. "If they were as thick as that wedding veil he wouldn't be able to tell what the light was."

"And someone fired the barbecue grill and set it on the covered patio and let the smoke come around the corner."

"Once, my neighbors at my apartment complex decided to grill in the rain on their covered balcony. They lived at the back of the building. They didn't know how to grill right. It rained and caused the fire to start smoking heavily. The balcony cover was trapping the smoke. It billowed around the corner of the building. Residents towards the front could not tell what was happening. More than one person called the fire department."

"Why didn't you ever tell me that?" Plate asked.

"It was a long time ago. I forgot about it."

"Come to think of it, a similar incident once happened where I live. Not as dramatic. I forgot it also."

"The heavy rain and fog, a little smoke coming around the corner and the lights behind the thick sheers convinced Tim Willhouse that the Pauliza house was on fire," said Daphne.

"The answers to the questions: Number one, Pauliza did not kill a policeman, not knowingly. He killed a man he thought was breaking into his house. That answers another question. He was telling the truth. And the other questions- Why Tim climbed to the balcony. He thought the house was on fire and that was the only way to rescue the couple he knew was sleeping in the bedroom. And it was an illusion. One more element that I'm missing."

"The word of a good friend," Daphne said softly.

Plate blinked. "It had to be a magic trick. A con artist or a magician behind it all."

"Or someone he knew and trusted. Confirming an optical illusion."

"Pauliza was just a weapon. Someone else pulled the strings, someone who knew them both and knew how both men would react in such a situation. Who? And Why?" Plate asked.

Daphne sighed again.

It was so obvious to her. She had her suspect. And she was sure. But she was afraid to say.

And the problem was, if she was right about who killed Timothy Willhouse then there were two killers.

Because her suspect in the police officer's murder could not possibly have shot Kate Traval.

Chapter 52

Thunder sounded and lightning split the sky.

"I had better go unplug the television. And the computer."

"Maybe it was Zopev who did the shooting. Maybe he never left Texas," Plate said half-heartedly.

"It all goes back to him. To Yolanda's death."

"What makes you say that?" Plate asked.

"Someone would have to have arranged the alibi knowing that Emilio Cardioxa was going to kill his wife using Zopev's MO and Zopev would need an alibi," said Daphne.

"So Zopev conspired in Yolanda Cardioxa's death? No, I'm grasping at straws. There was no connection we could ever find."

"Then it had to be an interconnecting link. Someone who knew the lawyer was going to kill his wife and someone who had access to the Zopev details. Who knew them both?" Daphne asked.

"The alibi had to be a setup. Had to be, but by who and why? Cardioxa? He had to have known how to kill his wife to make it look like Zopev did it."

"Why would Cardioxa set up an alibi for Pauliza or Zopev?"

*It is simple and he is trying to complicate it because he does not like the result,* Daphne thought. *He is going to have to add up all the details himself before he will be convinced.*

"Does not make sense, if the lawyer killed his wife, he would want Zopev convicted," Plate was saying.

"Ask yourself a different question. Who would know the MO details kept from the press?"

"Someone in the system. Klaus Lewegz, perhaps. It is possible that a child advocate could somehow access the information?"

"With no children involved?"

"He might have piggybacked a file onto a legitimate request. But true, it is not likely."

"What about a police officer?" Daphne asked softly.

Plate looked at her grimly.

"Peter, think about who else is dead," said Daphne.

"Kate? You think she was the intended victim? Not the princess? Or Elizabeth Lopez?" Plate asked.

"You did say that from the beginning."

"True." Plate bit his lip.

"Remember, Elizabeth Lopez wasn't there. You said the princess has nothing to do with any of this. If Cardioxa was the shooter and Elizabeth Lopez was the target, then why did he shoot? When she wasn't there?" Daphne asked.

"I don't know." Plate seriously did not like the direction the conversation had taken.

"I've sort of been grasping at straws myself to explain away something else I found out," said Daphne. "I was listening when you were explaining about the trap that it's easy to fall into when you're investigating. That you stop when you think you found what you need or want."

"I did say that," Plate admitted.

"There is one database we have not accessed with the new computer system."

"Law enforcement officer personnel records?"

"I may know who, Peter, and why. I just had not figured out how."

"And I figured out how." Plate's voice filled with irony.

"Earlier, I did a little more research into the incident where the other officer died nine years ago. Officer Fondrem. There were beneficiary records for a private life insurance policy."

"You think it could be someone from his family? No, Officer Fondrem had no family. Or did you find family members we missed?" Plate asked hopefully.

"Officer Fondrem was engaged to be married. Shortly before the accident, the beneficiary on the policy was changed."

"To a girlfriend? But who?" Plate asked, confused.

"Officer K. Fondrem, first name Kay, was engaged to be married."

Plate was silent.

"Her fiancé was a young serviceman who had recently lost his sister to a tragic murder. How do I know this? She had made him her new beneficiary on her life insurance."

Plate looked at the information that Daphne handed him. He stared at the name on the beneficiary line.

"He never claimed the money?"

"No, in fact the state is still holding it in their unclaimed property division. Insurance companies want to pay out legitimate benefits. They diligently try to find beneficiaries."

"So they are admirably thorough. What you trying to tell me?"

"Other than tragic deaths, and both originally living in adjacent communities in the Panhandle, Sally Monroe had something else in common with Kay Fondrem. They both left life insurance proceeds that were never claimed. Sally's beneficiary was not her husband. She had a $5000 policy taken out by her parents when she was a child. They were her beneficiaries but they died just after her murder and never filed a claim. The contingent beneficiary was her brother."

"Then you have his name!"

"At the time they purchased the policy, Sally's parents must have been planning on more children. There is a way to name future beneficiaries not born yet. You put in a phrase that means all children born ever to a person. So in the future when more children come, you don't have to redo the beneficiary designation. As policy owners, the parents could do that. So the actual name of the brother did not show on the application."

"I hate insurance policies," said Plate.

"At the time, records show Sally's husband attempted to claim the money, producing death certificates for the parents and saying the only sibling was lost in Vietnam. He gave the brother's name as he knew it. But the husband couldn't prove the brother was dead and it hadn't been seven years. No further claim was ever made."

"So Ted Monroe did not come back after seven years to try to get the money?"

"No. He did keep in contact for a couple of years. His last address the insurance company had was in Alaska. At the end of the seven-year period, they sent a letter and never received a response. They did locate a man they thought was her brother, but he denied being related to her," said Daphne.

"And the situation with Officer Fondrem?" Plate asked.

"The only explanation is that this beneficiary did not want to be found. The company should have been easily able to track him down but they could not."

"Don't beneficiaries have to put their birthday or Social Security number or something on the application?"

"No. Proof of identification is usually required upon claiming the death benefit. The legal relationship between policyholder and death beneficiary has to be proved then. Like you would have to prove you're my husband and that your name is Sinclair Peter Plate to collect a benefit from my policy if I died. Beneficiaries are changed so often. Most policyholders don't know their beneficiary's Social Security number and sometimes they don't even know birthdates. And you don't even have to notify somebody if you make them a beneficiary of a life insurance policy. Some clients don't want the beneficiaries to know."

"I see," said Plate, with a flat voice.

"Both Sally Monroe's brother and Officer Fondrem's fiancé cut paper ties to the policyholders, making his identity and relationship to each ambiguous. And they had the same name, as far as we can tell."

"Why would Kay Fondrem not list the full name of her beneficiary?" Plate asked.

"Maybe because she didn't know it. They weren't married yet. He seems to have dropped it legally somewhere along the line. He never told her his full name."

"You are right that she would not have asked him if she did not want him to know she was designating him," Plate reflected.

"And she was planning to change the beneficiary later if the marriage did not come off," Daphne concluded.

"I presume as her fiancé, the lack of a middle or first name would not be a hindrance to collecting?" Plate asked.

"The newspaper clipping about the engagement would have

sufficed as identification. He could have collected. People don't skip collecting life insurance proceeds unless there is a good reason."

Plate had no reply to that statement.

"This relationship with this woman police officer happened in 1973. It was in the few months before her death," Daphne said.

"The fact that he never claimed the insurance money means he was dead, too," said Plate stubbornly.

"No, it does not. You are letting your emotions cloud your thinking. Sally Monroe's brother was missing in Vietnam in 1972. Suppose he came back, finds his sister murdered, and decides to lay low. He wasn't interested in her life insurance money. He wanted to find her killer. He wanted to remain in the shadows. He grew a beard and long hair. He started keeping company with a police officer who worked for the department that investigated the murder."

"Fondrem worked near that department, not for it," Plate reminded her. "He would have had to follow her to East Texas."

"Don't quibble. Close, then. And it would not be hard to find and follow her. They became engaged and she made him her life insurance beneficiary. She probably did not even inform him when she did it. It might have just been routine paperwork as far as she was concerned. There is an engagement photo in the paper. Remember, he looks like a hippie at that point."

"Because he does not want to be known as Sally Monroe's brother? He fears this will stop Fondrem from confiding in him?"

"Right. Then she's killed in the car wreck. The insurance company attempted to deliver the policy proceeds but her fiancé drops under the radar. Total between the two wasn't much anyway. Just $15,000."

The annoyance that Daphne would consider $15,000 not very much money penetrated the dismay and denial Plate was feeling about the other information she was giving.

He shook his head in frustration.

"The hippie fiancé resurfaces cleanshaven?"

"Right," said Daphne.

"It's a common name. You said the ties to the man and Sally

Monroe were ambiguous. This information doesn't mean it's the same man," Plate insisted.

"I asked Darica to dig up any news stories concerning this female police officer. This is what she and her pals came up with. And only part of his name was common."

Daphne showed him the engagement clipping copy, complete with a small black and white photograph of the happy couple. It was a professional picture, degraded only slightly by being converted into dots for newsprint.

"It might be him," Plate admitted reluctantly. "It could be Klaus Lewegz. Or Zopev himself."

"Now that's just plain being in denial," Daphne analyzed.

"Humor my denial a little longer. We still cannot be sure that this is the same person. We can't be sure that just because Kay Fondrem was engaged to a former soldier, Vietnam vet, that it was the same soldier who was the brother of Sally Monroe. There's probably dozens, even hundreds of soldiers that served in Vietnam with this name. I admit the clipping resembles him. But we cannot be sure. I have still not dug through enough files to find out what Sally Monroe's maiden name was or if her brother was really killed in Vietnam."

"Isn't there a data bank kept by the government that would clear all this up? Military records. Federal tax information. Not to mention Social Security records and birth certificates kept by counties."

"Yes, of course there is."

"Do you have access to it?" Daphne asked.

"No, of course not. The chief doesn't even have access to that. And writing to a county get a birth certificate will take weeks."

"But you think the answer could lie there?"

"Yes. I already have requested information. It's coming. They're slow. What else can I do? I don't have time to drive to the Panhandle. Even then, it would take several days. I'm not going to make accusations based only upon this information you and your sister uncovered."

"What if there's another killing? Think about that. It could happen. Before you get your information from these slow moving government entities. How would you feel?" Daphne asked.

Plate was silent for a long time.

"I knew you would get around to that eventually. I have figured out your strategy. By the time you are finished manipulating the conversation, your prey is exhausted and confused. No wonder you're such a successful saleswoman," Plate finally said.

Daphne was quiet until he was ready to speak again.

"What would you suggest I do?" he asked.

"Find out for sure immediately. You might be right. You might not have to confront him at all if you are," said Daphne.

"If he ever knows I even suspect-"

"We might can get the information we need much faster."

"How can we get access?"

"I know just the person to help us. I called and left a message for him earlier. He called me back while you were in the shower and offered his assistance."

"A computer criminal? Is one of your insurance clients a computer criminal?"

"Certainly not!"

It was a clear and silent night. A car audibly pulled into her driveway. Plate opened the front door. A man got out of a taxi. It left and the man came forward.

"He's here right now," Daphne called to Plate. "Let him in while I get the computer started. If it makes you feel better don't tell him who we suspect, just tell him everything you have figured out."

"Thank you for coming," Plate said to their late night visitor. "Right this way."

Daphne looked up from the computer and blinked.

"Welcome to my home, Mr. Shiameto," said Daphne.

"It is my honor," said the Japanese agent. He pointed to Daphne's Franklin Ace. "This computer I hack with?"

Chapter 53

The area was under a severe thunderstorm warning. The clear night would soon give way to the chaos of spring.

The Japanese agent was concerned about his flight.

Still he took his time. He understood he was there to confirm an unpopular result.

Plate explained their theory of how Officer Willhouse died. Shiameto agreed that it made sense. This theory explained many otherwise inexplicable actions on the part of a number of people.

Plate feared Daphne's tentative identification of the killer explained everything else.

He was still trying to keep an open mind.

The winds had begun to exude a low moaning sound. A storm was on its way. This put even more of a sense of quiet urgency on the shoulders of the three people hovering around the small computer.

If they lost electrical power, all their efforts would be halted.

"So we know that Yolanda's death had nothing to do with Zopev except that somehow Cardioxa found out all the details that had been kept back about Zopev's modus operandi."

"So we are looking for the person who gave him such clues?"

"Yes that's right, Mr. Shiameto," said Daphne.

"You find nothing from pictures? Movies?"

"No, the only concrete information the pictures revealed was that an Italian journalist, called Fabrizio, was a groomsman both times. He's an old flame of the princess. And a thug sent by her jilted Egyptian fiancé was a groomsman first time, but did not come back. We do not suspect either of them as being the killer," said Plate.

Plate did not name the person he and Daphne suspected.

"Always start with basics. File on first killing available?"

"Not on a computer yet. But I have a copy. It was in a small town and their police department has not modernized yet. In fact, back in 1972 everything was still being handwritten. They didn't have a typist in their budget."

"I see." The Japanese policeman looked over the file on the

death of Sally Monroe for a few moments. His opinion of the skill of American typists was not improved.

"Much basic identification is missing here." He pointed out what he was talking about to Plate and Daphne. "Women especially are incompletely identified. Basic information on first murder victim does not indicate her maiden name or name of her brother."

"He has a point," said Daphne.

"Tampered with?" Mr. Shiameto asked.

"Possibly. We don't know. Many previous cases I've researched, I've had to scratch to find feminine first names," Plate said. "Until just a decade ago most women were referred to as Mrs. John Doe or just Mrs. Doe or John Doe's wife. Many clerks didn't take into account those nomenclatures could refer to more than one person. John Doe could have more than one wife."

"Mrs. Doe could be his mother," contributed Daphne.

"Right. Anyway, you see on the notation her parents were dead and her brother was lost in Vietnam. Nobody followed up on them because they weren't there. So no notation was made of their names."

"How soldier lost? Killed? Missing?"

"Missing usually meant killed."

"But not always," said Daphne.

"I have tried to find out. I have tried looking for any Sally born in that year that would have a twin brother. I looked at military records. A lot of them are still handwritten or typed. I've tried to find Sally Monroe's birth certificate. But not knowing her maiden name- we had been looking for records of her husband working as a police officer," said Plate.

"But my sister's research revealed he was a law school graduate. The only way she knew was that someone had the foresight to put a graduation announcement card in the file," said Daphne.

"I've contacted the law school but they don't have their own files on computer. I'm waiting on mailed information about a Ted Monroe they graduated in 1970," said Plate.

"There is a name we should search for. You know if that was her maiden name, that cinches it," said Daphne.

"Yes, I know. But I don't have any authority," said Plate. "All I can do is contact federal officials and request that they do some searching for me. They tend to be busy with their own cases. Officially, there is no case in Willhouse's death. Pauliza is expected to be no billed."

"You have line connection with this computer?"

Bending over her shoulder, Plate demonstrated Daphne's setup and Mr. Shiameto nodded approval.

"Crude. Nevertheless, it will work. Please to let me at it. My plane leaves soon. I like to get to the airport at least 15 minutes before departure."

Daphne stood up and let him sit down.

The Japanese man sat rigidly at the computer, immobile except for his fingers, which moved nimbly over the keyboard so quickly they became a blur. The gray screen with the green letters started popping rapidly, accompanied by the typewriter keyboard sound built into the system.

The result was now without question

After the computer was silent again, the three people sat at Daphne's dinette table and sipped Coca-Cola.

Plate was staring at the files spread out before him. He needed a little time before he could fully take in just what the Asian man had uncovered.

"Solid proof of who Sally Monroe's brother is?"

"Yes, that does prove it."

"I am sorry."

A taxi arrived to take Mr. Shiameto to catch his flight back to Japan. Plate and Daphne profusely thanked him again for his help. He expressed regret that he could not remain to act upon the information he had uncovered.

"I hate that you did not get what you came for," Plate said.

"As Cardioxa will be prosecuted here, we in Japan must await our turn. Get him good or we will extradite him if there is a quit-acquittal."

"Don't worry. We will catch him. And if by some infernal

technicality he walks, I will put him on the plane to Japan myself."

"You must watch out for others who may have figured out what you have figured out," was Shiameto's parting advice. "Such person would be in danger."

Plate suddenly had a good idea of who that might be.

"I want to write down exactly what we think happened before I present this to the chief." Plate expressed this desire to Daphne when they were alone again.

"I can type it into the computer. Just dictate to me."

"Feel free to help me fill any gaps or correct me if you think I'm wrong."

After about 30 minutes, Plate and Daphne had a short, succinct narrative of how they now believed Timothy Willhouse died.

Plate's numeric pager beeped. He debated whether to respond.

Time had run out, he feared. There was going to be another murder. *I wonder if there is a type of pager where people can leave messages, not just their phone numbers,* he thought.

The pager went off again. The number was different this time.

He called the chief from Daphne's office phone.

His worst fears were confirmed.

"Plate," said the chief. "Alice Willhouse called me on my car phone. It didn't go through like it should to my house phone but it did alert me. She was able to leave a message requesting me to meet her at the office. She said she tried to get you at your place but you were not there. She said she tried to page you."

"You told me not to respond to her any longer, remember?"

Brecken did not reply. Plate speculated whether his superior had indeed forgotten. And wondered if Brecken had just been a little jealous that Alice Willhouse had reached out to him, instead of her late husband's chief.

"I have some very bad news, Chief. We think we know what happened to Willhouse- "

Time was pressing but without Brecken's understanding and help, they would be fighting a losing battle.

With the chief listening over the phone, Plate read aloud the synopsis he and Daphne had prepared just a few minutes prior.

*"Jordan surreptitiously placed the Pauliza house under surveillance. He observed they left lights on downstairs all the time. Jordan also has noticed an optical illusion. The lights give the impression of flames through shear curtains and dense rain. From experience, Jordan knows a lighted grill located under a covered area can produce excessive smoke. Jordan and Tim have a prearranged fishing date. They meet and proceed in separate vehicles. Shortly before, Jordan has the scene set. It is raining and foggy. Jordan has lit the grill on the patio behind the Pauliza home, knowing it would soon start to smoke. Meeting in their cars, Jordan instructs Willhouse to follow him. Jordan drives by the Pauliza house. Stops. Willhouse stops behind him. Jordan exits his car, hails Tim, points to the house and says the Pauliza house is on fire. Remember Jordan supposedly has a bad ankle so it is up to Willhouse to alert the residents. Probably he even tells Tim that this is the Pauliza house. They've been under secret surveillance since the trial. And he knows they're asleep in the bedroom off the balcony. He timed it perfectly. The murderer only had to sustain this illusion of fire for a few minutes. People inside, trapped, upstairs, but the downstairs is flaming, cannot get in or out that way. Here was Willhouse's opportunity to redeem himself for his indecisive action 9 years ago and poor judgment 14 years ago. Tim is not going to stop and analyze the situation. He is going to act. He is going to jump up on that balcony and break in."*

Brecken listened to Plate with admirable patience. Plate could hear his breathing grow heavier over the phone.

Brecken was unaccepting until Plate pointed out one more piece of the puzzle.

"I always thought Jordan was faking his weak ankle. But Sally Monroe's brother broke his ankle in Vietnam. And remember, we found footprints indicating an odd stance at the Cardioxa house."

"Now you are saying Jordan killed Yolanda Cardioxa?"

"No. But suppose he was there. Watching to make sure it all came off. Or just planted the evidence."

"That's comprehensive and very imaginative. You're telling me

Jordan wanted to kill Tim?"

"Salray Eddy Jordan was Sally Edwina Jordan Monroe's twin brother. We got a hold of her birth certificate and his. Jordan was also involved with Kay Fondrem at the time of her death. He is pursuing a vendetta against the people he considers responsible for the murder of his sister."

"My God! Why didn't you tell me that first?" Brecken gasped.

"It's so hard for me to believe. But we have proof from the computers," said Plate.

"Never mind that right now. Alice couldn't get you or me. And Skaar is still with the actress."

"So you think Alice Willhouse contacted Jordan?"

"She's been using us all as therapists. Calling whenever she feels overwhelmed and I've been trying to encourage her to go to a real counselor. I stop letting her calls be put directly through. I've been giving her a little time before calling her back. Right now, I cannot get an answer at her home. The telephone operator says the phone's off the hook. County is tied up with a major wreck on Loop 610. And as usual, there are emergencies all over the city of Houston and throughout the county. I'm not sure this is one."

"It is. But I think I know where Jordan may be. Let me go after him and you go check on Alice. Just send backup when you can verify this is an emergency."

Chapter 54

The storm had grown worse. Warnings were posted advising people to stay home, stay off the roads as much as possible, stay off area lakes, and bring their boats in from the bay.

"Do you know exactly where Jordan's boat is?" Daphne asked Plate.

"I do. After I realized the address Kate gave me to give the two visiting policewomen was his apartment address, I realized he must've moved out and was living on that boat. You know there's a rule against unmarried officers living with a partner of the opposite sex."

"Actually, I did not know that."

"Jordan knew that I need to know exactly where my men live. He did talk about living on the boat but never officially notified me. Maybe because Willhouse was supposed to have gone on the boat with him the day he was killed, I made the subconscious connection. But I went out there and I found exactly where the boat is docked. I saw signs he is living there. Jordan never knew I did that. I didn't even tell the chief."

"Don't forget somebody else had to have shot Kate Traval. Tell me exactly where you are going."

Plate told her.

"I know that marina," she said. "I went out there to sell insurance one time. To a couple who lived on a boat. I thought they were crazy."

"I'm not going to wait for Brecken," said Plate.

And he left.

At Alice Willhouse's home, Brecken found her mother, who had come in from Wisconsin to be with her daughter, still awake, in a houserobe, having coffee.

"I assumed the storm had affected our phone. We had been getting so many calls after Timothy's death, it was almost a relief that it had stopped ringing," the woman told Brecken.

"It's off the hook, according to the operator."

"Oh, my goodness! Must be the extension in the hall."

"Do you know where your daughter is?" Brecken asked.

"She was having an anxiety attack. They are an almost daily occurrence since Tim died."

"Understandable," said the chief encouragingly.

"I know she wanted to see you. Or one of the other policeman," the elderly woman said. "I assume she'd gotten hold of one. A policeman came by for her. It was a little strange. I did hear her ask him something about a sailboat. I can see where a sail might calm her down. I can't think that they would be going sailing at this time of the night in this type of storm. It was strange, as I said. That is why I have been unable to sleep."

Brecken found an extension phone in the hallway. The receiver was in a position that indicated it had obviously been deliberately placed off the hook.

The chief went to his car and relayed all this information to Plate over the police radio.

Plate was already crossing into Galveston city limits. The traffic diminished the farther south he went. Soon Plate was on the freeway just short of the marina exit.

As the cars zoomed alongside him at illegal speeds of 80 and 90, Plate whirled off the freeway on to the middle ground dividing the highway and ran the car to the edge of what looked like a sheer drop down between the east and westbound bridges over the most treacherous storm-tossed waters, which flowed unimpeded under the highway.

He would have had to spend another 15 minutes maneuvering through Galveston city streets.

This was a shortcut.

The 80 degree drop down to the seawall, somewhat resembling a drop on a monster roller coaster, was designed for four wheel drive dare devils on dry days, not four-door sedan-style police cars in soaking rain.

Plate plummeted towards the Gulf, slipping and sliding. The

car spun completely around at the bottom but did not roll over. As he collected his brain and stomach, he sped across the sand to the marina. As he exited the car, he heard screaming on the dock.

He pulled his gun and dashed as fast as he could through the mud and rain. He reached the pier near the front of the marina. Jordan's boat was docked in a prize slip just past the front of the pier, on the side open to the channel leading to the bay. Alice Willhouse was halfway on the boat, fighting and screaming against the current and her captor.

Plate pointed his gun.

"Let her go, Eddy."

"Is that one of your orders, Lieutenant?" Jordan pulled Alice completely onto the boat.

"She can do you no more harm. Whatever she knows, it doesn't matter. We know everything."

"Everything? You think you're a genius. But you're not that smart. You don't know half of what I've accomplished."

"Maybe not. But I do know you used Eduardo Pauliza to kill Timothy Willhouse."

"Ha! Used is a tame word. I manipulated them. They were puppets. One paranoiac, one guilt-ridden. They were puppets on a string. I was their master puppeteer."

"Let Alice Willhouse go and you can tell me everything you did to avenge the death of your sister."

Eddy Jordan let his guard down just long enough for Alice Willhouse to get in a slightly better position for a sharpshooter to take him down without hitting her.

But no sharpshooters had arrived.

"You know about Sally? I thought I had erased everything that could track me back to her. Yes, the death of Willhouse was my supreme accomplishment. It was really an excellent use of the two personalities. I knew Pauliza, awakened and terrified in the middle of his sleep, would shoot first and ask questions later."

Alice Willhouse whimpered. But her spine stiffened as she heard how her husband died.

Jordan laughed. "I knew Willhouse would be anxious to prove himself brave even after all these years. So when I found out he was going on vacation, I put everything in gear. I faked a sprained ankle to get the day off. I had even gone over the diagram of the floor plan of that specific house with him not too long ago under the pretext that I would soon be looking to buy a home and I wanted his opinion. When we encountered the 'fire', all I had to do was remind him that was the same floor plan as the house I was interested in. That was where the Paulizas lived. He knew they worked nights and were asleep in that house during the day. The irony of him being there to rescue them was not lost on him. That was the last thing he said to me before he took off running to the balcony."

Alice had been silent during this long narrative. Jordan ceased talking. She started to cry.

"Let her go, Jordan. It is all over."

"Yes." He looked down at the choppy waters. "Yes, I guess you are right. I have done what I intended. I have not anything against Mrs. Willhouse. If I had been a different kind of person I would have killed her and let Willhouse suffer what I did. But he hardly knew her. Just married her on a whim. Like I was going to do that woman cop. But she had a car wreck, so- " He shrugged. "Grabbing a hostage like this, I guess was instinct, just the survival instinct, so strong." He shook his head. "Even when you don't want to."

"Do exactly as I say, first drop the gun, and then let of Mrs. Willhouse-"

"Don't tell me how to do it, Plate. I got that bastard serial killer off the streets. That ought to be worth something."

"Who shot Kate Traval? Where's Zopev, Jordan?"

Jordan laughed and indicated the Gulf of Mexico. Nothing but a long mooring line was tethering the boat to the dock, keeping it from the ocean.

"Where I dumped him the same day he was acquitted. Probably half way to Florida now, what the sharks left of him. There's nothing like a night sail to help smooth over your problems. There's been so much damn rain, I haven't been able to sail nearly as much as

I've needed to. Sailing is the only thing that has given me any peace these last 11 years." Jordan held Alice with only one arm now, picking at a rope on the boat deck with his free hand.

"So who shot Kate Traval? Her caring for you held no peace?"

"No. It was nice. But not enough. True love is overrated as the cure for a broken life. Something would've got her, just like Kay." He looked sober now. Almost morose. "I killed her. Oh, I didn't do the shooting, you know that. But I had a killer to do my bidding. That lowlife Cardioxa. He was my slave from the day he killed his wife."

"Why?"

"Kate read that blasted newspaper article, saw the old picture of Sally and I'll be damned if she didn't recognize me. So much older and fatter, but she saw the resemblance between Sally and me. I don't know how."

"You blackmailed Cardioxa into killing Kate? Tell me. You want Emilio Cardioxa brought to justice? We know he killed his wife but the case is not strong."

"You'll find I photographed that event. I'm an enterprising photographer. Had to assume an awkward position at the time, but I got great shots. The pictures are back at the apartment hidden in a picture album. Not on the boat. So don't worry."

Plate relaxed a little.

"That's my only request. Find the lowlife and nail him. I know I'm not much better. At least, I was after some justice. Zopev was sick. But Cardioxa's motive was pure greed."

"We will get him. Especially if you don't harm Alice."

"I really didn't want to harm Kate. But she would've stopped me getting Cardioxa. I would've accomplished nothing. He enjoyed killing too much the first time to stop at one victim. He would've killed again. So might as well get it over with."

"Tell me about Kay. Officer Fondrem."

"That was a long time ago. What about her?"

"Just for the record." Now that he had confirmed who shot Kate, Plate was just trying to keep Jordan talking about any subject.

The rope holding the boat was coming untied. The vessel

would inevitably become free of the dock area. Plate was trying to calculate how much more time he had, then how far he was going to have to swim if help did not arrive soon.

"I was trying to get some information about Zopev's first victim. I found a single policewoman originally from the town right next to where Sally had lived and died. I was not a cop then. I thought they were all one big happy family and I could get information about the way Sally's death was handled from any cop working nearby."

"You knew her earlier. From the Panhandle area?"

"It was ironic and my first stroke of luck that she got a job right next to the town where Zopev had attacked Sarah Pauliza."

"Officer Fondrem knew you were looking for your sister's killer?"

"Naw, she thought I was a journalist looking for a story. I did do some freelancing after Nam. Kay was looking for a husband. I was still rather nice looking back then. She was quite straight-laced. Only way I could get really close to her was to propose. She was a lady. Very private and wanted to keep our relationship quiet until she was sure I wasn't just after her as a source for stories. We had not known each other very long. Who knows what the outcome might have been? I might have married her."

"So how did you find out about Tim's actions in the Pauliza case?"

"Before she died, she told me about Willhouse and the Pauliza case. It was pure chance. She had made the connection from my sister's death to the Pauliza case. But she had said nothing. Neither were her cases. A woman cop, she had to be careful. It was not her place, she told me, to judge Willhouse. She feared I'd write a news story about it so she kept her information sparse. I was still prying it out of her when she was killed. It was so ironic that Tim was the first cop on the scene of Kay's wreck," said Jordan.

"You blamed him for failing to save her from the fire?"

"He did not try. All I could do was agitate Willhouse over not rescuing her, anonymously of course. It was small consolation if, as I suspect, his carelessness cost Sally her life."

"Why didn't Tim ever recognize you?" Plate asked.

"He and Kay were serving in adjacent towns but they didn't know each other. Only way he would've recognized me is if he had seen my picture in the paper from the engagement announcement. After Kay died, I cut my hair short and shaved my beard."

"You joined the police then?"

The rope slithered off the dock like a snake and its end vanished into the dark water. The boat was slipping farther away and both men now had to shout to be heard.

"I realized to ever find anything out about Sally, I would actually have to become a cop. So that's what I did. It was easy. You know the time. Desperate for recruits. I played it straight for a while. Then Sally's husband killed himself. That was worse than my parents dying. They were old, in poor health to begin with. Ted Monroe was still young, with a bright future in the law. He had been depressed ever since her murder. He'd taken his child and moved in with his parents. Some psychiatrist quack said that was unhealthy and tried to take the kid away. He failed but he got the child diagnosed as some kind of crazy. Said the child would never speak because he saw his mother murdered. Even though he was just a baby. It was too much for Ted. He took his life. And to this day the boy never has spoke, never smiles, doesn't know you're there. Couple of years ago they said he has something called autism. Zopev, and those that let him slip by, did all that. Destroyed my entire family."

Plate started edging forward. The boat was almost free of the pier. Jordan had not started the engine yet. Plate surmised Jordan was a good enough sailor and the waves were high enough that the muscular policeman would be able to manipulate the boat once he got it free of the wooden structures around it.

"And about-"

"You can figure the rest of it out!" Jordan yelled. A wave washed towards the marina and the boat scraped the last few feet of the dock. He pulled a string and the outboard motor started.

Jordan flung Alice aside. She landed halfway on the pier with a thump that sounded above the wind. Her feet were caught on the rail of the boat as it began to move faster but she had the presence of mind to grab a post, raise her feet, and kick the boat. It angled into a wave.

With a cry, she crawled onto the dock.

"Stay low," Plate cautioned her, trotting forward a little.

Jordan waved the gun a little, then smiled when Plate stopped.

"I'm not going to shoot her in the back as she slinks away," Jordan yelled. "What kind of a person do you think I am?"

Never taking the gun off Plate until he was out of range, Jordan maneuvered the boat farther and farther out, ignoring Plate's protests. The current snatched the small craft and took it into the storm. It vanished so fast it was hard to believe it had ever been there.

Plate was looking at a small maintenance dinghy with a 12-horsepower outboard motor tied at the far end of the dock.

"Peter! Don't you dare go after him!" Daphne yelled as she ran towards the edge of the dock.

She had followed, just now getting to the scene, having gotten lost briefly because she could not keep up with Plate. But she finally remembered the way her client had directed her several years ago.

She ran down the dock towards the sound of voices and got there just as Alice crawled onto the pier.

Alice Willhouse picked herself up and went towards Daphne instead of towards Plate, who was as far out as the pier would allow.

His gun drawn and aimed still.

At the empty water. At the darkness.

"Peter! Get back here! To go after him in that tiny boat would be suicide!" yelled Daphne.

She embraced the wet trembling woman.

Thunder flashed, the rain came down in heavy sheets, and the Gulf roared.

And for once, Plate listened to Daphne because she was right.

Chapter 55

Princess Joanna was being deported Friday morning for having lied on her temporary visa application.

"I had no idea she was only 17 years old," Stark Wynter had claimed when immigration authorities pointed out to him that her legal right to work in the United States was fraudulent. "She swore she was 23. She looked 23!"

There were several international personages shocked by this fact as well, not to mention Joanna's fans in Italy where she had starred in TV shows and minor movies for the past two years.

There was a tiny question about her claim to royal blood.

Her parents, facing possible charges in Italy, protested that she was extremely advanced for her age and so talented that the real crime would have been to have stifled her by keeping her in school until she reached the age of majority.

United States immigration authorities decided it was the simple and easy way out to just send her back, rather than try to prosecute her for the papers that falsified her age.

Due to her familiarity with Grant Skaar, he was chosen to take her to the airport along with a CPS agent, who had taken Elizabeth Lopez's place at the Wynter compound. As Skaar's rank was still only patrolman, Plate had to go along to supervise.

As he drove to the Wynter compound, Plate was thinking about what must have gone through Willhouse's mind as he climbed to the Pauliza balcony. Prestige, recognition, an award for valor. Redemption for a questionable performance 14 years ago and laziness that led to sloppiness that had possibly cost lives.

He turned the car onto the Wynter driveway and pulled up to the front door. It still felt odd to Plate going in the front door instead of to the back as the Yorks had designated.

Plate greeted Skaar, who wanted more details, now that he was being relieved of the princess.

"Why did Jordan go back and steal the barbecue pit? Would not it have been better to have left it there, and not draw attention to it by having it disappear?" Skaar asked as they waited for her. Her luggage had gone on before her but she was still gathering mementos. The CPS officer was helping her organize her carry-on.

The men waited in the foyer.

"That's a question. Perhaps he was afraid he had left prints on it. But we would have never thought of dusting that. Plus, Eduardo and Sarah are very meticulous. And since it's not yet summer, Jordan might have figured it was more dangerous to call attention to the fact that it had been used out of season, rather than just swiped. Barbecue grills are swiped all the time around here."

"You know, Lieutenant, I think waiting for the chance for revenge is what kept Jordan sane all these years. Then his long planned vengeance accomplished, he slowly started to crumble."

"You could be right."

"So what will happen to Pauliza?"

"Nothing. He was innocent. He sincerely thought he killed Willhouse in self-defense."

"Why he was yelling policeman when he came out of his front door? Do we have an explanation for that?"

"A simple one. Because he needed a policeman. He thought he had been attacked."

"I see."

"Two things led us astray immediately. The fake package Jordan left the same time he tampered with the grill. That was just thrown in for confusion."

"To make us think it was connected with the local wave of fake deliveries. And the second?"

"Remember Elisabeth Morgan probably really couldn't clearly hear what Pauliza was saying. It was raining. It was across the street. She was inside her home, playing with her puppets, listening to music. She certainly couldn't exactly understand his intonation. The idea that he was celebrating having killed a policeman just somehow fabricated itself in thin air and fell down on us like a blinding blanket."

Joanna and her escort were ready to go now. The foursome

made their way downstairs and into the sunlight. Skaar helped the princess into the car.

"If I be single and you be single I take you with me back to Italy." She kissed him on the cheek when they took custody of her for the ride.

With Officer Plate, she merely shook hands.

"You be good boss to my favorite officer," she said pertly.

Princess Joanna had learned enough English in her short stay in Sand Waves to chat amiably as she rode with the police officers who had been charged with protecting her while she was in their jurisdiction.

The CPS agent was unexpectedly relieved by an INS agent at the next stop. They had a scheduled stop to pick up Fabrizio who was being deported as well. There was a short turf tussle. The INS agent won. The CPS agent retreated to her office to prepare her complaint.

At a small hotel near the airport, Fabrizio, the dark skinned groomsman, who had first thrown out the student in the employee of the Arab prince, then later stood by Joanna when the shooting started, smiled happily when she greeted him.

"My wimp," she said proudly.

While she may have not been sure of all of the implications of the word, he had no idea what she was saying.

They were going back to Italy together. More red tape had been cut to allow the Italian journalist to get back into his own country without any repercussions of having slipped into Texas illegally.

On the way she chattered to him in Italian and despite not understanding most of it, the INS agent and the police officers accompanying them were certain she said 'cathedral' and 'wedding' numerous times.

Her intended was agreeing with everything she said.

They nestled in the backseat the rest of the way to the airport. The INS agent scrunched over to one side. Fortunately he was slender.

Fabrizio's dreams of working in American journalism and Joanna's dreams of starring in a major American movie were shattered.

They showed no sign of disappointment.

Arriving at the airport arm-in-arm, waving to her fans and posing for press photos, they appeared more the epitome of 1980s celebrities than illegal immigrants. Striding down the terminal, smiling radiantly, they proclaimed Texas a wonderful land of adventure.

"You know," Plate said to Skaar. "They can search the water for Jordan's body without me tomorrow. I think I did my share of work on this case."

Plate and Skaar were alone on the drive back to Sand Waves. The INS agent was dropped at the hotel where his car had been left.

"You've got a good point, Lieutenant," Skaar agreed.

"I am declaring myself officially on a vacation day."

"You've worked pretty hard these past few weeks. Must've taken a lot of thinking to figure it all out."

"You can say that again. Let's go get something to eat. And some aspirin. I've got a headache."

"My mother warned me about these things," said Grant, smiling.

"What?"

"All that thinking. Does it every time. Causes headaches."

"Was that a joke, Grant? A joke from you?"

"Yes, sir. I do believe it was."

"My headache's coming from the fact that my marriage is apparently in some type of legal limbo."

"I think your marriage will come off. The movie, maybe not. Do you think that movie will ever get finished?" Skaar asked Plate

"If it is, I'm not going to have anything to do with it. My movie career is over."

"How about a little wager on that, Lieutenant? The movie studio is still in the process of being built. One movie down the drain does not a studio financially ruin."

"Gambling is illegal, Sergeant."

"Sergeant?"

"Well, you have to pass the test."

"What test?" Skaar asked.

"I will find one." Plate smiled.

"I hope this means a raise in pay."

"I wouldn't count on that. Anyway, you can enjoy your new title on the way to Houston, then Galveston."

"I haven't been home in days. What am I going to be doing?"

"We located the motel that Jordan and Kate used on the island. And the one that Cardioxa and Elizabeth used in Houston. Plus, an old phone booth that calls from Jordan to various persons were traced to. The county is sending forensics and I want you to check them all also."

"Gee, thanks."

"You're welcome, Sergeant Skaar."

"Jordan and Kate met at motels? Why motels? Why not his boat?" Skaar asked.

"He didn't want her seen there. The affair was unethical. And I think, at first, they were concerned about her ex-husband finding them."

"Unethical? Says who? By what authority? But, anyway, she had a house. Why didn't they meet there?"

"It was for sale. And she wanted it pristine for the showings."

"So she moved out of her house into Jordan's apartment and he moved onto the boat."

"That's right."

"Okay. I understand now."

"You know, Cardioxa also had a boat. Everyone forgot that. So locate it first and check it out. Make that your priority. May be some evidence there. Even another crime scene. He and Elizabeth thought their romance could come out in the open once Zopev was convicted for Yolanda's murder. But they are on the run now. Last seen in Nevada but they slipped the net."

"And it was because Jordan was chosen to try to trap Cardioxa, who had fallen in love with Elizabeth and now wanted to kill Yolanda, that Jordan was able to make it all so intricate. He was in a position to instruct Cardioxa just how to kill Yolanda and make it look like it was Zopev," said Skaar.

"Yes," Plate confirmed.

"Man! If only we'd known Jordan was so brilliant we might could have put him to good use."

"You're saying that facetiously. But I do feel like maybe if we had gotten to know him a little bit better... Maybe- I don't know."

"Obviously he came here- when this job was open- Jordan wanted it so he could kill Tim."

"Possibly. I don't know that at first he had it all worked out just exactly what he was going to do. You know, he might have just been thinking he would ruin Tim's career. By letting it all become known. The reprimand concerning Officer Fondrem's death and the mishandling of the evidence in the Pauliza case."

"So you don't think he had it all planned out that clearly from the beginning?"

"Too much happened he could not have known about in advance. Too much he could not have predicted."

"So it just came together for him in the wrong way? He must've thought it was fate, or that he was incredibly lucky."

"His luck ran out when he set Pauliza and Tim up against each other."

"You don't think he was sure Pauliza would kill Tim?"

"He was 95 percent sure. If it gone the other way it would have been just as bad for Tim. On the surface, Tim had a motive. He would probably have been convicted of murder. Certainly would have lost his job."

"Did the job mean that much to him?"

"I think it did. Just because he wasn't the best at it didn't mean he didn't care. He was still in there trying. He died trying to help somebody, thinking that's what he was doing, thinking he was helping somebody who he was not sure deserved help. That's what we do. That's what Jordan did in the beginning of his career."

"You think that all of this might have been prevented. Don't you, Lieutenant?"

"Maybe. Maybe if Jordan hadn't felt alone in the world."

"He had Kate."

"Yes. But she came along at the end. And just one person, no matter how you love them, is not enough always. If she had come along earlier. Or, let's say, the girlfriend, the police officer, had not been killed in the wreck. Or maybe if he had just had friends."

"Not to be impertinent, but I disagree, Lieutenant."

"Do you? Tell me what you think," said Plate.

"I think that there has to be a foundation of right and wrong based on something more than relationships with other human beings."

Plate had never before regarded Skaar in any other way than as a fellow officer. A younger officer with less experience. Yet reliable and dependable with a lot of common sense.

Now he perceived Skaar had a depth that Jordan, and if he were honest about it- also Willhouse- lacked.

"Are you religious, Grant?" he asked. Then he added, "forgive me if I'm prying into your personal business. I have no right to."

"No problem. I don't mind admitting being religious. My wife and I are both Catholics. We attend church at least once a week."

"Indeed? I don't know how you find time to go with this job."

"My church has a Mass every day, several times a day on weekends. I can always find a time, no matter my schedule. Do you and- ah- is she, or is she not Mrs. Plate yet?"

"We're not sure but we're not counting on it. And to answer your question, we're still working that out in our lives."

"Any time you would like to talk to me about it, Lieutenant, I'll be happy to talk to you about my faith."

Plate suddenly felt like he was the junior of the two men. He did not quite know what to say.

"I say that because I often thought about making that statement to Eddy. But I never did. I was sure he would reject it. If he had not, that might have been the one thing that could have made a difference."

"I may take you up on your offer. When things settle down."

There was a silence between them for a short time that was not uncomfortable but was necessary for them to each process the implications of what they had just said to each other.

And the possible consequences.

"Lieutenant, what do you think eventually happened to the barbecue grill?" Skaar finally asked before the silence got too long. He made his question in a respectful manner that reestablished Plate as the superior beyond doubt.

"I imagine Jordan took it off on the boat and dropped it overboard same as he did with Zopev."

"And do we know why he went after Alice Willhouse?"

"Because she must've said or done something that indicated she was a danger to him. Opposite of why he didn't go after Elizabeth Lopez. Something had to have indicated she was not a danger to him."

"That makes sense."

"Also I think he had gone off the deep end by the time the episode with Alice occurred."

"I could see that. One other thing, Lieutenant."

"Yes?"

"I was going to say that if you need a place to stay while things are sorted out about whether or not you're really married, Geralyn and I can make room. We have a two bedroom house."

"Thank you. I'll keep that offer in mind," said Plate with gratitude.

In the back of his mind, he had been expecting such an offer from Robert Brecken. It had not come. The Breckens did have children and their house probably was crowded.

Plate had never been there so he was not sure.

The chief had found room for two visiting officers for Willhouse's funeral.

But that was only for two nights.

It suddenly occurred to Plate that he did not know how long it would be before he and Daphne would be able to get legally married in a ceremony she would consider approving.

305

Chapter 56

"So the minister was a fraud?" Daphne asked.

"He was an actor," Plate said.

"And you're not going to arrest him?"

"Acting is not a crime. He claimed he had no idea we were supposed to really be getting married."

Plate and Daphne had already decided to have another ceremony later in the year and consider this wedding as fictional as the movie, except for being legal permission to live in the same house. But it looked like they did not even have that.

"Of course he's lying."

"English is his second language and he doesn't speak it too well. There's no way he's going to be punished."

"And we're not really married?" Daphne asked.

"Well, this is Texas-"

"Have we got a legal opinion on whether or not this wedding was valid?"

"No. The colony and studio lawyers can't agree. But the marriage certificate cannot be valid. However, Texas has common law. If we say we're married, we are."

"Yes, I know. So basically we may not actually be married but if either one of us wanted to split up, and the other one protested, we would have to get a divorce."

"That's about the size of it."

"I am not going to enter into a common-law marriage."

"Sometimes they happen without actually being entered into."

"We have to get really married," Daphne insisted.

"I agree. I was joking."

"We need a legal wedding without stress."

"The only way to get that is to elope," Plate said.

Daphne's silent reaction to that suggestion was chilling.

"My mother would kill me if we did that," Plate said after a few seconds, trying to dispel the cold hostility in the air.

"My father would beat her to it. He would be mad at me also."

"So elopement would be doubly fatal for me and would earn you a scolding," Plate said.

"That's about the size of it," said Daphne.

"I guess we can't elope. Do you have any different plans?"

"What do you think we should do?" She felt creeping despair.

"The first problem is- I don't have anywhere to go," Plate said.

"Can we get away with you living here?" Daphne asked.

"I have already been informed that would jeopardize my job."

"So if you were to live here, it would have to be a secret."

"That will never work," Plate said.

"You cannot find another apartment?" Daphne asked.

"There isn't anything anywhere near Sand Waves. There's long waiting lists on everything, even efficiency apartments. I guess I can be one of the homeless and live under the bridge."

"There's hotels," Daphne suggested.

"That's going to cost a fortune. And what about all my stuff on its way?" Plate asked.

"You can move the stuff in here and take what you need with you," said Daphne.

As they spoke, Plate's furniture began arriving. Daphne directed most of it to her garage but one piece was destined for her office. Daphne reacted with awe as the Pulaski replaced her old desk.

Her good humor returned.

"This is so rightfully mine. This is truly why I am marrying you. To get possession of my property. It will take its rightful place where it belongs. Now that I have possession, I can remain single."

The desk was breathtaking with a decorative frame across the back containing an etched mirror and carved wood spindles. The corners were topped off by glass finials. A scalloped frame, sloping from each side, contained etched opaque glass with shorter posts at the front. The desktop was leather inside a square of wood. Three drawers had apothecary décor with glass ball drawer pulls and a door opened with a brass handle. The back panel covered the entire desk bottom, allowing the desk to be placed anywhere in a room.

"You cannot keep the desk if you don't keep me. I will,

however, leave you the cat," Plate said.

"Don't be silly. You know you love Vandal. And I plan to keep you for all time. It just seems impossible to actually marry you. We may just have to correspond from a distance," Daphne said.

"As I said, I have a plan," Plate reiterated.

"For a place to live?" Daphne asked.

"I've been offered a place in the home of friends. Grant and his wife. I suppose I have no alternative but to accept."

"That solves one problem."

"Not for long. I'm sure there's an ethics rule somewhere that says lieutenants should not live with their subordinates."

"And about our wedding? You have a plan?" Daphne asked.

"You wanted a church," Plate said.

"Yes, very much. I've already looked into that. It's impossible. Most churches, if they don't require conversion to their specific denomination, require a long drawn out pre-marriage class. Some require both. All churches in the area not imposing such requirements, are booked for every Saturday for the next six months. And if we don't have it on a Saturday, no one will be able to get off work to come. The best we could do is an unemployed minister marrying us in a secular location. Even then, I can't find anybody not booked for 60 days. And I can't find a venue available for a year, unless we wed at my house or out in the park. I don't want to get married here. It's too small and I don't want a bunch of people messing around with my stuff. And I think I'd rather just go down to the courthouse to get married than try to have a hot outdoor ceremony in a park with mosquitoes and people in shorts walking their dogs going by."

"Don't despair. I think I have a solution. I don't think we have to settle for anything less than a church wedding."

"How can it be possible?" Daphne asked.

"I know a church that has dates available. And there are no requirements other than we are committed Christians and willing to commit to each other," said Plate.

"In this area?"

"Sort of. Not that far away. Let me tell you about it."

Chapter 57

Plate was spending as much time at Daphne's house as he could, without actually living there.

He and Daphne were enjoying the quiet evenings and weekends leading up to their wedding when he would move in for good. The location had been decided.

The date had only been reset twice. So far.

Conflicts had been minor this time. Routine cases for Plate. A few unexpected problems with clients for Daphne.

And they were making sure all their family could come.

The newspapers were still getting mileage out of the recent and past tragedies that had come to light as a result of their first two attempts at a wedding ceremony.

The Sunday paper had sent an investigative reporter to Neches for a feature story on Officer Kay Fondrem and how she had been in the first wave of modern-day policewomen in Texas.

"Why did the paperwork disguise that Officer Fondrem had been a woman? I thought police departments are trying to get women these days," Daphne said, after reading the article.

"Some maybe. There was a push while Jimmy Carter was president."

"That's why I got my job. Governmental pressure."

"Having a policewoman in the early 1970s, especially in a small town, was really rare. Unheard of before 1972. The department probably didn't want to publicize it. Apparently her father and brothers had been police officers, both killed in the line of duty. She had successfully graduated from a private academy and a police chief, an old friend of her father's, gave her a start."

"Why 1972?" Daphne asked.

"There was a law passed in 1972 making it so a woman could legally be a police officer on the same level with men. I remember my father's reaction to it."

"So she really was one of the first. And the article says only two percent of women were officers then, but now it is more."

"Not many," said Plate.

"She had such a short time."

"And by all records found, for that short time Officer Kay Fondrem was an exemplary officer who had the misfortune to be in a fatal wreck."

"Willhouse probably could not have saved her?"

"Who knows? His actions were questioned," said Plate.

"But he wasn't fired?" Daphne asked.

"No, just reprimanded, but along with Willhouse's inaction in the Sarah Pauliza case... I suspect both of those reactions and their consequences tormented both Eddy and Tim. In very different ways."

"Did Jordan know at that point in time who Willhouse was?" Daphne asked.

"We're not exactly sure. We think so. He got information from Officer Fondrem," said Plate.

"So he didn't really care for her?"

"Who knows? I would've said he cared for Kate."

"Yes. I agree. I would've said the same thing," said Daphne. "So there were two secret romances."

"Three. Actually four in the end," said Plate.

"Three? Four? Who?" Daphne asked.

"Kate and Jordan-" Plate began, "a secret because they started seeing each other before she and her abusive husband got a divorce. And he was dispatched one time when she called the police. Unethical for him to get involved with her. He could have been fired."

"I imagine that's how they met," Daphne mused.

"Yes."

"And he seemed so happy about her. The first time they tried to shoot the wedding scene, he was practically showing her off as his fiancée, beaming about her."

"Yes, but he had her take out life insurance with you."

"She didn't put him as the beneficiary."

"He might not have known that," Plate speculated.

"No. I had the idea at the time she had a married lover who she expected to be free soon. And that he knew all about her taking out life insurance. In that situation, most men don't want their names on the policy. Since I was wrong about that, I would say that something changed. Something from the outside of their relationship affected him," said Daphne.

"Darica's story came out," said Plate.

"Right! And there was a picture of Sally Monroe on the front page."

"They didn't look anything alike. That's what Jordan said. Kate confronted him that he was Sally's brother but he didn't understand how she knew either. He put it down to her seeing a resemblance."

"They were twin brother and sister. They were bound to look something like. It's hard to see sometimes, like with me and my sister. But it's there."

"I don't see where they looked anything alike," Plate said.

"But- the pictures! We were so concentrated on all the computer data we ignored obvious right in front of our eyes. The pictures."

"What was important about the pictures? I never saw it."

"I looked at the pictures, the movies, and everything. I didn't find anything that pointed to anybody specific," Daphne admitted. "But I think the pictures we found in Jordan's apartment that Kate was living in were important."

"I never looked at those. Later we found the blackmail photos in behind them. The photos of Cardioxa killing Yolanda." Plate tried to recall any details about Jordan's personal photos. He could not.

"Exactly. Kate stopped you that day. What do you want to bet there is an old picture of Sally Monroe among them?" Daphne asked.

"And Kate found that, not the blackmail pics?"

"That would make sense. She saw the picture on the front page of the paper and then saw Jordan had either the same picture or pictures of the same woman and wondered why. "

"Might've even been a picture of the two of them together."

"I'll bet there was only one. He was efficient enough in his long planned vengeance to have gotten rid of them all. But there was probably one he could not stand to throw away."

"Why take that chance?" Plate wondered.

"Memories fade over time. He was probably afraid he would forget her face," said Daphne.

"Nonsense, you can never forget the faces of those you love."

"Don't argue. It's a moot point anyway. He started to fear Kate so she had to die." Daphne let the point pass.

"And the second secret romance was Elizabeth Lopez and Emilio Cardioxa. And that began when she worked as a translator during his courtship of Yolanda."

"Was she his accomplice?" Daphne asked.

"We think she at least knew about the murder and may have actually conspired in the killing. She will certainly be charged with kidnapping the Hollywood stuntman. That would have been murder if Grant hadn't found him in time Friday, after we sent the princess off."

"Yet Kate knew nothing. But Jordan had Emilio kill Kate. Not Elizabeth," Daphne mused.

"Elizabeth was no threat to Jordan. Cardioxa never told her about Jordan and how he got the MO knowledge and who set up the alibi. He saved her life by keeping her in the dark."

"I think Kate would have turned Cardioxa in if she had found the blackmail pics. Have they found the lovers yet?" Daphne asked.

"Not yet. But we will. They've been spotted. They're together."

"Don't forget. He's an agent. They might get away."

"No. They will be caught somewhere along the way. Mexico will cooperate. Yolanda's family wants him worse than we do."

"And then there was the third secret romance?" Daphne asked.

"Klaus Lewegz and Elisabeth Morgan. They actually met at the first wedding scene. They've gone off together. No crime there."

"Not exactly a secret. And the fourth?" she persisted.

"Princess Joanna and her Italian journalist boyfriend. Apparently, initially he hoped he would just get to keep her and also get a prestigious job with the Arab oil prince. He's just a kid. Barely 22. Very ambitious and rather brave. Covered the Middle East for a while. He was coming to her rescue, if he could figure out how."

"He probably thought it would make a good story as well."

"I'm sure it is. In Italy."

"How about Italy for a honeymoon?" Daphne asked.

"Italy, Texas?"

"That's probably the only Italy we can afford since Joanna's life insurance policy was void because she is a minor."

"We will be lucky if I can get a day off."

"You have to be off tomorrow night."

"I'll try."

"Remember what I said about the process. Introducing our parents to each other is part of the process."

"There could be a disaster or a murder, or several murders and several disasters."

"I don't care if there's a catastrophic earthquake. You have to be at the Toy Museum Restaurant tomorrow at 5 PM. Your parents are coming in from East Texas and my parents are coming from Katy."

"We don't have earthquakes in this area. It may not be too late for a hurricane, however."

"The tropical forecast is clear. I checked. And I don't care what happens, you have to be there."

"The Toy Museum Restaurant could burn down."

"If it so happens to burn down on the night that my parents and your parents and the two of us are going to have dinner there, planning to get to know each other better, I will turn you in for arson."

"That might hurt my career. I thought you were going to be supportive."

"I will visit you in Huntsville."

"That would probably be a federal charge, I might go to New York for prison time."

"It is cold up there. I'll just write."

"I suppose I would not like prison. At the moment it does sound preferable, but I do promise I will be at The Toy Museum Restaurant on time tomorrow."

Chapter 58

Plate was true to his promise. It was Daphne who was late.

Drake and Vivian Plate were waiting when their son arrived.

"We will go ahead and get a table. Daphne had an unscheduled appointment with a client and should be here shortly. Her parents are on their way. They're caught in traffic."

"Good. I want to hear all about this serial killer and what happened at the marina."

"Drake! We are here to meet Daphne's parents. Not to talk about crime and criminals," Vivian admonished her husband.

"They aren't here yet. The quicker Peter tells me, the faster we move on to social amenities. Start from the beginning, son," said Drake.

"Table for six, please," said Vivian to the hostess. "Hurry."

"Many years ago during the Vietnam War at the beginning of his serial killing, Castroe Zopev killed the wife of a young lawyer, who later killed himself. This was Jordan's twin sister and brother-in-law," said Plate, not noticing the strange looks from the hostess as she led them to their table.

His parents pulled out chairs and made themselves comfortable at the round table. Plate selected the chair opposite from them where he had a good view of the doorway and front windows

"What no one knew at the time was- this was not Zopev's first crime. During a short stay in East Texas, he attacked Sarah Pauliza. Zopev had no idea there was a man in the house when he broke in. Eduardo Pauliza managed to fight him off, but not before Sarah was seriously injured."

"And how did these people fit in with what just happened?"

"I'll get to that."

"Just listen. You wanted him to tell you this. So be quiet and let him talk," Vivian said.

"Eduardo never forgave himself for failing to completely defend his wife. They moved to Houston. He bought a gun. Shortly after he started a moving company specializing in moving furniture after hours. It filled a niche demand and was successful. With her earnings as a night nurse they were able to afford an entry-level house in Sand Waves. They bought into the idea that Sand Waves was a crime free paradise."

"No such place."

"Shut up, Drake!"

"They are not here yet," said Drake, unruffled. "And Pauliza didn't buy into the utopia concept completely if he kept his gun loaded under his bed."

"Back when the attack on Sarah happened, Castroe Zopev was actually questioned as a suspect. Zopev had in his possession a necklace he stole when he broke in. The rookie patrolman, Tim Willhouse, brought Zopev in and dutifully recorded this. Zopev claimed the necklace belonged to him and the patrolman never checked it out. It was, after all, 1969, and with the hippie movement of the late 60s, it wasn't uncommon for men to wear necklaces."

"Shut up, Drake." Vivian spoke this time before her husband even said anything.

Plate stifled a laugh.

He concentrated on the details of the case that most reflected how the police proceeded. He knew that would be the most interesting part to his father.

"Now, Sarah Pauliza had not reported the jewelry missing. She didn't miss it until later. By this time, Zopev was long gone and nothing could officially be done. But it was the first indication that he was actually guilty and the information should have been sent along to the police department in the Panhandle where he moved. But Willhouse probably became worried it might reflect badly on his career and covered it up. After Officer Fondrem's death, he came to Houston."

"Hold on," said Vivian. "Tell me exactly who Officer Willhouse was and who Officer Fondrem was."

Plate explained the parts those two police officers played in the drama.

"My goodness," said his mother. "Okay, go ahead."

"Zopev went on in a northerly direction, attacking and killing Sally Monroe in the Panhandle along the way in 1972. Then he came to the Houston area about 1978, having been drafted and served his time in the army in between. After Zopev was questioned as a suspect in Sally Monroe's murder and made the news, Willhouse began to feel guilty about his lapse of judgment. It affected his performance. Then Timothy Willhouse had a second lapse of judgment that possibly cost Officer Fondrem her life in 1974."

"Not enough supervision for police during the early 1970s. There was such a shortage. Standards became lax," said Drake.

"Meanwhile," Plate continued. "Sally Monroe's brother had finished his service in the Army. As soon as he possibly could, he started to try to find out everything that was known about his sister's murder. To make a long story short, he connected Zopev with the attack on Sarah. Maybe with Officer Fondrem's help. He realized it was Willhouse's negligence, lack of experience really, that inadvertently led to his sister's death. Had Willhouse been a sharper, more experienced investigator instead of a new recruit, not long graduated from the police academy and experienced only in patrol, he would have spotted the discrepancy in Zopev's story about the necklace and investigated a little further."

"How would that made a difference?" Vivian asked.

"Sarah, prompted by a question about a valuable necklace, would have looked for hers and discovered it missing earlier. Zopev's serial killing spree might never have happened."

"Pure speculation. They probably would not have even sent him to prison, the way things are these days. They would've said he had a bad childhood and let him go live in a halfway house for psychological counseling," Drake commented.

"Jordan didn't see it that way. Or if he did, he figured any deviation in the course of events might have saved his sister. And there was more," Plate continued.

"The death of Officer Fondrem," concluded Vivian.

"After Jordan became a cop, he found a path to revenge," said Drake.

"It was too much for him to absorb. He might have handled one or the other. He might have handled both if he had not just returned from hell in Vietnam. All three experiences mentally crippled him. He wanted his revenge. And he wanted to get away with it," Plate said.

"It got out of hand. He had to kill more people than he planned," said Drake.

"I still don't understand. You were telling me this officer was behind all of these murders? How? I will have lemon water," said Vivian.

"Are you not ready to order yet?" asked the server.

"No, ma'am. But I will have a Coke," said Plate.

"I will have tea," said Drake. "Sweet, with ice."

The server left and Plate continued.

"I think Jordan's first plan was fairly simple. Followed all the time, dogged everywhere he went by either police or private detectives hired by the families of his supposed victims, Zopev had stopped killing. I think Jordan's original plan was to set up a copycat killing with enough evidence that would get a trial. If Zopev was convicted, that would be good. If not, hopefully enough would come out to try him on the other murders that he did do."

"Sounds like he only had vague ideas at that time," Drake said.

"Then the perfect plum fell into his lap."

"How so?" Vivian asked.

"A somewhat secretive operation. The FBI approached us about one of our officers posing as a hitman. They had a tip that someone in our area was shopping around for somebody to kill his wife."

"That was the lawyer, Emilio Cardioxa?" Drake asked.

"Right. But we weren't privy to all information. Emilio Cardioxa was actually a foreign agent posing as a lawyer in the United States. He also worked for our side on a case-by-case basis. Because there was diplomacy involved, this was one of the traps set with the local cops. If it goes wrong, they can blame us. Jordan was selected. It was a one-day operation. He was to contact the foreign agent and present impeccable credentials as a hitman and make a pitch for the job," said Plate.

"They should've chosen you for that ruse," said Drake.

"Jordan reported back that the target of this trap was outraged at the idea that anybody thought he wanted to kill his wife. Jordan said he actually had to reveal he was a police officer to the man to stop him from calling the authorities right then."

"This was actually what the feds wanted to hear," said Drake. "I know from experience, they don't want to hear anything bad about one of their own."

"The man was a valuable operative and they wanted him to be clean. They had been hoping that rumors that the guy wanted his wife taken out were planted by the other side in hopes of flushing him out as an agent," Plate confirmed.

"And I suppose, to avoid any potential embarrassment and also to avoid blowing his cover, Jordan was instructed to never reveal who had been the man under suspicion," Drake concluded.

"Nothing could have been more perfect for Jordan's plan."

"So what actually happened?" Vivian asked.

"What actually happened was that Jordan told Cardioxa how he could easily murder his wife using the same MO and the privileged information that had always been held back about how the Zopev victims had died."

"Jordan told Cardioxa the truth that he really was a cop?"

"Yes. Saying he was willing to overlook the killing of one woman, a Mexican national at that, to get the serial killer off the street. He might have even told Cardioxa that his sister had been one of Zopev's victims. Probably did. He convinced Cardioxa that Zopev would be convicted for the crime of killing Yolanda Cardioxa."

"Clever," Vivian said.

"Jordan was more clever than we ever knew. He gave off a good old boy persona that belied his depth," Plate said.

"Cunning is the word, son," said Drake.

"Then he set about fishing in Zopev. Jordan knew the Paulizas now lived in Sand Waves. That was easy to find out. He had been tracking all of these people for a long time and he knew where all of them were. He simply made sure that Zopev and Pauliza were together at the time Emilio Cardioxa was murdering Yolanda Cardioxa," said Plate.

"Poor woman," said Vivian, reading the menu at the same time.

"Cardioxa was instructed in the details of Zopev's method of killing and directed to say that he glimpsed Zopev on the premises at the time of the murder," said Plate.

"He knew that if any connection was ever made between Pauliza and Zopev, it would even make Pauliza's testimony stronger," Drake concluded.

"These prices are atrocious. Makes sense. Why would the husband of a victim alibi him unless it was true," Vivian declared.

"Remember, Jordan was on duty when the emergency call came in from Emilio Cardioxa. Willhouse was asked to go instead. Chief Brecken knew about Tim's past. He wanted Willhouse front and center on the Zopev case, knowing that if Zopev were convicted, Willhouse would feel vindicated," said Plate.

"Jordan made sure Zopev was not convicted by setting up the alibi," Vivian said, understanding that point at last.

"Right. That was a great shock to Cardioxa," said Plate.

"But then Jordan still just told Cardioxa, 'okay, nobody really believes Zopev is innocent. Cops all over the country think the alibi was false and they're still not going to be looking at you for killing Yolanda.' Cardioxa relaxed, but not enough to bring out in the open his relationship with his girlfriend," said Plate, adding, "and that saved her life.

"An engagement announcement would have meant death."

# Chapter 59

"Sorry I'm late." Daphne suddenly stood before them.

"How lovely to see you again!" Vivian Plate stood up and embraced her future daughter-in-law.

"That was Elizabeth Lopez," said Drake.

"Correct," said his son.

"Drake! Peter! Daphne is here!" Vivian exclaimed.

Daphne laughed and sat down.

"They would have noticed me eventually."

"He's telling us about Elizabeth Lopez. Peter, go ahead. Hello, Daphne," said Drake impatiently.

Plate caught Daphne's eye and winked.

"She had been the translator for Emilio Cardioxa and Yolanda when their relationship first began. Emilio Cardioxa had fallen in love with her. As Yolanda had begun to learn English, she didn't want a second woman involved in the relationship. Elizabeth was let go. But Emilio Cardioxa could not let her go. He wanted her and his wife's money. He wanted to retire in style behind the gates of Sand Waves with the woman he loved."

"So what did the attack on the princess have to do with any of this?" Vivian asked.

"Jordan arranged that also," Daphne contributed.

"Mr. Shiameto found out a little information about that. Jordan contacted the prince and pretended to be a nationalist, manipulated the prince into thinking he had to do some kind of revenge against Joanna. The prince contacted the college student son of a friend and offered him an outrageous sum of money if he would do something that would make a few headlines. The college kid came up with the idea of a hazing stunt and enlisted one of his buddies," Plate explained.

"How did they get by security?" asked Drake.

"Elizabeth Lopez let them in. I assumed they broke the windows to get in but the Italian actress smashed the glass herself trying to get away. That part was lost in the translation. Since Ms.

Lopez was the translator," said Plate.

"But why go to all of this elaborate trouble?" Vivian asked.

"To make sure that the chief, Skaar, and me were all occupied behind the gates while Willhouse was being killed by Pauliza under Jordan's gaze."

"That was a risky scenario," said Drake.

"He was convinced everything he arranged was going to come out exactly as he planned it," said Daphne.

"So far, it was," Drake commented.

"The death of Officer Willhouse did," said Plate. "Even the weather cooperated. Of course, it had been raining for some time. And the forecast was pretty reliable. Betting it was going to keep raining wasn't much of a gamble."

"He planned meticulously," said Daphne.

"He knew the Paulizas slept upstairs with small lamps left on downstairs. He was counting on the haze through their sheer curtains, the haze through the rain that had been prevalent every morning for days. He was lucky there was heavy fog accompanying the rain that morning," said Plate.

"He knew how to light a barbecue grill so that after a short time it would start to smoke heavily," said Daphne.

"He staged the grill. Then he met Willhouse, who thought they were going to drive down to a boat. They detoured instead to Harbor Shadows," said Plate.

"Where he convinced Officer Willhouse the Pauliza home was on fire," said Daphne.

"How awful," said Vivian.

"Who knows what he told Willhouse? That he found a shortcut out of Sand Waves? Or that he knew somebody and just had to stop by and say something to them on that street?"

"Willhouse know whose house it was?" asked Drake.

"Jordan said so. Alice was not sure if her husband knew the Paulizas lived on that street. After all, there so many streets with so many similar names. The place is a giant maze. He could easily have known they live in the colony without knowing exactly where."

"He probably didn't want to know," Drake said.

"At first they didn't even remember him from the investigation of her assault. Then they saw him in a photo that accompanied Darica's Sunday morning feature," said Daphne.

"So we don't know if Willhouse thought he was breaking in to rescue a woman, a couple, he had failed to achieve justice for years ago? Or he thought he was rescuing strangers," Drake mused.

"I still don't understand why he thought the house was on fire," said Vivian.

"According to witnesses, Jordan must have pulled the car a few feet from the house. Stopping behind him, from his car Willhouse would've seen a dim haze of smoke coming around the corner of the house, hazy light inside that could be mistaken for flames."

"Jordan used Willhouse's past against him at an emotional moment," said Drake.

"We don't know how far Jordan ran with Tim from the cars, down the street maybe, not across the lawn, according to our witness. He certainly did not go up the tree," said Plate.

"Although it's probable Willhouse thought Jordan was right behind him," said Drake.

"And Pauliza woke up to someone banging on his door, just a few days after receiving scathing threats about his testimony alibiing Zopev. Plus, the memory of the assault on his wife. The odds were tremendous that he was going to grab his gun and shoot Willhouse," said Plate.

"Or Tim Willhouse, confronted with a gun unexpectedly, would have harmed either Eduardo or Sarah," said Daphne.

"Then Jordan would have disavowed any knowledge of Tim's actions. If Tim had survived a violent encounter with the Paulizas, then his story about Jordan having seen a fire would sound like he was expecting Jordan to back him up because he was a fellow cop," said Plate. "And Eddy would have played a good part. Initially lamely defended Willhouse, then allowed himself to be broken down and admit there was no attempted rescue, that Willhouse had snapped. Putting the icing on the cake."

Chapter 60

"No, we don't need a dessert menu, you have the wrong table," Vivian Plate told a new server. "We have not had our main entrées yet. All of our party has not arrived."

The lost server backed off, searching for the correct table.

"There's my parents." Daphne rose and walked over to greet her parents as they entered the restaurant.

Plate and his parents stood up as the Martins approached.

"My parents, Frank and Deborah Lynn Martin. Mom, this is Drake and Vivian Plate. And this is Peter."

Mr. and Mrs. Martin both shook hands with Plate and his parents. The amenities continued, stiff but not unfriendly,

The conversation turned from the recent lawlessness in Sand Waves to small talk about travel, traffic, and careers.

The two mothers had spent their married lives as homemakers.

Daphne's father spoke a little bit about his job as a manager of sales personnel at a car dealership.

Drake spoke up. "And I am a retired-"

"Police chief," Plate broke in.

"Oh, you were a chief? Peter told me you were retired from law enforcement. He didn't tell me you were a chief," said Daphne.

The right server came by to ask if they were ready to order.

As they each recited their menu selection, Drake and Vivian Plate took turns sending a few scolding glares at their son.

He ducked behind the menu.

"And if there had been no confrontation," Plate began speaking as soon as the waitress had taken the menus and departed.

"Peter, you need to let Mr. and Mrs. Martin know what we're talking about," Vivian said.

"Don't worry, Mrs. Drake, we know all about it. Both of our daughters involved. It's been in the newspaper every day for weeks. Daphne's kept us informed and Darica's told us a few things."

"I can imagine what Darica has told you, Dad," said Daphne.

"We're discussing what might have happened if Pauliza had

not gotten his gun when Willhouse climbed that balcony. If they had just been scared and froze or ran when Tim broke in," said Plate.

"Run to another part of the house, that is what I would have done," said Mrs. Martin.

"I don't know what I would have done," said Daphne.

"I would have reacted like Pauliza. I would have shot him. No way I would have given him time to explain," Drake admitted. "But that is the way I have been trained."

"Jordan was counting on Pauliza reacting as he did. And if he had not, well, Jordan would've come right up behind and then it would've been written off as an honest mistake. The police department would've had to buy them a new set of French doors."

"I read about the witness. Did she see the police officer climb up to the balcony?" Mr. Martin asked.

"Yes, but he was not in uniform," Daphne reminded him.

"And the other policeman, the bad one, had set this up to avenge his sister?" Mrs. Martin asked.

"He accomplished that and it should've been the end of it. At least, the end of innocent people getting killed," said Plate.

"Except for Darica," Daphne said unkindly.

"Kate Traval read Darica's story, but we think she found hard evidence that got her killed. Mrs. Martin, Mr. Martin, there's no way any blame can be attached to Darica," said Plate.

Daphne looked at him in surprise.

"Thank you so much for saying that," said Mrs. Martin. "It means a lot to us to know that no one blames Darica for any of this."

"Yes, indeed," said Mr. Martin.

Daphne's parents, heretofore a little hostile, experienced their first positive feelings towards their future son-in-law.

Plate glanced at Daphne, giving her a brief superior look.

She narrowed her eyes at him.

"I believe Jordan generally cared for Kate, as much as his bent mind could. He rescued her from an abusive marriage. I think he was planning to marry her," said Plate. "With Willhouse and Zopev dead-"

"He killed Zopev?" Vivian asked.

"Oh yes. Right after the trial. Lured him into a sailboat somehow, killed him and dumped him in the bay. We found his car with some of his belongings in a paid lot near the marina," Plate said.

"So Jordan truly blamed Willhouse for the death of Kay Fondrem just as much as he blamed Zopev for the death of his sister?" Drake's words were more of a statement than a question.

"That is sociopathic," Mr. Martin commented. "What were the odds that Willhouse would be involved in both cases?"

"Pretty good actually. The small counties there had few deputies. Wilding Falls and Neches, where Willhouse and Fondrem worked, had only three officers in their police forces. In such small towns they call on one another frequently," Plate explained.

"We live near Wilding Falls," Vivian volunteered.

"The real tragedy, against the odds, was that, in such a small town, two victims would be directly connected to Jordan. His sister and friend," Drake Plate said.

"But Officer Fondrem's death was an accident," Vivian said.

"Yes," said her son. "Unfortunately his next girl didn't have any chance. He had the perfect murder weapon to kill Kate Traval."

"He'd used Emilio Cardioxa to kill her," Drake said.

"Right. Before Kate became a danger, I think Eddy planned to marry her and spend several years blackmailing Emilio Cardioxa, maybe killing him later after a lot of time had passed," said Plate.

"Why did he have to kill Kate Traval the way he did. At the wedding?" asked Mrs. Martin.

"He needed her killed in such a way that no suspicion fell on him. The boyfriend is the first person we look at. What better way than to have her assassinated in public when he was in full view of dozens of people?"

"How did he know she was going to be kept on as an extra in the show? How could he possibly arrange for one of the bridesmaids to be sick?" Mrs. Martin asked.

"He didn't. The bridesmaid called in sick. Kate didn't know she was going to make a second walk down the stairs until then. She excitedly told Jordan and he got word to Emilio Cardioxa. We don't know if Emilio Cardioxa decided to wait for the second wedding march, if he got cold feet during the first, or if he just lined her up as the target, waiting for the second as a precaution," said Plate.

"You mean if the extra had not called in sick, he would have shot her during our ceremony?" Daphne asked, with surprise.

"How did he take the place of the original guy that was supposed to have fired the shot?" asked Mr. Martin.

"The second stuntman hired was new to the craft. Another Vietnam vet. Nobody on the set knew him. And he didn't know all the procedure. It was easy for Jordan to find out details and have Emilio meet him at IAH. Jordan was helping monitor Wynter's employees. Emilio had moved his boat from a marina to a private dock at a vacant Sand Waves house on the waterfront. Emilio imprisoned him on the boat," said Plate. "Grant found him, locked in the cabin, lucky to be alive after three days trapped alone with no food or water."

"I think we need to look at this as more of a rehearsal and not an actual ceremony since it wasn't a legal minister," said Mrs. Martin.

"About that-" Mr. Martin began.

"And the groomsman who quit?" Drake interrupted. "Was that because he was the prince's hired goon?"

"We don't know," said Plate. "We do know the oil prince had called off his plans to harass the princess between the two attempts at staging the wedding scene. So probably."

"I think the part about Princess Joanna is the most interesting part of the whole story. At least it's not as sad as the rest of what happened," said Mrs. Martin.

"Chief Brecken says rumor is that Joanna's Sicilian father let it be known that if anything happened to her in America he would be looking to Arabia for revenge. The Egyptian declared he was duped by Jordan into setting up the first attack on the princess," Plate said.

"He dropped it when he saw it went wrong. If only Jordan had possessed that much sense," Drake commented.

"It all went Jordan's way for such a long time. He might have stopped and reconsidered if he hadn't had such good luck for so long. His luck finally ran out," said Plate, not for the first time.

# Chapter 61

"So you have another son?"

"Yes, Mrs. Martin. Peter has a brother. And he also has two sisters. He's our youngest son, I'm afraid. Every so often I regress and call him Petey," Vivian said.

Everyone laughed.

"I go by Debralyn, myself," said Mrs. Martin. "It is a combination of my first and middle names made into one word. It's what I've always been called."

"You must originally be from East Texas," said Vivian Plate.

"Yes, I am. I was born there but moved to Houston as a child. I thought that was where all of you were from."

"Not exactly. Due to my husband's career, we had to move around a lot. When he retired, we settled there. Peter was just finishing up high school. Drake got a job as a chief at one of the small nearby towns before he finally quit working for good," Vivian said.

"As of the moment," Drake Plate said.

"My brother's name is Dell, after my great-grandfather, who was a character in the book," Plate said.

"I would like to read that book," said Mrs. Martin.

"I have a copy I will let you borrow," Daphne said.

"I understand Daphne also has an older brother," said Vivian.

"We try not to talk about him."

"Daphne! What will people think with you saying things like that? She's joking! Our son is currently living in West Texas."

"That's a coincidence. Our son moved off in that direction also. He's a dentist," Vivian said.

"A dentist?" Daphne ran her tongue across her front teeth.

"Our son is- uh, uh-"

"An educator," Daphne interrupted her mother.

"How nice," Vivian said.

"Then do your daughters live near you?" Debralyn asked.

"Yes, they do. They're both married. Each has two children."

"It does not look like we're ever going to get to be

grandparents," said Frank Martin.

"I'm sure Peter and Daphne will be having children," said Vivian Plate. "Won't you?"

Plate and Daphne looked at each other and there was an awkward silence.

"We haven't really discussed that yet," said Plate.

"Sounds like they have not discussed a lot of things," said Drake Plate. "Maybe it wasn't such a bad thing that this movie wedding didn't come off after all."

"Drake!" Vivian's tone could have been interpreted as deadly.

The server arrived with their food. She had an assistant that open the little folding table and the two of them made an elaborate display of making sure that everything was positioned exactly right on the table.

The six diners sat in silence as this ritual proceeded.

After the restaurant staff departed, everyone grabbed their utensils and started eating their food.

Debralyn Martin waited until she was sure everyone's mouth was full before she broke the silence.

"Exactly what do you two plan to do about your future?"

Daphne swallowed her baked potato quickly. "We will be married soon. Peter has found a site. We just have to work out the details and the date."

"You have been with the Sand Waves Police Department for some time?" her father asked Plate.

"Yes, sir. I have."

"You do have a high rank for such a young man," Frank Martin commented.

"It's really not uncommon in very small departments."

"Don't sell yourself short, Peter," said Drake.

"So is there very much job security in a department like yours?" Frank asked.

"There is no job security in law enforcement. Not on individual basis. But generally we have as much or more job security as any profession," said Drake.

"They probably have more job security than you do, Frank. The economy goes down, nobody buys new cars," said Mrs. Martin.

"I'm just making conversation," said Frank Martin.

"I do fairly well at my job in case anyone has never noticed."

Daphne knew her words fell on deaf ears.

"You do work on commission, Daphne. Your income is dependent on your next sale. Nobody knows that better than I do."

"Daphne has that big house with upkeep," said her mother.

"Are the property taxes real high?" asked Vivian.

"I think we will be all right financially," said Plate.

"As your parents, the only thing we worry about is your happiness. I'm sure that Mr. and Mrs. Plate will agree," said Frank.

"Absolutely," said Drake.

"You are both young and just getting started in life."

"Mother. I am 27, almost 28," said Daphne.

"I'm about to turn 30."

The four older people looked at each other.

"I think we are all just concerned for both of you," Vivian said.

"Your first attempt at a ceremony was called off," said Frank.

"Your bridesmaid was shot and killed at the second attempt."

"You lost your friend," said Debralyn.

"We did not have anything to do with those things. None of that was even because Peter is a police officer. And I didn't even know Kate Traval. She was actually an insurance client, not a friend."

"You get to keep your commission on that sale?" asked Frank.

"Only because she had paid an annual premium in advance."

"It was my fault we tried for that movie wedding," said Plate.

"We did get good pictures. Some of me as a bride with dark hair. And others with my hair pulled back severely. I refused to wear the wig the second time. I did decide to keep the veil."

"And, Mom, wait till you see me in a 1940s tuxedo!"

"You are missing the point," said Drake.

"We just want to see you happy," said Debralyn.

The four older people all looked at each other again, nodded in agreement, and then turned a united front towards their adult children.

"Maybe you should consider thinking it over and waiting a little while," said Frank Martin.

"Yes," said Drake Plate.

Vivian Plate looked uncomfortable and started eating again.

Debralyn Martin did likewise.

"Well," said Plate.

He did not know what else to say. He looked at Daphne.

"Have the four of you been in contact with each other before now?" Daphne asked.

"No."

"Of course not."

"Why would you think that?"

"N-no."

Daphne glared at all four of them, then said to her mother, "I need to use the restroom. Do you think you could come with me?"

Debralyn Martin rose reluctantly and followed her daughter.

They were barely behind the closed ladies' room door when Daphne turned her wrath on her mother.

"Darica got married when she was still in college to a man she barely knew. They had no careers, no money, and the two of you made no objection whatsoever. Here I am only two years away from 30, I have a successful career and the man I am about to marry is a police lieutenant."

"Daphne!"

"Will you never have any respect for me? Do you think I'm so flighty that I would just marry somebody that I didn't know was the right person for me? Maybe everything hasn't gone perfectly so far but when does it?"

"Daphne, it was the experience with Darica-"

"Darica has nothing to do with this! She got married and she got a divorce. It happens to millions of people. What she's done in her life is still weighing on what I've done in my life. Why? I love Peter Plate and I'm going to marry him. I am going to marry him as soon as possible and if my family does not want to be a part of it, so be it."

"Of course we want to be part of it."

*Peter Plate?* Debralyn thought. *With Sinclair as a first name! What was his mother thinking?*

"I knew just how you would react from the beginning. That's one reason why I went along with that movie wedding thing. So I didn't have to explain to my fiancé why my family would behave the way they do."

"Daphne, it's just that you've always been the responsible one. You have a house. This sudden romance. It's just so unlike you. I know he can't possibly make as much money as you do. That can cause all kinds of trouble between a husband and wife."

"If my making more money than Peter causes problems, I'll quit," Daphne declared.

"You'd quit?"

"I'd quit."

"You must love this boy then."

"Yes, I do."

Vivian Plate entered the restroom at that moment.

"The men are having a little conversation," she said. "I felt like I was in the way."

"I think perhaps we'll just get to know each other better and that will help," said Debralyn.

"I hope you do get to know each other better," said Daphne. "But whether you become mortal enemies or best friends is not going to make any difference."

"If it's any consolation, my dear, when Peter brought you to East Texas to get that hook, I knew the two of you were going to wind up together," said Vivian.

"Thank you."

"My husband is an ass," she added, laughing.

"Your father can be that way also," said Debralyn. "He wanted me to speak to you about this. I have to do all the dirty work. And after we get home he'll criticize me for doing what he asked."

"They are men," Daphne commented, calmer now.

*Now I sound like Darica*, she thought.

"Perhaps your father and I might have felt a little left out of all of this," said her mother.

"I have not meant to leave you out. Everything has happened very fast. Peter and I admit that. We have talked about it ourselves. And we've come to some conclusions," said Daphne.

"Conclusions?"

Both women looked at her expectantly.

"Among others. Mainly. The main conclusion is- we feel it was meant to be. That is- it is- uh- the will of God."

Vivian and Debralyn glanced at each other.

Neither mother had a reply.

Invoking God had stopped them cold.

"So shall we go back to the table?" Daphne asked. "If they have anything to say, I'd like to get it over with."

"Were they arguing when you left?" Debralyn asked Vivian.

"Did my father seem very angry?" asked Daphne.

"Not exactly. Petey- I mean Peter was saying the two of you have spent more time together then we all had realized and that the two of you were working together to get up on all this computer stuff," Vivian said.

"I haven't heard any loud voices," said Daphne.

"Does your husband still carry a firearm?" Debralyn asked.

"Yes, I'm afraid he does," said Vivian.

"We would have heard any gunshots," said Daphne.

"I'm sure they are having a civilized discussion," said Vivian.

"If there's any fuss, we will order dessert," said Debralyn.

"Yes, that will distract them," agreed Vivian.

Daphne followed her mother and future mother-in-law out of the bathroom.

The three women returned to their restaurant table to find the men genially discussing the latest news about how advancements in computer technology were affecting statistics concerning criminals and customers.

Daphne listened for a moment.

She decided to interrupt.

"Before we totally get off the subject of mine and Peter's

future life together, there's something else you should all know."

Everyone stopped talking and looked at her.

"Peter and I are seriously considering that if we have children he should give up his career and stay home with them while I continue with my insurance business."

Plate coughed a little and clasped his hands over his mouth.

The four older people all froze. Despite having different complexions under normal circumstances, all four of them turned a near identical shade of white.

Daphne smiled brightly.

Plate made a choking sound. He grabbed a napkin.

"Just kidding!" Daphne said in a cheerful voice.

Plate pushed his chair back from the table and burst into laughter.

"That was not very funny, Daphne!" Frank Martin exclaimed.

Debralyn Martin started to giggle.

Vivian Plate started laughing along with her son.

Daphne began calmly finishing her meal.

"You think it's funny?" Frank Martin addressed his wife.

She stifled her giggles.

Drake Plate scowled suspiciously at his son.

"Daphne's always been a great kidder," said Debralyn.

Frank and Drake regarded each other. They suddenly united in a cause and began roundly condemning the idea of men becoming househusbands.

Debralyn Martin was having none of that conversation. She nipped it in the bud.

"Daphne, Peter," she said. "Darica told me that she met a fascinating man, some kind of secret agent from Japan. Tell me all about him."

"Yes," Vivian Plate agreed. "He sounds like the most fascinating character. And we don't know anything about him. Peter, start talking. Don't give me any national security nonsense."

Therefore, for the rest of the evening the conversation was all about Mr. Shiameto.

# Chapter 62

"I just wanted to give them a glimpse of a future in which you and I make the actual decisions about our lives," Daphne said.

"You don't have to convince me. I thought you were wonderful. I was just trying hard not to laugh too soon. I wanted to say- 'it does make sense for me to become the househusband. Daphne makes a lot more money than I do'. But I had already started laughing so all I could do was pretend to be choking."

"How did you, and my father, and your father, all get on the subject of computers when we had been talking about our relationship?"

"I don't know," Plate said, with an air of innocence.

"You manipulated the subject. When you should have been standing up for us."

"Look. The less said about our relationship, the better. Our parents will come around. All we have to do is get married and be happy."

"You are a master manipulator."

"I wish. And look who's talking. That joke will remain in the back of their minds for the next ten years."

"Good."

"Actually, both your father and my father know a few things about computers that I hadn't thought of. I'm trying to learn as much as I can so I have as much control as I need. Think about what criminals will do when they learn how. Think about what Jordan could have done if he had known how to access computer files, if there had been any to access when he started his vendetta."

"What did you say he called himself right before sailing off to his doom?"

"A master puppeteer. I heard him make that remark once before about something. I didn't pay any attention to it."

"You must have paid some attention to it to remember it."

"True. I guess it stuck in the back of my mind. I never did analyze it. That's one of the important things you do for me. You analyze quirky things."

"At least I can be of some use."

They laughed.

"Jordan was no master puppeteer," said Plate. "He may have been a puppeteer of sorts but the only advantage he had was being unknown, not being masterful. He may have been clever but if we had just known more about him, he could've never manipulated anything. Exposing him for who he was would have negated all his power."

"In my mind, there's only one Master."

"Me?" Plate asked with a smile.

Daphne cut her eyes at him.

"I told our mothers that our marriage was the will of God."

"How did they take that?"

"They did not have anything to say."

"Were you serious?" Plate asked.

"Yes, I was," she replied.

Plate became serious. "Master, yes. But you know I don't think puppeteer is exactly the right word. After all, according to Christianity's teachings, we have free will. We're not puppets."

"True. It sort of comforting to think of Him up there directing every little movement. However, I suspect you're right."

"And with free will comes danger. I've been meaning to bring this up. My chief has pestered me about it. My father has mentioned it several times."

"What?"

"I suppose you have noticed being a police officer can be a dangerous profession."

"Yes."

"Some wives become widows."

"Most women outlive their husbands."

"Earlier than normal."

"I have noticed."

"That does not worry you? Don't make a joke about life insurance. I know I have plenty that you sold me yourself."

"I'm not joking," Daphne said.

"This is serious," Plate said.

"I know."

"You'll be taking a risk. Not just a romantic one."

"My profession is not without danger. I spent the early years driving all over the city of Houston. In terrible traffic. In all kinds of weather. Getting lost. Relying on maps I could hardly read. Having to stop at pay phones in neighborhoods that would scare off a bouncer. Going alone to the homes of total strangers late at night. And all of this with a serial rapist running around in my own neighborhood, possibly waiting for me when I did get safely home."

"I don't discount any of that. It all sounds very dangerous."

"It was."

"And you weren't afraid?" Plate asked.

"No. There was sometimes I was a little afraid. And I was always very cautious. I frequently drove to my appointment destinations hours earlier in the daytime so I could find them easily at night. I always did that if the people lived in an apartment complex. When I was coming home at night, even after they caught the rapist, or thought they had, I varied my route. Of course, I was never home at a predetermined time so I didn't have to worry about that. I lived on the third floor, my apartment being as far from the elevator as possible in the building so I rarely took it. I even varied which staircase I came up. I couldn't vary my parking slot. It was assigned."

"And you had a gun."

"Not at first. Not for most of the time I lived in Houston. Not until my friend in Austin helped me get a permit. By then I was almost ready to move here, where I thought I could safely cultivate clients in Sand Waves and my job would be a lot less dangerous."

"As I said, I don't discount any of that. Did you ever hear shots fired? Before you met me, that is?" Plate asked.

"No."

"And if you had, what would you have done?"

"Run."

"That's right. That's what you should do. Even if you do carry a gun. But I don't. I can't," said Plate.

"What are you trying to say to me?" Daphne asked.

"That you probably don't know anything about what it's going to be like to be married to a cop," Plate said, with some worry in his voice.

Daphne recalled a section about Jenny Plate's fears in *Murder as the Organist Plays.* Fiction or not, she had memorized the words.

*Jenny wondered after he hung up if he knew just how much she loved him. She wondered when, or if, she would ever see him again.*

*Making sure the child was settled, she took out her Bible, clasped it to her breast, and bowed her head in prayer for her husband's safety.*

"I may know a little bit," Daphne said.

*It is possible to learn from other people's stories, fiction or not,* she thought.

"How about asking Alice Willhouse about being a police officer's wife?" Plate asked.

"Peter, I'm aware of the risks."

"There may be times when I don't come home at night and you don't know exactly where I am and I might not be able to tell you or contact you. There's a lot of women that cannot handle that kind of lifestyle."

"Peter, I know we've only known each other a short time. You're the only man on this earth for me. It's you or nobody. You said once, sometimes you feel like I could never fully belong to you."

"Well, I know you have powerful clients in Austin."

"One is a cardinal in the Roman Catholic Church."

"What?"

"I ran into him absolutely by accident. I was in Austin for a mini convention meeting and I had a car wreck. Just a fender bender but it could have caused me a lot of trouble insurance wise, if the other driver, the cardinal, hadn't been so considerate and cooperative. In the end, we didn't report it."

"A car wreck with a Catholic cardinal? What are you saying?"

"I'm trying to tell you. I am confessing," said Daphne.

337

"Okay, I will try to listen," said Plate impatiently.

"This cardinal and I had a car wreck. We illegally conspired to not report it. He was out on an errand that he didn't want anybody to know about and I didn't want to stain my driving record. So we arranged to have the cars repaired on the QT. He knew some people that got that done for us and in the process we became acquainted. We had to spend a little time together arranging for the cars to be picked up and taken to repair guy and so on and so forth. He talked to me about his faith. Very unintimidating. And I sold him life insurance."

"I get the picture. You blackmailed a cardinal."

"Will you be serious? I'm trying to talk to you about religion. People about to get married should talk about such topics. We should talk about it now, before the wedding."

"Sorry. We never talked about religion much when I was growing up. We went to the Baptist church in whatever town we were living in. But because we moved frequently around the state, we never got fully involved for any length of time."

"When we were children we went to the Lutheran Church. Darica got married there. It was all very friendly and sociable. But not really spiritual. I somewhat always had a religious life alone, just to me. I've never talked about it."

"Go on." Plate was aware that Daphne had changed the conversation completely away from the topic of his dangerous occupation to religion.

He admired the way she was achieving the change. Even if her language was awkward.

*She is as good as me,* he thought.

And it was not a conversation that he necessarily wanted to avoid.

Daphne took a deep breath.

"I can relate that not much is ever said about such things in my experience either," said Plate encouragingly.

"I guess what I'm trying to say is that I think I could be a police officer's wife and be strong because of my personal faith. Can you accept that?"

"I was going to get back to that subject if you did not. The idea is that the lifestyle I lead is something you need exposure to for a long time to be able to adjust," said Plate.

"I may not have been born to this lifestyle but I believe I have faith and enough mental discipline to adapt," said Daphne.

"Remember our discussion about the mind?" Plate asked.

Daphne laughed a little. "My part in that conversation may have been a little- fanciful. I was trying to impress you."

"I gave you the technical definition, my technical definition, but I did leave something out. Something I've never told anyone."

"What?"

"I believe the mind is the manifestation of the soul. That is the mechanism through which soul inhabits the body. The soul, being spirit, expresses itself through the brain. That's what sets us apart from animals. We have minds that can calculate and reason."

"Although if animals have spirits-?"

"Let's not get into animals. Stick with people. I have enough trouble trying to think about this in terms of humanity. What I'm saying is- the mind is the manifestation of the soul, the soul acts through the mind and if the mind turns against spirituality or otherwise inhibits true expressions of the soul, which results in aberrant behavior and, frequently, criminality. If the mind is damaged or corrupted, the true expressions of the soul are then limited."

"So where does faith come in for you?"

"Faith is needed to keep the mind disciplined against despair at all the evil in the world."

"And incorporate discipline with faith to handle whatever situation comes our way?"

"Exactly! Faith is something we need and should strive for. It comes easier to some than others. I don't know why."

"So you are religious. Just sort of technical about it."

"Would it surprise you, Daphne, to find out that I have literally felt the hand of God in my life?" Plate asked.

"No," said Daphne, not quite truthfully.

"And like you, never talked about it with anyone else."

"When I first met you I truly knew God has sent you for me. Do you think that is crazy?"

"Not at all. I feel the same. It may have taken me longer to see it, perhaps."

The implication of what they had both just told one another thrust them into a thrilling silence.

Secretly suspected yet not openly expected. And the abundant anticipation of what it meant for their life together encompassed them in a cloak of familiarity that they might never have achieved otherwise if they had never known.

The moment relaxed with understated joy.

"So what are we?" she asked with a short laugh, holding him still. "Closet Christians?"

Daphne touched his cheek with her fingertips.

"I think everybody already assumed that we were not anything other than Christian, except maybe nothing at all," he said.

"It does seem to be the trend going these days," she said regretfully. "You said you felt God in your life. How?"

"Everyone thinks I became a police officer to try to follow in my father's footsteps. But that was the furtherest thing from my mind."

"Are you saying you were led? That police work is a calling for you?"

Plate nodded. "I believe so."

"Then it will all work out. It will work out for the best. From when and where we get married all the way to how we approach our married life."

"Yes, you're right. Spirituality can be our strength. But don't forget the physical must be dealt with. There are no guarantees."

"What do you mean? Physical danger? Risks of injury?"

"Yes, but not just that. Remember our conversation some time ago, the hypothetical one about other women."

"You don't have to tell me. I was being inconsiderate."

"Then I will ask again. I need to know. Can you consider my line of work, and that I might have had to have done things I didn't want to do to avoid losing my life. Considering my position, can you have faith that, in my heart, there's never been anyone else and never will be?"

Tears came to Daphne's eyes. She nodded.

"I know I can be a police officer's wife. Your wife. With God's help."

"Then, it is settled. I won't ever question you again."

"Never again?"

At that moment, Catherine and Vandal made a rambunctious entrance into the room, entangling their tails and running into each other in an attempt to reach Daphne's feet first.

Both cats then sat back on their haunches and looked up at Daphne and Plate with demanding expressions.

"Okay one more question. There's a long-standing debate about the elevated role of the feline versus human superiority in the cat-human relationship," Plate said. "Would do you think?"

"Royal highnesses, maybe. Deities, no," said Daphne.

"I will serve their majesties cat food," said Plate, going to the cupboard.

Chapter 63

"This is a disaster! An absolute disaster! I may just kill myself."

"Darica, whatever is wrong? Tell me. Do I need to come up to Dallas? What is it!? Did you have a car wreck?" Daphne gripped the phone receiver and tried not to panic.

It was only ten days before the ceremony. Daphne was on pins and needles, hoping no new catastrophe struck before the wedding.

The three weeks Plate had promised had turned into eight. It was now mid-July.

The time and place had been set for the third time. So far the date was holding. Family was all pledged to come, even Plate's maiden great-aunt, at 79, the only one of that generation still alive on either side.

If anyone could cause problems, it would be Darica.

"It's your fault!" Darica shouted over the phoneline.

"My fault? What did I do? Tell me!"

"I'm pregnant!" Darica burst into tears.

Daphne held phone receiver in front of her and looked at it as if she thought the device itself was lying to her.

"Pregnant?" She put the instrument back to her face so she could be heard.

"Yeah, and it's all your fault."

"I didn't even know you are seeing anybody."

"I'm not! It was a one night stand! And because of your abortive wedding."

"Oh no. My God, who was it?" Daphne's mind went over numerous possibilities. All she could remember about the men who were present at that scenario was that most all of them were either married men or criminals.

"Who do you think it could possibly have been? You invited him! You knew how I felt about it, but you invited him anyway!"

"Who?" Daphne had finally settled on the only possibility being Mr. Shiameto. She could not recall any other man that she had specifically invited. And their mother had been overly interested in the Japanese police officer and the details surrounding his visit.

A Japanese niece or nephew. An interesting addition to the family.

Or there was another possibility. Sadder but more practical.

The Japanese agent was married.

"Are you considering giving the child up for adoption?" Daphne wondered briefly how a part Asian, part white child would fair in the adoption market, despite the chronic shortages of babies since abortion was made legal.

"No! I've already told him. He's making arrangements for a marriage ceremony."

"You're going to marry Mr. Shiameto?" Daphne asked.

"Daphne. What on earth are you talking about? You totally lost your mind? You certainly weren't thinking straight when you invited Dan to that movie wedding you and your cop cooked up. This is all your fault. And his. I should make the two of you take the baby and raise it. Or at least sue you for some support money."

"Dan!" Daphne finally made the connection and felt herself caught up in a wave of mirth. She held her hand over the phone receiver so the Darica could not hear her laugh.

"Let me get this straight," she said, after she regained control of her voice enough that Darica could not hear the laughter. "You slept with your ex-husband and got pregnant. And it's my fault?"

"You invited him. I blame you. But, most of all, I blame Plate."

"Yes. I did ask Dan to come. After most of my own family told me they couldn't be there. You wouldn't have been there if there had not been a story you thought you could get. I always liked Dan. He was always really nice to me and I enjoyed having him as a brother-in-law. There was no reason for me not to invite him. That was the only good thing that came out of the canceling of it the first time. He was able to come for the rescheduled event. Which would have been a great experience had there not been a murderer loose."

"That's just the problem. He ran to me to try to help me when

343

the shooting started. I did need someone to help me with the camera bag. He was there. And one thing led to another. And now I'm pregnant!"

Daphne bit her lip and kept silent a moment.

"My life is ruined!" Darica wailed.

"This is 1983." Daphne had a sly note in her voice

"Daphne! If you make any insinuation that I would ever consider having an abortion, I will kill you."

"I'm glad to know that you are pro-life."

"I could murder both you and that cop over this," Darica continued.

"I was still speaking of adoption," Daphne said smoothly. "What will you do?"

"As I said, I've already talked to Dan. We will remarry until the baby is born. He's coming up to Dallas next weekend. I think the idiot is actually happy about it."

Daphne covered the phone's mouthpiece again and collapsed on her couch in laughter. Plate came in at that moment and viewed her with curiosity.

"Don't forget to tell Mom, Dad, and Scott. Sorry, I've got to go- can I call you back?" she managed to say in a choked voiced. "A client just came in."

"I thought you didn't have clients at your house. I've told Mom and Dad. I will tell Scott when I get ready."

"I break my own rules occasionally. Sorry, I have got to go. Your long distance bill is going to be astronomical, anyway."

"Oh, heavens yes! I forgot we were on long distance." Darica hung up the phone with a loud click.

Daphne put her receiver in its cradle and burst out into laughter again.

"Who were you talking to? What's so- so funny? And why did you call me a client?" Plate asked.

"You are a client. You bought insurance from me."

"Who was on the phone?"

"It was Darica. Darica is going to sue you."

"What?"

"She's pregnant. And she blames you."

"Me! I've never touched her!"

"And me. I'm responsible."

"What? Stop laughing long enough to explain this to me."

"Darica is pregnant. She and her ex-husband- well, he helped her out taking the pictures. And smuggling them out after the shooting started, and, as she told me, apparently one thing led to another."

Daphne had another fit of laughter.

"I see," Plate smiled a little. "And this is my fault- our fault- because?"

"Because it happened because we were getting married."

"Next time we won't invite them."

"She is my twin sister. And I like Dan."

"So Darica is going be your maid of honor after all?"

"She is. She has the dress. I suppose technically the bond between fraternal twins is not supposed to be stronger than ordinary siblings but maybe it is."

"Sally Monroe's twin brother certainly put his life on an equal basis with hers. When she died, he threw his away. Even though he loved a good woman, in the end, his feelings for her were not as powerful as his desire for revenge for Sally. He would have sacrificed anyone, done anything to see Zopev punished."

"Even love," said Daphne, her mind more on the upcoming wedding than the recent criminal events.

"Do you feel that way about Darica?" Plate asked.

"Would I do anything to see her punished?"

"You know what I mean."

"I don't think so. Maybe it is there deep down. But I think- you know how we agreed we could never completely belong to another person because we belong to Him? I think it is the same. Those primal instincts are subordinate once you know God."

"Yet He said the two became one," said Plate. "It's another mystery isn't it? So complex. Beyond our understanding. This life and the next."

"Perhaps, if he had felt some hope for the next life, maybe he could have overcome his instinct for revenge. Even if he could never fully forgive Zopev, he might have been able to come to terms with it and find some type of happiness on earth," said Daphne.

"Although I don't think any of us could say how we would react if we suffered the type of losses that he did."

"You're probably right," Daphne said, her mind reverting to the wedding.

"True forgiveness is rare in this world. And when it does come, it is frequently ridiculed or otherwise viewed as a weakness."

"It's hard enough to try to forgive people for all the petty things they do to you, much less a grave injustice," Daphne said.

"I don't bear anyone any ill will today, anyone anywhere in the world," said Plate.

"Neither do I. I feel full of goodwill and graciousness towards everyone and at the moment, I love all my enemies and all my relatives and all my friends," Daphne said.

"Do you suspect that these sublime states of mind are temporary?"

"I know they are in my case. I'm hoping they last as long as the honeymoon. No guarantees," Daphne said.

"Same here."

"All bets are off once the honeymoon is over."

"I agree. We start from scratch."

"I hope that doesn't mean we have another flood," Daphne said.

They caught each other's eyes and burst out laughing.

## Chapter 64

"Keep your eye on the road," Daphne instructed.

"Don't start backseat driving until after the ceremony."

"You are accelerating too fast. My car is fragile."

"We need to be on time for our real wedding. I'm going to let this baby roar."

"The wedding is tomorrow. You are going the 55 mile-per-hour speed limit. Just as you should. And you never told me your brother was a dentist," said Daphne. She was examining her teeth in the mirror on the flip down side of the passenger sun visor. That amenity was one of the reasons they were taking her car this time.

"Yes, I did."

"You said he worked in a dentist's office."

"He does."

"Not quite the same thing."

"Are you intimidated by dentists?"

"Yes!"

"There's one more thing. About my father. He is a retired police officer. He spent much of his years with the DPS. Then later as a small town police chief. But in between he was a- "

"What? A secret agent?" Daphne asked. "CIA? FBI?"

"Not exactly. A Texas Ranger."

"A Texas Ranger!"

"Yes."

"Did you think that would intimidate me?"

"Yes, it intimidates most people."

"You're right. I am intimidated." Her eyes widened and she turned to him. "A Texas Ranger? Really?"

"Yes."

"And does- And do you-"

"I have told you I am happy where I am. And don't mention it to Dell. It's a long story. Just please don't mention it."

"Okay. How old did you say Dell was?"

"42."

"Is he married?" Daphne asked.

"No, he is not."

"And Penelope?"

"She is 36. She is married and has two sons. Her husband's an electrician. Vivienne is 26. Also married, to an automobile mechanic, with two daughters. The kids range in age from 6 to 15. They're monsters but I am rather fond of them. How old is Scott?"

"He is 38. He is single."

"And he is an educator? What does that mean? A college professor? High school principal?"

"He teaches fifth grade elementary students."

"Oh. Well, a male elementary school teacher. Not unheard of. More common than it used to be, I presume. Like male nurses."

"In my parents' minds, he has my job and I have his career. Darica as well, but lesser, if you know what I mean. Because both of them make much less money than me, I'm the more guilty culprit. That's really a bit simplistic but not inaccurate."

"I make a lot less money than you do," said Plate, with a smile.

Daphne stretched. "Little do you know I'm planning to quit soon and let you support me."

"The income disparity is reversed but I have the same problem concerning Dell. Wrong career for the wrong son. Has to do with status and tradition. It's too complicated to go into but I promise to tell you all about it sometime."

"I think I can guess. Because he is older, that is what the root cause of it is?"

"Yes, in a nutshell. I hate being the youngest son."

"I'm the oldest daughter. But the shortest. That's worse."

"Darica was born second?"

"See, even you are surprised."

"I bet she hates that."

"You know, you are right. It really does bother her. When it could not possibly really matter."

"Now let's not worry about our relatives anymore. Let's talk murder, much less stressful."

"I have found one more piece of evidence that we overlooked in the insurance data."

"Really? What was it?"

"There's no real reason I should tell you. Because it implicated an innocent man."

"I would guess it was a strange beneficiary designation."

"Yes, and it's still in force."

"He has left the state, apparently with his new love. Wonder if he will make her beneficiary? He dropped his lawsuits, telling us that he was going away to try to find peace of mind. Like the Smith husband who became a missionary and remarried. But apparently with Elisabeth and her puppets."

"If this had been the only piece of evidence we had found, we would've been certain he did it."

"That's why we look at things in context. One single piece of evidence against one individual does not usually suffice."

"It is still rare to designate someone else besides your wife as your life insurance beneficiary."

"Maybe he was afraid she would kill him."

"I hadn't thought of that."

"She might have been tempted if she had known it would bring her a windfall."

"So I guess you don't worry about having all that life insurance I sold you. That it could motivate me to murder you some day."

"Let's not go that far. I'm only human."

Daphne was silent for a moment. Then she gasped.

"Peter! Your brothers-in-law! They have names!"

Plate remained calm.

"Why yes, as a matter of fact they do."

"But you didn't mention their names just now."

"No, I guess I didn't."

"Why not? Don't make something up. Think about it for a minute. Why didn't you mention your brother-in-law's names?"

Plate reflected as she asked.

"I guess because my focus was on my sisters. I thought you would be most interested in them. Plus, I know my brothers-in-laws' names. They are important members of the family. But they work all the time like most men and they are kind of in the background. And, while not really thinking about you not knowing their names, I guess I subconsciously thought you would just find out in the course of time and events. Same for the kids," said Plate.

"Right. That all makes sense. Do you realize that no one has ever mentioned the last name of Jan Smith's husband? He's never been on the scene. He went off to make a new life for himself. He has rather been in the background in the past. We probably thought his name would come up in the course of time and events. But it has not."

"What are you saying?" Plate asked.

"Do you know the man's name?"

"Not off the top of my head. I am sure I have seen it."

"Is it some version of Edward?" Daphne asked.

Plate was silent.

"Ted, Eduardo. And the other guy's first name was actually Edward," Daphne said.

"We can probably find out on your computer."

"Too bad we don't have it here in the car."

"A computer which you could take on a road trip. That would be something."

"Yes, it would."

"I'll call Chief Brecken as soon as we arrive."

"Won't we be coming to a town soon?" Daphne asked.

"Right."

"Also, just an idea, ask what was Zopev's father's first name," Daphne said.

Plate stopped at the next town and found a pay phone.

He gave the chief a phone number where he could leave a message with the results.

A short time later Plate pulled his car into his parents' yard. He was going to stay with them while Daphne was going to stay at the motel where her family was registered.

Everyone was meeting at the elder Plates' home that evening for a pre-wedding supper.

Drake and Vivian embraced the couple and Plate introduced Daphne to his sisters and their families, explaining his brother would arrive later that night.

"Oh, and your chief left a message for you. I really hate it that he's not going to be able to come to the wedding."

"Me too, Mom. What was the message?"

"It didn't make sense. Edward Soap Peas and Edwin Sits. He didn't speak very clearly. He was calling from a car telephone. He said you would understand what it all meant. Some kind of code?"

Plate looked at Daphne.

She repeated the names correctly.

"Edward Zopev and Edwin Smith."

"It was as simple as that," Plate said softly.

"And so ironic. And the puppeteer's middle name... The name we all knew him by..."

There was no time to discuss it. Daphne's family arrived and Vivian Plate began serving the food.

Chapter 65

As her mother helped button the wedding dress, Daphne repeated the story of Jenny Plate and how after years as an undercover agent's wife, she was able to come out in the open and joyously attend the small church at the hilltop.

"So that's why you and Peter chose this out-of-the-way location for your wedding?" Debralyn asked. "I had no idea this little church existed. It is so off the beaten path."

Sunlight streamed through the window of the small side room in the church where the bridal party was preparing.

"Yes, and it has a good airconditioner. And a nice reception area with room for dancing," said Daphne.

"I cannot believe you are playing Frank Sinatra and Dean Martin records in this day and age," Darica said.

"We have a 1940s nostalgia theme. I am wearing a dress from that era."

"I think you chose well," said Debralyn.

"And it's in close proximity to his family. Most of them live around here. There's a lot more of them than there are us."

"Soon be one more of us," said Darica.

"It's a start," said their mother.

"I'm just glad I have not started to show yet."

"You look lovely, Darica. Daphne, you look breathtaking."

"I love the simple yellow gown. I do appreciate, Daphne, that you didn't make me wear that uncomfortable pink taffeta contraption from the movie scene. Not that I can get into it now anyway."

"My dress is the only thing I kept from that movie studio wedding. We gave the rings back. Peter needs a plain band so he can wear it at work. I decided to go with the same. We accepted the dress as our payment for the work we did for Stark Wynter. I don't think I could've ever found a more beautiful gown if I had looked all over the country."

"It does not bother you that Plate has already seen it?" Darica asked.

"We are not superstitious. I haven't seen him in his dress uniform," said Daphne.

"Times have definitely changed," Debralyn Martin commented. "I picked out your father's suit. He had no idea what I was wearing. Except that it was a wedding dress of course, long and white with a veil. My style totally surprised him. Now, instead of the groom being surprised, it is going to be the bride."

"Peter hasn't seen my veil. He doesn't know his mother gave me her veil. So, he'll have a bit of a surprise there. I fibbed and told him I was wearing the same tulle headpiece as before. This one is much nicer than that thick layered mosquito netting that I wore in the movie scene. This one has no netting. It's completely antique lace."

Darica unwrapped the treasure from its tissue-lined box and placed it over Daphne's curls. The lace fell down her shoulders and softly framed the full skirted dress, almost perfectly aligning its handwoven edging with the hem of the gown.

"It's held on with that jeweled clip in the little box beside it," Daphne instructed her sister while she clasped the veil to her head with her fingertips.

Darica fixed the clip, gathering the layered top section behind it. Daphne relaxed her arms.

Mrs. Martin put the finishing touches on the bouquet.

The photographer from Sand Waves Perkins Photographics arrived and began taking pictures, each shutter click producing a blinding flash.

"This is a lace handkerchief carried by your Swedish grandmother," Debralyn told her daughter. "It almost matches the veil."

"Why didn't I get that at my wedding?" Darica asked, referring to her first ceremony a decade ago.

She twisted the new ring Dan Daniels had gotten her for their remarriage, making the diamond flash.

She had pawned the original years ago.

"I didn't have the handkerchief then," said Debralyn. "Your grandmother had not died yet. She was there at your wedding, remember? She was still using it."

Daphne cradled the bouquet inside of the small cloth.

The photographer took a close-up.

"It's beautiful. No one would know that they were not a totally complete set. Thanks, Mom."

The music started.

"It's time!" said Darica excitedly.

The three women made their way into the church foyer. Daphne's brother and father joined them. It was a small church. Even though they had kept their guest list limited to close family and friends, the sanctuary was full.

Daphne's brother escorted his mother. The other usher, her about to be brother-in-law, had already seated Vivian Plate.

The photographer interrupted every action with a new flash. Nobody minded.

Darica made her way slowly and confidently alone down the aisle.

Then the music changed and Daphne took her father's arm.

Standing at the front of the aisle, two uniformed men came to attention.

"Here comes the bride," whispered Grant Skaar to the groom standing beside him.

"Hush," said the groom to his best man.

Plate was seeing Daphne's face, framed in the antique lace with her blonde curls peeking out, for the first time.

He barely dared to breathe.

She looked more enchanting than ever before.

*He looks like a prince in that dress uniform, an American prince*, Daphne thought as she slowly stepped forward.

Bride and groom smiled happily as the distance between them began to diminish, finally to vanish.

The congregation stood up and the music got louder as Jeanne Daphne Martin came down the aisle of the small hilltop church in Wilding Falls, Texas, to be united in marriage with Sinclair Peter Plate.

## Published by Ruskras Corner

By Deborah DR Kralich

### Fantasy
*A Cat Whisperer\** humorous futuristic murder mystery romance

### Historical Fiction
*The Mystique Woven in Our Land* 1792 murder mystery
*Murder as the Organist Plays* 1904 murder mystery thriller
*Interlude of Carelessness* 1930s intrigue romance espionage
*A Spy Come to Town\** 1950s intrigue espionage thriller
*The Mystery of the Missing Persons* 1960s cultural drama

### Lt. Plate in Sand Waves Mysteries
A series of mysteries set in the 1980s
*An Innovative Murder for the Season* traditional cozy
*The Ruler of the Toys* murder mystery cultural drama thriller
*A Kaleidoscope of Masquerades* traditional mystery thriller
*The Unknown Puppeteer* traditional murder mystery romance
*Poised Like a Knife* short story anthology including 2 Lt. Plate stories

*I Lift Up My Heart* a book of Christian poetry

\*\*\*

By Carl S Kralich

Young Adult Science Fiction Series
*Karl Sabers Space Knight Adventures:*
*3748 A.D. The Return of the Cat*
*Auction of Worlds*
humorous adventure with space pirates, princesses and feline
\*\*\*

## Available on Amazon and Kindle

\* Published under the pseudonym Deborah Denise